BILLY MCGU
the Shop, h
sends him on a relentless quest to save it . . .

ZILKIE THE COSEX—A mysterious plant-like information broker, his real merchandise is secrets and plots, one of which threatens Billy's life . . .

DING DO-WORT—One of the oldest and wisest of the Shop's merchants, she gives Billy lessons in the hardest part of his trade—survival . . .

SOLAQUIL—Leading member of the savage, lizard-like Tets, he's determined to eliminate Billy—even if it means the destruction of the Shop and all who inhabit it . . .

—

RETREAD SHOP

T. JACKSON KING

POPULAR LIBRARY

An Imprint of Warner Books, Inc.

A Warner Communications Company

POPULAR LIBRARY EDITION

Copyright ©1988 by Thomas Jackson King, Jr.
All rights reserved.

Popular Library®, the fanciful P design, and Questar® are registered
trademarks of Warner Books, Inc.

Cover design by Don Puckey
Cover illustration by Tom Kidd

Popular Library books are published by
Warner Books, Inc.
666 Fifth Avenue
New York, N.Y. 10103

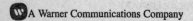A Warner Communications Company

Printed in the United States of America

First Printing: August, 1988

10 9 8 7 6 5 4 3 2 1

This book is dedicated to my children, Keith, Karen, and Kevin, who I hope will grow up to enjoy it, and to my wife, Paula Downing, a fellow writer who saw herself in another.

I gratefully acknowledge the inspiration, help, and encouragement of the following people: Rudyard Kipling, Robert Heinlein, James White, my eighth grade geography teacher, Dave Wolverton, Kathleen Woodbury, Orson Scott Card, Ian Monson, Cara Bullinger, Shayne Bell, the Xenobia group, and my mom and dad, Thomas J. and Sarah L. King. They were all there when I needed them.

NOVICE

Chapter One

"Caught you, little thief!"

Billy, still clutching the stolen fruit, looked up at the alien whose tentacles firmly gripped his right hand. He saw a forest of blue-green cords sprouting from a three-meter-high fleshy green trunk. The trunk stood on hundreds of small, wiggling, worm-shaped toes that apparently could move the shop owner very quickly. No face was visible on the giant anemonelike alien. He didn't recognize the species.

He was hungry. His last few Garbage parts scavenged from several Tokay habitat hulks were valueless, burned-out chunks of silicon, germanium, and quartz crystal. Even their base mineral value was not enough to pay his oxy and suit jet reactant bill at the station's Dock Six, let alone feed him. And he certainly didn't care to work on the open alien Farms—his last such stint left him with a skin rash that took all his remaining barter credits to cure.

Billy hadn't eaten for two days, and a lanky, gangling sixteen-year-old human male needs calories and protein far more often than every two days. So he'd scouted out a new section of the Grand Arterial, off near the space station's Orion end. Perhaps the merchants would be less alert than those around the compressor plant where he usually slept.

Not so, it seemed. Time to go into his pitch.

"Please, Honorable Sapient, I'm very hungry! I'm an orphan without Clan or House support. I am the only one of my kind here. Release me and I promise to never bother you again!" The plea made, Billy alertly watched his captor, waiting for a moment of inattention, a loosening of the

3

tentacles. Then he would be off, dodging and running among the awnings, shop front stands, and crowded glideways of the Grand Arterial.

But the giant tree-anemone had other things in mind. The whiplike green tentacles tightened around his wrist, pulling him closer to the alien.

"No, little thief, you don't escape Zilkie the Cosex so easily! You know the Rule—no Sapient gets something for nothing! Make your choice—two light cycles of service and two meals, or sensory flagellation at the local Enforcement station."

Damn! And he'd thought picking this shop—a vendor of specialty D-L–class fruits and vegetables—two blocks off the primary glideway of the Arterial would be safe.

A wave of lightheadedness swept over him. His muscles felt weak. No way could his body stand even the lowest level of punishment reserved for petty offenses on the Retread Shop space station. If he worked here at least he might eat.

The huge alien stood waiting before him, strong, implacable. He could see a small translator comdisk affixed to the green skin where the tentacles sprouted out from the top of the trunk. Several small vertical slits just below the tentacles periodically opened and closed—perhaps its speech and breathing organs. Enough delay—time to make a decision.

"Honorable Sapient, I accept your offer of local labor and food. How soon can I eat?" He had to eat soon or pass out.

"First, little thief, what is your name and species? I must know whom I employ."

"Billy McGuire, human, omnivore, and I'm D-L food-chain-based. I pledge my bond of Service—but I must eat! Please!?"

He didn't like to beg. In fact he would do almost any job, any errand in order not to beg. Mom and Dad had taught him to be proud of his heritage, of his race. But they were gone, leaving only their memory crystals as his inheritance. And survival by whatever means are available is a basic human trait. Basic, in fact, to all known sapient life.

The alien called Zilkie swayed toward him, bending the topknot forest of tentacles in his direction, close enough for him to see something new. Eyes. Scores of them clustered about the base of the two-meter-long tentacles. They looked like iridescent silvery fish eggs.

"Billy Human, I must close my shop for the day. But go up to my quarters above the Shop. Ask Melisay to fix whatever you wish—meat, fruit, vegetables, grains, whatever. Just be sure it stays down," the alien sardonically instructed him.

Billy pushed into the dim-lit shop interior, his eyes quickly adjusting to the orange radiance emitted by the ceiling panels. Piles of fruit and vegetables were arranged on long rows of refrigerator units. A few aliens walked, hopped, or slithered about, picking up and examining the merchandise. No one paid him any attention.

Against a side wall of the twenty-by-ten-meter room he saw a sloping ramp leading up through the metal ceiling. Evidently the way up to the Cosex's apartment—and Melisay—and food.

He tugged at his dirty brown jumpsuit, trying to make himself presentable. Then he walked slowly up the ramp reminding himself one did not break Service with one's benefactor.

Billy emerged into a forest.

Forest was really too grand a word, but the upstairs apartment was crammed with plants. Giant green ferns, purple trees, yellow toadstools, orange moss-covered rocks, grassy pathways—it was dreamlike. Reaching out he touched the blue-veined trunk of a nearby tree.

"Yes, it's real, little one. You must be the helper sent by Zilkie. What will you eat?" asked a warm, musical voice behind him. Billy's head jerked around, followed more slowly by the rest of his body.

A fat panda bear sat on its haunches before him, its fangs bared in a pseudogrin.

Of course the alien wasn't a panda. It looked to be 2.5

meters tall with black-and-white-striped fur. The ears were four long, pointed fans, two to each side of the blocky head. And four limpid brown eyes stared out at him over the muzzle of a carnivore. But the alien did look vaguely mammalian—and it had approached him utterly silent.

"Who are you?" How could the alien know so much about him? There was no sign of a spy-seed monitor screen.

"I am Melisay **brach-ahn** Corhn, Tellen race, carnivore and also dextromolecular-levomolecular food-chain-based. Again, what will you eat?" asked the bass voice.

"*Jacquil* fruit, a porridge of *esay* grains, and a large chop of D-L synthflesh," Billy hopefully asked. His stomach rumbled slightly. The prospect of food was enticing, alluring. At least he'd get basic proteins, carbohydrates, and most human trace elements with his meals if Zilkie's friend was to be trusted.

"Then follow," said the Tellen.

After a brief walk through the green and purple foliage, they arrived at a replicated cliff face fronting an open pool of water. Melisay reached up and touched a spot with a three-fingered hand on the rock face. A false stone panel slid down to reveal a standard food automat control surface. Her sucker-tipped fingers stabbed out a pattern on the automat's twinkling black surface.

A few seconds passed while the machine hunted among the apartment's stores, selected the proper ingredients, and cooked them with microwaves and infrared. The meal appeared on a black plastic tray that slid out of a slot below the control surface, the steam rising. Billy licked his lips. Then he looked at the alien, waiting for permission, encouragement, something.

"Good, little one, your mind still controls your desires. Perhaps you will provide good Service. Now, eat," Melisay encouraged him.

Billy grabbed the tray, stepped away from the automat, and sat down next to the pool. He pulled an aluminum spoon out of his right pocket and began with the *esay* porridge. He ate slowly, mindful that one did not waste food in the closed ecosystem that was the Shop. Glancing sideways, he saw the Tellen patiently sitting against the rock wall, watching him. Obviously Melisay didn't belong to one of the Florescence races for whom personal eating was a private ceremony, shared only with mates, fellow hatchlings, or progenitors.

That was fine with him. He could achieve privacy in his mind, shutting out all external sounds and images. Creating his own world peopled by images of other humans, humans seen in the memory dreams of his parents. The only other humans that he had ever seen in his life had been their four crewmates, now dead, aboard *The Pride of Edinburgh*. Jane, Zwaka, Tenshung, Malen, Mom, and Dad—the crew of the Garbage Hunter ship he'd been born on 16 bioyears ago.

As he ate the medium-rare synthflesh from one of the Shop's culture tanks, Billy mentally compared the variability of human individuals with aliens and with the alien races of the galaxy's Forty-Seventh Florescence. He thought of Florescence history, culture, and Trade lessons learned from MemoryNet crystals during his six precious years aboard the Shop space station before the accident. The years when he had belonged to a family. The years when he could afford the luxury of school.

Zilkie and Melisay were strange in appearance, but then so was he. Evolution and natural selection made for a strange, wildly variable universe. One in which morphoform variability was of little consequence. What counted was whether an alien's mind was structured similarly to human arrow-of-time referents, whether they were oxybreathers, and whether they were D-L, L-D, L-L, or D-D molecular-based lifeforms. The four patterns in which organic molecules arranged themselves to make up other bioforms determined if you could eat someone else's food. But most important was whether they were curious. Curiosity, the school lessons said, can overcome morphoform differences, weird social and cultural patterns, bizarre traditions, aggressiveness, almost any factor. So long as the alien was curious about the lifeforms inhabiting the galaxy, a basis for cooperation existed.

He tasted the amino-acid rich spices sprinkled onto the steak. Savored their hot, slightly sour flavor. The chop finished, Billy bit into a *jacquil* fruit, slowly chewing its bittersweet flesh. Hunger along with curiosity was also a basic motivator for any sapient.

The water in the pool was cool and refreshing, with little chemical aftertaste. With Melisay's nodded permission, Billy fastidiously washed his spoon, knife and fork, cleaned the tray, washed his face, and politely turned back to Melisay the Tellen. Aliens appreciated the rituals of social etiquette, the ingrained mental responsibility exhibited by observance of such simple daily patterns. Tenshung's Zen Buddhist colleagues, he suspected, would have approved his understated focus upon embedding the macroworld in the small world of washing dishes.

Melisay still watched. "Billy Human, I offer you a Trade. Your Service for Zilkie will be delayed until tomorrow with an additional two meals if you will Trade me some memories of you Humans in exchange for this meal. Agreed?"

He wasn't surprised. An alien wouldn't usually be on the Shop unless it was curious about other aliens. But could he, did he want to share his private heritage? He was also a little surprised that a shop owner not living in one of the single-species Habitats would possess its own MemoryNet terminal. Such devices were complex, almost self-aware constructs that were of great value no matter which Florescence or species manufactured them. But it had been over a year since he last accessed his crystals—and he ached for the memory of home, of family. *Mom, Dad, please understand.*

"Agreed, Melisay. But I'll pick the memory sequence and I will also take the same senseflow you get. Do you accept?"

The Tellen bear gave him a strong, sharp look. Perhaps he'd overplayed his hand. Taking the same senseflow as Melisay meant he would get a double set of memories—

his parents' memories and fragments from the Tellen's mind.

"It is satisfactory, little one. I hope you enjoy the flavor of my existence."

Melisay pressed the rock wall and two low, padded couch-pallets extruded. One side of each couch was in contact with the wall; between them lay a blue crystalline device. A filigree skullcap containing the neuron exciters and transducers lay on each couch, connected by a thin, metallic cord to the blue terminal between the couches.

A Kokseen MemoryNet! Nearly six million years old! Where did they get it from?

Thrusting the question aside for the moment, Billy reached into his jumpsuit and pulled out his most prized possession, a gold wire necklace from which hung electron beam encoded memory crystals recorded by his parents. Six crystals contained their memories of service aboard *The Pride,* their lives back on Earth before Departure, their private thoughts about each other, their advice about how to exist and survive among the aliens of the Retread Shop space station, and recent memories of the two years they had all shared aboard the Shop after arrival.

He chose the crystal containing their Shop memories. Their memories of a happy time when, with great effort, they were succeeding in fashioning a life and living among the aliens of the Forty-Seventh Florescence. The memory of a family picnic in the Park of the Hecamin aliens near Dock Three, two years after their arrival. The memory of their happiness in telling him—a twelve-year-old—of their luck in buying a used, third-hand service lighter of the Hecamin that was only two hundred years old.

Billy, somber, slipped the yellow crystal into the turquoise blue receptor, lay down on the couch, and fitted the cap over his head. Like all memory crystals, it would run sequentially through the memories, like an old-fashioned sight-sound record, but far faster than the memories had been experienced. He composed himself, sought the alpha state, and mentally keyed the crystal to that innocent time. As he faded into the dream, he could hear the faint rustle of fur upon fabric as Melisay readied herself for a Lesson on humans.

The memory came, bringing with it love, caring, his family and a sense of belonging. He saw yellow-leaved trees waving in a breeze . . .

Chapter Two

The McGuire family often came to the Hecamin Park for its tranquility, and for its similarity to Earth. They sat beneath a tree which looked much like a weeping willow with yellow leaves and a dark russet red trunk, surrounded by golden alien daisies. There was no grass analogue, but the daisies were thick enough to cushion them.

Sarah Yoritomo-McGuire was a thirty-nine-year-old, sixth generation American Rokusei who retained only the almond eyes and straight black hair of her ancestors. Like all immigrants the Yoritomos eventually intermarried, creating Eurasian offspring of striking appearance. It was in her third graduate year abroad at Cambridge—studying the processes of proton decay for her doctoral dissertation —that she met Jason McGuire, a Scot from Edinburgh who could build almost any kind of subatomic particle or wave detector. Quarks, tachyons, neutrinos, even gravity waves—Jason McGuire took the best of the new Compact alien technologies and infused it with Scottish practicality to create mechanical wonders.

(Billy's heart ached at the sight of himself with his parents. Spectator and participant, he remembered.)

Sarah looked appraisingly at her husband of fourteen years. The curly dark-haired, slightly brooding man had convinced her to sign up for Earth's Garbage Hunter crew competitions. He told her that someone whose father had only just missed earning a slot in the Human Compound colony aboard the Compact asteroid starship *Hekar* stood a good chance of getting into space on her own. He was a special man. The man who had taken a third in the European all-around gymnastics competitions in 2074. The man whose quick actions saved her and Billy when their Garbage Hunter ship started vaporizing around them.

Jason McGuire's deep blue eyes glanced at her as he set out the meal they had grown, bartered for, and scavenged to celebrate the special occasion. Next to him sat Billy, already at home among the non-Compact aliens of the Retread Shop. Billy's world was one where alien was normal, where claws, tentacles, pseudopods, graceful multijointed fingers, and prehensile tongues were all the same—simply part of the shapes of his neighbors, his few playmates, his parents' customers. Jason met her eyes, knowing her thoughts, reassuring her with his gaze, and conveyed a sober encouragement that they would prevail, would live until *Hekar*'s Crew of humans and Compact aliens got around to visiting this outpost of the Forty-Seventh Florescence. It might be decades, they might have to go into Suspense, but they both knew that eventually other humans would visit the Shop. The Compact aliens' starship had learned 240 years ago of the Florescence. Now *Hekar* was on a roundabout course down the spiral arm toward the core. Eventually the ship would come to the Retread Shop.

Sarah gathered her hopes about her and looked out upon the rolling hills of Hecamin Park, at the streams of blue water glistening under a whitish yellow ceiling radiator, at the great catlike, golden-haired Hecamin aliens lounging in family packs beneath shade trees. So different from humans, so alien in many values, but there was overlap, there were shared values. Family. Tradition. Competitiveness. A technology orientation. A common D-L life basis. And a sense of humor...

"Craaackk!" A yellow lightning bolt sounded outside Melisay's ancestral cave.

Her four night-adjusted eyes were momentarily blinded by the flash, but not before she had picked out the shape of a great metallic globe silently descending into the tall trees of her forest.

Is it a Voice? Are they come at last?

*Her mind touched the rest of the awake Corhn Clan. Aunts, sisters, mothers—all those whose Voice had watched over the cubs and males since time immemorial. They knew of the faint Voices from the sky, from the twinkling yellow, red, and blue stars that stretched in a broad band from horizon to horizon. They too wondered—are there People out there? Will they come to visit the **brach-ahn** of Homeworld?*

(Billy's ghostmind was shocked—the Tellen was female *and* telepathic. Her memories drowned him.)

*Sisters Mimen, Doriel, and Lamen were on the Hunt in the forest for tomorrow's food. They were closest to the great globe. **We will scout for Corhn Clan. Our eyes will be your eyes.***

*Melisay maintained her guard post, watchful for a stray hakken or demirel. The other carnivores of Homeworld might be larger, quicker, and more numerous than her People, but Melisay and the six million other **brach-ahn** ruled the planet—at least as much as they wished. The Balance must be maintained, she knew. Let there be too many **brach-ahn** and the rest of the food-chain would be affected.*

*Mimen's mind flashed steady color pictures of the globe, settled on six great trunks that sank deep into the red-brown soil of Aachen Plateau. She saw a tongue of metal protrude from its base, dip down and gouge to a stop in the sod grass of the meadow. Her nik-sense saw the globe overlaid by pale purple bands of string, wound fully around it. **How is it a Device can possess the magnetic field of Homeworld?***

Melisay felt her younger sister's uncontrolled reaction before elder Lamen imposed strict mind discipline. They were there as Recorders, and as bait to see whether this globe held unthinking predators. They were not cubs or *young males struggling to control their emotions. They were **brach-ahn**, the only self-aware members of Home-world's lifechain. Their duty was paramount.*

Mimen saw a round, bright eye iris open in the side of the globe, and shapes moving about, preparing to come down the ramp. The first shape she could make out . . .

(Billy's ghostmind jerked back to his memories.)

Twelve-year-old Billy watched his mom and dad looking at each other with that special look, the look of two against the world. The look of love. A look with many meanings.

Billy munched on a ham-and-cheese-analogue sandwich, relishing the unusual flavors after years of mostly alien foods. He knew about dietary supplements, about trace elements, and that they had to wait here until the other humans came. He knew much about physics, comparative xenosapientology, Earth history, human social customs, chemistry, biology, astronomy—all the factual things one can learn from MemoryNet crystals. But he only vaguely remembered Jane and Zwaka, Tenshung and Malen—the other two couples who, with the McGuires, had made up the Garbage Hunter crew. He remembered their last Hunt on the Forty-Fourth Florescence world of the Zikich for the cast-off technological debris and devices, or Garbage, left behind by the extinct Zikich civilization less clearly. Little useful Garbage had been found. That Hunt ended when he was six years old, and they had been on their way to a promising Forty-Sixth Florescence world called Doreen when disaster struck.

He mentally shrugged, dropping the old memory, and wondered what other humans would be like. What special news did his parents have? This picnic was rare—they seemed to work continuously, Trading raw materials, devices, and Garbage. He felt something important was going to happen. His mom turned to look at him.

"Billy, your dad and I have news for you," said Sarah. "This morning we completed a barter Trade with the Hecamin to buy a service lighter from them at Dock Three. We'll have a ship again!" Sarah smiled over at her son.

His dad flashed a quirky grin at him.

"It means, son, you'll have to study up on Hecamin Power systems and less on the General Trade principles you like so much. We must know how to repair it ourselves. But it will greatly expand the numbers of customers—we might even give the great Houses a run for their Trade."

Billy finally smiled, shaking his head.

There was no way the McGuire family could be a threat to the great Houses, those mostly single-species Habitats whose members were in the hundreds. But they could go from a hand-to-mouth existence into a sort of petty bourgeois status, a status where they could get the credit so rarely extended to lone-wolf aliens.

(Ghostly Billy, caught between two memory worlds, noticed a shape recorded in his subconscious memory—an orange form in a nearby grove. He started to wonder what it was when his mind was rudely jerked into a different senseflow.)

was a jumble of eight legs connected to a central body that seemed to glitter with a thousand small eyes.

The figure slowly, carefully pranced down the ramp, the central body swaying with motion. Other forms followed. Weird shapes, tall things, long skinny things like a hakken, a cluster of soft balls that rolled over each other, several walking trees with writhing tops, and many, many different forms. Some of them shapes out of the nightmares of cubs.

Mimen's mind was Recording, her personal Self withdrawn in shock.

Doriel and Lamen lay near their frozen sister, ready to aid her if she lost control, ready to mentally dampen the wild emotional swings that could drive whole Clans into a frenzy before they were mercifully killed by their neighbors. The infection of hysteria, of unreason was close.

Melisay stirred and lumbered out to the front of the cave. She let the rain beat down on her. She let the booming night sounds buffet her ears. She tried to help her sisters and herself.

Here is Reality. Here is your anchor. Here is Home-world!

Her feedback over the common Clan senseband began to awaken a few males, slumbering deep in the cushion-lined recesses of the cave. But it reached Mimen, and Doriel and Lamen. It helped. Mimen's Self returned, began to wonder, began to seek for Voices.

The strange shapes clustered in the dark meadow moved around with apparent purpose. Some collected pieces of soil, plants, and rocks. Others set Devices upon the meadow and started them to thumping away at Home-world. A few roved about the perimeter carrying glittering Devices as if they were Scouts or Guards. A group of three night-darkened forms, one holding a Device, headed unerringly for the three **brach-ahn** hidden several thousand paces away in a Hunting overlook of clustered boulders.

Her sisters began to feel concern. There were no true Voices here. There were minds, whispers of sapience, stray thoughts crashing against the ordered senseband, but no one like the **brach-ahn.** They knew these were People of a sort, not animals, but so strange! The shapes of their minds varied wildly, and even those with a common form (as much as the dark, moonless night let them see) did not share a common mind-shape. It was all disorder to the watching **brach-ahn.**

But Lamen picked up something, someone, a half-Voice still inside the globe. A Voice of raw emotions, who sent and received only emotions. This half-Voice quested for the three sisters, seeing but not-seeing, knowing only a part, crippled but thinking itself whole.

The group of three new People suddenly halted, looking straight where the three **brach-ahn** lay, the black of night one with black fur.

The Person of loosely connected balls set down a tripod Device, aimed it with pseudopod hands at her sisters, and it made sounds louder than the thunder of the stormy night.

The last coherent sense-image Melisay got from her sisters was a wailing scream of pain, of agony, of sound that ripped and tore at their ears. Then deadness.

She thrust herself out of the cave on all four limbs toward her sisters, her Clan alerted by a single mental scream. Melisay...

The McGuire service lighter hung in the square cavern of Dock Three, waiting for the arrival of the Torsen aliens. The silvery block of the lighter, flanked by three tubes containing the chemical thrusters, reflected the multicolored lights of the airless dock. Then the great clamshell doors of the dock began to split in the middle, a sheet of metal two kilometers wide by one high began to recede upward into the outer skin of the Shop. A similar lower door slowly sank. Billy stood watching behind a merchant's gallery window, ready to order from the common bond warehouse any item his parents could convince the Torsen to buy.

(His ghostmind screamed *No! No! No!*)

The great, pitted nose of the wedge-shaped Torsen ship gradually entered Dock Three, pulled by tractor beams spotted about the back interior wall. The massive gray bulk, nearly a kilometer long, slowly swung around toward Portal Six. This ship was too large for the half-kilometer-long cradles used for smaller starships, so it would dock nose-in, plugged into one of the ten interior Portals that could adjust to any ship morphoform. There it would stay, hanging in weightlessness, until its lithium six primary Trade cargo was off-loaded for barter sale on the Grand Arterial.

(I don't want to see it. I can't. Please, NO!)

In simple slow motion, like a dream, the McGuire service lighter exhausted monomethyl hydrazine and nitrogen tetroxide in a golden flare of gases. The lighter moved slowly up toward where the ship's forward cargo hatch would be once it docked. His parents wanted to be on hand, ready to Trade the moment docking was done. Other lighters crewed by the Ketchetkeel, Tet, Hecamin, and Bareen aliens also moved through the Dock cavern toward the Torsen craft.

(He was crying in his mind, trying to close his mind's eye.)

The human ship, drawing near as the Torsen ship approached from the left to enter the Portal on the McGuires' right, flared its nose reaction control system to slow it to a halt meters from where the Torsen ship would be after docking. But the expelled gases abruptly flickered out. Only sixty meters from the Portal rim, the McGuires approached at a deadly twenty meters per second.

They had three seconds to live.

Billy, watching from the gallery, had just begun to guess there was a problem, to wonder if a pressor beam operator could stop their inexorable rendezvous with inertia, when it happened.

(NOOOOO!)

The Torsen ship's nose was brightened by a ghastly white flare as the McGuire service lighter was crushed between the slowing tons of momentum and the Portal rim.

(No! No!)

"NO!! I didn't want to remember that!" he cried, sweat-drenched, as he jerked upright on the MemoryNet couch, tearing the skullcap off his head.

Billy's whole body was shaking, aching, and hurting. He was crying. He was feeling again the loss he had spent the last four years trying to forget. He looked over at the Tellen female, a questioning look on his face.

"I sorrow for your loss, Billy McGuire. To lose one's progenitors so young is very hard. I also have suffered," she said, reaching out a furry arm across the MemoryNet terminal to lightly touch his hand.

Wiping the tears from his eyes, feeling the stubble of a young beard, Billy withdrew some of himself, trying to protect his inmost spirit. But Melisay's comment reminded him of the senseflow memories she had leaked to him. Something about three telepathic sisters hurting, in agony...

"What do you mean, Melisay. What happened to you, to your sisters?"

"They died, little one." Four brown eyes stared sadly across at him. "Without knowing it, a Florescence Research and Trading ship killed my sisters with ultrasonic vibrations from the comdisk Device they were using to contact us. It was a tragic mistake—they didn't mean to harm us—but they had no way of knowing how sensitive our species is to sound waves in the 30,000 cps range. Their Hokken empaths still within their vessel immediately detected the pain, but it was too late. My sisters were brain dead."

"What did you do?" he asked, wondering how Melisay's strange race of low-technology telepaths had reacted to their first Contact with other beings.

Melisay flicked her fan ears at him and fur rippled to muscles below the skin. She looked back at him, her eyes now both sad and sorrowful.

"I acted like a beast. I ran around the globe ship roaring, screaming, yelling my pain and anger, daring them to come out. Daring the crippled Voices to pay for their harm. Finally one of them did come out. It was Zilkie." The Tellen panda bear closed her eyes, remembering.

"Zilkie the Cosex came fearlessly down the ramp, standing before me, waiting. I sniffed this new being, sensing a kind of plant, but also a predator in a way. I made toward him, ready in my sorrow to take a life for a life. In my haste I stepped on one of his longer tentacles. It happened then."

Melisay rocked on her hips on the couch, her stocky legs gathered up cross-legged. She opened her eyes and stared sightlessly out at the apartment forest.

"In a flash I was in his mind, hearing his Voice, tasting his feelings. I knew him and he knew me. It was Contact telepathy—very rare between different species. But we spoke together. And in mind Voice there are no lies." The black-and-white-striped bear looked over him. "From that moment on we have been Voice bonded, always in each other's thoughts, always comforting each other. I came with him into space and eventually to the Shop. In a way we are mated."

Billy stirred as he sat on the couch-pallet, his tears dried, the ache inside receding. "Perhaps that memory is what kicked me forward to the accident. Your recollection fed the machine and my mind a particular cue, and the rest just happened."

"How long ago did you lose your sisters?"

"Nearly two thousand Homeworld years ago."

Billy looked more closely at his host and newfound friend. She couldn't be that old in bioyears. *Perhaps they've been in Suspense many times.*

Taking his memory crystal out of the Kokseen machine, he got down to routine business. "Where do I sleep?"

Chapter Three

"Master Zilkie, where do you want these *yorgave* fruit displayed?"

The Cosex tilted its topknot toward him from the rear of the shop. The watchful alien spoke little, but it always noticed everything that happened. Including how well Billy carried out its terse instructions to unpack, unload, lift, carry, stack, and display the valuable perishables that many species used to vary a frequently dull diet. The Cosex, like any good merchant, bought low and sold high. It was also very particular about the marketing of its wares.

"Over there, to the left side of your upper left manipulator. Place the *yorgave* by the bundles of *flis* nodes so their natural scents will mix and enhance each other." Silvery fish eyes peered at him from within a tangle of green whipcord tentacles. "Have you never studied basic Trade principles? You must entice the customer's perceptor stalk. You must arouse the digestive juices by tickling their pheromone sensors. And don't call me Master—Sapient will do!"

Billy kept his peace and controlled his temper. While Melisay acted friendly and seemed to empathize with his plight, Zilkie was distant. Fair, but not overly friendly. Like most aliens aboard the Retread Shop, Zilkie seemed to show only passing interest in a lone human male.

He built squat pyramids out of the round, delicate-skinned, orange-colored fruit. His fingers—most often he was hired for the sake of those precision manipulators—carefully wove bundles of *flis* nodes around the grouping of pyramids, adding a touch of asymmetry to complement the visual and smell attractants so favored by Zilkie. He was educated, he told himself. He knew General Trade principles. He knew Hecamin Power Systems, IR and RF sensors and signaling devices, the principles of interspecies Trade, and many, many other things. But Billy wasn't about to enlighten this money-grubbing tree. Two days of Service and he would be gone.

Back to his compressor station hovel. Back to wonderful freedom among the seventeen thousand aliens of sixty-four Florescence species who periodically awoke from Suspense, lived hurried, frenzied lives aboard the 120-kilometer-long by 30-kilometer-wide tube of the Shop, and then went back to sleeping the cycles away. Until new alien Traders came again to this five-million-year-old relic left by the Kokseen. Back to the freedom to starve. His parents had told him, living in a Retread Shop astride the main Trading route of Orion Arm was a hard existence. *Someday*, he whispered softly to the ghosts in his mind, *I will make a name for myself! Someday a human will be a Merchant!*

"Billy Human, work faster! I open in a short while for the day customers. We must be ready." The Cosex scurried into the main Food shop display area from the back. "Here, move these stasis cubes out for unpacking," it said, pointing to a pile of yellow-metal boxes recently deposited against a near wall by a preprogrammed transport sled.

He hurried to comply.

The stasis cubes were to Food Merchants what tools were to a Power Systems engineer—they replicated the great wonder of Suspense on a small scale using broadcast power. The cubes suspended biological processes—like enzyme breakdown, bruising, or nutrient leaching—of any organic item for a day, a year, millennia. It gave perpetually fresh food.

He carried the now empty cubes back to the rear storeroom, put them in an airtube conveyor to the shop's subbasement, and snatched a moment of rest while Zilkie turned off the pressor field at the shop's wall-to-wall open frontage. A glance around the storeroom told him only a little.

Several spare refrigeration units, tiny devices no larger than his hand, sat on nested wall shelves. Beneath them, piled on empty packing boxes, he saw a dozen reels of organic fiber rope, a laser cutter, and a dozen record crystals. A Forty-Fifth Florescence video Imager stood on its pedestal in the far corner. As Billy walked back to the door, something glittered among the record crystals, a blue flash. He walked over on silent bare feet, keeping an ear cocked for the Cosex. He looked down at the stack of record crystals and saw a sapphire blue cube among the standard brown and gray crystals.

A star chart record crystal! What use would a Food Merchant have for astronomical data?

"Do you Humans always laze about, or are you atypical for your species? Come out at once, we're opening," said the Cosex, leaning its green tentacle topknot through the storeroom's open door to glare at him with tiny silvery fish eyes. Billy jerked guiltily.

"Coming, Sapient Zilkie. I was just being sure the cubes arrived safely in the subbasement." A stupid answer really, but better than letting the Merchant guess he was looking for valuable, portable items that could be bartered for food, tools, suit maintenance, and a little MemoryNet time. After all, this Service would last only two light cycles, and he had to plan for future needs.

He walked out after the swiftly scurrying tall form of the

Cosex. Out into a throng of aliens, of weird shapes, of beings who spoke in light bands flashing on their bodies, of beings large, small, and in-between, of beings fast and slow, even a few beings in mobile habitat tanks—the methane and chlorine breathers, most likely. Billy sighed. It was going to be a long day on the Grand Arterial.

That evening, just before the shop briefly closed then reopened for the nocturnal customers, Billy saw something not routine, not ordinary. He was standing behind a vegetable-laden pedestal repacking some ice-cold tubers into a stasis cube, when the blue praying mantislike form of a Ketchetkeel entered the shop. The six-legged insect hailed Zilkie and retreated with the Cosex into the back storeroom. Seconds later Melisay descended the ramp to attend to customers and to supervise the changeover to the low-chlorophyll, high-sucrose content fruits favored by many nocturnal species. She looked over at him as her comdisk swung from a chain around her squat neck.

"Billy McGuire, will you stay awhile to help with the changeover? You may take your leave for rest and recreation once the evening produce is displayed."

"Yes, Melisay. There are only two more rows to complete."

She, at least, showed some kindness, some thoughtfulness for him. He wouldn't steal from her, but anything of the Cosex was fair game.

Billy's mind worked furiously as his hands automatically moved delicate vegetables to storage, unpacked the replacement fruits, and carefully arranged them in pleasing patterns, wondering what business the Cosex had with a member of one of the most powerful single-species Houses aboard the Shop. The low gravity-evolved Ketchetkeel controlled most star systems within thirty light-years of the Retread Shop. Their Trade alliances stretched two thousand light-years further up the spiral arm away from the faraway galactic core. He also knew the Ketchetkeel controlled two of nearby Cebalrai's gas giants, and the deuterium, tritium, and helium 3 they harbored. An endless supply of deuterium, his dad had said long ago, can give any species a sense of confidence. So what business did a Power Merchant have with a Food Merchant?

His forehead furrowed with the effort of his concentration. Perhaps the simple information of who was meeting with whom would be of barter value among the Ketchetkeel's competitors? He filed away one more datum into his scavenger memory.

Melisay let him leave a short while later.

Billy looked at himself in the reflective metal wall of the next-door shop. His brown jumpsuit was clean, thanks to the use of Melisay's cleaner alcove. His long black hair hung bound in a tail over his left shoulder. The memory crystal necklace lay hidden below a high collar. A blue sash belt hugged his narrow waist. The appearance seemed presentable and unthreatening—time to pick up his sparse kit at the compressor station before some other scavenger found it.

The two block walk to the Grand Arterial itself and the public glideway was uneventful. A few aliens of the Bareen, Tet, Hecamin, Dok'aah, Sorep, and Gordin species shared the metal-plated street with him. He ignored them, intent on getting back quickly from the errand so he could eat and sleep awhile before his daytime Service began.

Billy entered a jam-packed Grand Arterial.

A broad corridor 120 kilometers long, one kilometer wide and high, the Grand Arterial amazed his parents when they first saw it. Bordered by one- to ten-story buildings on either side, the intervening open space was crowded with metal shanties, fabric awnings, and small open plazas. And aliens scurried everywhere. The shops sold, first and foremost, rebuilt devices from any one of the last thirty Florescences (this was after all a *Retread* Shop). But they also offered everything from semiliving spacesuits, to antiaging drugs, to genetically tailored narcotics, to faster than light-speed tachyonic communicators—even a complete starship could be bartered for from the great House of the Ketchetkeel. The insectoids would also sell you the fuel too—at a nice markup.

Mom and Dad had mumbled something about "a weird mix of India's Grand Trunk road and the bazaar at Marrakesh," and then recorded everything they saw on their wrist comunits. When Billy had bartered those devices from Earth long ago on this same Arterial, he had received a two-month supply of D-L food and three suit refills. Without the refills he couldn't keep scavenging in the attendant cloud of technological Garbage left orbiting around the Shop over the last five million years.

Telling his mind to leave the past in the past, Billy wove through the crowd, searching for the central glideways running down the middle of the Grand Arterial. The first indication he was near transport were alien bodies moving from right to left beyond the crowd in front of him. Billy stepped around the transparent pressurized habitat tank of a barnacle-encrusted, tube-shell ocean creature.

The outermost, slowest lane of the glideway moved past him. It carried dense local traffic of aliens going from the Dock Ten Sector to the Dock Nine part of the Arterial. He stepped onto the moving strip and leaned into the direction of travel. Step, lean, step, lean, a final step, lean and he stood on the fast commuter strip near the central cargo glideway, traveling along at ninety klicks an hour. Billy would reach the Shop area near Dock Three in an hour. Slow transport, but it was free.

Nobody stood near him. Most Sapients needing to get somewhere fast usually had access to one of the magnetic repulsion taxi ovoids. He looked up as a shadow passed between him and the orange-yellow ceiling radiator strips one kilometer above his head. A yellow-and-red-striped taxi swiftly flew down the crowded airspace of the Grand Arterial. It reminded him of yesterday's MemoryNet sequence with Melisay—of what he had once had. *Memories!*

"Excuse, Sapient, this one must pass. Excuse, excuse."

"What?" he blurted out, looking behind him.

A small, one-meter-high bush with blue leaves, yellow

branches, and a gray trunk floated behind him on the narrow glideway. *A Melanon!*

"Certainly, Honorable Sapient, you may pass me," he replied. "But first may I ask a question—how do you move at all, let alone quickly?" Billy moved to one side just in case the alien had little interest in idle conversation.

The bush stopped its glide and shook its leaves at him. He heard a metallic chiming sound just before his comdisk translated.

"A curious being? Well met we are then, for we Melanons seek Answers to every question. So far, we have Archived Answers only from the Thirty-Third to the Forty-Seventh Florescence. Your question? I move quickly by use of this lodestone gripped in my taproot. See." And the bush lifted its outer fringe of dark gray sucker roots to show a thick, pale gray root wrapped around the rim of a flat, black, dinner plate-sized stone.

"I see."

He didn't really; how did the Melanon achieve linear induction levitation—maglev—above the metal of the glideway? Or did it work by magnetic repulsion at all? Billy did what his parents said humans do second best— ask questions.

"But how do you induce repulsion? The natural magnetism of the stone isn't strong nor is it polarized."

The bush rocked back to level, lowering its sucker roots. He thought it might leave, bored with the brief novelty of talking to someone from the animal phylum. Instead it answered.

"A logical query. I use electricity generated by small metallochemical photocells in my leaves to first polarize the stone, then I induce a high gauss field"—Billy started at the Earth term; most comdisks were not programmed in human languages—"in the stone by passing electricity around it in a circular manner. You are, I assume, familiar with the technique for generating an electromagnetic field by rotating iron oxide within a copper coil? Basically I move my field around a stationary core, creating a stronger, single pole field in the stone, which then levitates above the glideway. To travel, I simply lean toward the direction I want to go, unbalancing the repulsion, and my stone moves, carrying me with it. Simple, isn't it?"

Billy grinned, enjoying himself. He couldn't help admiring a species that used a renewable, nonpolluting energy source for personal transport, taking free energy from the station's ceiling radiators. The technique probably also served to build up an internal charge to maintain life processes after dark, when the sun set on whatever world it originally came from. *Perhaps it's time for company.*

"Can I accompany you? We're both heading for the Sagittarius end. And I have more questions to ask."

"Agreed," the bush chimed back to him, "but only if I can ask a question for each one you ask. Melanons are quite curious, especially about why entropy seems to favor the animal phylum over the plants when it comes to selecting for sapience. Do you have an opinion?"

An hour later they parted company. Billy thought he had a new friend—at least Zekzek the Melanon offered him its comdisk personal access code and an invitation to visit it.

The Melanon, he had learned, belonged to a mind gestalt, to a parent Tree mass hidden away deep in the earliest parts of the Shop, near the remains, it was said, of the original Kokseen Shop craft. Individually sapient but capable of a tremendous combined mentality, Zekzek and his fellows had access to an Archive of electronic, electromagnetic, and subatomic physics data that dwarfed the combined resources of every other race aboard the Shop. Zekzek could literally design a tachyonic communicator from scratch, devise an eighth-dimensional tunnel for feeding an antimatter-matter drive impulse safely into this existence, or create the algorithms necessary to give self-awareness to an inorganic construct. That was daunting enough to Billy. But it also belonged to the only race still extant who had some direct memory of the Kokseen, progenitors of the current Florescence of galactic civilizations.

His brain hurt after leaving the bush.

Which was probably why his usual predator alertness didn't notice the small signs that someone or something had traveled his private path among the automatons of the compressor station.

He noticed nothing odd until he saw that the hatch to his oxytank hideaway hung partly open. Not closed as he had left it four days ago.

Billy backed up among the forest of pipes that writhed around the tank and the whole compressor facility. A glance about him at the pale yellow dust he had scattered about the area. A sniff of the air. Ears concentrated on the low hiss-wheeze of hot and cold fluids as they passed in nearby pipes. There they were—tell-tale signs that someone had scuffled into and out of the tank. No clear tracks —just disturbed areas. The question was—did someone still Hunt him?

His right hand reached silently behind to a juncture nexus of six pipes and felt for his dad's Krupp steel bowie knife. It was a small heirloom and a modest weapon. He had used it to defend his home in the past. He would use it again if necessary.

The knife felt cool to his fingers. The rough elk-horn handle scratched his calluses. Lifting it before his eyes, he quickly glanced at the silvery white stainless steel blade.

"To Billy—Hunt well. Dad," read the laser-cut inscription along the blood runnel of the blade. Hunt he would.

A scrap piece of metal coupling lay to his left. It would do.

The coupling hit the inward-opening hatch with a sharp, loud clang, swinging it half-way open. *Anybody still there?*

Nothing happened.

His left hand reached to grip the interweaving pipes at his side. Billy climbed into the pipe maze, gradually moving toward and above the oxytank. When the position was right, he dropped a meter down onto the tank, bare feet gripping its cold surface. Still nothing came rushing out.

Moving the knife to his left hand, Billy pulled a small hand mirror out of the sash belt, knelt, and leaned over the lip of the tank. Angled carefully, the mirror reflected a decent view of most of the interior of the hideaway.

He saw an upside-down image of the dimly lit tank with small clothing items scattered about. No aliens. Nothing lying in wait for him. Time to go inside.

The hatch swung inward on well-oiled hinges. Billy bent down a little, stepped inside, and moved quickly to the left, ready for a rush from behind the hatch on his right.

Nothing.

Slightly shaky from the adrenaline rush brought on by anticipating danger, he stepped warily toward the far end of the five-meter-long tube—toward where his duffel bag lay hidden in a floor trap installed by some prior occupant of the tank.

The shock of it all stopped him cold. Billy's chest expanded with pent-up emotion. Eyes watered with tears for the second time in as many days.

Everything was a mess. The duffel bag lay in slashed green pieces flung against one side of the flat-bottomed tank. Papers giving him his entry permission into the Shop were torn apart. Two 3-D cubes of his parents were scratched and starred as if someone had tried to smash the nearly indestructible plasticine. His mom's white wool sweater was rent and discolored with what smelled like urine. And excrement had been splattered everywhere about the curving metal walls—even onto his crude drawings of Earth, Sol system, and some mountain scenes drawn from an old discbook.

Damn them, damn them. "DAMN YOU!!" he shouted out at all the aliens, all the strangers, everyone who didn't care.

I will survive! I will not give up! And whoever is my enemy—you will know human revenge!

Hours later Billy emerged from the tank, carrying the roughly cleaned picture cubes, the sweater, and his knife. His eyes held a terrible dull look as he gazed around at the pipes, then beyond them to Dock Three, and out across the rest of the Shop—seeing in his mind's eye a world of foes and few friends. His lips curled up slightly at the corners. *Today is the first day of my Hunt, alien. Look upon me and know your defeat!*

Billy walked away. Lonely except for his hate.

Chapter Four

"I offer you long-term bond Service in my employ, Billy McGuire," said Zilkie the Cosex. "In return you will receive two meals a day, access to educational vidcrystals, and training in specialized Trade matters. Do you accept?"

Billy pondered the offer. Zilkie and Melisay had called him upstairs to the pond eating area during the day-night produce changeover. It was his second and last day of Service under his original agreement. A quiet somber day he had worked, the memory of the compressor station incident still burning inside him.

Did he want to stay? Did he want to give up the lone-wolf life forced upon him by the aliens, which he doggedly tried to turn into a virtue? Aside from food, what else could he gain by staying here?

Zilkie stood on one side of the small pool, while Melisay reclined near the tree-anemone on her stomach, her muzzle turned to look at him across the small abyss of water. They were so alien, but they had been somewhat friendly, not indifferent. A blue pebble in the pool's sand tickled his memory.

Why would a Food Merchant have a star chart record crystal? Perhaps there was more to these two aliens than was obvious, he decided.

"I accept your offer of long-term bond Service. Do I stay in the downstairs storeroom where I've been sleeping?"

"Yes, Billy McGuire," said Melisay before Zilkie could respond. "At least until we get to understand each other better. Our ways are not your ways, and it has been a long time since we shared our personal quarters with another sapient. You understand?"

Oh yes—how he understood! A sapient's personal quarters—particularly outside the single species Habitats—were its refuge, its place for mentally adjusting to the constant psychic shocks of seeing, smelling, hearing, empathing other aliens. Which was why he still ached over what had been done to *his* quarters, *his* home—small though it was.

"Sure, Melisay. I understand. I work two shifts in the shop, come up here for meals, run errands, scavenge materials for a bed, and huddle in the storeroom like a pet!"

Sarcasm was something his parents had told him to avoid as unproductive, besides being impolite. But he still hurt.

Melisay sat up on her haunches and looked directly at him. Zilkie slightly bent his tentacle topknot toward him. Oh, oh—perhaps two alien minds could make sense of human sarcasm. He kept forgetting they both were constantly, irrevocably in each other's thoughts, so that Zilkie had also shared in Billy's memory transfer.

"No, Billy McGuire Human, *not* like a pet. Like a sapient employee who thinks before it reacts," admonished Zilkie. "The loss of your progenitors is regrettable. Your presence as the only Human aboard this station is probably lonely. But life is not fair. You will either adapt and survive, or you will die."

It sounded harsh to Billy, but he knew the alien was correct. Along with "You don't get something for nothing," the lesson that "Life is not fair" had been one of the aphorisms constantly drilled into him by his parents. He mentally fingered among other lessons on humility, honesty, principles, and chose one marked *cunning*.

"You are correct, Honorable Sapient. I intend to continue adapting and surviving, as I have since I came to the Retread Shop. What are your instructions?"

The constantly writhing tentacles separated to expose the Cosex's numerous silvery eyes. They seemed to stare right through him.

"My instructions are simple but explicit. First, you will return downstairs to finish laying out the nocturnal produce. Second, you will requisition a rest unit from the common bond warehouse to place in the storeroom for your use. Third, you will review the Station's basic overview of the Forty-Seventh Florescence and the Station's history. Fourth, you will derive three Trading concepts from this history. Fifth, you will sleep. Sixth, you will present your concepts to me in the morning over the day's first meal. Then you will work two shifts as usual and repeat the process with a new vidcrystal lesson, until I am satisfied with your basic education. Understood?"

"Understood," Billy quietly replied. What had he got himself into?

The rest unit was a compact, one-meter-square cube that cost the Cosex precious barter credits. It sat in front of him in an alcove of the storeroom, awaiting programming and activation. His family often saw such devices in the homes of customers, but all three of them made do with hammocks. They had too little credit to waste on expensive, nonproductive devices of the Forty-Seventh Florescence.

Billy looked confidently at the control panel on the cube's upper surface. The panel had Braille-like projections, various ideogram groupings, IR emitters, UV lightbands, sonic and ultrasonic speakers, and several other control/interactive options that lay outside of his sensory capabilities. Whether a species saw by infrared light, communicated by touch, or controlled a device with precise jets of pheromone gases, the unit could adjust to any user. He touched a panel illuminated in his visible light range, rubbed a finger across the size controls, and pushed a pressure sensitive triangle to activate the unit.

The cube shone with a low-level blue light. Then it

started enlarging. The base lengthened to 2.5 meters long, the head and foot panels rose on metallic tubes, a vidscreen dropped down to cover the foot of the bunk bedlike unit, and a pale yellow light panel in the roof of the rectangular box came on. He pressed his comdisk against the headboard control panel to program in the basics of human physiology, Earth gravity, circadian cycle, and English. Then he climbed in.

Billy relaxed in the cushion-bed, enjoying the feel of comfort, of relaxation after a day spent mostly on his feet. Now to his next task.

The unit's internal controls were now keyed to simple ideograms visible in yellow light. He could easily reach the panel section above his head containing the Educator vidcrystals. He picked a purple crystal he hadn't reviewed since that day six years ago when the McGuire family arrived at the Retread Shop—a refugee group of two adult humans and a ten-year-old male child. Castaways with few resources. But determined to survive. They had all sat through this history lesson after entry into Dock Three. *Memories.*

Mom, Dad—I miss you. The vidcrystal slid easily into the receptor slot. He lay back, ready to remember. Ready to learn. Ready to adapt.

"Greetings/fair-eating/good-hunting Sapient. I am one of several self-aware constructs located in various parts of this Station. One of my chosen duties is orientation for Sapients new to the Forty-Seventh Florescence, or first-time visitors to this Trading Station," said a humanoid morphoform from the vidscreen that vaguely looked like Billy McGuire. "You will note my illustrated appearance is similar to that sensed by the study environment within which you now reside. This is intended to reassure you, as is my use of your primary communicative mode of modulated sounds. As you learn, I learn, and your vital specifications are even now being entered into our transient population data Repository. Are you comfortable? Please respond verbally."

"Yes, I am." Boring, boring, boring. *This part I remember.*

"Good. This is an interactive orientation program where your verbal queries and cues can cause our standard data presentation to expand upon any issue you wish. However, the subsystem I use for this duty is nonsentient, so please be patient. You may access me in real-time by touching the flashing cursor at the bottom of the screen, or give oral instructions."

Billy decided to be impatient. After all, the use of self-guided interactive programs like this was common among humans, let alone among the aliens of the Retread Shop.

"Construct, instructions are understood. Advance to your first data presentation. Execute."

"Complying," said a neutral metallic voice. The color screen flashed momentarily, and the standing humanoid form reappeared against a background of stars. It spoke.

"Imagine that the galaxy is alive with Sapient life, with civilizations old and young, with curious, questing people of all shapes, thoughts, and histories. Imagine that there is a natural cycle to all things, including civilizations, including Sapient life. Each cycle of birth, growth, maturity and senescence is one-hundred million of your years long, until the galaxy's three kiloparsec arm falls again into the central black hole, producing the Extinguishment radiation front that kills off most Sapient life. Such a cycle is called a Florescence. The present is the Forty-Seventh Florescence known to home galaxy," said the screen humanoid.

"Imagine that while Sapient life can communicate instantaneously by tachyons, and manipulate all things by subatomic particles and fields, our flesh—*can a robot have flesh?*—"and all matter must trek the chasms between the stars at slow lightspeed. Imagine a present where all life talks to itself, but only slowly, laboriously can it visit other islands of life."

Billy closed his eyes to the visual image of a slowly rotating galactic lens. He knew most of this already. Why did he have to repeat it for the Cosex?

"—realize that you come to self-knowledge in a trough of perception, aware only of the basics of communication, while all about your species conversations pass in the night. You must understand that just as life proceeds from the simple to the complex, that adaptation is crucial to survival, so too does technology, does communication, does growing awareness proceed in stages. It is—"

Time.

Time hung heavy on him, along with memories. Even this redundant recorded message could not erase his fears, his worries. What could?

"—a universe of unbelievable truths, of wonderments only now visible to your eyes, of fear, of argument, of survival in a new environment. It demands much of any Sapient. It takes its price in lives lost, loves forsworn, and veils lifted. But because it exists, it is worth the doing."

What do you know—a poetic robot!

"This Trading Station"—Billy came back to attention with a struggle—"was established five million, six hundred and sixty thousand years ago by the Kokseen aliens." Finally, something good. He never tired of hearing about the Kokseen. "The Kokseen," droned on the humanoid image, "were a three segmented, six-legged arthropod lifeform, with acute hearing in the ultrasonic range and sight in the yellow to blue range of the spectrum. They were known as very efficient omnivores. Their K3 orange star is located twenty thousand light-years around the core from this Station. A visit by a Repository memoryship built by the Glakh Conglomerate of the Forty-Sixth Florescence gave the Kokseen—through mind gestalt of the memoryship with the planetary population—much knowledge of our predecessors. The Kokseen then lit the cultural flame of this Florescence with their curiosity, their desire to know, and established tachyonic communications with most new species then coming out into space after the fallow period between galactic civilizations." *What a strange idea, that intelligent life must go through repetitive cycles of death, fallow, and rebirth!* "—and as part of their sublight expansion into space, they built the Station as a Trading nexus for this part of the spiral arm. It became and still is a multispecies entrepot where Trade in knowledge, concepts, cast-off Garbage from earlier Florescences, biologicals, fuels, and many other things is carried out. Then four million years ago, they moved their planet to a black hole after millennia spent crossing deep space. They sought the eternal dream—immortality for themselves, a way to beat the coming senescence of their race that was the price they had to pay for being the first, for being the forerunners of this Florescence." *Immortality—would it be this lonely?* "—then with planetary stasis fields never equaled before or since, the Kokseen held their Home together as it touched the event horizon, and disappeared from this universe."

It was a heroic story. Often he thought of them, of the Kokseen, alone in a newly reborn galaxy—at least until other races joined them. But now they were gone. Had been gone for four million years. Lying with arms folded behind his head, Billy dutifully watched the vidscreen.

"—some say the Kokseen entered into another parallel world of new life," said the construct. "Some say they circle endlessly, frozen in time. We do not know. But we who have minds hold this Station in trust for them, awaiting their return. And among us are the Melanons, last to see the Kokseen. The Melanons keep alive their memory, while the rest of us go about our tasks, Trading, debating, sometimes fighting, but always remembering our debt," concluded the computer's persona analogue. It then started to go into a boring description of local space Trade sectors, Clans, Houses, the various Docks, bonded warehouses, indentured Service rules—he stopped it with a touch on the cursor. Anyway he already knew these basics. But he had to develop three Trade concepts for presentation to Zilkie in the morning. And the Kokseen always fascinated him.

Billy set to work interrogating the sentient part of the program. Asking questions. Generating hypotheses. Being curious.

He fell asleep three hours later as the construct droned on about the tradeoffs between scarcity, mass, and cultural preferences.

Zilkie was eating as Billy wove his way out of the encircling green ferns of the apartment. The Cosex stood in a sandy basin, its many small worm-tentacles roiling the liquid nutrient-rich sand. It stuffed small fish into the topknot of tentacles. Perhaps Zilkie digested the animal protein with enzymes, like Earth's Venus's-flytrap and pitcher plants. However he did it, this alien was omnivorous.

"Honorable Sapient, I did as you instructed. I derived three General Trade concepts from the Trading Station's orientation lecture. Do you wish me to proceed?"

Zilkie continued to stuff small minnowlike fish into its head as it stiffly bent over to look directly at him. Yes—he could see a dark, tubular, central void among the tentacles that glistened with green fluid. A stomach where a brain ought to be! *That's really alien.*

"Yes Billy, describe your derived concepts for me. Unless you object, I will continue eating."

A tree-anemone gobbling down pint-sized pisceans didn't faze him after two years aboard the Retread Shop. He began.

"My first concept is the self-evident one of scarcity and implied value. Obviously whatever is scarce in a culture has a value, and that value provides a basis for Trade if another species shares a similar value concept. Put simply, scarcity yields value in a cultural context and it is the foundation of all Trade. Satisfactory?"

The Cosex stopped feeding a moment to respond.

"As you say, it is self-evident. The mere existence of this Trading Station that you and some others call a Retread Shop demonstrates scarcity and value as valid Trade concepts. Most infants understand this. Can't you Humans do better?"

Billy's face felt warm as a flush began to redden his skin. *Patience and control—I must be calm.*

"Yes, Zilkie, I can do better." Standing by the pool he briefly closed his eyes to aid his recall, then opened them. "The concept of synergism suggests that when two or more species combine their knowledge bases, the resulting product is greater than the individual parts. Such a multispecies knowledge product is more valuable, and hence has greater Trade value than the concepts of a single species. In sum, interspecies cooperation yields both new knowledge and greater Trade value."

Zilkie paused once more in its eating.

"Not too bad. That concept has been recognized since the First Florescence. But it is new to races who do not know of the Florescence. What is your third concept?"

Billy wondered if he could do *anything* that would please this arrogant tree.

"My third concept is not so simple. Given that all life grows and adapts through the processes of evolution and natural selection, then the striving for more knowledge, more concepts, more raw materials for Trade with other species should serve as an evolutionary stimulus to any species or grouping of species. To be succinct, Trade among species is a useful evolutionary growth mechanism because Trade involves competition, and competition forces greater and greater adaptive responses from any sapient species. In this role Trade is as useful in the evolution of a race as is violence and the use of violence to compete for living space and food."

Zilkie, he saw, had completely stopped eating halfway through his recitation. Melisay had silently drawn near to her mate, a black-and-white paw touching several loosely hanging tentacles. They both regarded Billy in silence for a few seconds. Zilkie spoke first.

"Very good, little one. You show some original thought with that concept. The evolutionary utility of Trade to a species is known to many in the Florescence, but it is not something we expect to hear from a newcomer race such as yours." The Cosex leaned its topknot toward Melisay and caressed her ears with a tentacle. "I think he has earned his first meal, don't you?"

"Yes, Zilkie. Billy is perceptive, and his progenitors obviously provided him with a good mentational foundation. You may have found yourself more than a day-laborer," mused Melisay as she handed Billy a bag of *jacquil* fruit.

A day-laborer he was. Also a human. And also a predator.

What does she mean by "more than a day-laborer"? He took the bag of fruit and began his breakfast, pondering Melisay's comment.

The answer did not come until a week later.

Chapter Five

Dwelling in past memories, Billy lay in the rest unit when Zilkie came in unannounced. Why couldn't he knock? Why no appreciation of *his* need for privacy? Of course the building did belong to the Cosex.

"Billy," peremptorily began the tree-anemone, "tomorrow you won't work in the shop as usual. Instead you'll go to Dock Twelve, find the Merchant's Refuge and present yourself to Sapient Ding do-wort. She's an oxybreathing omnivore predator like us."

"And what shall I do when I find her?" he asked. Zilkie loved playing this game of giving only part of the information needed to do anything. The Cosex always assumed everyone else was either touch-telepathic or should be. Nine days of this left him with little patience.

"Why, whatever she tells you, of course! I promised you instruction in specialized Trade matters. She is your instructor. When she is done with you, return here."

"How long will I stay with her?"

The Cosex's topknot tentacles grew still. A sure sign of irritation. *Damn! You got to watch every word with aliens!*

"However long it takes!" thundered the alien through all four sound sphincters. "And don't bother me with more questions. Comply!"

"I will comply. I understand my bond Service is under this Sapient's control," he quietly said, turning to look at the vidscreen at the foot of the bed. He shut out Zilkie, shut out all the aliens, and withdrew his perceptions inward. The screen's nonaware lesson on the food Trade preferences of the nocturnal Slizit passed before unseeing eyes.

"Billy, I think you'll like staying with Ding do-wort," said Melisay the following morning as they sat by the automat wall. "She's an old friend of ours from when we first came to the Station."

Why is she bothering to reassure? He was just an indentured laborer. Why waste time catering to his feelings? But her Memories told him otherwise. She cared.

"Thanks, Melisay. I guess I'll adjust. What's she like?"

"She is of the Kerisen species, a low gravity, arboreal-evolved omnivore from the Hercules Cluster. They've been in space for 200,000 cycles, and they're spread across both Orion and Perseus spiral arms. You'll like her," the Tellen bear reassured him.

"Thanks. I'll try to please you and her."

Melisay watched Billy speculatively as he ate a breakfast of *esay* porridge and *jacquil*. He wondered what her alien life had been like after going into space. But he wasn't ready to Trade more memories. Not yet.

The trip to Dock Twelve was so simple he put his mind on autopilot. Walk down the street. Push his way through the crowds. Find the public glideways. Step onto the local commuter strip. Then anonymity as he passed buildings, locks, tunnels, machine shops, local Farms, and anything else someone chose to build in the Retread Shop. His duffel at his feet, he retied his black hair into an offset tail on the left side, tightened the sash belt, and prepared to leave at Dock Twelve.

The Dock, he saw as he nimbly stepped off the gliding bands, was almost identical with the other eleven standard Docks at the Retread Shop. It was simply a large, cavernous space bordered on the one side by the interior Grand Arterial corridor and on the other by the two-kilometer-square spacedock cavern. Starships, local Garbage lighters, and taxis to the external Habitats would enter the Dock, connect to a cradle or Portal, offload their cargo to a common bond warehouse, and then make deals with a Merchant's Guild, Clan, or House. Afterward they'd visit the commercial area, and sometimes crew would ride the Grand Arterial for sightseeing or business. Billy used to spend long hours at the Dock Three Trade gallery window-watching the panorama of aliens, dreaming, wondering if ever other humans would come to visit. He grew up dreaming that wistful dream, always hanging around the gallery window in his brief spare time.

Today he was grown up. Today he wasn't a child anymore. Today he had duties public and private, food and shelter, and a long-term vow to keep. Maybe the Kerisen could help.

A flashing sign with the Trade ideogram caught his eye as he stepped off the glideway. It was over five kilometers away, across the commercial sector, on the spacedock side of the cavern. Billy headed toward it. At least he had good calluses on his bare feet.

The Trade ideogram loomed high overhead, flashing its image in IR, UV, and visible light to tell everyone who cared—*Here are the Traders*. He stepped through the open archway leading toward the Merchant's gallery, looking for the fractured spiral circle that denoted the Merchant's Refuge area within the larger warren of shops, offices, corridors, fuel dumps, and warehouses.

The circle shone quietly in purple light two hundred meters down a side tunnel. In minutes he stood before the bronze portal of the entryway. Billy announced himself.

"Hello, I'm Billy McGuire, in Service to Trader Zilkie the Cosex, to see Trader Ding do-wort. Please allow me entry."

The monitor eye above the entry arch gleamed red as it examined him, compared him to its file of every known sapient aboard the Shop, confirmed he was expected, and then opened the entry. Since it was not self-aware, it didn't speak to him.

Billy stepped into the lobby-bar that was part of every Refuge. He ignored the glances of the several alien Traders sitting, lounging, or hanging from the ceiling, and passed into the private quarters/offices section. He walked past the circular doors in-set into the metal walls, looking for one with a tree ideogram on it. Six offices down he found it. Before he could press the entry pressure switch, the door irised open.

"Enter Sapient, you are expected. Tell me Human, what is the meaning of existence?" called a high-pitched, alto voice.

What a question!

Billy walked in, looking for the source of the voice. A low gravity field lightened his step. Ten meters across the circular room he found it. Or her. Or something.

The alien who'd spoken sat on a giant blue-and-red cushion, surrounded by blinking terminals and computer entry stations. It looked like a giant flying squirrel from Earth. Except that this squirrel had yellow fur, six limbs, flaring fan ears, a bullet head, and six eyes that encircled the forward-protruding head and jaw. Purple cats-eyes looked at him from under the chin, top of the head, and where a human's ears would be. This alien not only looked in all directions at once, but while in horizontal glide-flight it could look both up and down simultaneously. An open tool harness seemed to be the only clothes on the alien.

"I'm waiting for an answer, Human," said the creature's mouth, revealing a fine collection of incisors and molars arranged in a V-shaped snout.

He had to collect his wits. Still standing by the door, Billy felt his feet sink into the rich carpet of the office. He concentrated on the sensation. Seeing new aliens for the first time always threw him off track for a moment.

"Are you Trader Ding do-wort?"

"Of course I am. Are you brain-damaged and unable to answer my question? Friend Zilkie told me you possessed some hint of creativity. Perhaps he was mistaken," said the Kerisen alien.

"NO!—No, I'm not brain-damaged, or anything wrong,

or . . ." He paused, hearing the confusion in his speech. Get it together! Be sapient!

"Trader Ding do-wort, my response to your question is this—the meaning of existence is said to be propagating one's genetic code. Why do you ask?"

The Kerisen tilted its head on a stumpy neck and gave a low whistle.

"Not good. Any Sapient knows the standard evolutionary rationale for existence. That is why animals exist. What about us? Why do thinking people exist all across the galaxy for billions of cycles? Do you or your species have an opinion?" asked the two-meter-tall squirrel, flexing her mid and upper arms to spread the skin between them.

Billy thought a moment and then decided to be honest. He was, after all, only sixteen years old.

"No, Trader, I don't know the answer, and I'm still trying to develop my own opinion. Actually I'm more concerned about survival than philosophy."

"Better," said Ding do-wort, "at least you admit ignorance when it exists. But let me share with you your first lesson—at least about us Kerisen. The meaning of existence is to have fun—life is a big joke played upon some poor, unsuspecting, self-aware chemicals. What do you think?" she asked. Purple cats-eyes glinted at him.

"I think that's a novel concept. Why do you believe this?" *Was that diplomatic enough?*

"Why, because it's better than believing there is no purpose to life, or that everything is predetermined, or that some crazy deity created us and then went away leaving us orphaned. It's best to have some purpose in life. We Kerisen have—over the millennia—seen so much absurdity in the cultures of two spiral arms that we concluded long ago everything is a joke. But," the squirrel conspiratorily whispered, "we pretend to take things seriously so other species won't feel bad about not knowing the meaning of life. Logical, isn't it?"

How do you deal with a crazy alien? Not crazy maybe —just very, very weird. This recitation was definitely one of the more unique points of view he had yet heard aboard the Retread Shop.

"It's logical, given your assumptions. However, I came for further training in specialized Trade matters. Is this discussion part of my training?"

Before Ding do-wort could answer, a side door irised open to admit a one-meter-long duplicate of the Kerisen. The smaller yellow alien silently glanced at Billy, faced the bigger Trader, and scampered toward her on all six hand-feet, its three small fingers and thumb curled in on each foot so it was walking on its knuckles. Billy was about to speak when he saw the smaller Kerisen climb onto Ding do-wort's back.

"Billy McGuire Human, this is Keen so-thorn, my senior husband. We Kerisen prefer nearly constant mating behavior, but don't pay any attention to him. I conduct business day or night whether he's here or not. And no, this is not part of your training. That comes later. But we Kerisen are curious—aren't you Humans?"

Ignoring the male Kerisen still atop Ding, Billy forcefully turned his attention to business. To his new master. Who liked having fun, it seemed.

"Sure, Trader, we're curious. Most sapients are curious, aren't they? That's how I came to be here. My progenitors were part of a human-only Garbage Hunter crew looking for new knowledge and Devices at abandoned worlds of previous Florescences. Their disabled ship was brought in tow here by the Bareen aliens. They died four years ago in an accident, leaving me the only human here." Billy paused, considering his options. He took a chance. "I want to be a Merchant someday!" he confided.

Ding's two fan ears flicked forward at his statement, and Keen so-thorn even glanced up.

"That's difficult for a Sapient without House or Clan," she said. "But to begin your training, then, what are the five stages in Trading which lead to this lofty position?"

"Novice, Runner, Apprentice, Factor, and Merchant," he swiftly replied.

"And how long does it usually take to reach Merchant status?"

"Ten years if you are going to make it. Otherwise you get stuck at a lower stage."

"Well, Novice, you've a long ways to go. Go into the study hall to your right and respond to whatever Trade situation the teaching construct presents you. You may leave your bag here. Go!" she commanded.

Billy did as he was ordered.

After one step into the room next door, with the iris door closed behind him, he stumbled in sudden darkness. There was no light, no sound, nothing. He stopped walking.

"Construct, what's going on here? Illuminate this space immediately!"

No answer.

"Construct? Construct! Answer me!" Billy demanded. But the self-aware computers—the algors—of the Retread Shop were just as alien as the organics, and none of them took orders willingly. They were "damned cursed obstinate algorithms," as Jason McGuire had once told Billy years ago.

This one seemed to fit that description.

Yellow light suddenly blinded his eyes. Blinking, Billy looked out at the newly revealed hall. But the expected tungsten steel walls were missing.

He saw instead a wide sandy beach with blue-green waves curling up onto brown sand. His toes dug into the moist wetness of the sand. Overhead some kind of seabird screeched at him. A yellow sun blazed down from a blue sky. His nose smelled wet salty air.

Earth? A memory of Earth? Some other planetary sea? Then he knew—this was a 3-D training environment, which the construct was creating by nuclear magnetic resonance reading of his neurons. Invisibly feeling his brain, the construct read his memories. And this beach scene was the result of laser holograms and direct neural stimulation. Billy started to object—then he saw the shape in the water.

A black shadow lay just below the waves, slowly coming toward him. Then a dull black dome broke the water. A large limpid eye stared out at him. Billy stood very still.

The black dome moved toward him, gradually exposing more of itself. A large octopoid lifeform with three-meter-long tentacles crawled partly out of the surf, advanced to within two meters of him, and plopped down in front of him with a squishing sound. The eye looked up at him from the one-meter-high dome. Now what?

Oh yeah—this was a Trade lesson. The alien must be here to Trade. What were the Trade Protocols? Billy remembered the basics.

He abruptly sat down, crossed his legs, and looked over at the alien. *Put yourself on the same level with your customer*—that was Protocol 2 he remembered. Other lifeforms might not like an overlarge sapient that could be similar to an unthinking local predator looming over them.

Billy relaxed his muscles, kicked himself mentally, and tried to be serious. First things first. *Establish communication*—that was Protocol 1.

"Hi! I'm Billy McGuire, human, your friendly local omnivore predator. Actually I'm here to take your barter credit—not eat you. How about some dealing?" Better, even though he knew he was in essence talking to the construct controlling this simulation.

No answer. Evidently this Trade scenario didn't allow for simultaneous translation by comdisk. This was going to be really basic.

"Well, that's okay if you can't talk. But you saw me and came toward me, ergo we both share a common visual range. Now what else do we share? You're curious—not hungry, otherwise you would have attacked by now. Hmmm. How about my sash? Want a blue sash to take home?" No response.

Be systematic in your Trade offer said Protocol 3. Billy thought a second, then he reached forward to draw a circle in the sand.

A finger drew a bisecting line from left to right, dividing the circle into two facing halves. He untied the blue sash, cradled the bowie knife in his left hand, and pulled the memory crystal necklace over his head. No way would he ever give up the crystals, but the gold wire might be of Trade value. He stripped the six crystals from the necklace, storing them in a thigh pocket of his jumpsuit. He was ready.

The sash he piled on the left side of his half circle, the knife in the center, and the gold wire went to the right. Billy looked over at the octopoid alien. Would it understand? Did it share the concepts of value, scarcity, and Trade? Pretty soon he would know.

The octopoid pulled its tentacles together, humping up the domed central body. A sucker-festooned tentacle curled around to reach under the mantle dome. It reappeared, carrying with it a glistening black bag about the size of a small pillow. He couldn't tell if the bag was of organic or synthetic material.

The black tentacle reached into the bag, poked around, and came out with several items. The alien, ignoring the knife and sash, put a beautiful conchlike shell, a round glassy globe, and six black pearls opposite the gold wire.

"So you like the wire? Okay, let's clear the board and put the wire front and center. Now, you display three different things for Trade. Do I want any of them? Let's see." Billy bent forward, looking closely. *Don't be too eager—* Protocol 5 was always good advice. Stall a bit. The glassy globe caught his eye. It seemed to be a miniature seafloor scene frozen like a fly in amber. Beautiful, it tugged at his heart.

"Well now, friend, I like your pearls and your globe. To show you I want more than the globe, I'll put the wire in front of the globe and draw four pearls in the sand. There! Do we have a Trade?" he asked the silent octopoid.

Billy's heart raced. This wasn't a computer game anymore. Somehow, someway, this was a real Trade encounter from someone's past, being recreated for him now. It caught him up.

The octopoid's black tentacle slowly curled toward the

circle drawn in the sand. It lifted the shell and put it back in the bag. Then it slithered over to the pearls, each as big as a walnut. The flared tip of the tentacle deftly picked up four pearls and dropped them into the bag. The remaining two pearls were pushed over to join the globe. The octopoid stared at him, then a translucent eyelid slowly slid down over the single eye.

"So, Mr. Octopus, you like to bargain? One globe and two pearls for my very rare, hand-crafted gold wire necklace. Does it matter to you if it came from Earth? Probably not. So I won't lie—I got it at Dock Three from a Hecamin cub I once knew. But it does have some sentimental value. How about three pearls?" he asked as his finger drew the shape of a third pearl in the sand next to the offered objects.

The octopoid stayed motionless so long Billy wondered if he had overplayed his hand.

A tentacle reached into the bag, pulled out a lustrous black pearl, and dropped it beside the globe.

"Ah hah! We have a Trade! My gold wire necklace for your globe and three pearls. You drive a hard bargain, but I accept. Here, take the necklace," he said, pushing the wire across the dividing line into the octopoid's Trade territory. He didn't, of course, lay a hand on the octopoid's possessions.

Two tentacles reached out. One collected the wire for the bag, while the other pushed the globe and pearls toward Billy.

Gathering up his materials into his sash, Billy remembered Protocol 7—*Always agree to a follow-up Trade meeting*. He rubbed out the bisected circle and began to draw. Soon it was done.

Before him was a profile picture of the beach, with Billy and the alien on it, and the arc of the yellow sun in a curving half circle over them. The half circle was divided into eight pie slices—he hoped the octopoids used a base eight numbering system. A curving arrow beginning at the high noon fourth-fifth quadrant juncture sliced through and around all the segments, passing under the beach scene and returning to stop in the fourth quadrant. It said come back at high noon tomorrow.

Was his symbolism clear? Did the octopoids divide their day and night into eight equal parts, for a sixteen "hour" day? Would the octopoid return?

"I hope you understand. Let's Trade some more. I like your pearls, and maybe I can find something else to Trade. Good-bye," he said, standing up and moving back a few meters.

The alien humped up on its tentacles and angled its eye up to look at him. Then it slithered fully into the surf, sinking below the waves, its single eye still watching him until the waters covered it.

The Trade was done.

The yellow sunlight flashed off, on, off, and then he was looking at a standard residence cubicle. Discshelves, a low cushionbed in one corner, and a toilet well in another corner. Spartan accommodations. Maybe he could get his rest unit shipped over.

"Sapient Billy McGuire," said a disembodied voice, "your Trade lesson for this light period is done. Next to you is your duffel bag. Trader Ding do-wort requests that you sleep and then meet her in the morning to discuss your actions. I am called Amadensis, and you may access one of my Repository nodes by simply speaking aloud. Good-night."

Billy looked at his fingerwatch. He was astounded to see it was already late evening. Mind gestalt training with a self-aware computer evidently took a while. He started to wearily walk toward the cushionbed when his right big toe hit something that clicked.

Looking down, he saw the seascape globe and the three black pearls. The gold wire necklace was nowhere to be seen. He leaned over to pick the items up, still partly wrapped in the blue sash.

Lying flat on the bed later, Billy pondered the presence of his first Trade goods. What was real? What was unreal?

Had it all just been Amadensis playing with his mind? Whatever the answer, he planned to keep the Trade goods. Especially the seascape.

Billy fell asleep watching the seaweed forests wave in an invisible current as pods of miniature octopoids hunted for minuscule crustaceans.

Chapter Six

Ding do-wort's office the next morning was unchanged. Keen so-thorn—or another male—groomed Ding's yellow fur. The Kerisen, apparently, only mated most of the time —not continuously. Ding didn't bother with a greeting or introductions.

"Billy McGuire, what do you think the objective was of yesterday's Trade lesson?"

Questions. Every damn alien loved to ask him questions. Oh well.

"The objective was to test me on primitive, nonverbal Trade modes, Trader Ding do-wort."

"Adequate, but not complete. You retained your Trade goods. Why?" she probed. This he could handle.

"To emphasize that Trade is real, not hypothetical, not theoretical. It is something real Sapients do for a specific reason. To develop the proper Trade instincts, I should always be prepared for Trade, and the keeping of my Trade proceeds reinforces the realization that Trade is for keeps, Trader Ding do-wort."

The six purple eyes all looked at him from their stubby, conical mounts—like a chameleon can when it turns an eye to look backward. The look reminded him she was much more than a cute-looking, overlarge flying squirrel. She thought, she felt, she acted alien—no matter how good a job the comdisk did of translation.

"Good. Another part of your training is real-life encounters, not just interactive bouts with Amadensis. Another Trader is coming shortly to discuss business with me. Sit and observe—you may learn something," she told him.

Billy sat on a purple-and-green cushion at one side of the circular office. Sitting, he cast his eyes about, observant. The rich, multicolored carpet on the floor, the random scattering of cushions, the 3-D light pictures on the wall of alien scenes—it all seeped into him. He was far, far from his natural home.

Ding do-wort concentrated on data manipulation at her terminals, ignoring him while six eyes coordinated four handfeet in a symphony of motion. Well, he could be patient too. He recalled a few safe memories, memories of earlier alien friends and acquaintances.

Time passed.

The door hissed open to Billy's left, shattering his reverie. A blue-leaved Melanon floated in on its levitating lodestone. Its leaves chimed.

"Good light to you, Trader Ding do-wort. Shall we compete?"

The Kerisen looked up from her terminals, sixteen fingers suddenly still.

"May your Answers be Deep, Melanon. Yes, let's compete. But first, may I offer you refreshment?" she asked.

At the Melanon's chimed concurrence, one of Ding's husbands hurried into the office with a broad flat bowl of glistening red liquid. It set the bowl down in front of the floating Melanon.

The gray sucker roots loosened their tight grip on the lodestone, and a fringe uncurled into the bowl. The liquid level visibly declined.

"Excellent, Friend Ding! The potassium trace element is just right! But now, to business," said the yellow-branched bush. "We are informed that a previously unknown Sapient culture approaches in an ATMM starship with delectable Garbage in tow. They seek Trade obviously. The Tree proposes a joint venture with you and Friend Zilkie. We get the Deep Knowledge, you get most Devices, and the Cosex gets the Shallow Knowledge and a market for its Food. Interested?"

Properly Ding do-wort didn't immediately respond. Billy observed that she took her time, tasting in her mind the fit of the proposal. Finally Ding replied to the patient bush.

"Friend Zekzek"—what? this was the friendly Melanon from the glideway—"your proposal has much merit. I do have extensive reserves of deuterium and a few modern appliances from the Forty-Seventh Florescence that the new aliens might desire. Zilkie of course can attend to replenishing their Farms with new seeds and food varieties. But what does the Tree offer as its share of joint Trade goods?" asked Ding.

"What we always offer, Friend Ding—Knowledge. Specifically, we know the exact arrival time, the likely Dock they will use, the physiological makeup of these Sapients, *and* their language. Surely you appreciate the advantage this offers, even when competing with the House of Ketchetkeel, the Tet, or other single species Habitats. Are we agreed on Service?" the bush ritualistically asked.

Ding do-wort didn't immediately accept the offer to close the deal. Instead she laboriously discussed options, percentages, risk allocation, bonded warehouse fee sharing —every aspect of a Trade involving physical and intellectual Trade goods. By the end of the day Billy was exhausted from listening. Zekzek's refreshment bowl had been filled four times, and Keen so-thorn had been summoned five times. Apparently, she drew inspiration from being with her senior husband.

Both Billy and Zekzek left for a long night's rest. He had much to do in the next six days before these new Hisein aliens arrived at the Retread Shop.

His dreams were restful, almost pleasant except for an orange phantom always lurking in the corner of his dream eye.

* * *

The Hisein starship appeared as a bright white metallic dot on Ding do-wort's wall-mounted Imager screen as it approached the Retread Shop. Its antimatter-matter main drive shut down, the four-kilometer-long ship approached slowly, using mercury-based ion thrusters to station it well outside the encircling nimbus of abandoned hulks, Garbage, and occupied Habitats sharing the local space area with the Shop. Billy felt alone, despite the presence in Ding's office of Zekzek, Melisay, Zilkie, and three of Ding's eight husbands—who alternately shared conjugal bliss with a preoccupied Ding do-wort. All save Zilkie sat or reclined on cushions.

The group was not at Dock Ten, the projected Contact point, because of a last-minute hitch. The Hisein had earlier told Port Authority they would not accept the standard regulating visit of BioSystems and Defense representatives, nor would they deactivate whatever they used for weapons. Accordingly they were ordered to halt 1,100 kilometers out from the Shop, well beyond the encircling Garbage debris cloud. Self-aware and nonaware Defense Devices even now kept close watch on the Visitor. The Florescence aliens might be greedy, but they weren't fools—not after millions of years of Trading.

Billy shifted on his cushion, feeling very much the Novice. Ding do-wort broke the quiet.

"Friend Zekzek, brief us. What are these Hisein like? Why don't they follow Protocol and approach under Standard Restrictions?"

"Friend Ding," began the Melanon, "the Hisein are low-gravity, L-L based, chemovore predators from an F2 white star four-hundred, eighty-three light-years away, and toward the galactic south pole. The morphoform is a ground-hugging, eight-limbed insectoid form with hard upper exoskeleton and soft underbelly. They use four compound eyes to light-percept in the ultraviolet through green part of the spectrum. In common with most other insectoid races in the galaxy, the Hisein manipulators are evolved mouth palps; they have a hive social structure, and they breed excessively. Where they are different," the Melanon emphasized, "is their food-chain reliance on direct underbelly contact absorption of nutrient chemicals from their prey. Instead of digesting, they simply exude an acid that quickly reduces most matter, from which they imbibe their meal. How they avoid harm from the acid is unknown." The diminutive bush paused, rocking slightly on its black lodestone before continuing.

"As to why they refuse Standard Restrictions, this is something the Tree did not predict. Perhaps their centuries in Suspense have disordered their minds. Perhaps they are simply overly cautious. Or again, they may have something to hide." The Melanon sounded thoughtful.

"More likely they are brain scrambled," rumbled Zilkie, "after such a long voyage. What of their Garbage cargo—where did they find it?"

The Melanon responded, offering up more of its Trade goods.

"Brief Port Authority contacts by the Hisein over the last few cycles indicate it is an amalgamation of Twenty-Third, Thirty-Seventh, Forty-Second, and Forty-Fifth Florescence Devices and hulks. The Hisein say they stumbled across a beacon world out towards Perseus arm. Once there, they gathered up a random sample with their tractors and headed for this Station. They say they knew of us earlier but chose not to visit until they had desirable Garbage," concluded Zekzek.

Desirable Garbage! Billy thought. That was an understatement. A beacon world, rare in any Florescence, was a planet regularly used by several Florescences. That made it very valuable. The Hisein might even prefer an arm-wide tachyonic auction of the coordinates, rather than sell such fresh Garbage knowledge to the Shop. This was a special visitor.

"That's unusual," said Melisay. "Most Sapients, particularly those new to the Forty-Seventh Florescence, can't restrain their curiosity. Usually they come out of curiosity, and only later do they become Trade partners. Could there be danger?"

"Maybe," spoke up Keen so-thorn, "but life wouldn't be any fun if it was always safe. Right?"

Billy irritably eyed the senior husband, riding Ding's back. Seeing the Kerisens remind him how alone he was. Such a relationship was impossible for him—at least until other humans came.

"There may be danger," said Zilkie to the group, "but we face danger here on the Station. And yet our different species get along, more or less. War is rare and we usually coexist. These new aliens can be absorbed—or at least Traded with. But"—the Cosex paused, laying a tentacle across Melisay's white-striped black fur—"we need to observe this Visitor closely. We need someone to inspect the Garbage while one of us attempts Factor contact." The tree-anemone tilted its green topknot toward him, exposing Billy to the stare of scores of glittery fish egg eyes.

"Friend Ding do-wort, is this young predator ready to Run for us?"

"He needs more apprentice-time," Ding do-wort said in a deep melodic voice, "but he has a certain natural aptitude. Also, he adjusts quickly to morphoform change. Billy McGuire Human may do."

Being the center of attention was not what he had planned. Anonymity was better, especially for a light-fingered male on a Hunt. Still—credits don't crawl into one's lap.

"What's my Trade share?" he stoutly asked Zilkie.

Zilkie hooted, Melisay barked, Zekzek chimed, and Ding howled with spine-tickling laughter.

"What an arrogant Novice!" Ding chuckled. "Well Zilkie, have I trained him well? He is certainly arrogant enough to become a Merchant—if he lives."

Billy sat quietly on the cushion, patient despite his excitement. He had ached the last few months for the chance to use his suit again, the chance to scavenge among the orbiting, already picked-over Garbage surrounding the Shop. Now he had the opportunity to see, first-hand, fresh Garbage from a beacon world. Would they use him?

"He will do," boomed Zilkie. "Let him partner with

Zekzek—that way one of them is always in mind-touch with the Station. As for your Trade share"—the green tree trunk loomed over him—"you may have two percent of profits after joint expenses are deducted. Our best offer—and of course," reminded the Cosex, "the cost of your rest unit will be deducted."

Two percent! On a deal of this magnitude that could be enough credits to buy his own MemoryNet terminal—certainly enough to feed and house him for at least a year. Billy felt weak, trembling. It was good he was seated.

"That's fine with me, Zilkie. When do I go?"

"Patience, patience. It will be a light cycle or two before the Port Authority allows anyone to approach. Bring your suit gear here from Dock Six, refuel, and stand by. By the way—have you ever ridden on a Melanon taxi?" Zilkie asked.

Everyone started laughing, hooting, and barking again. All except him. An inside joke apparently.

Billy ignored them for the moment. For the first time since his parents had died, he looked forward to a more immediate future than the arrival of humans. Survival on the Shop was hard, with little sympathy, but there was camaraderie. There were a few friends. And he very much wanted to be a Merchant.

He mentally cataloged his suit supplies, preparing for the future. This orphan would be ready. This human would make a name for himself. This lonely boy finally belonged to something again.

It felt good.

" " he blurted out, looking behind him.
" small, one-metre-high bush with blue flowers

RUNNER

Chapter Seven

Billy felt sick to his stomach. His eyesight was disoriented. And he was floating. Zero-G nausea hadn't bothered him in years. But now he understood the joke about the Melanon "taxi."

He hung in the middle of a large, crystal clear globe with Zekzek. The taxi was frantically darting hither and yon in three dimensions as it transited the free-floating local Garbage cloud around the tubular shape of the Shop.

"Zekzek—*please*—slow down! I feel sick!"

The pygmy bush, its taproot connected by metal cables to the C-cubed package that controlled the demonic machine, chimed back at him the answer he kept getting.

"Sapient Billy—I *am* going slow. Our speed is a paltry 120 *nicks* per *dicom*. We missed that Gorchen hulk by a full two meters! Don't you enjoy being a part of a simple three-body mathematical relationship?"

"NO! But if you must go so fast, polarize the shell! If I can't see onrushing destruction, maybe I'll survive. Please!"

"But Billy, you know we Melanons are photovores—I need the sparse photons available out here, even if Cebalral *is* a light year away. I'm hungry," explained the placidly floating plant.

He shut up. To the Melanon, this kind of transport *was* simple. Just your everyday magnetic repulsion space taxi that happened to be hectically dodging floating debris like a marble in an archaic pinball machine. He took several deep breaths, recalled Tenshung's Zen *koan* lesson to an eight-year-old, and fixed his eyes on the stationary Command, Control, and Communications package stuck to the inner wall. The C-cubed package was the only nontransparent part of the globe, other than the field coils below his feet. Billy also pushed against the invisible pressor fields protecting him and Zekzek from sudden vector changes. The feeling of pressure, of resistance helped calm his adrenaline-washed heart. In a few more minutes they were out of the cloud and heading toward the Hisein starship.

"Zekzek, what are your Factor plans with the Hisein? How do you want to rendezvous?"

"I plan to tempt their greed of course—standard Trade procedures," said the plant. "Offer a Sapient a deal so light-filled they don't care if you do look like lunch! Our group controls many resources, Runner Billy," the bush reminded him. "And I will rendezvous with you after negotiations are completed. Your suit transponder is working of course?"

Billy looked down inside his suit to the neck ring indicators. The transponder monitor showed blue—satisfactory. He looked out of his clear globular helmet at the blue-leaved Melanon, who still clutched its lodestone. No suit was necessary for it since it would enter by airlock. Anyway, if necessary, Melanons could endure vacuum for several minutes.

"It's fine. I plan to just skim through their Garbage cloud to get a feel for what they have, with a few spot inspections. Maybe five hours of work. OK?"

"Satisfactory, Runner. But be certain your chest vidcorder is working along with the RF, UV, and EMF sensors—we need at least a basic electromagnetic spectrum readout besides your visible light observations. Above all assess how likely the Garbage is to be in working order," the bush chimed. "Remember, anything we don't have to subcontract out for rebuilding is more profit for us."

"Everything's fine." He had already told the Melanon five times the suit was his dad's spare, kept in excellent repair. But it still persisted—can a four-hundred-year-old alien plant be nervous? "What about you, Zekzek—is *your* vidcorder working? Switch it on so I can check its feed to my neck ring monitor screen."

The Melanon didn't reply, but one of its sucker roots did activate the ultrasmall vidcorder attached to the main trunk below its yellow branches.

A view of nearly empty, white-speckled blackness with a large central white dot appeared in the lower left quadrant of Billy's helmet globe, projected against the one-way polarized plasticine. The check completed, Billy looked out at the white dot. He winked his left eye twice to tell the helmet's heads-up electroptical controls to go to telescopic magnification. The white dot enlarged in form.

The Hisein starship showed a peculiar design. Billy saw three long, rounded, linear blisters that ran along a lanceolate-shaped core tube. Each blister lay offset 120 degrees from the adjacent one. And all three formed a Y-axis pattern, with the core tube at the center. He saw no sign of a waste-rock shield at the nose, so the Hisein must use a forward-deploying dustbag to prevent being cooked by encounters with near-lightspeed particles and hard radiation. The standard magnetic mirror housings of the first-stage, fusion pulse exhaust could also be seen. The radiators for the gas laser-pumped primary drive stretched out from the ship's wasp-tail like wings on a dragonfly. The second stage ATMM modulus that completed the stardrive hung below the fusion pulse exhaust, ready to accept the white hot plasma, mix it with antimatter, and eject the product at one-half to nine-tenths lightspeed. Nothing unusual in the standard ATMM drive design, he noted.

But on the one-half-kilometer-long nose of the lanceolate core Billy could see dozens of half-dome blisters ten to twenty meters across. Were they sensors? Were they weapons projectors? Or were they something as simple as ship-wide Suspense stasis field nodes, rather than the individual-sized units most species built to sleep the light-years away? He couldn't tell from forty klicks out, but maybe Zekzek could figure it out once the brainy bush got on board.

"Coming up on the Defense screen, Runner Billy! Please

do nothing unusual while we are being scanned," the Melanon cautioned him. He didn't need any warning—the destructive capabilities of the fourteen Devices arranged in a blocking octagonal pattern just before the Hisein starship were daunting. The least of their capabilities included the ability to erect an eighth-dimensional entropy screen which could absorb the output of all known matter and energy weapons. The self-aware device in charge of the Shop's defensive efforts still refused to give the secret of the forty-kilometer-wide screen to any organics. But Billy knew it had to be a variant of the basic entropy globe that safely contained the ATMM reaction just outside a starship. Unfortunately no organic sapient of the Forty-Seventh Florescence yet knew how to generate an entropy field larger than a three-meter globe. Until a silicon asteroid Zotl came, or someone in the galaxy found the secret, or the algor culture of self-aware devices changed its own secretive rules, only inorganics would know this trick.

"Melanon transit globe 4XZ312, you are being held for scanning. Disengage your controls," one of the devices ordered. Zekzek complied, letting go of the cables. They floated weightless.

"NMR and boson deep-scanning are complete, Melanon transit globe. You may proceed with your visit," announced the dutiful construct a few minutes later.

Zekzek reattached the control cables. The globe sped up to cover the remaining thirty kilometers to the Hisein. And Billy positioned himself on the upper globe surface, readying for ejection.

When the globe drew within ten kilometers of the Hisein ship's nose, it suddenly moved upward at a right angle to clear the massive, two-thirds-kilometer-thick body of the starship, then again changed vectors to parallel the long axis of the alien ship. He looked up at the circular primary hatch in the globe's roof.

"Ejecting," said the Melanon.

Billy tumbled forward out of the hatch when it suddenly opened. As the globe slowed sharply, Billy continued forward at the previous speed and course in a free-flight trajectory that would eventually place him among the Hisein Garbage cloud thirty kilometers behind the starship's main drive. Until he arrived, all he could do was watch Zekzek's approach and entry into the Hisein ship on his monitor screen.

The Melanon globe curved down toward a great circular hatch in the starship's nose that glowed blackly against the white metal of the ship. Zekzek approached the empty cavern, cut power, and waited for a tractor beam to bring him inside. A jerk in the transmitted image on his helmet monitor told Billy the globe was being drawn inside. Since the vidcorder was forward-pointing, Billy couldn't see the spacelock shut behind the Melanon. But a sudden, slight fuzziness in the transmitted image suggested the metal of the Hisein ship had some effect on the very powerful, Ketchetkeel-made vidcorder.

The image now showed blinking UV lights, a docking dimple, the suggestion of pressurization, and then a harsh, purple light glared out on the Melanon as it floated down a connecting tube—out of the globe and on its way to meet new customers. The Melanon halted before a closed, truncated triangle door, and chimed a greeting in Hisein.

"Brood Mother, this hatchling is lost and begs the gift of new scent. Will you bless me?" the Melanon's translated voice echoed in Billy's ears. He looked up to take a sight on the approaching Garbage—still five more minutes to go before braking. He turned his attention back to the monitor, anxious to see what the Hisein looked like.

The door slid up in its frame and they both saw Zekzek's new customers.

"Hatchling, you are severely deformed and stunted in growth. Are you sure you do not wish the blessing of death to ease your torment?" asked a monstrous, hulking, four-meter-long alien that looked to Billy like a giant blue-green scorpion. Only this alien sported six waving mouth-palps, a whisker-fringe of chitin spikes on top of its four-eyed cranial globe, raised triangular spinal plates on the thorax, and a series of black liquid-weeping spiracles along the length of the abdomen. The metal floor of the hallway steamed where a few small drops hit it. Billy wanted to yell, to warn the Melanon to get the HELL out of there. But Zekzek stayed calm.

"No, Brood Mother, I'm resigned to my deformities. However the gift of new scent so I can pass among your young ones"—Billy shuddered, he could see six more of the monstrosities moving about in the purple shadows behind the lead Hisein—"would ease my torment. The opportunity to see perfection is rare, and I hope to learn from you and your hatchlings the proper Dance of Communion." Billy watched with one eye on the slowly approaching Garbage.

"Hatchling, you are strange, but we accept you into the great Race. Come before me," the Brood Mother ordered. Zekzek floated up to the erratically weaving mouth-palps. Which was better—the mouth or the poisoned stinger tail even now arching over the Brood Mother's back toward Zekzek? Billy mouthed a silent Zen chant, hoping.

"Accept your new scent, Hatchling. It will give you passage among the Workers of the inner Hive only—do not venture out to the *gar*-backs," warned the Hisein. A small tube below its mouth-palps pointed at Zekzek and sprayed a fine, red-dust mist upon the Melanon. The bush shook its leaves, chimed some untranslatable sounds, and resumed its Contact bargaining without missing a beat.

"Your blessing is most generous, Brood Mother. Your Race shows great wisdom in coming to bless this poor outpost with its presence. Tell me—are there any gifts you desire from us? My associates, too deformed to pass your gaze, have access to deuterium, L-L synthesized chemicals, life-extend, new Food varieties, and similar cast-off rubbish. Shall we discuss this further in your abode?" the Melanon asked.

The Brood Mother reared up on the back four of her single-jointed legs.

"Hatchling! Your gifts are minor, but the intent is well received. We do have certain gifts of our own . . ." WEEP, WEEP went the proximity alarm on Billy's suit. *Damn!*

Billy slowed his approach by touching the chest pack

thruster controls, then added a lateral vector to allow him to miss the looming, partly dismembered hulk of a He-lithex h3 factory from the Forty-Second Florescence. New Garbage! Now he could really Run!

Setting the vidcorder on wide-screen scan, Billy aimed his suit into the miniature asteroid cluster of technological junk and began to skim the cluster, happy at the sight of so much alien Garbage.

Four hours passed quickly.

Chapter Eight

Toward the end of his inspection Run, Billy's eye caught the jewel in the lotus of this Garbage cluster. Until then his Run had been an eventful but normal Run cataloging by vidcorder and sound the size, shapes, number, and degree of intactness of the Hisein Garbage. But a distinctive form caught his attention.

The jewel was a small starship only eight hundred meters long, with the usual protuberances. But what was not usual were the decorative details on the ship's frame-work. Several distinctive lines of burrs spread out from the wasp-tail main drive area like the feathers of a peacock. Midships he saw three tubular rays extending rearward at an acute angle on the port and starboard sides of the ship. At the front a distinctive teardrop shape sported five—and only five—half-domes arrayed on the upper dorsal surface. In short a three-segmented ship with six lateral pro-trusions at midbody floated before him. *A Kokseen starship!*

His heart beat quickly. His throat tightened. For him, the myth had become real.

Pressing forward in the suit, Billy aimed for the central

halfdome—which represented one of the five compound eyes common to the Kokseen species. It quickly loomed before him, twenty meters across. Just below its rim, near the nose, a small, open airlock offered access to the long abandoned and airless interior. He wasn't about to turn away when faced with such fresh Garbage—and that belonging to the race who had begun the Forty-Seventh Florescence six million years ago.

The bronze color of the outer hull retreated past him as he carefully dove into the dark, unlit interior. Yellow lights affixed to each suit shoulder came on to illuminate his way. A giant worm tube twisted before him into the innards of the five-million-year-old ship. According to the histories all Kokseen installations were basically chambers connected by tubeways, harkening back to the pack social organization of the semi-subterranean dwelling Kokseen. He eagerly followed the tubeway.

The yellow light suddenly splayed out from the confinement of the tubeway, partially revealing a large, open chamber. Billy floated upward into it.

It must be the chamber underlying the central halfdome. Turning slowly in the middle of the chamber, he saw strange metallic shapes partly appear, loom in profile, and then retreat as his lights passed by. A flicker of color, of shapes appeared in the upper corner of his eye. There! Up on the dome surface above the machine crowded chamber floor. He saw the miraculous.

Beautifully colored Kokseen, brilliant in their gray, lavender, and yellow body colors, frolicked across the painted halfdome ceiling, engaged in obvious and obscure pursuits. He turned on his back.

It was a picture history perhaps. A depiction of their orange K2 star occupied one quadrant of the dome, attended by the planets and moons of the Kokseen home system. A gradually enlarging column of varicolored Kokseen spun out from the home planet like a thread from a spinning wheel. There were groups, there were devices brought along, but it showed the race together, going out among the stars. The great wheel of the galaxy was their object, its four primary arms pinwheeled in amazing detail and exactitude. The spun thread of their race spread out, going to all the arms, even into the core and the giant black hole beast at its center. Then on an opposing quadrant, the home planet reappeared, without a sun, sailing the stars. Headed toward nothing—or something.

Billy shook his head, amazed, wondering and hopeful. *If they can be the first, so can I!*

He pulled his hopes back inside and started the standard catalog Run. Here in this ship, sticking to the routine patterns that ensured knowledge, ensured success was even more important. Billy spent the next hour combing the thorax section of the ship. He documented living quarters, Suspense canisters, storage rooms, great empty echoing ballroomlike chambers, mountains of electronic and sub-atomic-based equipment—all in prime condition, preserved by the vacuum. It was on his way out through the forward halfdome chamber that he found his prize.

Checking the pedestaled work stations, the sliding floor panels, and the alcoved chamber walls one last time, Billy found the library.

A curved wall segment of bronzelike metal slid up at the touch of his glove on a pressure sensitive part of the wall. Inside were rack upon rack of memory and vidcrystals. Multicolored, the crystals shone with the sapphire blue of star charts, the brown of food sources, the gray of procedural patterns, the blue-green of history, the red of science, the yellow of memory crystals, and a cyan-colored crystal without any content analogue he knew of among the other races of the Shop. His gloved hands lovingly caressed the crystals, holding a treasure beyond compare. Billy turned to head out to the rendezvous with Zekzek when he faltered.

I'm a Runner now—but will it last? I survived on my own because I grabbed every chance for survival I could find. Maybe a little insurance would be good?

Then he remembered the suit vidcorder silently recording everything he did. He remembered the gruff good-naturedness of Zilkie. And the warm caring of Melisay. He put the crystals back carefully, but he made a note of the cyan-colored crystal, a lone yellow memory crystal off by itself, and a sapphire blue astrogation crystal—perhaps he could ask for them as his share of the Trade profits. Billy closed the library panel, turned, and passed through the airlock wormtube. He tried to bury the feeling that he had passed up an opportunity for security. But he couldn't. Having a conscience was a burden sometimes, he thought.

Coming out of the lock into space, Billy spared a glance at the repeater screen monitoring Zekzek's Factor contact with the Hisein. It was blank, without image. *Had they eaten the poor bush?*

He rotated the suit on its vertical axis, the electroptical homing systems looking for the red-gray colored metal of the Retread Shop. With a hiss of reaction gas his rotation stopped, and Billy saw home. Or the best home he was likely to know for quite a while. Zekzek's taxi was nowhere in sight. He glanced down at the transponder indicator—still blue and working.

"Billy Human—where are you? I have been searching for twenty *dicoms* for your transponder signal. Answer please," came the reassuring, educated, comdisk translated diction of his partner.

"Here, Zekzek—toward the outer end of the cluster. Can you pick me up now?"

"Yes, all of a sudden your monitor signal came on. Have you been playing with expensive equipment, Runner?"

"NO! Not at all. Maybe there was interference from my last inspection. You won't believe what I've found."

"Well, if I won't believe it," came the cultured speech of the Melanon from the suddenly enlarging transparent taxi globe as it rocketed to a halt meters from him, "why do you insist on telling—Oh! I see what you mean. Do not speak of this on audio circuits, please. You've trace-tagged it, I assume?" asked the bush as the globe slowly circled around the Kokseen starship. He supposed the bush must be doing its own survey with globe instruments—or perhaps the unusual arrangement of the main drive magnetic mirrors piqued its curiosity. Whatever, the bush now had before it tangible remains from the mythological first creators of the Forty-Seventh Florescence. Given the near worship the Melanons had for the Kokseen, the bush might spend a year out here.

"Yes, I tagged it. Hadn't we better get back to Dock Twelve? The Run report will be extensive anyway, even without this object. The Garbage here is pretty fresh, even with later occupants of the beacon world salvaging some of their forerunners' leavings."

"What? Oh yes, I'll come get you. Prepare for insertion," warned the preoccupied plant.

Billy curled into a fetal ball as the open hatch of the taxi globe rushed toward him. The clearances had damned well better be adequate, or he would bill the group for damages to his dad's suit.

Even a preoccupied Melanon can achieve perfection, he found out. While Zekzek might seem to him to be a kindly old uncle figure, Billy was reminded again that the comdisk translations hid more than they revealed. Body language, idiosyncratic customs, a species' basic ethos—it all took time to learn, and he had only had six years of parttime study to begin understanding of the myriad variations and patterns common to the sixty-four alien species currently occupying the Retread Shop. He'd never even seen some of the Shop's aliens, let alone studied them.

"Billy—that is a most precious piece of Garbage! My leaves are aquiver! I hear the voices of the rest of the Tree in rejoicing—this promises the most sublime of Deep Knowledge," rhapsodized the entranced plant. "Were there . . . any remains? Anyone left in a Suspense canister, perhaps?"

"Nope. I checked. The ship is deserted, but all fittings and Devices are present—it's as if they just stepped off for a vacation, but then never returned."

"That's just what they did, Billy. Remember? Now for the exit through the Defense screen."

He was so preoccupied himself with his memories of being where the Kokseen had been, of treading their pathways, of sharing their special places, that he completely forgot to ask the Melanon how the Factor contact had concluded.

They both returned quiet and somber to Dock Twelve.

"Well little one, how was the Run?" asked Zilkie as the group gathered again in Ding's office. "Find anything interesting?"

Billy looked around the crowded circular office of Ding do-wort. Now was his chance to prove himself, to show he was not only a Runner, but an up-and-coming sapient who would one day be a Merchant.

"Pretty normal—except for the Kokseen starship and library I found," he nonchalantly commented. Zilkie wasn't the only one who could play the partial information game.

"What?!" hooted the tree-anemone. "Explain yourself! Does the Kokseen starship work? Were there any remains? What did you—"

Billy interrupted. "Do you want my report or just disorganized lumps of data, Zilkie?" he smugly asked. The Cosex shut up, but the tentacles were still. This little impertinence wouldn't be forgotten. But it felt great to assert himself.

"Billy, you're a Runner," said Ding do-wort from her cushion as Keen so-thorn looked over at him from his usual perch on the Kerisen's lower back. "Give your report, please."

Assured of their attention, he did just that.

"First, there are twenty-seven hulks from the various Florescences, including the single Kokseen piece. These break down into three h3 synthesis plants in poor repair, fourteen C-cubed-type satellites in poor to excellent repair, three starships, one formerly self-aware deuterium processing plant, two small habitats that are completely stripped of everything but their base metal, a transatmospheric lander that has been holed several times, and two fragments that could be specialized Devices of some sort." He caught his breath, switched on the remote feed from his vidcorder to Ding's wall Imager screen, and continued. "Second, as you can see from these images, the species represented are the

Helithex, Zorsen, Machen, and Da' ubadah from the Forty-Second Florescence; the Torrilex, Lesser U:mtak, and Glakh Conglomerate from the Forty-Sixth; the Melisuk from the Twenty-Third; the Nornep and tsa'Lichen from the Thirty-Seventh; the Damen from the Forty-Fifth; and of course the Kokseen from this Florescence."

He looked around, proud of his mastery of the obscure science of galactic species identification based on distinctive design features of their technologies. No one commented. Such expertise was common and expected on the Retread Shop.

"Third, of the twenty-seven hulks, I found six that were in such good condition that they will need little or no repair—including of course the Kokseen ship and its library. These were trace-tagged for any later auction that might be held," he said, finished with the report. The rest of the data, including the spectrum readouts and remnant field patterns, could come later. This was the core of the Run.

"The library—tell us about it, Runner Billy," asked Zekzek.

"Sure. Based on the standard cross-Florescence color codes of the vid and memory crystals, both Deep and Shallow Knowledge is present. Especially attractive may be the scientific, historical, and astronomical crystals. The memory crystals"—that caused both Ding and Melisay to lean forward from their seated floor positions—"are of unknown content. However, Zilkie, you have a Device that can read them, don't you?" he asked the Cosex, wondering if this was a trade secret of the tree-anemone.

"I do," replied the Cosex shortly. "But that is not to be known outside of this group," he warned Billy.

"OK. Maybe it's time for Zekzek's report on our new customers," he suggested. "Any chance we can get what we want?"

The Melanon bush moved toward the center of the office, inserted its vidcorder disk into one of Ding's terminals, and began its report.

"The Hisein species is typical insectoid—arrogant, paranoid, condescending, and potentially very dangerous if anyone at this Station makes the wrong move." Billy paid close attention to the mention of danger—after all, there was no place else for him to go but the Shop. "Besides my visit there have been six other delegations from various Station consortia, including the Tet, Ketchetkeel, Bareen, and House of Skyee groups, to visit the Hisein. No one else has quite our knowledge of Hisein mores and language, so only the Tet and Ketchetkeel are still in the running. The rest either failed to gain entry, failed the initial Contact or made some error in interaction with the primary Brood Mother. I hear the Bareen taxi was partly damaged by digestive juices squirted its way as it fled the starship." It paused, as the group dwelled upon visible light images of the Hisein, the Brood Mother, and the geometrically shaped interior of the starship. They all knew the risks in Contact with a new sapient species, but they were practiced at it. Still that didn't ensure perfection every time aliens came calling.

"The Trade approach I used was a variant on the 31K style of Deprecative Inferiority—they respond well when you stroke their abdomen with light-filled phrases of their superiority as a lifeform. Like most predatory insects the Hisein identify Hive members on the basis of an applied Hive scent rather than strictly morphoform shape. Once carrying the scent, I could safely pass among the occupants of the central ship core. For some reason never explained, the outer blister tubes of the ship contain a group of Hisein for which this scent does not provide free passage."

"Interesting," said Melisay, "but what of their social organization—they must have something in order to have built the ship and to have survived the trip. What is it?"

"The usual—a group of genetically bioengineered Brood Mothers controls specialized castes of Workers, Thinkers, Drones, Defenders, Technicians, and something called Seeders," said Zekzek. "It is strictly hierarchical, with most species members in servitude to a small control group. The other *gar*-backs group is probably similar in makeup—but I never met any of them."

"Those halfdomes on the nose—what are they?" asked

Zilkie, pointing with a green tentacle to one of the flickering exterior ship pictures being projected on the Imager screen.

"Unknown," replied the bush. "I asked, but the Brood Mother ignored me, just as she ignored my questions about the *gar*-backs." It paused to consider further. "The Tree gestalt warns me that the selective data restrictions which the Hisein engaged in probably indicate other motives are operating here besides Trade."

"Every species always has other motives!" asserted Keen so-thorn. "So what—there are no pure-of-heart among the known Sapient civilizations. That's reality. What's the point?"

"The *point*, male Kerisen," Zekzek somehow shouted, "is that the unknown can be dangerous, and the purposefully veiled unknown is almost certain to be dangerous. The Tree suggests extreme caution. It has also transmitted to Port Authority a Class II Beta alert."

That got Billy's attention. A Class II alert meant some visitor was likely to attack the Shop, while the Beta designation meant the time frame for the attack was unpredictable. What would the arrogant algor culture of self-aware Devices on Defense duty make of this organic warning? Not for the first time he wondered just how this strange Retread Shop of organic and inorganic sapients had managed to survive in one form or another for five million years.

"Enough!" hooted Zilkie. "Your Factor report is accepted, along with Billy's Runner catalog. Ding—why don't you check with the Arbitration Guild to see if anyone has called for an open auction broadcast to the Hisein. If they haven't, request it in our group's name." Zilkie turned back toward the Melanon. "Zekzek, the Tree's warning also concerns me. Will you ask it to check its Answers for any analogue to the current Trade Contact? And Melisay and I will check with the Hecamin, Bareen, and anyone else who has data on the part of the spiral arm where the Hisein originated—maybe someone's old data crystals contain a passing mention."

Zekzek chimed its blue leaves in accord and exited the office. Zilkie and Melisay turned to depart also, leaving Billy rushing to ask the question uppermost in his mind.

"Zilkie! A question—do I stay with Ding do-wort, or is my training now complete?" As much as he appreciated the familiarity of mammallike Ding, Billy wanted to be back with the Food Merchant. He had a feeling there was much more to know about this particular alien.

"Stay! Until my tentacles uncurl from your insolence, your presence is not desired," said the Cosex as it continued its exit through the iris door. Melisay twisted her broad head to look back at him in sympathy, but she didn't say anything.

Left alone with Trader Ding do-wort and Keen so-thorn, Billy dejectedly watched them sway together as Ding's sixteen fingers entered Billy's and Zekzek's reports into her database. There was a lesson here about dedication to one's work, but right now he didn't want to think about good advice or appropriate Trading practices. Right now he was just homesick—for his parents, for his racial home, for someone he could possess.

Billy closed his eyes, trying to sleep. Instead he wondered about the upcoming auction and what it would be like.

Sleep eventually did take him, but only after a male Kerisen dragged him into his own rest unit. His dreams were of humans, of people like himself.

Chapter Nine

The Arbitration Guild's main auction hall near the Central Dock was sparsely occupied, considering the unusual aspects of the Hisein Trade encounter. Billy wondered if others were licking their scarred teguments from unsuccessful Contact attempts. He looked around the hall, fixing in his mind's eye its shape and form.

The hall was a simple circular chamber with a domed roof and concentric circles of flat open benches cut into the poured stone. In a way it was like an ancient Roman stadium—except it had a roof. And except for the fact that the action to take place in the central stage area several levels below him would make use of highly advanced hologramic projections direct from the Hisein Garbage cloud and from the Hisein ship. And, he thought, the old Roman stadiums sure as hell never had variable gravity and atmospheric controls built into each Merchant's alcove. In that way it was like the old New York Stock Exchange where only certain people were members; they paid a stiff fee to hold a seat on the Exchange; and they all knew just how cut-throat the competition could be.

"Billy, have you ever been here before?" asked Ding do-wort from his left. This time she was abstaining—no husbands, and no sex. *She must really be serious about this auction!*

"Once, but only briefly. It was right after we got here and the Bareen chief Merchant brought our Garbage Hunter ship remains up for auction. We sat in the observer's gallery up there." He motioned with his head, pointing toward a high circular strip of quartz crystal glass above the top row of benches. "I was only ten at the time."

"Billy," interrupted Zilkie from his right, "tell me what you conclude from the Sapients you can see in attendance."

He looked around. The hall could hold several score sapients—even if they came in methane, ammonia, or deep ocean personal habitat tanks. But now he saw only six other sapients—a six-limbed Ketchetkeel mantis, a Tet amphibian, a Hecamin felinoid, two individual clumps of connected furry balls that were Bareen aliens, and a twelve-legged, giraffelike Mycron from the House of Skyee.

"I conclude that the Bareen either don't give up easily or they are stupid," he playfully commented. "To be candid, I would have thought more species would be present—even if direct physical Contact was unsuccessful or not attempted, you don't cede territory to a competitor without a fight. The species who are present are logical, considering the resources they control. We face tough competition," he concluded.

The Cosex's topknot tentacles swirled and curled about as the Merchant pondered Billy's answer. Zilkie was usually quick with his comments, but not this time.

"Perhaps what is thought by some to be valuable may in fact be otherwise," mused the Food Merchant. "Ding, any word from Zekzek on his background research on the Hisein?"

"Only the word that the Tree totally lacks any Archived material on this species or on the area of space they *said* they came from," replied the over-sized yellow squirrel. "Zilkie, I sense much more is present here than meets the nose."

For a two-hundred-year-old senior Trader like Ding dowort to be worried, things must really be out of kilter. Billy couldn't restrain his curiosity—he had to know what his senior partners were worrying about. Even if it irritated Zilkie.

"Sapient Zilkie, your and Trader Ding's concern is obvious. What are you worried about?"

The tree-anemone angled its upright green body down to focus its fish-eyes on him. But at least the tentacles still moved—like hunting snakes.

"Since the auction will not start until the Hisein activate their hologramic carrier wave, I will take a moment to explain." *Great! Maybe the Cosex was taking him more seriously now.* "Many things are wrong here, but they are in the background—for the moment. What is most important is that while we often get Wanderer-type aliens dropping in on the Station from time to time, they always contact us well in advance and provide us with full data readouts on their culture. The Hisein have not done this to the extent common in the Florescence. Second, we know nothing about the region of space the Hisein say they come from; very peculiar since sapient life is quite common in this spiral arm and the Hisein should have run into someone else before they met us." The Cosex paused, looked around at its quiet competitors spaced some distance away about the hall, and then continued. "Third, and most seriously, they will not comply with the Standard Restrictions. *Everyone* accepts them—they are so self-evident as basic security and coordination requirements that anyone refusing to comply is highly suspect. It could be a simple cultural aversion, a taboo, or a mind-set that cannot abide strangers on home territory. But I doubt that is the case here."

Billy decided to press his luck a bit. The tree-anemone was almost garrulous compared to its usual tactiturnity.

"But what about the history of past Trade Contacts with the Shop—surely some species have acted like the Hisein. How many refused Standard Restrictions and what happened?" he asked.

"Armed conflict," replied the Cosex tersely. "Of the forty-seven cases similar to this one, two-thirds of them ended in violence. The other cases derived from the cultural factors I mentioned earlier."

He didn't ask what had happened to the aliens who engaged in violence against the Shop. The Shop still existed. Ergo it was a very dangerous thing to pick a fight with the Shop aliens.

The master of ceremonies appeared. "Merchant Sapients, welcome to the Arbitration Guild's offering of Trade goods from the Hisein of Torax Hive," blared a voice from a black ovoid that had silently floated into the central stage pit on maglev repulsion. Was the speaker a deep ocean or nonoxy atmosphere type? Billy wasn't likely to know unless the sapient chose to make transparent its transport vehicle. The ovoid stayed black.

"Standard bid procedures will be followed, and the right of direct communication with the Hisein Brood Mother is guaranteed. All bids must however be public—no encrypted comlines are permitted for this auction," said the black ovoid. "The commensal carrier signal is now arriving. May the bids be grandiose!"

As the hall partly darkened, a globe of purplish light began to appear in the center of the stage pit. It expanded outward to ten meters wide, wavered as the signal heterodyners kicked in, and solidified into the horrific shape of the Brood Mother. She appeared to be on the control bridge of her starship, although background detail was poor—perhaps intentionally. He thought she looked as ugly and dangerous as when he first saw her on Zekzek's vidcorder.

The alcove audio repeater adjacent to his, Ding's, and Zilkie's positions came alive with a hissing, sibilant noise that modulated itself in unnatural rhythms. Just before his own comdisk kicked in to translate—using Zekzek's Hisein language algorithm—Billy realized he was hearing the natural speech of the Hisein.

"Sapients of the Forty-Seventh Florescence Trade Station"—at least she knew basic Trade courtesy—"we of the Hive bring Gifts to exchange. Are there any among you who dare to share Gifts with the *gar-hach-aachen?*" Why hadn't the last phrase been translated? No time to wonder —the Trade was afoot.

Zilkie led the way for the auction group. "Radiant Brood Mother of the Torax Hive, this one is malformed and not even good to eat. But we beg the boon of your beneficence. Perhaps we may review your Gifts one by one, since such splendor is surely beyond the ability of any one of us to acquire totally?"

The Hisein insectoid reared up on her back four legs. "A plant speaks! Disgusting! But I see our honorary hatchling with you—perhaps your words have some use." The Hisein paused, lowering her forebody to the floor. "Very well—we will go from that part of our Gifts closest to you to that farthest away. Who dares bid first?"

"We-us, your Eminence," said one of the Bareen ball-clumps. "For the first Gift of an archaic, interesting but nonworking h3 synthesis plant, would you consider the Gift of some second-hand environmental Refreshers?"

"YOU!! You belong to the slime spawn that insulted us once before! How dare you compound your insult by—"

Billy cut off his comdisk feed; he wasn't interested in alien epithets. Once they got down to real bartering, he would tune back in.

It took four hours of acrimonious bartering before they got to the Kokseen starship.

"Billy!" asked Zilkie, "how many crystals were there in the library?"

He thought a moment to clearly recall the image.

"Fifty-five, Trader Zilkie."

The Cosex nodded its tentacle topknot and turned its attention to the solidifying image of the Kokseen starship. Ding do-wort leaned forward from her seat, flexing the membranes between her limbs.

But the orange-skinned Tet amphibian beat them to the first offer. "Radiant Brood Mother, this one understands the sublime significance of your visit to us, and our respect for ancient traditions compels us to admit we have no Gift which can began to equal this rarity you share with us." The Tet's long, flat, orange snout slowly turned to sweep the gathered Traders in one glance, exposing them all to the basilisk gaze of two utterly black eyes with orange iris slits. Its upper and middle arm pairs held three-fingered palms together, but not in benediction. Billy felt a cold wind rise up his spine. "However we Tet make a free-will

Gift of a complete overhaul of your primary ATMM drive modulus as a sign of our respect."

Zilkie loudly interrupted the smoothly subtle pitch of the Tet. "Brood Mother, founder of Hive Torax, and superior to all beneath your gaze, I implore you to not be misled by my illustrious competitor's simple offer." The blue-green Hisein scorpion turned slightly in the floating 3-D image, placing her attention fully on the Cosex. So far their consortium had secured three of the six Garbage items they wanted. The Hisein would listen to them—for a while.

"What Trader Solaquil does not mention in his free-will Gift offer is the fact that your ship will be completely immobilized during such an overhaul. Perhaps there will be delays. Perhaps a certain part may not be available. Perhaps what seemed to be freely given will become laden down with obligations, like lice upon the tegument of your least Worker?" The Hisein hissed—an ominous sound. Billy wondered if Zilkie was overdoing it. Generating distrust of the Tet could easily overflow into distrust of the Shop itself.

"So?! What do you offer as a Gift, plant?" The Brood Mother was rearing up on her back four legs—not a good sign, he felt.

"Careful, friend Zilkie, this sapient may not be stable," finger-signed Ding in *lyol* Trade speech from Billy's left.

"Oh fertile Brood Mother," continued the tree-anemone, "I speculate upon matters best left to your wisdom. However our group can offer that which is safe to use, while you retain all your options. First, we will replenish your Farms with genetically and molecularly altered food plants matching your L-L food-chain requirements. Second, we offer four-thousand *torons* of deuterium fuel. Third, our hatchling says it can secure starcharts for suitable bioenvironment planets within the surrounding two-hundred light-years which you may wish to visit." Zilkie finished. Billy and Ding both watched the transmitted image of the Hisein, wondering if their small group had managed to outmaneuver the redoubtable Tet Clan.

The Hisein engaged in a curious, prancing dance about

the starship's bridge, as fellow monsters scattered from her path. He didn't know if it meant she was confused, frustrated, insulted, or just getting ready to close the deal. There had been little repetitive patterning to her behavior during the earlier Trades.

"DONE! My eggs may shrivel for dealing with a plant, but the safety of the Hive is all important. You may deliver your Gifts in eight *hicahs* and receive your own Gifts from us." She scuttled around again. "I hunger. This degradation of the Hive is at an end!"

The purplish light sphere quickly shrank to a pinpoint and then disappeared. The Trade was at an end. Billy was tired. But he was also curious about how the Tet Solaquil would take its recent defeat by a predatory plant.

The bipedal Tet, he knew, numbered nearly four hundred sapients aboard the Shop, making them common sights around the Shop. They had been dominant in fusion-based implosion drives and antimatter-matter overdrives for the last two million years of the Florescence. While they, like all sapients aboard the Shop, went into Suspension frequently to sleep away the ages until new customers came calling, they were reputed to be the second oldest organic occupants of the Shop still around. They also had a reputation for cold-blooded ferocity that made every sapient aboard the Shop mind its manners when around a Tet. Solaquil not only fit this mold, but Melisay said he was also one thousand bioyears old, having been hatched nearly a half-million years ago in a distant part of the galaxy's Perseus Arm. All the ancient knowledge, traditions, and ethos of the Forty-Seventh Florescence lived and breathed within Solaquil.

The Tet gave one withering glance their way and then swiftly exited the hall on two kangaroolike legs, its scaled tail whipping the air.

"Zilkie, do you think it was wise to take that last Garbage item from the Tet?" asked Ding. Good. He wasn't the only one worried.

Zilkie still stood on its worm-toes, looking perhaps to

where the Hisein had been. It didn't reply immediately. More strange behavior by the normally self-assured Cosex.

"Right or wrong, we had to have the Kokseen starship. Not just for the Deep and Shallow Knowledge, but for a special use I have in mind for the ship itself." The tree-anemone turned to look past Billy and down at the Kerisen. "Tell me Ding, do you think you could pilot a Kokseen craft?"

"What? You must be joking. Oh, how clever of you to grace me with a Cosex joke. I must tell my husbands that you Cosex savor the fun of existence as much as we do," she barked.

"I wasn't joking," said Zilkie as the three of them slowly left the hall, heading for the Grand Arterial glideway to Dock Twelve and Ding's office. "I'm serious. But enough of that for now—we have Trade goods to move from the warehouse to spacedock for modular linkup with my service lighter. Billy"—oh, oh, probably the scut detail for him—"it's time you earned your keep and your Runner rating. Surely you can see to the proper transfer of the cumulative Trade good Gifts we offered for our four purchases, their storage in cargo modules, and the leasing of a remotely piloted lighter to tractor-haul *our* Garbage from the Hisein location to Dock Twelve?"

"Sure Zilkie. I'll get right on it."

Damn! No sleep for the next six hours at least—on top of a ten-hour day already. But that was the way of things on the Shop—produce and succeed, or screw up and starve. Anyway at least he would once again see his envy, his dream, the Kokseen starship. This time he would be bringing it home.

Billy felt reasonably happy, despite the hard work. He had a decent, interesting job. He had enough to eat, even if some of it wiggled on the plate. And he was anxious to find a quiet time to privately view the vidcorder tape of his Run.

Chapter Ten

"Billy! Are all humans as slow as you?" asked Zilkie as he, the Cosex, and Ding floated in the gravity-free cavern of Dock Twelve, waiting for Traffic Control to pressor-push the RPL craft over to Zilkie's service lighter and the waiting cargo modules.

Damn! Every time he started to feel ahead of the game, some alien would burst his bubble.

"No—yes, I mean I'm working as fast as I can, Zilkie. Here it comes."

Billy floated in his suit, alone among aliens, but looking forward to seeing the Kokseen starship again.

The RPL craft silently curved to Zilkie's rhomboid-shaped service lighter, coming to a halt behind the high-pulse ion jets. The RPL automatically began attaching the modules to itself. Billy had already given the Cosex the list of L-L foods, deuterium, Refresher units, and seeds that were packed into the modular segments of the RPL. His job was carefully done. But the Cosex seemed too impatient to give compliments.

"Come," said the tree-anemone, "let's get on board. The Tet, Ketchetkeel, and the House of Skyee are already out there getting their Trade goods. I don't trust my *honorable* competitors to not try to hijack our goods."

Billy, Ding, and Zilkie jetted over to the dorsal lock at the lighter's nose, entered, pressurized, and took their stations on the control deck.

"Zilkie," asked Ding do-wort from her cushion-chair at the Tractor controls, "did Zekzek secure final approach ap-

83

proval from the Hisein?" Billy glanced over at the Cosex from his post at the Tracking console. He wondered if the tree-anemone was as irritable with the Kerisen as he was with humans.

The twisting, snaky tentacles remained in motion, unperturbed. "Yes, of course. It's all laid in with Port Authority and with the Defense screen Devices. Now tractor-grab the RPL while I exit the Dock."

Since his duty didn't begin until they arrived at the Hisein Garbage Cloud, ready to track the trace-tagged Garbage they had bought, Billy sat back and watched their departure from the Shop. This time the speed was much more sedate. He didn't get spacesick. In the pleasure of watching the glittering jewels of occupied Habitats, hulks, and miscellaneous local area transport traffic, he almost forgot how dangerous it was dealing with new aliens.

Like an archaic Earth truck pulling a trailer, Zilkie's service lighter and the attendant RPL pulled up to the Defense screen, were checked out, and then passed beyond, on their way to Trade with the Hisein. Billy's heart began to beat a bit faster.

"Aliens! Who goes there? Halt or be vaporized!" screamed a hissing voice in translated Hisein.

"Illustrious Torax Hive, it's only the Zekzek group bringing Gifts for the Brood Mother, as agreed," Zilkie quickly replied. Ding's six purple cats-eyes met Billy's two as they both wondered if the deal had gone sour. But the Cosex was very sharp. "Young one, would you destroy the property of the Brood Mother?"

That shut the nervous Hisein up. But the chemovore's touchiness bothered Billy.

"Very well, you may approach the Garbage. Locate and cluster our Gifts that you desire. Place your Gifts nearby. Go, plant!" ordered the unseen Hisein speaker. Zilkie complied.

On the way aft of the Hisein starship's main drive, Billy thought he saw the magnetic mirrors brighten, then dim, then brighten. Could they be reactivating the main drive? If so, why? It was not something you did in a crowded space like the node around the Retread Shop. He was about to mention it to Ding when he saw a three-kilometer-long Ketchetkeel dreadnought slowly pass across their path, moving toward the Shop with its Trade goods in tractor tow. Billy checked the Tracking console; no trace-tagged items of theirs had been hijacked by the powerful Ketchetkeel.

As they approached their first target, the tsa'Lichen transatmospheric lander that would need only modest rebuilding to make it usable, a cluster of a dozen orange globeships moved in front to block their approach. Billy looked down at his repeater screen to see the vid-signal Zilkie was now getting from their Tet competitors.

"Greetings, Sapient Zilkie," said the wavering, watery image of Solaquil, black basilisk eyes staring into his heart. "Have you come to buy from me?"

The Cosex kept his temper quite well. Even the tentacles kept moving.

"Perhaps *you* wish to buy from *us*, Tet." Good; if the Tet wouldn't even give the Cosex its proper title of Trader, it deserved no title at all. "But such negotiations can be done back at the Station, when our goods are in the common bond warehouse under proper *security,*" the tree-anemone emphasized.

"And why should we move? We think the Radiant Brood Mother will accept our offer now that she has had time to recover from your insults."

Billy watched the screen carefully—things were starting to get dangerous. And all they had for defensive weaponry was an antique helium-argon gas laser sticking out from a ventral weapons blister. Not much to fight off a dozen individually manned Tet globeships.

"In the end, force of course," calmly replied Zilkie. "We can at least take you with us, now that our firecontrol has locked onto your signals. But to be polite, Trade deals reached in the chamber of the Arbitration Guild have traditionally been final and irrevocable. Do you wish it known that the Tet do not honor Tradition?"

The upper body of the orange-colored, salamanderlike amphibian shook, perhaps with repressed fury. Its forked tongue flickered repetitively from side to side. The orange irised eyes glared out at them from the watery screen image.

"NO! We Tet are civilized, unlike *plants*. But," hissed the flattened snout of their enemy, "such insolence to us will not be forgotten or forgiven. Get your goods! But beware, they may become too warm to touch." The orange image vanished from Billy's repeater screen, and the globeships silently rushed off, probably to garner their own Trade goods.

He let out a pent-in breath in a loud woosh. Ding glanced over at him, an unreadable expression on her six purple eyes.

Zilkie leaned toward him from the Control Nexus command seat between and behind the two of them. "Human, why do you expel so much internal gas? Its aroma is not conducive to relaxation," the Cosex criticized him. "Prepare for tractor lockon of the target. Ding, comply!"

Billy had never been told in quite so crisp a manner that he had bad breath, but he got too busy to feel insulted. In truth, strange body odors were only a minor peculiarity associated with living among sixty-four alien species. Ding do-wort complied with the Cosex's instructions and locked the port tractor beam onto the tsa'Lichen TAL. She hauled it into stern position, alongside the RPL.

Over the next hour they picked up a Glakh Conglomerate C-cubed satellite and a Melisuk specialized Device. He didn't know why Zilkie wanted the Device—it was in poor repair—but maybe it had some antique value as an object of veneration for one of the Shop species. Then they were before the Kokseen starship. It shone in the front glassine window with a golden glare, reflecting starlight. It tugged again at his heart.

"Billy," said Ding do-wort from her post at the Tractor controls, "I'm almost at maximum capability with the tractors. Can you pressor-push the Kokseen Garbage into starboard position for me?"

"Sure, Trader Ding. We humans do have a deft touch with energy fields," he modestly teased her. Zilkie, he saw while touch-adjusting the pressure sensitive controls, watched the EMF readouts; probably wondering if the old starship still had any working automatons.

With their attention all concentrated on the difficult tasks at hand, it was no wonder they failed to notice the universe start to go to hell.

"*Hisein Starship!*" blared the loud voice of the primary Device maintaining the Defensive screen. "Explain your actions! What are you doing?"

Billy, Ding, and Zilkie jerked up from their tasks and looked at the main Imager vidscreen at the bow of the service lighter. Billy's stomach clenched, flipped over, and he started a cold sweat. He tried to understand what they were seeing.

The magnetic mirrors of the Hisein stardrive shone radiant silver as they came up to full power preparatory to generating the entropy globe necessary for main ATMM propulsion. But what was worse, he saw, were the long, *gar*-back blister tubes. They were no longer attached to the main Hisein starship. Instead they had been cast away like a seed-pod throws out its feathery seeds. He now understood what they were—spaceships. That were now arcing outward from the mother ship. Shortly they would exceed the arc-angle of entropy screen protection provided by the Devices, and be on an unhindered firing line of sight to the Shop.

"Miserable slime lice!!" screamed a Hisein voice over the main comwave, "you betray our Brood Mother's generosity! Come back! Come back!"

Billy looked at the screen, trying to figure out what was happening. The *gar*-backs continued their swift outward curve, angling toward the Shop. Between them and the Devices darted several small orange globeships and a service lighter from the House of Skyee. The Hisein mother ship was starting to rotate on its axis, striving to turn its stardrive toward the Shop. Just as he was about to point out to Zilkie they were in the line of fire from the Shop, the tree-anemone acted.

With a sudden jerk the lighter, RPL, and their four trac-tored Garbage hulks swung toward galactic south, out of the common plane shared by the Shop, the Devices, the *gar*-backs, and the Hisein starship. Then the Defense Devices pulled back in unison toward the Shop, covering the enlarging Hisein arc angle and buying a little time.

He didn't know who fired first, but in the end it didn't matter.

The interior of Zilkie's lighter suddenly lit up with brightness as a proton beam speared past them two kilometers away. It also missed the few remaining pieces of the Hisein Garbage Cloud. Then everything happened at tachyon, electron, and photon speeds. When it was all over four seconds later, they found themselves alive below the rapidly expanding gas balls of the Hisein starship and its three *gar*-backs.

The Hisein were no more.

"Zilkie, what happened?" yelled Ding from her automatically enclosed crash seat.

"Yeah, and where are we going?" Billy chimed in, his voice also muffled by the billowy cushions of the crash-protection device. Zilkie, he saw, was also enfolded, but its tentacles lashed around to various controls with lightning speed.

"The Hisein attacked the Shop. Those *gar*-back ships—I heard a Hisein shout something like 'Life to the Seeders!' —were unarmed, but they were heading for the Shop without clearance. The mother ship however shot everything it had. Proton beams, neutronic-antimatter beams, torps, plasma balls—everything." The Cosex paused while it adjusted their return course to the Shop, setting up a wide, curving trajectory that would give Port Authority time to ID them as friends, not foes. "The Defense screen contained it all of course. And then simultaneous neutronic antimatter beams shot out to the four ships from the Shop's Central Dock area and three of the Devices." The tree-anemone paused, checking to be sure their Trade goods were still following them. "I'm surprised by the Dock beam—it speared through two perfectly salvageable Haakeen hulks and narrowly missed an occupied Bareen habitat. They must have been really worried to take such chances."

"Zilkie," interrupted Billy, "I'm picking up an emergency transponder signal from some wreckage that's transiting in front of us. It's standard Shop ID—someone needs help."

The Cosex's silvery eyes spared him a look from within busily writhing green tentacles. "I'm too busy manipulating this craft, the RPL, and the hulks. Ding can't help either. What do you propose?"

He looked back at his Tracking screen, seeing the steady transponder light that signaled someone was alone, maybe hurt, in need. It definitely wasn't one of the Hisein, but it could be someone from one of the other Trading groups that were around when the fight began. Maybe they had information on how it all started. Maybe not. But he couldn't abandon another orphan.

"I'll use my suit," he replied, releasing the crash protection locks and heading toward the lock and his dad's spacesuit. "It's still got enough reactant to intercept the object. If anyone's alive, you can pull us in with a tractor. I'm going!"

"Wait, Billy!" began Zilkie, but the tree-anemone shut up as it saw him enter the airlock. The suit went on fairly quickly. He exited the lock and was on his own again.

Billy jetted toward where the transponder said the wreckage would intersect the lighter's course. His left eye blinked, flipping on the helmet's IR filter. His right eye blinked, activating the telescopic lens. It brought his objective into abrupt, shocking detail.

It was the House of Skyee service lighter he'd seen moments before as it headed toward the Defense screen. The triwinged craft, better suited to atmospheres, looked like someone had—as Jason McGuire once suggested to him —put a load of number 10 buckshot through it. Two of the wings were lazily flapping in weightlessness, their support pylons nearly shot away. The ventral pylon and wing were still intact, but the lifeglobe that usually occupied center position in the Y-shaped ship of wings and pylons was badly damaged. Some kind of kinetic energy weapon must have hit the lighter; otherwise it would now be a ball of gas from one of the energy beams. The transponder signal came from the lifeglobe part.

He made his way through the blown-out natural vision dome of the control deck. There were only rapidly drying spots and smears of green-yellow blood showing around the dome's rim. Apparently the control deck occupants were unsuited and had been blown out the quartz-crystal dome by explosive decompression. Billy pulled himself into a rear corridor that connected with the ventral pylon. He found his survivor there.

It was a Mycron, a twelve-legged, giraffelike herbivore and member of the pacifist herder-browser social pattern. The alien floated unconscious in an emergency bagsuit. A C-cubed package was stuck to a polar end of the transparent bag, blinking away in mute testimony to the condition of the sapient it protected. Looking closer, Billy stared. He hadn't seen a Mycron at all until the Arbitration Guild auction, and never one close up. While he attached a haul rope to the bagsuit, he satisfied his human curiosity.

The Mycron was about three meters tall from elongated head to its three-toed, hoof-clawed feet. The six pairs of legs that supported a ribbed, scaled, light blue body had at least two main joints per leg. They could probably run pretty fast. As the bagsuit jerked after him, following Billy out the corridor and through the dome portal into space, different parts of the alien came into his view. He saw a long, prehensile tail with poisoned talon for defense, a chest pouch for second-term gestation of the young, and twelve eyes. Scattered in a broad band about the head, they were covered by blue-skinned eyelids.

"Billy," called Zilkie over the comlink, "what do you have?"

"A Mycron in a bagsuit. It seems to still be alive. It's also painted in House of Skyee colors." He looked appraisingly at his fellow survivor, wondering what he, she, or it was like. "Can you grab us?"

"Not easily. There are only five tractor beams, and they're all holding something," said the tree-anemone.

"Well, let go of something! We live, objects don't! Come on!"

The service lighter was passing just a few hundred meters away, but unless it grabbed him, he couldn't change his inertia enough to intercept. He would be stuck out here with an unconscious alien until someone from the Shop came after them. It could be hours or even days. He wondered just what choice his greedy alien benefactor would make—assuming he made a choice.

The Melisuk Device suddenly peeled away from the miniature Garbage cloud around the Cosex's lighter. It was nice to know he was worth more than a defunct Device. Billy felt the invisible jerk of the remaining tractor. It pulled them in—slowly—to the lighter's dorsal lock. He finished the job by hauling the bagsuited Mycron into the lock, sealing it, repressurizing, and pulling the Mycron into the gravity-free hold of the lighter. It came awake just as he was tying down the bagsuit.

"Predators!" screamed the Mycron as all twelve eyes opened to glare redly at him. "Predators! Why did you attack! Why are you always attacking!? The Hisein were peaceful—until you attacked. WHY?"

"What, how—what do you mean?" Billy mumbled, completely taken aback by the burst of angry emotion from a normally placid species. "I—we didn't do anything, we were just Trading when the beams started going off."

"What?" asked the Mycron. "You predators didn't start this? *We* didn't start it. We were trying to get out past the Defense screen when the beaming started. We saw a proton beam shoot out from the Garbage Cloud toward the Hisein main ship. You didn't do this?" The Mycron struggled in the weightlessness of the bagsuit, trying like all herbivores to reassure its secondary spinal brain that solid ground was under it. Unfortunately the only thing that happened was a whirling cloud of clawfeet, until Billy, floating by a wall panel ecocontrol, slowly applied artificial gravity up to eight-tenths G—normal for these aliens.

The Mycron and bagsuit slumped on the scratched deck plates. Then the suit split down the middle and a very angry blue-skinned giraffe stepped out into the oxy-nitro atmosphere Billy had conveniently switched on. It twitched its two floppy ears at him.

"You're a *Predator*," it said, disgust coming through even with the difficulties of comdisk simultaneous translation. "Why should I believe you?" It took a few jerky steps, trying to get its multiple legs in sync. How could a brain coordinate all those legs? How could it be so natural? And maybe it thought humans crippled with only two legs.

"Because," he said, coiling up the towline and stowing his suit in a nearby locker, "this lighter only carries a helium-argon laser—no proton accelerators on this craft."

"Oh—but if not you, then who? Only a *Predator* would attack after a peaceful Trade." The Mycron flicked out its three-segmented, prehensile tongue to grab a bag of personal effects from within the bagsuit. Billy watched with distracted fascination as he saw just how well a tongue in three parts with individual fine motor control could mimic the utility of fingers and thumb. A red glare from the twelve-eyed alien reminded him of the question.

"I don't know—only you, us, the Tet, and the Ketchetkeel were out in the Garbage Cloud. And I thought I saw the Ketchetkeel passing the Defense screen as we entered, an hour before the fight started." Billy looked appraisingly at the yellow, lavender and red body-paint on the forechest of the Mycron, representative of the only multispecies Trading House on the Shop. The House of Skyee, he had heard, gave every sapient a hard run for the Trade. "You're sure it was a proton beam that started the fight?"

"Yes!" shouted the Mycron. "That kind of energy beam is unmistakable. It struck first at one of the Hisein blister tubes, then it fired back into the Cloud. We couldn't see where it came from—anyway my progenitors were too busy trying to escape the conflict plane." Reminded of its loss, the herbivore glanced away from Billy, distracted, memories striving to overwhelm the need to carry on, to survive. When he realized this was really an alien orphan, Billy felt horror. It was too much. Death again, a death that had narrowly missed them. But in the depths of his frozen mind, a glimmer of an idea broke surface.

"Mycron, I'm Billy McGuire, human, predator, and omnivore. But I'm friendly. Is there anyone you want us to call at the House of Skyee?" he offered.

"Your caring is appreciated," said the somber voice of the alien. "I am Tsorel trill-aa, herbivore, browser pattern, and peaceful L-D plant eater. No," said the lonely voice, "the only one left of my family is my neuter parent, Tsorel ak-aken. But it may not live when it learns of our disaster. I may not live," said the morose blue giraffe softly, depression beginning to set in. Its legs started to buckle.

"No! I mean—don't think that way. Please! I—I too am an orphan, the only one of my kind here. And yet *I* survived. You can too!"

The band of twelve solid red eyes looked down at him from below beautiful long lashes. The long mouth opened again.

"You survived? After the loss of your progenitors? Perhaps so can I, although we herd types feel the group loss in a deeper way than you Predators." The Mycron slowly moved toward him. Looking up, he saw the scaly long neck bend down slightly; the purple tongue flicked down to taste the air around Billy, getting his scent.

"Enough about violence," it said, dismissing firmly the minivision of hell he'd just lived through. "Who is controlling this lighter? Are there Friends with you?"

"Sure there are. Come on and I'll introduce you to a crazy plant and a sex-starved flying squirrel."

Billy and Tsorel trill-aa headed out of the hold into the corridor connecting to the control deck. He felt good about helping another sapient. And his heart felt scraped raw by the realization it was another orphan. Living aboard the Shop was not all sweetness and light.

But as they headed in to see his alien partners, he turned over in his mind the ugly thought that if they and the Ketchetkeel hadn't started the fight, it must have been the Tet. And that made him wonder whether the Tet would start a very dangerous battle just to cover their attempt to hinder or kill a Trade competitor. Could Zilkie really be that powerful?

"Well, partners, that was a very successful Trade," said Zilkie a light cycle later as Billy, Zekzek, Melisay, Ding do-wort, and Keen so-thorn gathered in Zilkie's rear storeroom at the Food shop. "We not only got most of the Garbage we wanted, but we didn't have to pay for it."

"*That* kind of Trade I can do without, thank you," said Ding, lying with Keen so-thorn atop a purple-and red-cushion. "Violence may be natural to evolution and survival, but I don't have to like it!"

"Agreed," chimed Zekzek, floating near the consortium group. "But it was inevitable, given the excessive paranoia of the Hisein. Whoever started the fight just 'lit the fuse,' as my friend Billy might say."

At the mention of his name he looked up from his task of organizing the Kokseen memory and data crystals after their copying by Zilkie's MemoryNet. Earlier Zilkie had paid Billy his profit share—which included the three special library crystals he'd earlier noted on his Run. Now they all relaxed around a small water pool that the Cosex had installed in Billy's absence. Getting the rest cube to fit now would be difficult. Would he be returning?

"I think the Tets started it. On purpose. Because Solaquil resented the fact we got the Kokseen starship," Billy quietly stated to the gathered aliens. This time he got respectful attention.

"Billy, you may be right," rumbled Melisay from her prone position near the tree-anemone, opposite the entryway from the shop front. "But we can't prove it. Proton beams are used by *both* the Tet and the Ketchetkeel, along with about one-third of the other Sapients on this Station. But"—she turned to look up at her tree-green mate—"starting a battle *is* a bit overly competitive, don't you think, Zilkie?"

The tree-anemone's topknot bent down toward the group, offering its standard view of writhing tentacles and silvery fish eyes. Then the tentacles went still. Billy alertly watched, knowing the Cosex had a deadly temper. At least *he* wasn't the object of the predatory's plant's anger.

"It *is* my dear. And, my Friends, it will not be forgotten. I will speak to the Council about it." That made Billy really sit up and take notice. The Council was the nearest thing the Shop had to a central government. Actually it was a self-help, self-interest group of the most powerful Merchants aboard the Retread Shop. They enforced a rough but usually balanced discipline of strictures and penalties against any sapient who got too rough. Tricking, cheating, stealing, even some physical harassment was permissible, but murder and organized violence was something the Council reserved to itself.

"Billy," called the Cosex. "Is the Deep Knowledge separated out for Zekzek?"

"Yes, Honorable Sapient, it is. Here." He handed fourteen multicolored crystals over to the tree-anemone. A green whipcord tentacle deftly snatched them from his open palm. The Cosex deposited the priceless crystals at the base of the Melanon's floating lodestone.

"We honor our Trade agreement, Melanon," said the Cosex. It turned its topknot toward Ding do-wort, still encumbered by Keen so-thorn. "And for you, my Friend, the tsa'Lichen TAL and the Glakh C-cubed satellite." Billy wondered if that were a fair share, but the Cosex added a codicil before he could speak up.

"Also I propose you and I share joint ownership of the Kokseen starship. I have a very special project in mind for a joint expedition to a Kokseen outpost now passing only four light-years away. The starship could get us there if you, the Human, and Zekzek can overhaul it. Interested?"

Ding do-wort was so excited by the Master Trader's proposal she pulled away from her senior husband. Keen so-thorn sat on his haunches, looking nonplussed.

"Zilkie! So that's what you meant by asking whether I

could pilot the starship. Yes," the Kerisen squirrel mused, her purple eyes alight with humorous merriment, "it would be great fun. But where is your planet? We all know there is no nearby sun with a Kokseen outpost—that's the purpose of this Station." Billy wondered the same thing. Although the idea of an expedition to a planetary surface was a fantastic dream he'd never thought could come true, he knew their local space astrophysics well enough to know the Kerisen was right. And where had the tree-anemone found the star chart for the planet?

"True," said Zilkie, "there is no Kokseen sun nearby. But there is a planet. It's a rogue, without sun or other planets, roaming the interstellar abyss. Probably a death-star approach ripped it from its home system millions of cycles ago. But whatever its origin, it has atmosphere, warmth, and a world ocean."

"Highly unlikely," chimed Zekzek from across the store-room as they all sat or reclined in discussion. "A star is necessary to warm a planet."

"Usually that's true," hooted the Cosex, evidently amused at getting one up on the Melanon. "But this planet formed around a sun, developed a nitrogen-methane atmosphere and an ocean, and then maintained it through the heat generated by radioactives in its crust. It barely supports a lifezone, but the planet lives.

"Anyway," hooted Zilkie, "the expedition is still in the future. Let us adjourn and I will be in touch with you about the joint venture. Good Trading." Taking the hint, everyone except Melisay started to leave. Including one lone human orphan.

"Billy," called Zilkie, "stay awhile. I think your training as a Runner is over. Ding has done well."

He hoped. Maybe there was a place for him here after all.

Billy followed Zilkie and Melisay up the ramp to their forest-room and the eating pond. Melisay went over to the pseudorock wall and began to order food. Zilkie, its worm-toes churning the moist sand around the pool, stared at him a moment. But at least the whipcord tentacles still moved.

"Human, what do you think I am?"

"What? Oh—you're a very rich Food Merchant who does strange things." How much could he tell the tree of what he suspected? Should he mention the sapphire blue star chart crystal he'd seen in the storeroom that day months ago when he'd been hungry and desperate. *Hmmm*.

"Try again," the Cosex invited him.

"Well, I think you're involved in a lot more than just Trading. For example, why would a Food Merchant have a star chart crystal sitting around on a shelf? Why would you have secretive meetings with a Ketchetkeel?" He paused, eying the tree-anemone. No outbursts, and the tentacles were still writhing. Time to go all out perhaps. "Also no Food Merchant is likely to undertake a Garbage Hunt expedition. Food Merchants *supply*, they don't explore. Whatever you are, it's not *just* a Food Merchant."

"Good, you show basic powers of observation and deduction," commented his master. "Then again, as Melisay once said, you are more than a day-laborer." The Cosex paused, accepting a few fresh fish from Melisay as she waddled over to them. The Tellen bear's brown eyes also looked sharply at him. Expectantly, he thought.

"What I am, in part, is an operative for the Council. I buy and sell information. I maneuver certain sapients into power positions. I get jobs done, even if they are sometimes violent. How else do you think this conglomeration of sapients has held together so long?" asked his mentor. Billy had long wondered about the same question. Now he was suddenly discovering the Cosex had connections so powerful it could withstand the wrath of a group like the Tet. He knew little about the Council, except that what they wanted done, was done. Period.

"But to test your mind is only part of the reason I asked you to stay behind. The expedition," hooted the the tree-anemone softly from its sound sphincters, "will take place soon. But I cannot lead it—Ding will as Pilot-Captain. But you and Melisay could accompany her, representing my interests and those of the Council. It means also that you will be an Apprentice to me. Think you can handle it?"

Billy abruptly sat down on the sand, stunned. He? An Apprentice? It was what he wanted, but it was all coming so quickly. Normally the transition from Runner to Apprentice took a year, not months. He looked up at the towering, strong tree-anemone. Actually his way had been charted long ago, back when he'd discovered he had an alien enemy. One who desecrated his home. The boy finished becoming a man.

"YES, Zilkie! I can handle it. When do we start the overhaul work?"

APPRENTICE

Chapter Eleven

Overhauling a starship was not the easy job Billy had thought it might be when they started. It had taken him, Zekzek, and Ding three months to repair and reactivate the cranial and thorax segments of the Kokseen starship. They contained the command functions and living/Suspense quarters. Three hours earlier they had begun on the abdomen segment containing fuel and propulsion. He felt tired beyond belief.

"Billy!"

He jerked his head up at the comdisk call, banging it on the deuterium-lithium six main fuel tank. *Damn!*

"Zekzek, don't do that! We humans have jumpy nerves, particularly when we're concentrating on Power System diagrams. What is it?"

"Sorry. Just a status check with you. Does your EMF sensor panel show this power feed?" asked the Melanon bush from its position next to the primary capacitor banks, up by the abdomen-thorax juncture.

He looked down at the orange, purple, and green light-glowing gas dynamic screen. The complex Hecamin device used magnetic fields to detect the passage of electrons or photons through the machinery in front of him. And then used miniature pressor or tractor beams to correct any physical malfunction, even down to the repair of a chip pathway. The blinking readout lights registered a particular pattern for him.

"Yes. Looks fine. The pellet preparation system, the freezer, and the injector portions of the fuel feed system look fully functional. Want me to check out the rest of the system down to the ATMM modulus?"

"Please."

Billy set the panel to neutral and then free-floated down the central feedway tube. A gravity-free berth in Dock Twelve did make things easier. Looking through the clear quartz crystal of the tubeway, he could see the complex innards of the stardrive and the abdomen interior.

On either side of him and below in a Y-axis arrangement that surrounded the pellet tubeway were the 130-meter-long, 10-meter-wide cylinders of three hydrogen-fluoride gas lasers. They provided three primary beams for the split-up into twenty-four subpulses that fed the basic deuterium-lithium six fusion reaction far ahead of him in the first thrust chamber. Back toward the juncture with the thorax he could see the electron beam exciters that could pulse with up to 300,000 joules of power at 200 picosecond intervals. Also near the juncture and close by the capacitor banks were the four magnetohydrodynamic power systems that would start up the electron beams. The MHDs were, he remembered from his Hecamin Power Systems course, far more efficient and safer than the old fission power plants used by humans. Passing by the antique rotary pellet injector, Billy slowly traversed the 100-meter-long pellet injection tube, checking out each optical sensor and course correction CO_2 laser as he passed. The reactivated EMF panel blinked orange-OK at each step in the stardrive.

"Are you at the first thrust chamber yet, Billy?" called the Melanon on the comdisk.

"Not yet—I'm just coming to the end of the pellet runway. Give me a few more minutes."

The last collar of sensors-course correctors passed around him as he floated down the five-meter-wide tubeway. Taking care to avoid jostling the pellet feedline that speared down the center of the tubeway like lead through a pencil, Billy stopped at the massive woven circle of the first set of superconducting magnetic coils. Beyond them lay the fusion reaction vessel, the outer optical mirrors that deflected the twenty-four laser subpulses into the reaction vessel, and then the rear SMC—the one that directed the fusion products into the ATMM modulus. He opened a tubeway service hatch to pass into the interior abdomen chamber, then floated over to an inspection port on the reaction vessel.

"I'm at the vessel, Zekzek. What do you want to know?"

"Check the SMC coils, the vessel lining, the radiators, and the pickup coil for structural integrity, please," directed the Melanon from its comfortable post inside the main engine room, just inside the thorax-abdomen juncture. He had to tell himself that scutwork wasn't always reserved for humans; it just happened that the Melanon, in linkage with the rest of the Tree, was simultaneously checking out the electrical, photonic, and tachyonic controls for the mechanical guts he was inspecting. He wondered if this job was what his Dad would have called grease-monkey work.

"Right."

After demagnetizing the local field around the port, he unscrewed it like a cylindrical thread screw coming out of a wall. Billy poked his naked head into the globular vessel, trying for a bare-eye inspection before he used the EMF panel for UV and X-ray diffraction passes to check for stress fractures.

The alternating layers of beryllium and beryllium oxide looked fine to him—no evidence of pitting or plasma whorls on the vessel's inner surface. The single pellet injection port and the twenty-four laser entry ports all looked free of dust or debris. He glanced toward the rear SMC and the exhaust funnel for the charged particles that rocketed out of the encircling magnetic fields at nearly 160 million meters per second. The rear SMC looked in good shape.

Pulling his head out and screwing the inspection port back in, Billy prepared to check the radiators.

The paired, rectangular tungsten steel metal radiators rose up from the front and rear SMCs in massive shield walls. The walls, carrying liquid nitrogen coolant, passed up and out through the abdomen hull to end in vacuum forty meters later. The flat, rectangular radiators looked fine to him. The structural tie bars that ridged their surface also seemed intact, although the liquid nitrogen cooling tubes that paralleled them and hugged the SMCs probably had pin-prick leaks given their five-million-year age. Billy looked down to the smaller, petal-shaped radiators attached to each of the optical mirrors. The little radiators, lying between the great wings of the front and rear SMC radiators, rose only five meters beyond the outer pressure hull, and gave the exterior of the drive wasp-tail a burred image. Billy looked for the pickup coil.

He found it situated quite near the rear SMC coil, positioned just right to pick up and drain up to 10 percent of the energy carried by the expanding magnetic field pushed outward past the SMCs by the repetitive fusion blasts. It played a minor but critical role in feeding converted electrical energy forward to the capacitor banks. In case a few pellets failed to fuse and implode, the storage capacitors could initiate up to ten laser firings before they needed the incredible energy generated by the main fusion reaction. Billy passed the sensor panel over the pickup coil. A purple light flared.

"Zekzek, I get numerous fractures among the pickup coil windings. Looks like neutron and x-ray embrittlement to me." Billy paused a moment, weighing the difficulties of dismounting the coil in the crowded innards of the abdomen. "Better put this down for total replacement."

"Fine. The Bareen owe the Tree a pickup coil for some Shallow Knowledge we gave them 1,988 cycles ago. Meet me outside at the ATMM modulus."

Pushing over to an external hull port that led outside to the oxy-nitro air of the Dock Twelve drydock, Billy paused a moment to mentally prepare himself. Inside the abdomen his visual orientation was constrained and comforted by the illusion he was in a room with a regular up and down orientation. Outside, in the busy cavern of the Dock, multiple gravity fields prevailed beyond their local drydock; things could be upside down, right side up, and everywhere in between. Local transports would be passing above, below, and around them. In essence he would be floating in a multienvironment space filled with disorienting visual cues. It took some adjusting.

He opened the access hatch and pushed out into the transparent, rectangular drydock enclosure, not forgetting to attach a safety line to a hull prong. Billy resolutely tried to ignore the sights of everyday disorder in a busy spacedock, and instead pulled himself hand-over-hand down to the glittering Gordian knot of the ATMM modulus.

"Where are you, Zekzek?" he called to the Melanon, needing the reassuring sight of the familiar, the friendly.

"Over here, my Friend. Come see our little beauty."

Billy floated past the rear SMC exhaust port to the ATMM modulus. The modulus, consisting of englobing magnetic mirrors, black hole storage reservoirs inside the englobement, and a final exhaust port opening, looked like an unattached assortment of curving shields and cannonballs. What held them together, his dad had marveled years ago during their first sight of an ATMM drive, were invisible pressor and tractor fields, which also attached the modulus to the abdomen of the starship.

"Can it generate an entropy globe?" he asked Zekzek.

"According to my panel readouts, yes," said the Melanon. "Let me check the black hole storage reservoirs. Without any black holes, we have nothing to hold the antimatter fuel," the blue-leaved bush reminded him. He watched the Melanon wave its own EMF panel in front of the modulus.

"I count sixteen pin-point black holes in the reservoirs —a standard charge. Now for the key question—do they contain antimatter?" Billy watched entranced as the Melanon took an attachment that looked like King Neptune's trident from under its gray root fringe. He watched as the plant's sucker roots attached it to the EMF panel. Then a hair-thin line of inky blackness uncurled from the trident prongs to slowly weave down into the modulus, heading for each of the black holes. In a few seconds the only form of reality that could easily pass through the event horizon of a black hole finished its task and withdrew into the trident. He was too impatient to wait.

"What's it say, Zekzek? Do we have fuel?"

"Unfortunately," chimed the Melanon, "we do not. Antimatter fuel, that is. It must have leaked out through subatomic tunneling over the millennia. Now the holes contain nothing but normal, supercondensed neutronic matter. This is a problem."

Damn! Where are we going to get antimatter fuel?

"Billy, we have done enough here. Let's head back to Zilkie and Melisay to report. Only the Cosex can arrange for AM fuel."

He followed the Melanon down to the floor of the drydock area, got his mag-soled boots under him, and walked after the floating bush. He wondered what Zilkie would do.

"What! It has no AM fuel! Great coils of Syntha!" cursed the Cosex after Zekzek factually reported their problem.

Zilkie, he saw while standing behind the Melanon in the forest apartment, was roiling the sand around the food pool with furious worm-toes. Only this time it wasn't eating. Come to think of it, he'd never heard the Cosex curse in the six months since that first thievery of his. The tree-anemone was even pacing—a human affectation it must have picked up from Billy.

"What can we do, Zilkie?" crooned Melisay from her perch high up in a miniature pine-fern tree that overlooked the pool. The Tellen bear seemed to like heights these days. He saw the tentacles of the Master Trader split open to stare up at its mate.

"Even the Council can't help on this, my dear," explained the tree-anemone. "The only Sapients who control AM fuel are the algor culture, which uses it exclusively for the neutronic antimatter beam projectors; the Ketchetkeel, who synthesize it in an AM factory satellite around one of Cebalrai's gas giants; and the Tet, who synthesize it out at their free-floating Habitat near the Sagittarius end of the Station."

"But what about those Sapients that use AM weapons?" Billy interjected. "Don't they make antimatter?"

"No. They barter for it from the Tet or the Ketchetkeel. The algors don't Trade it at all. It seems," mused the Cosex, "that either Dorken da-sub of the Ketchetkeel or Solaquil will be a gentleman-partner on the expedition. And maybe both."

"What!" yelled Billy, astounded at the possibility any Tet might accompany them. "You can't let a Tet come along— it'll probably kill us while we're in Suspense!"

"*Apprentice*, who commands this expedition?" the Cosex emphatically demanded. The tree-anemone's tentacles had gone still.

"You do, Master Trader Zilkie," he quietly replied.

"And what are the common principles involved in Trading expeditions, little one?" the Cosex asked as if it were speaking to a naive budling just learning about the real world. The world of hunger, needs, desires, and power.

"They are that the Pilot-Captain leads and commands while in space, the gentlemen-partners accept her authority in space, and on the ground it's everyone for themself or for whatever cooperating group they can agree on," he boringly responded. This he'd known for years, ever since they'd come to the Retread Shop. Most alien Garbage Hunter expeditions were not like the central government-controlled human ones. Instead they were like that followed by England's Sir Walter Raleigh, Sir Francis Drake, and some Spanish Dons, according to his dad's memories. Basically it was stay together while the common need demanded it, but once among the treasure it was rape, pillage, and grab whatever wasn't plasma torch-welded down.

"And what is the role of the Benefactor?" Zilkie asked him, driving the point in even more. The tentacles, he nervously saw, were still quiescent. The Cosex evidently didn't care for anyone to question its authority.

"The Benefactor provides supplies, approves the gentleman-partners, assigns crew duties among the partners, and sets the Charter for the expedition," he very quickly, very carefully, and very respectfully replied.

"Then if I decide it is necessary to accept a Tet—even Solaquil—as a gentleman-partner in exchange for AM fuel, who is to question me?"

"No one, Master Trader," he very quietly replied.

"See that you remember that, or you may yet stay here. As a Runner again."

Billy slumped down by the pool, letting Zekzek provide the technical readout report on the Kokseen starship. He knew the Cosex was correct and within its rights. It was just that his human intuition silently screamed at him every time he saw a Tet. A sense of unease lurked in the back of his mind, growing.

He fervently hoped the Ketchetkeel were interested in partnering with Zilkie.

Chapter Twelve

"Billy," asked Pilot-Captain Ding do-wort from her Control Nexus chair, "are we clear of the Station's local Garbage Cloud?"

He carefully looked at his Detection pedestal and its varied EMF, UV, IR, and yellow visible light screens, nimbly reading the morphoforms and ideograms of the Kokseen equipment. His job only mattered when leaving or arriving in a planetary or matter condensation system, and he was determined to prove himself a superior Apprentice.

"Clear in 2.1 *dicoms*, Pilot-Captain. We are heading down spiral and twenty degrees up toward galactic north on the general heading Master Trader Zilkie gave us," he reported. Billy looked over at the Kerisen. She had a double-seat Control Nexus chair so Keen so-thorn could be with her while she ran the control deck. He smiled at them, then looked around, silently evaluating the other Crew.

At the bow Navigation pedestal was black-and-white-striped Melisay, comfortably ensconced in a form-hugging accel chair. She winked her two left brown eyes at him in friendly acknowledgment. To port under the painted high dome were the Mycron Tsorel trill-aa at Life Patterns, a Hecamin female dominant at the Remotes, and a Bareen fur ball clumping at Supplies. To starboard he saw the blue praying mantis form of Dorken da-sub at Power Systems, the slate gray manta ray triangle of a cloud-dwelling Dor-sellien at the Defense pedestal, and orange Solaquil at the Attack pedestal. The four-armed, two-legged salamander looked ready to devour any opponent. He sighed—at least the Tet was appropriately placed; it could only harm someone or something outside of the starship. Billy glanced to the stern. He saw the two-meter globe of Amadensis the algor floating at the Tech Assessment console and the tracglobe of a methane-breathing monitor dragon settled before the Comlink console. The Ta-Aaken dragon handled the tachyonic and EMF communications with fiber-optic controls—there was no way it could ever exist in the predominant oxy-nitro atmosphere of the control deck. The last Crew post was Tactical. It integrated the Defense and Attack pedestals, and all other useful inputs. Ding herself would handle that pedestal; four handfeet with sixteen fingers did give her a slight advantage over Billy.

"Melisay," called Ding, "please feed in the final coordinates for the Kokseen rogue planet to NavMentat." The Tellen bear looked distracted for a second, perhaps reaching into her mind for that perennial link to the tree-anemone, and then one sucker-fingered hand quickly touched in the three series of numbers.

His first Friend looked back toward them. "Done, Pilot-Captain," Melisay said. "You may commence full stardrive at any moment."

Several thousand kilometers beyond the Shop, Billy felt the rumbling vibration of the deuterium-lithium six fusion pulse drive start up, pushing plasma reaction products out past the rear SMC exhaust port into the ATMM modulus. Then the whole ship jerked as a high-pitched whine heterodyned up into inaudibility. The antimatter-matter reaction had just taken hold, he knew, hidden deep within the modulus. And plasma reaction products hotter than any sun and more violent than a nova were streaming out behind the Kokseen starship, pushing it up toward nine-tenths lightspeed. The flare of utter matter-antimatter annihilation fingered out 1,500 kilometers behind them, a deadly stream of radiation. The Shop histories said some species had used it as a weapon in local wars of conquest.

Billy looked up and to the right to watch the maglev suspended shape of the Dorsellien as it lazily flapped its broad, delta wing-shaped gray body in the instinctual physical motion of a low-gravity cloud-dweller who had never lived on land. Who couldn't live on land. And who, he remembered, must always move its body to push its large, gaping oval mouth through the plankton-rich, soup-thick atmosphere of its home planet. Here it was fed with a pump-mask that provided its own special diet. The Dorsellien, Melisay had told him upon reporting to the control deck, manipulated the free-floating Defense console with short-range telekinesis since it lacked appendages for physically controlling the solid world. Mentic lifeforms like the Dorsellien, he knew from his studies, were only one of the several manipulative patterns evolved by sapient life. There were also the Technological types like himself, Ding, Zilkie, and the majority of the Shop aliens, the Non-Technological like Melisay, and the Biogenetic like the ill-fated Hisein and several other species. However it was done, external reality was manipulated by sapient lifeforms. It was just that dealing directly with such weird lifeforms, having them share his own living space—that took some adjusting to.

"Billy, you may put the Detection pedestal on automatic.

We're clear of all local Garbage and facing a long, boring trip," said Ding do-wort from her Control Nexus chair. "Crew," she called out to the rest of the gentlemen-partners on the control deck, "you may go to shifts. We enter Suspense in 600 *dicoms*. Comply!"

He keyed in the automode on his console, stood up and swiftly walked back into the thorax segment, seeking his personal room. His own space and rest cube he'd paid Zilkie for. Billy ignored the dark stare of Solaquil, the indifferent looks of most of the aliens and Melisay's swift brown glance.

This human needed rest. He needed time to mentally adjust to the aliens on the control deck and the twenty other gentlemen-partners hanging about the thorax section preparing their equipment for the Garbage Hunt. Being surrounded by twenty-nine aliens and an algor was not his idea of comfort. He wanted to dig out the yellow Kokseen memory crystal that was his payment for his Run on the starship, now renamed *Star Riches*. He needed the contact with the Kokseen, the encouragement of those who had been alone like him. Being part of Zilkie's consortium as an Apprentice was great, but a part of him needed something else. Something only the lure of the Kokseen could satisfy.

The yellow memory crystal slid into the rest unit's Bareen-made MemoryNet. Billy had bought it with some of his share from the Hisein Trade profits and installed it in the library alcove above the head of his couch-bed. The red filigree skullcap came down in his left hand, trailing its attachment cable. Glancing around one last time to be sure the iris door to his room was secure and Defense safetied, the orphan lowered the cap over his head. He hungered to know the Kokseen, to know their thoughts, to know them as People.

His mind slowly became alien, became that of the Kokseen whose memories were encoded on the crystal as something called *The Tale of Ayeesha* . . .

* * *

Ayeesha the orphan felt lonely.

She knew she was lonely because the company of her band of *stretzels* did not comfort her. The dumb, six-legged animals hopped around the tumbled rocks of her mountain pasture, nibbling at the moss-lichen as usual. They managed to avoid falling off the ever-present ledges only due to her ultrasonic warning whistles signaling danger. But the glistening of their iridescent scales under the orange midday light of Lamiseen did not move her.

(A morsel of Billy's conscience struggled to preserve his identity, his Self, his existence amidst the flood of alien perceptions. He struggled.)

An orphan she had always been. That verity of existence would never change. She would never know which pack of the Kokseen had been her birth-group. Like several score other packs they had been destroyed by the eruption of Gallisay that buried her home village, killed all but herself, and destroyed the Administrative alcove with its mundane record of crop yields, taxes owed, duties done, packs formed, and children birthed.

The port cities had belatedly sent an Air-Sea rescue unit once they worked out which of the various erupting volcanoes was Gallisay. The hovercraft, using precious hydrocarbons, had floated over the stinking, smoking ruins of home, of industry, garishly lit by the setting light of Lamiseen. Searching here, searching there. Never finding life amid the piles of ash, the sulfurous fumes, the aftershocks of magma seeking new balances. So they had left. After all the ports had high waves and a crumbling breakwater to deal with.

She watched them go from her refuge in the rocks of the southern foothills. Uncaring, benumbed, hungry, oblivious to the fate that had sent her south that day on her lifequest. Not east into the searing blast of flame, gas, and rock that burst laterally out of Gallisay upon the home cluster of domes. A youngling when she went south, all she possessed was her name, her language, and the instincts of the Kokseen.

(The searing trauma of another orphan, another who had lost home and parents, tore at Billy's mind and soul. Would he always lose those he held dear?)

Through the passing cycles those instincts found her prey food, and they led her to shelter amid the cordillera's regular eruptions as the oceanic plate subducted beneath the coastline of Azaire continent. They also taught her to be cautious. She had carefully chosen contact with a traveling Merchant leading a string of burden carriers inland from the coast to a nearby settlement. Acting as if she belonged to the village he sought, she obtained books, pictures, record tapes, and a reader in exchange for her *stretzel* herding.

The blood serum of the *stretzels*, suitably fractionated, dried, and photoactivated, was a powerful antiaging drug that allowed a Kokseen to experience nearly 150 cycles of Lamiseen rather than the usual eighty. The Merchant had several such arrangements with hinterland groups, and each party profited. The Merchant grew rich in precious metals, allegiances, and concubines. Ayeesha learned of the Kokseen about her, of the pioneering efforts on Azaire, and of the complex industries, towns, and transport centers on the home continent of Akahah. It was enough.

She had grown into an adulthood, making do for herself, rarely seeking extended contact with other Kokseen. Not that she was an ascetic—she joyed in the pleasures of life, of competition, of learning.

It was just that she felt at ease among the quiescent and active volcanoes of her mountains. They had taken from her, but they had also provided. They were Home, her touchstone, the place she lived.

Still, she felt lonely.

An epoch ago the Repository had landed on Azaire, unaware that sapience was rising on the other continent of the world Hamiden. It had settled upon an aged stretch of shield rock, gathered its fields about it, powered down, and begun waiting. The only outward sign of the last product of the Forty-Sixth Florescence was a dull gray ovoid and an immaterial psych-alarm. While it waited, the two continents slowly moved back toward each other, narrowing minutely the world sea between them. A coastal cordillera burst up through the shield rock, engulfing the Repository, burying it in molten granite. Climates changed, coastlines were inundated, continental shelfs were exposed, and life adjusted.

The Repository persisted, immune to most forces short of a neutronic antimatter beam. But now its attention had been pricked. The psych-alarm barely pulsed its notification. A Subject had been found. The minimally self-aware construct spoke to its masters.

"*Alert, Subject detected! Alert, Subject detected! Instructions required,*" it pulsed against the sleeping minds. Slowly, slowly, the one chosen as first sentinel left his reverie to contact reality.

"*Alert acknowledged,*" said the sentinel.

Ages ago he had been a respected historian of the Glakh Conglomerate, that last best hope of the Forty-Sixth Florescence. Now he was less than that and also much more. "*Report Subject observations,*" he instructed the eager but relatively dull-witted device.

"*Subject is a three-nakt-long, six-legged, three-segmented arthropod lifeform. Local habitat coloring of Subject is gray on the abdomen, lavender on the thorax, and yellow in the cranial area. It possesses acute hearing into the ultrasonic range, sees predominantly in the yellow to blue range of the spectrum, and is an efficient omnivore. While possessing technological devices and good basic mentational capabilities, it currently pursues herding as its vocation. Are readouts on the planetary sapients desired?*" it inquired.

"*Of course, fool, what is the culture like? What is the level of technology? Explicate!*" the sentinel Gamafore prodded. If only he were back home, he thought, among kindred minds, reaching out endlessly to know.

(Ghostly Billy, feeling yet *again* the self-perception of

another alien, felt his identity stretch. Would the memories shred him?)

"Conscious mind scan shows Subject belongs to a species called the Kokseen. There are nine hundred million sapients on the planet, nearly all concentrated on the other continent Akahah. Their industrial revolution began five hundred cycles ago, their information revolution two hundred cycles ago, and they currently rate as a Type 1.6J inquisitive-creative culture. Colonization of this continent began only one hundred cycles ago, being delayed by extensive volcanic activity over the past half-million cycles," the conscientious machine replied. *"The Kokseen possess fusion power, extensive automated industries, a basic level of biological-scientific research, and they have landed a small craft on the nearest of their two moons. Their society is organized about the pack, a breeding-work unit which engages in trade, industry, and research. A fairly weak central authority exists in the main trading city/capital of Lamkok. Lastly there is no sign of prior Florescence contact—they appear to be an indigenous sapience well suited to this ecosphere."*

Interesting, Gamafore thought. To see sapience again rise in a form so unlike his own—and yet it was the way of life. Wherever a suitable ecosphere existed for several billion cycles, some organism would ascend to know itself. And perhaps others. Time to work.

"Construct, establish an augmented psylink for me to the Subject. I must percept directly," he ordered.

With the closing of a few molecular pathways and a surge of electrons, the helpful device gave him the gift rare in any Florescence, that of direct mind link with another sapience. Not being a Zotl, an empath like the Tokay, or a gestalt mind member, he had brought only his normal abilities to his duty as an engram within the Repository. But now came the reward for eons of waiting.

Moving out over the link, he touched the curves, flows, fears, and hopes of another mind. He percepted another world view. Seeing, he tried to understand.

* * *

The *stretzel* band had begun to instinctively move in the direction of home pasture when she felt—something. It was a light, cool, somewhat pleasant sensation in the medial ganglion of her five-lobed brain. It wasn't a memory, a dream, a hunger, or a worry. She really couldn't classify it.

(Ghost-Billy empathized with Ayeesha—her struggle was his.)

All she knew was she felt funny. And she felt as if she were being watched.

A silly idea really. Her hearing was acute enough to detect the rasp of fresh magma moving up a fumarole, let alone the approach of the few large predators daring enough to compete with the Kokseen. Her eyesight through her three major and two minor compound eyes was also superb. Ayeesha was known as an efficient hunter and careful band protector. Nothing on land or in the air came near her that she did not detect, evaluate, and classify.

Halting her following of the rear of the band, she looked around to see whatever was watching her.

Ayeesha saw huge tumbled slabs of granite, cracked from the faces of the uprearing crags that encircled her. Pale orange in the light of Lamiseen, they hid nothing. The col ahead through which they would exit the little upland basin was unpopulated. More boulders, slab rock, talus, and patches of lichen, but nothing with a mind.

CRAAACK!!! A large slab broke off from a cliff-face to her left, just ahead along her line of travel.

Scanning quickly with her eyes while tracking the *stretzel* with her ears, she expected to see the usual—a freshly exposed face of granite newly born by the heat of the day. Such slabbing from cold or heat was a normal, regular part of existence in mountains that lived, that moved, that were forever seeking new stress release points. What she saw wasn't the usual.

Now freshly exposed was a curving, gray-black bulge. A shape out of harmony with the jagged edges of cold rock and the sludgy ripples of cooled magma. Looking just below the anomaly, she saw on the fallen slab the negative imprint of the bulge. Obviously whatever it was, it wasn't granite.

Whistling the *stretzel* to a halt, she cautiously moved toward this novelty in a life dominated by the routine. Behind her the band fell to munching on clumps of lichen, content for a while.

Excited, intrigued, cautious, she was still a curious being. All Kokseen loved to poke, to prod, to see the hidden designs within reality. No different from her kin, Ayeesha nimbly sidled toward the bulge, approaching of course from the side. The direct advance was used only when you knew what opponent you faced.

Reaching out with the sensitive tip of her left foreleg, she touched the bulge.

Smooth like obsidian, and without friction. Also it vibrated. It felt like something animate rather than misplaced metamorphic inclusion in ignitic rock. She was puzzled.

With a brief hum a part of the bulge fell away inward, creating an oval entry quite large enough for her low, long mass to pass through.

"Hello," said a Voice in her mind. *"Please enter. We have much to discuss, my child."*

Startled, interested, and puzzled, Ayeesha showed courage. She resolutely walked into a dark cave of crystals, of palpable surging lights that flickered orange, yellow, light blue, indigo, purple, and other spectrums she couldn't name. She entered wonder.

Gamafore marveled at the sense feelings he was percepting, at touch, smell, taste, sound, and body. To have a body, to feel the gravity well again—such was the stuff of dreams! Seeing with five eyes instead of two, touching with six tactile pads rather than four, moving horizontally across land rather than upright—strange, he thought. But it was real, was sensation, was real-time. Touching only the surface of Ayeesha's mind, he began the small Dance.

* * *

"Welcome," Ayeesha heard from all about her. *"This is our home, our Repository. What do you feel?"* asked a resonant Voice in her mind, one with a sense of maleness, but also a sense of the pack leader about it.

She halted inside the cave, swaying on her six outthrust legs atop a curving smooth pathway that went before her into the twinkling black depths. A Test, she thought, how like the learning tapes of her early years. Curious to know more, she responded.

"Voice, I feel excited, cautious, curious. Now you answer my query—who are you and what is this place?" she probed.

"I am Gamafore, sentinel mind of the Repository, once a historian of the Glakh Conglomerate of the Forty-Sixth Florescence of the galaxy. This place is the Repository, a humble spacecraft seeded outward as the last great offering to entropy of our people. In it are myself, and nearly seven hundred other minds of seventy-three different races and forty-two varied civilizations. We came to your world two million cycles ago, to await you, and your people," explained the Voice in her mind.

(The Remembering Billy, adjusted now to the senses of aliens, felt excitement. Here was direct knowledge of the predecessor Florescence. Here were their *real* Forerunners!)

Ayeesha was startled. Space travel she knew about. The likelihood of other races beneath the canopy of sky's egg cluster was a given long understood. That the moment for Contact with such Life had finally come, out of the past, was something else. Noting there was no new query, she pressed ahead.

"But where are you?—all I see are colored crystals. And what is this Florescence you speak of? Why did you seek us out?" she querulously asked.

Gamafore understood. Others had faced what she was now facing.

"Ayeesha, we are all about you. We are engrams im-

pressed into the crystalline matrices about you. Space voyages of lifetimes can be in the flesh, but voyages across the millennia, across epochs, require only the essentials— thought and identity. We think, we live within the crystals, but our reality is far more than what you see before you," he explained.

"The Florescence is—was—the Forty-Sixth known to home galaxy. It was trillions of beings from thousands of sapient races, all webbed together by tachyonic communications in the Dance. The Dance of wonder, of curiosity, of creation, of knowing, and of mutual humbleness. We spoke to each other, joyed with each other, and touched the face of creation across the four spiral arms and into the depths of the core right up to the radiation front of its black hole. Across nearly a hundred million cycles the Forty-Sixth Florescence arose, grew, stumbled, thrived, matured, and finally grew old. Races lived, died. Civilizations lived, died. Stars flickered out here and there. And amid the occasional disagreements, the wonderful achievements, and the thrill of discovery, we finally yielded to entropy. To senescence. Our time had been, and the wheel of life had turned full-circle. The Zotls went from us. Dead zones began to appear. The Extinguishment radiation blight spread," Gamafore remembered. Oh, how we remembered! Like members of his own body, his alien friends went away, one by one. The loneliness came. And with their remaining resources they did something about it.

(Ghostly Billy also felt the loneliness. It was something he always knew, no matter how caring Zilkie, Melisay, and Ding.)

"My child, our civilization is gone, but yours is just beginning. In the only way permitted to organics, our Florescence determined to send a Gift down the ages to our successors. As has been done since the First Florescence, we put the best of our minds into these crystals, launched ourselves out at barely lightspeed, and hunted life abodes. Then we waited for sapience to arise, as it always does. Waited until we could give our Gift," Gamafore said.

Ayeesha, enthralled by the vision of images, of fleeting alien shapes, of eons populated by Life, was still alert. Sharp enough to know you don't get something for nothing.

"Gift?" she said. "What is this Gift? And what is its price?" she forthrightly asked.

"This!" said the Voice as chaos engulfed her.

Gamafore ripped apart the veil separating Ayeesha from the 692 other, now-awake minds of the Repository. As he joined the growing chorus, the epiphany of identities, he hoped she would survive. There was simply no other way in which it could be done, by which a mind could join the Dance. A being either leaped fully into the unknown of this reality, or it perished by the wayside, unhinged from all moorings of sanity.

Enlarged, expanded by gestalt with his mind cousins, their physical enclosure evaporating to their combined perceptions, Gamafore awaited the outcome of the true Test.

Ayeesha felt agony.

Many voices battered her. Dozens of senses invaded her. Reality perceptions revolting to her, wondrous to her, or simply incomprehensible assaulted her world view. It grew and grew and grew until she felt as if she would explode.

And then she Transitioned.

Suddenly the fragile chips of her identity coalesced amid the tossing waves of her neighbors. She knew not where she was. She could not feel her body, but her self, her identity was there. And her neighbors were applauding her, shrilling their approval, humming their acceptance; in scores of ways they welcomed the newest mind to the Dance.

Using the instrumentalities of the Repository, tools she could now perceive, she began to explore her home world, accompanied by her new friends.

(Billy, also caught up in the unique feeling of mind gestalt, went with Ayeesha, wondering at the touch of other minds, other beings. He saw a view of reality that made books, disks, and all other data sources pale and two-dimensional.)

Gamafore, riding along with the others, skimmed from planetary magnetic pulse to pulse, riding the fields that had long sheltered the potentiality gestating within. They saw the Kokseen through Ayeesha's eyes, knowing the race as only one born to it could. Dipping down, they saw a family pack of twenty at work in a *gliss* field. Six of the group carried younglings on their backs as they directed the furrowing machines, while the rest seeded the black soil. Nearby another pack worked in an underground factory assembling thermionic isotope power units for satellites and remote sensor stations. Far above in the black embrace of space six packs moved panels, girders, and lifeglobes about to construct the Kokseen's first Transit station. The charged electron beam drives of their ships volatized water into hydrogen and oxygen which, sparked by an afterburner, slowly moved cargo about in low Hamiden orbit. And in a small dome on the moon Hogen a single pack gazed with calculating minds out into space at the microwave immanence remaining from the birth of the universe seventeen billion cycles ago.

Around and around the planet they went, percepting tidbits here, touching minds there, enjoying the reverie before the last choice.

"*Ayeesha*," said Gamafore to his newest cousin. "*You have paid the price; now will you accept the Gift?*" he asked.

His question puzzled Ayeesha.

"Gamafore, isn't this communion of minds your Gift? It was hard to accept, but once I did, it felt like an old, well-used work harness. What do you mean?" she asked.

Telling himself that all children must eventually grow up, Gamafore pressed ahead with his hard, hard task. Dimming the light of childish but intelligent delight he could feel radiating from her, however slightly, was not something he wanted to do.

"Ayeesha, a duty remains. The duty of the Repository. We exist solely to ignite the coming to being of the Forty-Seventh Florescence. Our tachyonic communicators are silent except for brief whispers. In all the long eons, no other Repository has yet found a race with which to begin the new Florescence, to start anew the Dance. Our Gift to you and your race is this mind touching, this access to all our knowledge, this knowing of how what was can yet be again! The price for you was simply a momentary mental joining to us, after which you could yield and return to your body. But the price for your race is to help us bring all nine hundred million of them into full mind-link, to perceive directly all we can offer," Gamafore said, doing his duty. He knew he must finish what he had started.

"You Kokseen will be known as the founders of the Forty-Seventh Florescence, as its first and greatest civilization. From you will arise a blazing wildfire that will sweep across the galaxy. You will be honored nearly forever. But such glory claims a last, final place. The Forerunners of a Florescence survive as a race for only one or two million cycles, not the five to ten million common to many. Then your culture dies out, prematurely exhausted by the struggle to lead a galaxy. What is your decision?" asked the alien, familiar, friendly, horrible, and wise Voice of Ayeesha's mentor.

Ayeesha floated in a timeless mental space in which she had nearly forever to consider the choice before her. No longer alone. No longer an orphan.

How could she choose for her race? How could she determine their destiny? What was her right to do so? she asked herself in echoing tones that beat against the chambers of her mind.

Absently caressing the beating lifepulse of Hamiden, she chose.

And glory burst about her.

* * *

"Mom! Dad!" Billy shouted out loud to the cubicle as he jerked awake from the memorydream of Ayeesha, of Gamafore, of aliens and of incredible choices that could begin Florescences. Sweat-drenched, he sat upright in the rest cubicle, physically shaking. His eyes slowly focused, bringing into sight the normal reality of this-time, this-space.

It had been a long time since he had called out for his parents.

But he had been frightened by the memory. It hinted at a vast tide moving the affairs of civilizations, of whole species. He wanted none of that kind of knowledge. Give him the usual, the normal, the understandable alien verities of greed, anger, jealousy, curiosity, and competition.

The Apprentice looked at the timekeeper blinking yellow on the vidscreen at the foot of his bed. Nearly six hundred *dicoms* had passed. Soon they would go into Suspense. Soon only the automatons and Amadensis would roam the starship's tubeways.

Billy slowly got up, locked the yellow memory crystal away in the rest unit, left the cubicle, and headed for the Suspense canister storeroom. Melisay would be there. So would Ding and three of her husbands. The friendly Mycron Tsorel trill-aa would be there. His few alien friends. They he could trust to set his Suspense controls, while Amadensis would keep guard over Solaquil. It was time for the organics to die awhile in the long sleep of Suspense.

Passing down a tubeway by the slowly flying form of the Dorsellien, the tracglobe of the Ta-Aaken monitor dragon, and the myriad shapes of the other gentlemen-partners as they all heeded the EcoMentat's call to Suspense, Billy McGuire walked alone, carefully shielding himself from caring about the other sapients. He folded his feelings in upon himself, afraid to care, afraid to lose a friend as he and Ayeesha had lost their families.

Finally he arrived at his Suspense canister. Billy got in.

The canister shell closed over him. Alone, he began a five-year sleep. Billy wondered if he would dream.

Chapter Thirteen

Billy woke up unable to breathe. His vision was blurry. Suspense wasn't supposed to be like this. What was happening? Where was the air? Where was help?

He looked up and out the crystalline direct-vision portal at a diffuse yellow-orange light. Vague shapes moved about above him. He scratched at the portal with his fingers, then pushed, then tried to yell—but he had no air. Dizziness overcame him and he passed out, visions of aliens haunting his dying thoughts.

"BILLY! Are you all right? Answer me!" yelled a mosquitolike voice in his ear. He wanted to sleep forever, free from worry. But the voice wouldn't leave him alone.

"Melisay, try again. The MedMentat says his biofunctions are stable."

Was that a voice he recognized? And Melisay—she was special. He peeled open one eye. Light dazzled him.

"BILLY! Come awake! You're all right now. Billy!"

He opened both eyes and looked into four concerned brown ones framed by black-and-white-striped fur. Sharp incisors showed in a partly open snout. Fan ears briefly flapped to either side of a blocky head. Melisay's comdisk hung on a chain around her short neck.

"What happened?" He struggled to rise up on his right elbow.

"A malfunction of your Suspense canister," said Ding do-wort from behind Melisay. "For some reason the transponder didn't signal the problem, and Amadensis was occupied with reanimation duties for others."

Billy McGuire the human looked around more alertly, restored by the oxygen mask cupped to his mouth and nose. They were in a small Life Patterns room adjacent to the main Suspense storeroom in the center of the ship's thorax section. Tsorel trill-aa stood on the other side of him, all twelve red eyes looking down at him. He sat up on the cold steel of the examination pallet.

"No way! You know Zekzek and I checked and re-checked every canister on board this ship. In fact we checked out every system. It took forever." He looked around at his one new and two old friends. He missed Zilkie and Zekzek, but they were back at the Shop. "This was intentional. Does Amadensis have any record of who was last to Suspend and first to arise?"

"Yes, organic, I do," announced the beryllium globe of the algor as it floated in from the main storeroom on mag-lev. "The last organic sapient to enter Suspense was Sola-quil the Tet, while Dorken da-sub, Solaquil, and the Ta-Aaken dragon were first to awaken."

Billy looked at the sensor-festooned globe of the algor. He had spent many hours with the algor in General Trade principles training and he felt it would not intentionally lie to him. Like all sapients however it could mislead through incorrect or partial information.

"You may be correct," said Melisay, "but there are too many choices of sapients who could have changed your Suspense controls. How can you know?"

"Billy," quietly murmured Pilot-Captain Ding do-wort, "you must be sure of this. I know we all feel the Tet were involved in the Hisein battle, but why attack you? Why not me and take over control?"

"I don't know, but it *was* the Tet." He swung his feet around and sat on the edge of the pallet. Billy started pull-ing on his brown duty jumpsuit. A blue sash and his per-sonals pouch lay nearby.

He looked sideways as Melisay glanced at Ding, then Tsorel, and then Amadensis. They all suspected. They all believed him. But there was nothing to be done without absolute proof. Particularly when the Crew were gentlemen-partners with great personal autonomy. The Pilot-Captain had to be very careful, even with the slight advantage of a telepathic link back to Zilkie through Melisay. Four light-years away from the Shop anything can and does happen. Particularly when multiple alien species are trying to out-Trade one another.

"I'm sorry, Billy," said Ding do-wort. "This incident must await more proof. Anyway we're coming in-system, and I need all of you on the control deck. Particularly my Detection sapient. Come!"

They all followed her out of the Life Patterns room, no one willing to put words to the worried thoughts that loomed before them. If Billy *had* been attacked, who would be next?

"We're two light-hours out from the rogue planet, Pilot-Captain," called Melisay from her bow Navigation pedestal. "Standard Approach option?"

Billy again sat before his Detection station, trying to ignore the orange form of Solaquil to his right at the Attack pedestal. Everyone else was on station, tense and alert. Coming into an inhabited system or planet, particularly one used by the Kokseen as a base, is not done without precautions. Machines built to last for eons could still be active. There could be an asteroid cluster remaining from a tidally fractured moon, or planetary defense systems could be operative. And, he knew, there could be other aliens picking over the Garbage heap just as you drop in.

"Yes—slow to one-twentieth lightspeed and corkscrew in. There are sapients here, and automatons. We must approach them carefully," said the Kerisen.

Billy saw her look past him to their right at Dorken da-sub on Power Systems, the Dorsellien on Defense, and Solaquil on Attack, then to her left at the golden Hecamin on Remotes. The female dominant flicked her two sensitive ears at the Pilot-Captain, caressed the Remote controls pedestal with two of her six neck tentacles, and settled down on her clawed fore and rear legs. The silvery wires of neurolinks to the four self-powered Remotes gleamed brightly. The Remotes preceded *Star Riches* into the rogue planet's local space, on watch for trouble. It reminded him of his duties.

"Billy?"

"I'm ready, Pilot-Captain." He put on his own neurolink skullcap and settled back into the accel couch, striving for a steady alpha rhythm. For calmness. For a centeredness, a Zen-sense he remembered from long ago—taught by Tenshung.

Closing his eyes, Billy began to work. To seek patterns. To apply his father's knowledge of anthropology and archaeology to alien modes of existence. He saw infrared, ultraviolet, radar, and visible light images of orbiting debris about the four moons of the rogue planet and in low orbit about the lifeworld. They were the former desiderata of a species. These things orbited the planet and moons, so they had meant something to the Kokseen. Perhaps there were also artifacts from the recent deep ocean-dwelling sapients. When they were closer, he would know.

Patterns.

Billy sought patterns of behavior, of association, of absence, of congruence, of existence. All minds, his dad had told him, order the universe. All life seeks to bring order out of apparent chaos. All sapients do something for a reason. And since they almost always do it repetitively, they create a pattern of behavior. An underlying unity of order therefore exists in the physical remains of any culture, any species. Billy's job at Detection was to be a sponge, to suck in data, all types of data. No factor was too small, too incidental, or too complex not to be important to him. Eventually he knew he would hit the inflow saturation level where ideas precipitate out. He would start to see that certain things always occur in certain circumstances. He didn't know why, he might never know why an alien ordered its worldview a certain way. But once he could see the pattern, he could predict danger, success, boredom, and simple insolubility.

A rash twelve-year-old, he had once objected to his dad that it all sounded like voodoo psychology. Jason McGuire, serving double-duty as the Xenosapientology–Archaeology or XA officer aboard *The Pride of Edinburgh*, gave him a stern look and then explained.

"Billy, it's real. We archaeologists train our eyes to detect certain shapes on the ground that signal artifacts. We xenosapientologists train our minds to detect cultural patterns. And we humans adapt to certain planetary seasons, certain faunal habits, certain floral growth cycles in order to eat. In order to survive. We XAs just take a common human talent and sharpen it up."

Pattern seeking was a MemoryNet-taught talent, almost the last legacy of his parents. It complemented his hard-earned Hecamin Power Systems training and his General Trade principles knowledge. Put together they made a young human orphan attactive to the veteran Traders of the Shop.

"Billy! What do you See?" asked Ding do-wort from the invisible world outside of the neurolink. He opened his eyes and looked left, seeing Keen so-thorn atop Ding. Was she nervous and needing her senior husband's reassurance, or was she confident enough to accept the slight distraction of continuous sexual play? Aliens had different ways, and this wasn't one he needed to worry about.

"Mostly metallic junk. The patterns are consonant with sublight communications relays, meteorological sensors, traffic control monitors, partial Transit stations, powersats, o'neills, and the usual automated factories generated by spaceborne industry." He paused looking forward at the attentive Melisay and remembering Ayeesha's *Tale*. "It's mostly Kokseen stuff—it has their distinctive design signature."

"Any evidence of activity by the current sapients?" Ding called over to the Hecamin at Remotes.

"Reverend Mother, there is only a comlink transmitter in low orbit. It is active and transmitting encrypted data downward and outward."

"Outward?!" called the Dorsellien manta-ray from starboard Defense in a musical voice full of wind chimes. "Where?"

That was Billy's job. He bent over the Detection console, tracking the linkage, using the Hecamin's Remotes to triangulate the maser tightbeam. In a few seconds he had the answer.

"Out of system, Ding," he called. "It's directed at forty degrees north of the galactic equator and above the local planet's ecliptic." Billy checked another red-orange, argon gas dynamic screen readout. "Its pathway doesn't intercept any of the Garbage or the four airless moons. It just heads out into deep space."

"Solaquil!" called the yellow, six-limbed squirrel to the Tet. "Status report on our weaponry!"

"Proton beamers at port are charged, the free-electron lasers amidships are powered up with blisters rotating freely, and the dorsal kinetic kill vehicle launcher is exposed and on autotrack." The black basilisk gaze of the orange salamander paused a moment to shift slightly down to lock eyes with Billy. The orange slit irises widened slightly. The four, three-fingered hands clenched. "Pressors and tractors are normal. Attack is ready!"

Billy wrenched his eyes away from the Tet's stare. He looked forward toward Melisay, still navigating their corkscrew approach to the ocean world. Ding sat quiet beside him for a moment.

"Crew, stand down to Modified Alert status. We will ask Amadensis to develop a translation algorithm that will let us talk to the ocean sapients through their own comlink." The Kerisen began instructing the algor in both speech and data feed from her busily flying sixteen fingers at the Control Nexus console.

Billy, his duties still present but easing, went back into neurolink, wondering what the ocean world sapients would be like.

The tsa'Lichen transatmospheric lander clattered and vibrated around him, penetrating even the crash-cushioning that smothered Billy, Melisay, Tsorel, Amadensis, the

Dorsellien, three Bareen fur balls, two Ketchetkeels, and the single Ta-Aaken dragon in its tracglobe. Of course for a billion-year-old Device it was doing rather well at penetrating the nitrogen-methane atmosphere of the planet. The red-colored, bathypelagic-dwelling worms who lived about hydrothermal vents scattered along the planet's tectonic plate boundaries called the ocean-world Silsilaa. He wondered how the two other groups of gentlemen-partners—one headed by Solaquil and one by the Ketchetkeel Dorkan da-sub—were doing. They had preceded Billy's group in their own TALs, heading straight for the small island continent where the Kokseen outpost was quietly entrenched. Their group had chosen to first visit the Sileen tubeworms. Native sapients might know something worth discovering about a Kokseen outpost that had been there during their entire rise to sapience.

The atmospheric skip-glide of the hypersonic lifting body slit the planet's upper atmosphere at Mach 23, then slowed to Mach 15 after a few circumplanetary passes. The ramjets cut in and Amadensis began maneuvering the craft toward the north polar thermal vent where they had an invitation to visit.

Billy looked through a small quartz crystal port, hoping for a view of the slightly saline, three-mile-deep ocean that covered all but a few islands and archipelagoes. But it was perpetually dark on Silsilaa. There was no sun to light it, no photosynthesis, no green-glowing chlorophyll plants, no lifeform at all dependent upon the food-chains generated by stellar heat engines. There was only the dark abyssal ocean studded with hot spring oases of life. The oases, Melisay had told him, clustered about mineral-rich undersea geysers that shot up out of the radioactives-rich molten core. And life fed on the geysers in weird chemosynthesis.

Amadensis had patiently explained to him how a special form of bacteria lived in the internal organs of the more complex lifeforms and thrived on the hydrogen sulfide carried up by the geysers. The bacteria produced carbohydrates and other chemicals as by-products, which fed the sapient tubeworms, shellfish, bottomrunners, and floaters that sought refuge from the lifeless desert of the abyssal floor. The algor said such forms of life were a major life-mode in the galaxy on planets lacking oxygen-nitrogen atmospheres, or which were in early atmospheric evolution. But only a few such worlds ever developed sapience.

The glare of their ramjets briefly illuminated a sheet of water, and then they hit the water at a very shallow angle. Fortunately the tsa'Lichen built well, and their TAL took to water like a submarine. The lifting body thrust downward, pushed by isotopic heat-transfer water jets. And shortly Billy looked out upon a scene from Dante's Inferno, a scene of active vulcanism as red-glowing lava sludgily pushed out against a water pressure of three-thousand kilos per square inch. Billy was so entranced he started when Tsorel's tongue lightly touched his shoulder.

"Coming, Billy Human?"

"Yes, Tsorel—it's just that I've never seen the bottom of an ocean."

"I understand," said the blue-skinned giraffe, stirring its six pairs of legs in rhythmic syncopation. "It is a first for me too and for a few others. Like the Dorsellien."

"Who's staying behind to con the TAL?" Billy asked, getting up from the accel seat.

"A Ketchetkeel named Namidun ka-tun. The rest of the company are suiting up."

"I'll be there in time for the pressor field englobement. Go on ahead." The peaceful herbivore briefly flicked its tongue at him to get his scent and then flowed down the broad aisle toward the rear of the TAL and its off-loading ramp.

Billy slowly followed, wishing he had one of the skin-tight, semiliving pressure suits like the other sapients. Such a suit literally breathed for you by direct osmosis with whatever liquid or gas one passed through. Or fed oxidizer-starved tissues with concentrated oxygen when in vacuum or a poisonous atmosphere. And those were only the least of its capabilities. But his dad's backup suit had worked fine for him at the Shop, and it could handle the cold seawater of Silsilaa's ocean. He hoped the pressor field englobement was controlled by Amadensis—no suit, mechanical or semiliving, could cope with the crushing pressure found five kilometers below the ocean's surface.

They were a strange group, the gentlemen-partners gathered around in a huddle on the volcanic rock of a mid-ocean mountain ridge below the invisible halfdome of the pressor field. Maintained by the algor, the field moved with them as they headed slightly upslope toward the black smokers. The smokers, Billy knew, were simply the hottest thermal geysers, shooting fountains of black or white material up from the vents. Lighted by nearby flows of blood red magma, the 420-degree-Centigrade-hot smokers wavered and billowed in front of and above them. On this world they were the "tree of life," raining down hydrogen sulfide and dissolved minerals upon the lifeforms gathered at the oasis.

Then they saw the sapients.

"Billy! Look at them!" yelled Melisay, looking like a giant teddy bear in her form-hugging suit. "Aren't they incredible?"

The Dorsellien, swimming in near weightlessness in the cold seawater, flapped and moved forward toward the edge of the field, attracted by the slowly writhing shapes of twenty-meter-long, rusty red tubeworms who waved filter fronds in the water. The Ta-Aaken monitor dragon, traveling outside the pressor field in its own tracglobe, fell behind the advancing group of Florescence aliens. He wondered if the sight of so much heat worried the frigid-dwelling methane-breather.

"I see, Melisay. They are remarkable. How do we talk with them?"

"With light, organic," replied Amadensis from the center of the group. "See, they talk to us now."

Looking back to the vent and the tubeworms, Billy's dark-adjusted eyes were briefly dazzled by a sudden symphony of green-glowing light. All up and down their length the tubeworms pulsed dots of light at the aliens, in rhythmic and arhythmic patterns. In joint harmonies and in individual arpeggios they spoke to the space-dwellers. His interior suit comdisk, like those of the others, quickly switched in with simultaneous translation.

"Who comes, who comes, who comes
To the warmth of the sea, to food, to company.
Who comes, who comes, who comes?"

they sang in various ways to the gathered group. And below his feet Billy saw the oasis.

It was a miniature Grand Canyon, a Valle Marineris of Mars, a deep cleft in the world's crust from which rose billows of black-and-white smokers. A thin runnel of reddish magma three hundred meters below signaled where the tectonic plates were pulling apart, separating, making new seafloor. And all about the deep cleft, stuck to the walls and benches in tubular shells concentrated from the mineral-rich waters, were the tubeworms, holding on to the rock with flexible anchor-cords.

"The Group of the Tree, honored elders," replied Melisay, speaking for the group in the absence of Ding do-wort waiting in orbit. The duty of the Pilot-Captain was hard—she must hold the ship for either a glorious return laden with fresh Garbage or be prepared to escape should the Garbage Hunters run into more than they could handle. For such sedentary duty she would receive one-tenth of all the Garbage gathered by the three groups.

The tubeworms near the cleft edge at the highest ridge above the nutrient-rich floor talked back with flashing lights as they quickly exposed or hid with skinfolds certain groups of bioluminescent bacteria. A kind of Morse code it was, Billy thought, but rich in symbolism and harmony.

"What seek you, what seek you, what seek you
Strange ones of metal, cold and sound,
What seek you, what seek you, what seek you?"

Melisay, following an agreed upon script, posed the basic questions.

"The Predecessors of Land—what can you tell us, venerable Elders?" barked the Tellen bear. "Do their representatives still live? Are there Protocols for entry into their niche? Do you have Devices of theirs which you wish to Trade with us for knowledge, food, songs, or wisdom?"

Billy hoped their reliance on the low-technology lifemate of Zilkie would help them deal with these Non-Technology sapients. The tubeworms were self-aware, they moved slowly about their planet on tame snaillike molluscs, and they used the comlink communicators left by the Kokseen and subsequent technological visitors. But they could not manipulate the physical world of Silsilaa. They simply lived—a rich culture, Amadensis said, of longlived organics who handed down their history in photonic Memory Songs of great complexity, rhythm, and subtlety.

He raptly listened as they sang their reply.

"Careful, careful, careful
Approach the sentinels of the Predecessors of Land.
Careful, careful, careful
Touch their silent places, their Niche, their still-humming Songs,
Beware, beware, beware the sentinels,
Living, living, living
Still are the Predecessors of Land,
But gift us with the Song of your journey long
Across the waterless Deep, Deep, Deep above,
Gift and grow richer, Gift, Gift, Gift strange ones."

Melisay looked around in the red-lit dark water at Billy, Tsorel, Amadensis, the manta-ray Dorsellien, the three Bareen, the Ketchetkeel, and the nearby Ta-Aaken tracglobe. Reading her body language, Billy could see she was pleased with the information of the Sileen, but unsure how to respond. They seemed to want a gift of song. Except the Tellen bears only sang in their minds, in Voice.

"Amadensis, please leave Ding's shiplog here, suitably transposed into photonic communication mode. Gentlemen-partners," Ding addressed the group of ten, "it's time to return to the TAL and seek out our competitors."

As the group swung around under the pressor field to rejoin the TAL, Billy thought he saw the small panda bear quickly reach up to the field's edge and try to touch the nutrient-sifting fronds of one of the tubeworms. For a second he thought she was trying contact telepathy, trying to share Voice with a People called Sileen. But that was impossible—the field prevented actual physical contact, and the tubeworms weren't telepathic.

But as he walked back to the lander, his back to the vent oasis, a blaze of greenish light flared up suddenly, startlingly, backlighting the group of aliens.

Were the Sileen just saying good-bye? Or was Melisay's Song, the song of a sister still mourning for three dead sisters and a lost way of life, being sung outward to the other denizens of Silsilaa?

Perhaps not even the Melanons had an Answer for that question.

Chapter Fourteen

"Over here! A roomful of MemoryNets!" called the musical chimes of the Dorsellien Memra to Billy, Melisay, Tsorel, and the Bareen Ika/Ikam. He wearily headed toward the sound of avaricious discovery.

The trip to the transparent-domed outpost city of the Kokseen had been uneventful. No defenses challenged them. No automaton barred their way. The dome's triangular doors opened quietly at their approach. Oxy-nitro air refreshed them. Brilliant orange lights came on to light their way in the planetary darkness. And their competitors —working opposite quadrants of the city—could barely spare time from hauling in mounds of fresh Garbage to acknowledge their signals. MemoryNets, vid and mem-crystals, C-cubed service units, MHD power generators of remarkable subtlety, artwork, sound disks with whistling songs, vials of chemicals they thought were a universal biomed healer, simple jewels of blazing colors—all the riches of a lost race had been found by their group. They transported their booty on Kokseen repulsor platforms that pulsed with artificial gravity waves but were barely the size of a large bed. Never before had Billy seen Devices of such sophistication. But then, he remembered, the Kokseen had enjoyed gestalt access to the knowledge of the Forty-Sixth Florescence.

"Amadensis—report," called Melisay to the other scout team from their group. The two other Bareen furballs, the Ketchetkeel mantises, and the Ta-Aaken that made up the original TAL group had gone with the algor once they saw the tranquility of the outpost.

"There is endless Garbage here, friend Melisay"—Billy started; he'd never heard an algor call an organic friend— "and we are gathering a representative selection. Unfortunately none of the Mentats are aware. There seem to be none like me here."

Did he detect a mournful sound in the algor's voice? It was something to ask Zekzek about when they got back to the Shop.

"Billy McGuire Human, will you lift that liquid to me?" asked Memra. "It's in an alcove I cannot reach from my maglev disk."

They were in a circular room underneath a massive dome, somewhat like his dad's memories of the Pantheon in old Rome. It held alcove niches, floor vaults, and recessed pedestals galore. The domed room seemed to be the only structure in the powered-up outpost that stood on a raised platform—all of the others were semisubterranean, harkening back to the pack burrows of the Kokseen. Strange memories rose up to haunt him, but Billy easily pulled out the vial, uncapped it, and held it up to the sensor tendrils fringing the gray manta-ray's oval mouth. Finding vials with liquids four millions years old had ceased to astonish them after they realized most of the alcoves worked like Zilkie's stasis cubes, miniature versions of Suspense.

"As I thought, land-walker, it is Life-Extend! I am rich! Oh, how that windless groundhugger of a Bareen will hum when it finds out I will be first to market this on the Grand Arterial!"

Billy looked at the slowly flapping body of the cloud-dweller, not surprised that greed was part of the Dorsellien culture. Where there was scarcity, where some had more than others, avarice, competition, and greed existed. Trade would exist. And that great engine would drive the culture outward and eventually upward into space, into the greatest Trade game of all. He supposed a 4.6-billion-year-old cultural pattern shouldn't prompt his disapproval—after all, he wanted to be a Merchant. But there were certain side effects of Trade that weren't attractive to him. Like violence and war, Trade was a two-edged tool that could both help and harm a species.

"Billy, come to me for a moment please," called Melisay from the far side of the echoing chamber. Leaving the rest of the group loading Garbage onto the repulsor pallets, he headed over to the Tellen bear.

"What is it?"

"Zilkie is calling me."

He was only a little startled. The constancy of Melisay's telepathic link with the Cosex across the light-years was simply part of reality, simply something some aliens could do that he couldn't. And he felt a bit reassured to know that, in a way, his mentor still watched over him.

"What's he got to say?"

"Some remarkable news," she replied, uncharacteristically evading a direct response. "Let's go into the access hall where we can speak privately."

Billy followed, wondering what news couldn't be shared with the other gentlemen-partners.

"Billy." Melisay turned around to face him. Four brown eyes looked down on him from a half-meter height advantage. "Zilkie says the Shop has received a tachpulse signal from *Hekar*, from your Traders of the Compact—they're coming to the Shop soon. They'll be there in only six years."

"Fantastic!!" he yelled. "That means they'll arrive shortly after we return from Silsilaa. Can I talk to them on *Star Riches'* tachyonic communicator?"

"Billy..." Melisay paused, obviously in a quandary; what was wrong? "Our way at the Shop is to accept all Visitors, but to save most information exchange for when they arrive. The Council prefers that no one from the Shop engage in extensive tachpulse communications with *Hekar*. Do you understand?"

He understood. Simple greed meant that those who controlled the knowledge of *Hekar*'s coming wanted to maintain as much of a Trade advantage as possible until the asteroid starship arrived. And no alien wanted the last human survivor of a lost Garbage Hunter ship to gain any advance favor with his kinsmen.

"Yes, but I don't have to like it!"

"Billy, Zilkie says he understands. He has promised to advise *Hekar* there is a Human at the Shop waiting to see them." The bear hugged her muscular abdomen with two wiry arms, absently fingering the tool belt harness that hung from her furred waist. "We have shared memories, Billy. Trust me. You *will* know your own people again."

He nodded and turned back toward the domed chamber, toward the riches of the Kokseen, toward the anonymity of successful Trading. He left the Tellen behind, knowing that he shouldn't tell any of the other aliens the news. In a way his dad had once told him, Trade knowledge on the Retread Shop was like scientific knowledge in the ancient, pre-Renaissance world. Back on Earth in the Baghdad of 52 B.C. some priestly researcher had developed the world's first electrical battery out of a clay vase, a copper tube stuck down its center, lemon juice for the reacting acid, and wax to seal the top. Copper wires running out of the wax seal and the copper tube provided an output for the electrical current. And the use this marvelous device had been put to? Probably, Jason McGuire had said, it simply served to give a convincing shock to believers who took hold of the silver hands of a particular local god or goddess. It showed the priests really *were* in touch with the divine. And then the knowledge, held to a tight group of acolytes, was lost to humanity during one of the regular social upheavals common to all human history. Until its rediscovery in the eighteenth century by the Frenchman Volta.

Billy sighed. At least the Forty-Seventh Florescence civilization was widespread enough to survive any local catastrophe. But that was poor solace to any sapients in cultural fugue, dying with the memories of ancestral greatness. It reminded him again how hard life was. That there were no guarantees, no security without price. Without eternal vigilance.

"Memra! Watch out for that pedestal—it'll upset your disk!" he heard Tsorel call out to the Dorsellien as it flapped low above the central floor, searching for hidden vaults. Only this time Billy saw just as he reentered from the hallway a pedestal the size of a Suspense canister rising slowly out of the center of the floor, directly underneath the cloud-dweller.

"Help! Assistance! Help!" it called in wind-chime tones as the rising tube of the pedestal tipped over the repulsion disk the low-gravity dweller was riding. Billy saw the Dorsellien slide off the two-meter-wide disk and fall toward the floor. At the last moment the Dorsellien slowed unnaturally in its local-gravity fall. Perhaps Memra had used its powerful TK to slow its own body just before contact. Still it hit the floor with an audible thud.

Melisay rushed from behind him, Ika/Ikam the Bareen rolled toward the motionless alien, manipulator pseudopods flailing, but Tsorel reached Memra first. Billy came up a few seconds later.

"Memra! Can you communicate?" asked the blue giraffe, its twelve red eyes staring in all directions. It was obviously unnerved.

The gray manta-ray lay silent. Unconscious, dead, or seriously injured, they didn't know. Melisay took control and bent to speak into the multi-function comdisk on her wrist.

"Amadensis—there's been an accident and Memra is injured. Please bring the rest of the group here immediately," she ordered the algor.

Billy was the first to notice a quiet scratching sound behind them. He turned, looking back at the place where the troublesome pedestal had arisen. What he saw sent nightmare chills down his spine.

"Melisay! Look!" he yelled, eyes still locked on the sight of a Kokseen. But then he noticed a metallic shimmer to the body. It was only an automaton. But a damned lifelike one.

The Kokseen automaton dropped down out of the vertical tube of the pedestal to the horizontal position normal for the Kokseen, for Ayeesha the orphan. Its five compound eyes looked at the Florescence aliens from a yellow head. A lavender thorax and gray abdomen followed behind, all supported on six outthrust spider legs. At three meters long, it was the size of an adult Kokseen. And a hell of a lot bigger than any of the Trade group. Billy's heart beat fast, fearful. He wrenched his head around to look at Melisay and the rest of the frozen aliens.

"Melisay! Put Memra onto one of the repulsor pallets and let's get out of here! Now! I don't like this at all. Remember the parting words of the Sileen—the Predecessors of Land still live?" He shivered, cold despite the relative warmth of the city outpost. Memory Dreams were not supposed to come alive. "It's time to retreat and to reevaluate."

The Tellen nodded her head in a human gesture of agreement, quickly loaded up the Dorsellien, and they all slowly, carefully retreated out of the domed chamber. They left behind several pallets of fresh Garbage and a silent Kokseen sentinel.

Billy, leading the group back to the TAL with an inertial direction-finder, wondered how the other groups headed by Solaquil and Dorkan da-sub were doing. Had they too uncovered sentinels?

Chapter Fifteen

"Melisay! Help! We're under attack!" Billy heard Amadensis call over his own comlink as they hurried down an underground tubeway on the pallet. It sped toward the landing field where their TAL rested. He had already called ahead to Namidun asking the mantis to power up for possible retreat. The algor's call reminded him they carried only hand weapons—the forty-centimeter beam of the xenon-fluoride heavy laser riding on a self-propelled air cushion mount had been left behind at the lander. He looked over at the Tellen bear.

"Billy, give me the DF and go try to help Amadensis," ordered Melisay. "We must get Memra to the TAL and check the landers of the other groups. Solaquil and Dorkan da-sub haven't answered, nor have their pilots."

"OK. I'm going."

Melisay, bent over the pallet controls, gave mim a tooth-filled grin of appreciation.

"But lend me your sonogun—my hand laser lacks focused power at a distance," Billy asked. The Apprentice grabbed the outthrust weapon, jumped off the swiftly gliding pallet, and turned left at a branching tubeway, wondering why he was doing this for aliens he hardly knew.

"Billy, I'll come," called Tsorel trill-aa from behind him. "I'm fast even if I can't handle weapons."

The Mycron's assistance surprised him. While the herbivores would fight in immediate self-defense, they were basically pacifists. Predatory violence was very alien to them. Apparently courage was not.

Running down the tubeway he saw ahead a familiar shape, a form out of Ayeesha's dream. The human orphan quickly jumped onto a flat-bed air cushion transport and started it up, fingers deftly remembering his Memory Dream. Billy looked up to a staring Tsorel, obviously puzzled by his facility with Kokseen devices. He ignored the look since the blue-skinned giraffe was on board, twelve legs splayed wide for support on the railingless transport. Billy twisted the steering yoke to run them out into the center of the tubeway. The six-meter-long transport quickly sped up to forty klicks an hour, the pastel-colored tubeway walls flashing past as they headed for the algor's last bearing.

"Amadensis, I'm coming. Are you above or below ground? Answer!" There was a long pause before the algor responded on the comlink. Static blurred its voice.

"Billy Human, hurry! We're on the surface. We've destroyed two automatons, but organics are hurt. Hurry please!"

In seconds he steered the transport into a rising tubeway that should, he thought, lead to one of the numerous open plazas scattered around the automated outpost. He wondered if the standard central fountain would be working, throwing water jets into the air amid violence. Then they burst out of the burrow hold into the orange glare of artificial daylight.

Billy's stomach clenched.

The scout party lay partly hidden behind three overturned pallets at one side of the plaza. Out toward the fountain he saw the body of one of the Ketchetkeels— blue limbs spattered with yellow blood. It was quite dead. On the other side of the fountain he also saw two rapidly approaching Kokseen automatons rushing to the attack. Cyan-colored laser beams burst from mechanical mouths, spearing toward the barricade. Before he could help, one of the beams punched through and impaled a Bareen.

The blood of the diminutive, brown-colored ball-cluster was hemoglobin red—like his. Another remembered instinct lifted the hand holding the sonogun. A finger twirled the cps setting, aiming for high ultrasonic. Billy's right finger depressed the firing stud. The weapon was silent— but its effect was spectacular.

The yellow cranium of the leading automaton blew apart, shattered by sound waves. Like its organic builder it was also attuned to ultrasonic signals as its hearing mode. Such an attunement could be a weakness. The second mechanical nightmare reared up on its mid and back legs, trying to elevate its mouth laser above the sparking wreckage of the first. Billy found its head before the mouth could fire at him. A second, five-eyed, yellow-painted cranium burst apart.

The sound of silence across the plaza was deafening.

"Billy, over here," called Amadensis. "Can we ride on your transport?"

Tsorel, having watched the violence, stoutly dismissed it and took hold of the steering yoke to move the flat-bed over to the rest of their group. Billy, standing at one side of the platform, fought to keep his balance on the transport as the air cushion skirts crinkled in a sharp turn.

He watched with combat fatigue detachment as the algor, the Ta-Aaken dragon, the remaining Ketchetkeel, and the last Bareen clambered onto the transport. There was plenty of room even for the cases of biomed and Life-Extend vials the Ketchetkeel quickly salvaged from the overturned, smoking, partly melted pallets. The tracglobe of the Ta-Aaken, Billy noticed, also held several sacks of vid and memcrystals tied down to exterior lugs. Greed, he realized, defied even sudden death. His adrenaline-pumped heart slowed as he started to get the shakes, began to realize it could have been him instead of an alien lying in a pool of yellow blood below the innocuous water jets of the plaza fountain.

Billy's last sight of the plaza was of water mist settling over the Ketchetkeel and sparkling rainbows dancing over the praying mantis body. He wondered if entropy was giving a benediction or just being sardonic.

* * *

An hour after their rescue of Amadensis they all sat strapped into their TAL accel seats, ready to depart, ready to escape. But Ding had other ideas.

"Melisay, Billy, Partners—we must check out the other two TALs," she ordered from orbit. "We can't leave anyone if they're alive. Will you check the other groups and see if there are any survivors?"

Pilot-Captain Ding do-wort could not command those on the surface, but he knew she was right. Billy also knew she was probably frantic at the thought that two of her junior husbands might be lying dead at the feet of an automaton. The Apprentice looked up front at Melisay sitting in the co-pilot seat next to the blue praying mantis form of Namidun ka-tun. Four brown eyes looked back while the Tellen's sucker-tipped fingers nimbly fed instructions into the Nav-Mentat console.

"Ding, we'll go!" said Melisay. "But power up *Star Riches*—we may be followed out of this gravity-well by planetary defenses yet to awaken." She brought the TAL up on its belly jets and angled the lander toward the quadrant where Dorkan da-sub had landed.

A curling ribbon of blue smoke guided them in without need for a DF signal.

Billy, watching an Imager screen from his accel chair near the XF laser by the rear loading ramp, saw alien bodies scattered randomly about the other TAL. The golden fur of the Hecamin female dominant was a glaring contrast to the lavender thorax of an automaton as both lay still, entwined from a last battle. The blue angular limbs of Dorkan da-sub were scattered near the burning remains of its own laser mount, while the snakelike bodies of four Dok'aah lay in pieces, sliced by laser beams. The surrounding concrete of the landing field was laser-scorched by Kokseen vengeance. The Mycron-made TAL, he saw, also burned, its wing pylons broken and the central lifeglobe blasted apart. It was obvious there were no survivors.

"Help! Assistance! Help us—the Kokseen are killing us!" called Solaquil's group over the lander's comlink.

Billy looked up the middle aisle past the quiet survivors

from his group. Tsorel trill-aa stood midway in an accel harness. Thinking of the call, he wondered if Solaquil was dead or alive. The Hunter in him wished to see an orange salamander form splayed out on the ground, dead.

"Coming, partners. We have your transponder signal. Prepare to board by the rear loading ramp," Billy heard Melisay respond. Namidun ka-tun chittered something to the Tellen. The protruding green globes of its two eyes looked back at him from the cockpit nacel.

"Billy, Tsorel—will you help again?" called Melisay. "We need someone to operate the XF laser to cover Solaquil's retreat and someone to help the survivors on board."

Billy sat frozen, fearful and angry at being asked to risk himself for aliens, for weird creatures who had never given him a break on board the Retread Shop. Especially now that he knew *Hekar* was coming, that he would soon see his own kind. It wasn't fair!

The Mycron's tongue-touch on his shoulder brought him face-to-face with the choice. He looked up at the blue giraffe, its long-lashed red eyes focused on him. Tsorel couldn't— wouldn't—operate the laser, but it would expose itself to danger in order to help others. Could he do any less?

"All right, Tsorel—let's go." He reluctantly got up and slowly walked into the back storage hold to wait for the ramp to lower. "I'll run the laser down onto the field and cover you. Remember, this TAL is old—it can't stand much laser fire, let alone anything more powerful. When I say close up—we retreat even if we don't get them all. Agreed?"

"I understand, Billy. You are fearful." Twelve light blue-skinned eyelids blinked in syncopation. "But we have both lost our Progenitors—the worst is past." Tsorel's tongue flicked out, sensing his emotions, tasting human pheromones, perhaps reassuring himself in the Mycron way.

"Billy, we're landing," Melisay called over the comlink. "They're retreating toward their own TAL. Be ready."

Two orphans stood looking at the reddish brown steel of the drawbridgelike loading ramp. Then they felt a shudder as the TAL's six hydraulic landing legs thudded onto the pavement. The ramp suddenly fell down four meters, hitting the concrete below with a loud clang.

"HELP US! HELP US!" Billy heard as he drove the laser mount down the ramp, its rubber skirt partly collapsing as it hit the field at a sharp angle. But then the vehicle righted itself. Looking quickly to his left he saw Solaquil's party. They rushed toward their orange globeship TAL on pallets laden with Kokseen Garbage. And behind them, firing cyan-colored lasers that barely missed, came four Kokseen automatons. Cursing the greed and stupidity of the Tet, Billy put the laser on autotrack firing mode and shot a beam of green hellfire at the lead automaton.

It blew up with a satisfying explosion.

"Over here!" he called out to the Tet, the three Sorep anteaters, the four Gordin methane-breathers in their tracglobes, and Ding's two junior husbands. The party was several hundred meters away and closer to their TAL than his. They kept heading on the pallets for the orange globeship.

Billy moved toward them, dodging return laser fire from an automaton and squirting ablative mist ahead of the mount to reduce the Kokseen laser strength. Then his blood chilled as he saw a gigantic Kokseen robot emerge from a hole in the ground behind the smaller automatons. It was at least ten meters long and four high. He wondered if this was the Kokseen version of a tank.

Helpless, he watched as the giant reared up on its hind legs, opened a palp-fringed mouth, and fired at the globeship. Brilliant red balls of light puffed out, slowly arcing toward the orange TAL. Then they hit. And the globeship exploded. There were secondary explosions from the nearby Gordin tracglobes. Methane atmosphere mixed with blue and orange smoke.

"Melisay!" he called out, eyes briefly light-dazzled, "that was a plasma weapon—we can't stay here! We've got to go!"

Billy started to turn the laser mount back toward the tsa'Lichen TAL, wondering if they could escape before the behemoth attacked, when he saw a pallet rushing out of

the billowing smoke and gases toward him. It held Solaquil, Ding's two husbands, and a Sorep anteater, its green
fur smoking from a near miss. The black eyes of the Tet
caught and held him from across the carnage-strewn field.
He stopped the mount and aimed the heavy laser behind the
aliens, waiting for a target.

The first target was a normal automaton. Billy blazed
away at it before the robot could sight on him. But from
around its smoking ruin came the last two Kokseen automatons. They both fired at the Tet's pallet, missing it, but
the blasts knocked the pallet over onto its side. A hundred
meters away, aliens called for help. He saw Solaquil run
away from its partners, heading toward the last TAL and
safety.

Billy gunned the mount forward, weaving in evasion,
his left hand firing the sonogun at one automaton. The aim,
fortunately, was good. The laser cannon's autotrack also
worked well. He heard the ping of a lock-on and hit the fire
button, leaving the steering wheel uncontrolled for a second. Amid the explosion of the last small automaton, the
mount slewed around to a stop by the green-furred Sorep
and two Kerisen. They needed no urging to clamber on
board.

"Moren aa-thorn, look to the rear and tell me when the
monster appears," Billy asked Ding's number three husband. Still wrapped in his harness he rose on his two lower
legs and looked back, watchful, fearful.

Just as Billy pulled up to the TAL's ramp and the blessed
help of Tsorel, Moren called out, "The monster comes!
Look!"

Billy, ignoring the rush of bodies carrying last minute
Garbage trophies up the ramp, looked back wearily at the
giant Kokseen as it slowly pranced out of the smoke from
the globeship. Seconds remained before it would fire. He
decided.

Keying in the laser's autotrack with a last command, he
jumped off the mount and ran up the ramp yelling to Melisay to take off laterally. Behind him the laser mount waddled toward the Kokseen, its motion briefly distracting the

plasma-thrower. Then the mount fired its entire capacitor back-charge at the automaton's head and blew up from overload.

Billy flopped down in his accel seat, feeling the shockwave of the mount's destruction shake the TAL. Had it damaged the Kokseen? Would the smoke of the explosion provide brief cover for them before the robot switched to IR sensors and regained its firing lock? All he could do was hope.

The forward Imager screen showed the field dwindling in size. The TAL's dorsal laser fired, blasting an exit hole in the outpost's dome. Then he saw the scarred Kokseen automaton fire its red plasma balls at them. They fell behind. Billy noticed however that the entire orange-lighted city outpost pulsed with diffuse light. Something else was awake besides the first minor sentinels. The outpost of the Predecessors of Land might yet reach out to them, to *Star Riches*.

He sighed. Planetary defense systems he couldn't offset. That was for Solaquil and whoever would run Defense in place of the Dorsellien. He had done as much as he could. More he felt than the indifferent aliens deserved. Billy closed his eyes and waited for rescue or disaster, for life or death.

"Melisay, I'm coming to meet you," he heard Ding promise over the comlink. "Prepare for ventral lock docking to *Star Riches*. The tractors are on automatic."

He listened to the sounds of frantic survival, images of Ayeesha and her pack cousins intermixing with searing memories of deadly automatons. Why had the outpost attacked? Had the other groups fired first at the sight of an activated Kokseen automaton rather than peacefully retreating like Billy's group?

The TAL shook and shuddered about them as the tractors locked on, pulling the smaller ship into *Star Riches'* ventral lander hold. The gentlemen-partners were back home, carrying a few riches, an antigrav repulsor pallet, and the transport, but without the bodies of fifteen sapients. The price of fresh Garbage was too high. Tears of regret ran down his smoke-darkened cheeks.

Then the rush of able-bodied aliens pulled him out of the TAL into the tubeways, and they headed toward the control deck. They all knew there was no escape until a full Crew could help Ding and Keen so-thorn. Billy, his dark brown jumpsuit in tatters, slipped into the Detection accel chair. His screens showed death reaching up toward them. He fell into Crew tempo.

"Ding, there are two AG battlestations rising up from Silsilaa's poles." An orange blinking light drew his attention. "Plasma torps have been fired from the outpost; there are fire-and-forget high-accel rockets coming around the planet's curve; and two ground-based free electron lasers just barely missed us. There are multiple fire-control radar lock-ons of us from the planet."

"Namidun, activate Defenses! Eject ablative mist. Throw out the decoys!" harshly barked Ding do-wort, her ensexed senior husband furiously copulating with the canny Trader. "Solaquil, fire every solid projectile you've got! Attack with the dorsal and ventral energy projectors. Melisay, get us *out* of here!"

Billy quietly watched his screens as the ATMM modulus kicked on, pushing them all deeply into their accel seats before the local inertial control field could catch up. They would probably escape he saw. He looked around at the rest of the Crew.

Solaquil's four arms furiously manipulated its console, attacking the death thrown at them by a Kokseen outpost that didn't know its makers were dead, or gone from this universe. Brief flares of nuclear and high-energy explosions from behind *Star Riches* seeped in through the polarized forward direct viewing portal above Melisay.

The orange salamander form of the Tet, preoccupied with violence, raised a determination in him. *This* time *he* would be last into Suspense and first awakened. Amadensis owed him that much. And when they got back to the Shop, when he could talk to Zilkie, Billy would carefully describe the perfidy and cowardice of the Tet as it abandoned fellow gentlemen-partners, running for its own safety. He was determined to dent the powerful armor of the House of Tet.

A melancholy feeling stole over him. There would be Trade goods for him from his trip, and he would probably gain some Life-Extend antiaging drugs for himself or for sale on the Grand Arterial. And he would insist Solaquil's group pay him a Rescue fee out of their shares. But the prospect of gaining power and influence among aliens had an empty taste. His inner self lacked something. What, he didn't know.

Billy McGuire finished carrying out his Detection duties, his thoughts far from the control deck. The lone human felt ever more alone, more abandoned. Zilkie's Garbage Hunt was over for him.

Paradoxically, he longed for the surcease of five years of Suspense sleep that awaited him. Maybe, in his dreams, he could be happy. And when he awoke, *Hekar* would be there.

Chapter Sixteen

"Ready for your Factor test, Billy?" asked Zilkie

He looked up at the Cosex, seeing the tree-anemone's green tentacles writhing in concern. The master Trader stood with him before the massive bronze doors of the House of Skyee compound outside Dock Six. Today, two months after his return from the rewards and terror of the trip to Silsilaa, was graduation day. Today he faced the opportunity to go independent, to no longer be under the tutelage of a Food Merchant who dabbled in alien power politics and spying.

"I'm okay. Tsorel trill-aa filled me in last night on what to expect." Billy stuck nervous hands in his blue sash belt and eyed his sponsor. "And with endorsements from Tsorel, you, and Ding do-wort, I'm confident."

"What—you don't like being an Apprentice?" the Cosex teased him, knowing that was only part of the problem. What Billy really wanted was to be in control of his life, to have the power to make his own decisions.

"After Silsilaa I think I'm entitled to move up. I learned more on that trip than most learn in a year of training."

"So you did."

The tree-anemone turned silent, not pressing, which Billy appreciated since he was nervous enough already. Dressed in a formal red jumpsuit with sash belt, bowie knife, Garbage Hunt earring, brown scaleskin boots, and his hair tied in a tail over his left shoulder, Billy McGuire was as dressed up as he had ever been.

"Who desires entry to the House of Skyee?" boomed a voice like tissue paper being crumpled up. The metal doors stayed shut, awaiting a response.

"Elder Merchant," began Zilkie in a five-million-year-old ritual, "the Merchant Ten'ta'ta-hep Nacem Zilken the Cosex comes before you bearing an Apprentice who seeks to become a Factor. Will you give shelter, testing, and sponsorship?"

The harsh white light of the apex radiator shining high above the isolated walled compound of the House of Skyee burned his brow, making him squint. It had been a strange walk, leaving behind the spacedock, the commercial urbus, and the Grand Arterial glideway as the two headed inward toward the ten-kilometer-wide chamber that was solely occupied by Skyee. Once inside, small automated food Farms had closely bordered the metal roadway that turned and twisted its way to the seat of ancient power.

"The candidate may enter."

The eight-meter-high metal doors slowly opened inward, revealing a narrow inner courtyard of blue bushes, yellow flowers, and purple trailing vines before a colonnaded hallway that stretched endlessly to his right and left. No one was in sight. Billy looked back at the Cosex, his mentor, his sponsor, probably one of his few true friends despite the predatory plant's gruffness. Today the tentacles were extraordinarily active. The tree-anemone leaned over slightly, eyeing him with scores of silvery fish egg eyes.

"Go Trade 'em out of House, Home, and Fortune!" the Trader softly hooted.

Head high, holding close recent MemoryNet images of his parents, he walked into the compound and stepped onto a pathway leading to the hallway. Once he began walking down the flagstone-paved hallway, which was open on the courtyard side and walled on the inner side, he was sure someone would turn up.

The bronze doors quietly closed behind him.

As Billy turned to the right down the hall, a shape out of a nightmare loomed before him. He quickly stopped and looked, wondering if this was his greeter. The four-meter-high shape looked like a mobile Venus-flytrap with yellow vines trailing from its pink mouth-head. There were no eyes to be seen, no hands or pincers, no clothing or harness—in fact, little but the fact of a walking plant.

"Candidate—classify!"

"Predatory plant, Mekanen race, thanavore, Mentic and D-D molecular-based," Billy automatically replied to the unseen voice of the Elder Merchant.

"Proceed."

He slowly walked forward past the Mekanen death-eater, shivers running up and down his spine. Studying general Trade principles had taught him about sapients who subsisted solely by telepathically feeding on the psychic deaths of others, but he'd never known any were on the Shop.

White light suddenly flared above him as a trapdoor in the roof of the hallway suddenly opened. Billy looked up, wondering what new surprise the House of Skyee had for him.

A giant jellyfish with transparent skin slowly floated down toward him. There was a slight hissing sound he took to be outgassing of helium so the flyer/floater could descend to his level. Hundreds of glistening ropes hung below the float-sack. In seconds they would contact him.

"Candidate—classify!"

"Facilitator-absorber mollusc, Ti-keel race, omnivore" —he backed away from the rope fringe—"Non-Technological and L-L based." The rare representative of the third major social pattern found in the galaxy, a race neither predator nor herder-browser, but one which lived for linkage between other lifeforms, which gained its satisfaction from being an eternal intermediary, softly floated before Billy. He looked with true curiosity upon the Ti-keel, but he was not ready to be facilitated; especially since connection with the fringe ropes was physically permanent.

"Proceed."

He wondered just how long it would take him to walk around the kilometers-long hallway if every few steps he ran into another sapient lifeform. Surely the House of Skyee knew his training in current galactic species, their life patterns, food patterns, social patterns, and external manipulative patterns was comprehensive. Zilkie and Ding had seen to that.

This time he was able to walk several hundred meters, enjoying the yellow flowers of the open garden, before something happened. The flagstone floor opened up before him this time.

A massive hydraulic tube rose up in front of Billy and stopped at his eye level. A clear crystal dome covered the solid tube's top, enclosing some kind of artifact. He leaned over to get a closer look.

"Candidate—classify!"

He was in shock, unable to believe what lay before him. Billy's heart pounded, his head throbbed, and his gray eyes stared hungrily at the most delectable Garbage artifact he had ever seen, or ever would likely see.

"Uh—it's a Quail-en-kalumen soul flute from, . . . from the First Florescence!"

"Do you wish to play it?"

Billy's enthusiasm suddenly drained out of him as if he had been hit by a cold shower. He drew back from the

4.6-billion-year-old artifact, fearful. The soul flute, rumor said, created the most extraordinary sounds any living being could hear, so wonderful one's soul would leap at hearing them. Unfortunately the rumor also said any sapient blowing the flute would become its soul slave forever, eternally trapped even after death in the mysterious metal of its forging.

"NO!"

"Proceed."

He had the shakes now. Billy had never guessed such unusual, rare, and deadly lifeforms and artifacts even existed on the Shop. His early confidence felt like a drop of water before the plasma torch of an ATMM modulus.

The ground began to vibrate. He looked out into the garden, wondering what was next. A giant strode into view.

"Candidate—classify!"

"Predatory thallophyte-animal, two races—a Zorell dominant atop a Bichuen drone, omnivores both, Biogenetic and D-L based." What the *hell* was a parasitic symbiont sapient like the Zorell fungus and its recombinant DNA-bred biped host doing this far from Centaurus arm? The trip to their home on the innermost arm of the galaxy reportedly took 24,000 years, one-way, on an ATMM drive ship cruising at near lightspeed. Until now the race had been mythical to him and to most other Shop sapients he dealt with.

"Proceed."

With a long look back at the headless Bichuen drone as it stood like a colossus, six meters tall at the shoulder, Billy almost didn't react in time to his next test.

"Candidate—evade!"

He quickly looked around, then up, and briefly froze in horror. A nonsapient electrical gasoid, its self-maintaining plasma field a red whirling miniature cyclone, dove down at him from the garden. He instinctively dropped down, folded himself into a ball, and died.

Or at least to the gasoid Billy McGuire Human died. The predatory electromagnetic field, native to a Jupiter-sized world where deadlier beings existed, wavered, searching for the lifefield it had initially detected. But it was unable to detect anything above the background pulses of the plants and bushes. The gasoid rose up and drifted off over the compound, hunting for thinking food.

"Candidate—enter the next room for food and rest."

Billy, nearly devoid of Self in a wonderfully peaceful Zen humming-chant, barely percepted the external world, the world of illusion. But a small tiny memory of Self still existed, still wished to participate in the absurdity of life. He opened a bleary eye on the shifting shadows of the hallway, seeing an open doorway next to him. A bed beckoned.

His body protesting at the sudden demand to re-energize, Billy shakily stood up and walked into the spartan stone room, happy with the thought even of a cushionless bed. He felt a light touch at his shoulder.

"Billy! You made it! Congratulations, my friend," said the suddenly visible form of Tsorel from a corner of the room. He hadn't seen the Mycron as his body single-mindedly headed for the anomie of sleep.

"Tsorel—what the hell is this all about?" His stomach growled, reminding him he hadn't fed it anything in six hours. "I thought it was going to be an interview, tests, and field work-study, not the chamber of horrors."

The Mycron, its red eyes flickering from below blue eyelids, flapped its two long ears at him. Perhaps in the Mycron version of amusement.

"I couldn't tell you about this, Billy. Everyone must go through the Walk of Recognition. Afterward it will be as you expected. Rest, and tomorrow I'll come to escort you before the Elder Merchant. It wishes to see the sapient who saved its House-nephew."

Billy, sitting down on the lightly padded bed, nodded his head in agreement, not caring if the Mycron understood human idiosyncratic gestures. He was exhausted from the mental strain of the last few hours, the stress of being on alert, sensitive to the unexpected. He had had enough of aliens for this day. The orphan closed his eyes as his ears heard the syncopated patter of twelve hooved feet carry the blue giraffe out the front door. He slept without dreams for the first time in many years.

"Billy, are you awake?"

Sleep felt good. It was a refuge he didn't want to leave. A slightly wet, pine-scented tongue lightly touched his nose.

"Billy, come on. You must be on time for your appointment. Wake up!"

"I'm awake, Tsorel."

Sitting up, still clad in a now rumpled formal jumpsuit, Billy looked around the stone bedroom. It was illuminated only by a beam of white light spearing in from a narrow window slot on the inner compound side and held only the bed, him, and the yellow, lavender, and red body-painted Mycron. He hoped that after joining the House of Skyee he could avoid smearing its distinctive House colors over his face. It just wasn't his style.

"I didn't know I had an appointment. When is it?"

"In about four *micoms,* Candidate. So let's go."

"What—no food or water? I thought I was supposed to eat in here."

"You were," replied the giraffe as it headed out the open door into the shaded hallway, "but you overslept. You can eat after your interview. Come on!"

He followed the quickly moving herbivore down the hallway, hoping there wouldn't be any more jack-in-the-box surprises on his way to see the Elder Merchant. They turned left through a high arch set in the circumferential hallway, and he finally saw the *real* House of Skyee compound.

A gigantic, stone-paved plaza a kilometer wide stretched before him. To the right and left he saw two, three, and four-story stone towers built from monolithic blocks of black granite. Beyond them stretched the bonded warehouses, long rectangles looking like his dad's memories of old airplane hangars. Glancing back at the center, Billy noticed that the administrative compound looked fairly standard—a pile of steel, glass, masonry, and connecting tubeways that resembled a Gordian knot. Several null-grav taxi ovoids soared over the complex, while far away what looked like three armed merchantmen starships towered up from behind the complex like lanceolate blades. Swiftly walking behind the Mycron as it headed straight for a main entry ramp, Billy wondered how the starships could ever get out of this interior chamber of the Shop; so far as he knew they were at least six kilometers below the outer skin of the space station. Did these Traders have their own exit and entry Docks?

"Tsorel, tell me about the Elder Merchant. What's the species?"

"Noktoren." The swiftly moving Mycron entered the first of a series of open archways at the top of a ramp. It didn't volunteer any more information.

He wondered if taciturnity was genetically inbred in all the aliens he knew, or was it just the personality type that *became* Traders. Zilkie, Melisay, Ding—even Zekzek were often long on silences and short on volunteered information. The epochs-old tradition of closely controlling all data about a particular Trade partly explained his experiences, but he felt there was more behind the tendency to secrecy than anyone was telling him. But speculating about aliens was both unprofitable and usually erroneous.

Instead he considered the fact that the Elder Merchant was a Noktoren. The species was a water-breathing, whale-like omnivore that cruised the littoral seas of a waterworld in the Sagittarius arm. What was peculiar about the species was that, in addition to eating tons of plankton each day strained through its massive mouth, the Noktoren were also partly photovores. Or at least the photosynthetic-active bacteria inhabiting its translucent upper back skin subsisted on sunlight. Traveling in great pods of sapients, the Noktoren used powerful Mentic abilities to mind-talk, teleport, and telekinetically move physical objects about as desired. It was rumored they were even slightly precognitive, able to foresee several minutes into the future. Soon he would encounter an alien able to read any thoughts projected at it and sophisticated enough to be running a powerful multi-species Trading House.

"How long have you been with the House of Skyee, Tsorel?" The silence had been growing on him and, walking toward a great geodesic dome in the middle of the complex, Billy guessed he had only a few more minutes in which to pry out whatever helpful data he could.

"Only a year, as an Associate." The Mycron swiveled its eye-studded head about on a long scaly neck to look back at him. "You will learn that the House is organized into three hierarchies—Associate, Partner, and Elder. While everyone operates free-lance within the strictures of House association, the ones in real control are the ones at the top—as in most societies." The blue-skinned herbivore turned its head, evidently figuring Billy would learn by trial and error, like all the Factors, just how his House operated.

"But how many—"

"QUIET," interrupted the Mycron as they stopped outside the dome's entrance. "Sorry, but the procedures for approaching the Elder Merchant are very specific and very strict. We must show proper deference." The alien reached up with its long prehensile tongue to touch the sentry monitor panel adjacent to the circular door. It irised open, revealing a dimly lit chamber with a gigantic water habitat tank. Underwater lights broke the turgid surface, casting green reflections about the interior walls of the marble dome. They stepped in and walked up to a small veranda that projected ten meters over the three-hundred-meter-wide pool.

"Oh most wise and excellent Elder Merchant, Associate Tsorel trill-aa of Herd Myden comes as ordered, with the new Candidate." Billy and the Mycron stood on the veranda. The soft lapping of surface waves against the side of the tank was a soothing sound.

As in a dream long past, but really only two bioyears ago when he had first walked into Ding do-wort's office, Billy saw a long, black torpedo shape loom just below the water's surface fifty meters out. It lazily came toward them, massive flukes barely breaking the water as it slid through its natural element like a hot knife through butter.

"So you are the Human!" bellowed the crinkly-sounding voice. He realized with a start that the voice—which he had assumed came from remote speakers in the hallway—was in his head. In his mind.

"Yes, Elder Merchant, I *am* the Human Billy McGuire, former Apprentice to Zilkie the Cosex." Young he might be, an air-breathing mammal he might be, but *no one* ever again would intimidate him! He had paid his dues to the Shop on Silsilaa and he *would* be treated as an equal by the aliens! Billy looked the Noktoren squarely in its two small eyes, just barely visible above the water level. The fist-sized eyes looked back at him from a wrinkled, leathery black skin that sported small barnacles and parasite symbionts.

"*You* will be my equal?!" asked the Noktoren, apparently voicing what it could feel in his mind. "Sapient, I am two thousand bioyears old. I have seen races die. I have fought the mind-vultures of Haaken Cluster. My Trade goods fill half the bonded warehouses of this compound. *How* are you equal to me?"

Tsorel looked at him, perhaps skeptically, its twelve red eyes unlidded and equally divided between him and the Noktoren. It prudently kept quiet.

"In *Will*, Elder Merchant!" he shouted with his voice and mind. "I have survived here, the only one of my kind. I set myself the goal of being a Merchant. And I *will* attain it!" Billy paused, wondering if Zekzek would approve of his use of the Dominant Assertive 12M-style approach to one of the most powerful sapients of the Retread Shop. "*That*, Master Trader, is how I am equal to your illustrious self."

"Good, Factor Billy McGuire Human." The whalelike form of the Noktoren rolled slightly onto its massive, thirty-meter-long side, exposing its white underbelly hide to Billy and Tsorel. "You are no use to this House or to me if you do not believe in yourself. You are accepted. No more tests. After two months of work under Tsorel, you may free-lance as you wish."

The Noktoren was halfway through its riposte before it hit him. The Elder Merchant had called him a Factor. Emotion swept up from inside, filling him with happiness and a fierce determination.

"Thank you, Elder Merchant." He turned to go with Tsorel, the matter of his membership in the House of Skyee solved, when he remembered a question he wanted to ask.

"One moment, Elder Merchant. It is the human custom to call a friend by name. What's yours?"

"What—what—you ask my name!" The voice in his mind felt indignant, then amused. "Well met we are then as the Melanons say! Little thief, my name is daa-lumkaliche ka-ka-Hak! Good Trading!" The Elder Merchant sank down into the tank, perhaps wishing for the opportunity to deep dive, to call across the world ocean to podmates, or to simply sing the song of life.

"Billy," whispered Tsorel as they walked out of the dome, "why did you ask his name? It has *never* been done before! Even I didn't know the Elder Merchant's name until now. That was dangerous!"

"Why?"

"Because in Noktoren society, anyone who knows your true name holds power over you, over your mind."

"Oh." That was something he hadn't known about the Noktorens. "But he told me. So it must be all right. Don't worry!"

Billy quietly followed his guardian-sponsor down the causeways and avenues of the House of Skyee. If he had understood the Noktoren correctly, he was in effect an apprentice Factor under Tsorel's tutelage for the next two months. Then he would be on his own, able to order up House services, to use House facilities like the warehouses, and free to claim the House's protection over himself and his dealings. And any other member of the House would come to his aid—for a fee later, of course. More than likely he would have to pay Tsorel a fee for his supervision.

But the new Factor didn't care that once again the universe was reminding him that "you don't get something for nothing." That was a lesson he had learned long ago in the embrace of his parents, when he still had a family. Gone though they were, other humans were coming soon. By then he wanted to be a Merchant!

A haunting laughing echo in his mind made him wonder if the Noktoren still listened in on its newest Factor.

He didn't care. He would prevail. He would survive as always until his race came to the Shop.

For the moment Billy followed Tsorel.

FACTOR

Chapter Seventeen

As Billy floated in space outside the Central Dock of the Retread Shop, the stars betrayed him. Beneath him other lights on the Dock cast a brighter glow than the distant stars and shifted in broad sharp movements as tiny multi-formed figures of the Dock personnel moved about on the interior service platform. Billy floated outside, a self-contained moonlet of the Shop among others, watching the steady colored light of the stars. He watched their panoply, and wondered what it would be like to walk again on the surface of a planet. Not a space hull. Not the Shop. But a planet.

To feel a steady gravity pull rather than the shifting, adjustable fields of the life habitats scattered through the Shop. To feel a natural, scented wind and hear uncontrolled thunder and lightning, rather than the fabricated and alien environments of each Florescence species. To be able to walk toward a boundless horizon rather than be hemmed in by the multicolored awnings, shops, Factor's offices, food dispensaries, and Trade platforms of the Grand Arterial. Other humans, if there had been any aboard the Shop, would have understood instantly that he was homesick.

For a home he had never seen.

To Billy the three gas giants orbiting Cebalrai only one light-year away didn't count. Organics can't walk on the frozen gas surfaces of such monsters, lifeless attendants to the orange K2 giant star. They were only useful as nearly inexhaustible suppliers of deuterium, tritium, and helium-3 to fuel hungry Trading ships, Garbage Hunters, the rare Wanderer who found the Shop without direct tachyonic communications, and the Shop's own fusion plants. And his own Garbage Hunting trip to Silsilaa was one bioyear in the past. It had given him a taste, but only a taste, of the many worlds outside the Shop. He hungered for more.

Billy sighed, tired of fantasizing. Survival came first. And to survive he had to make Trade deals, to buy and sell things, to put his own Trade goods in the compound's bonded warehouses, and make a place for himself among Factors already ancient before he was born. The last year of work as a Factor for the House of Skyee had taught him well—he'd mastered the intricacies of alien Trade relationships in half the time usual for most Shop sapients. And one of the lessons had been the need to be practical. He determinedly turned his eyes back to the Central Dock located opposite Dock Six.

"Billy McGuire Human, do you have any Answers about these Chellaquol?" called Zekzek from among the rough line of other Factors waiting next to him outside a nearby service portal. The Melanon's miniature taxi globe gleamed crystalline white with subdued photons from the Milky Way. Billy tongue-keyed his suit comlink to respond.

"A few, Mr. Bush, but they are for sale by the House of Skyee. Interested?"

"Perhaps later. The Tree is always curious, but we will await our first encounter with these beings." The Melanon hung silent, as did fifteen other alien Factors clad in pressure suits, habitat globes, or enclosed in opaque black pressor fields. They all waited for the new alien visitors to arrive.

Everyone wanted to directly see their craft. To assess their refitting and service needs. To note whether they had any Garbage in tow. And to see how they were armed. All these things and more, he'd learned during his early work with Tsorel, were important to a Factor and his House.

A bright purple-yellow flare caught Billy's eye, and he shifted his suit's attitude to squarely face the oncoming visitor.

He saw the visitor approaching from beyond the cometary cloud of civilized Garbage, from the direction of the shimmering gas cloud of Orion. Its one-half lightspeed velocity had long ago been reduced to a slow fourteen thousand klicks per second, then a thousand, and now a very sedate two kips as it approached the Traffic Control boundary where the tractors would take over and move it inward. Past the local Garbage and into a parking station only ten kilometers out from the docks. The visitor wouldn't dock immediately—that wasn't permitted by the Shop. And he knew first-time visitors always needed time to adjust to the Shop. To adjust to the new forms of life who would tend to their needs, refuel their ship, and take a steep commission for every service provided.

Another flare and he could see the ship. Billy raised his gloved left hand and started the vidcorder attached to his helmet. He looked toward where the glistening pearl-colored shape of the visitor was visible. Its delta vee killed, the ship was in tractor-tow now, growing gradually larger. He tripped the telescopic lenses with his tongue and punched an IR overlay for his right eye. *Time to leave memories behind. Time to earn a living.*

"Namidun," he called out. "The House of Skyee has a device which will enhance your contact with these Chellaquol. For a fee I will encrypt it with your House's comlink code. Do you wish the service?"

The blue praying mantis successor to Dorkan da-sub floated near to him in a loose, transparent pressure suit, its upper grip-arms free to move. It turned a long, narrow, burr-toothed mouth toward him. Two green compound eyes stared silently at the orphan.

"No. The House of Ketchetkeel has no need of minor services." Was there a hint of disdain there, of remaining resentment at his role in saving their group during the escape from Silsilaa? "These sapients will need fuel. The deuterium from Cebalrai always has customers."

Billy didn't press. The Ketchetkeel was of course correct—their fuel reserves were why they controlled most star systems for two thousand light-years ^{U}parm. He hoped the alien still wasn't peeved about the Rescue fee he'd demanded from the group—after all, he was just following tradition. Billy looked back at the Chellaquol ship.

The dull infrared glow of the exhaust funnel swung slowly away to present the ship broadside, then head on. The newcomer ship fit the general design of many Florescence ships—a bell-skirt fusion drive at the stern, a micrometeoroid shield device at the nose, a variable choice of habitat-shape between, here a ring of long cylinders. But it had some differences. Adjacent to the central stem core hung long, reddish-colored cylinders, over twenty of them in a ring around the stem core of the ship. Billy studied them, wondering about their function. A cluster of dull gray globes also followed each other from stern to nose between the core stem and cylinder ring. Faint metal crossties connected the cylinders to bearing sleeves between the globes. As he watched, the cylinder ring rotated slightly. Centrifugal gravity, he decided. Most Florescence species used artificial gravity, either web- or plate-generated, and the technology was very old. Not very advanced sapients, he thought, if they lacked artificial gravity.

As the ship swung fully into a head-on attitude to the Shop, the thrust-absorbing bell-skirt of the fusion pulse stardrive disappeared. The broad, flat disk of a micrometeoroid shield gradually eclipsed the cylinders and globes hiding behind it. *Could the Chellaquol be so primitive they didn't use a self-renewing Dustbag cloud or magnetic repulsor field ahead of them? No, impossible. No one was stupid enough to subject their cellular structure to the hard radiation produced by one-half lightspeed impacts of molecules upon solid matter. It must be a backup device for tangential vector dust not caught by the Dustbag. Particles like those that had crippled* The Pride. Billy resolutely thrust old memories back into his mind's closet.

The IR showed hot spots at two locations—the main drive area, of course, and the cylinders. Apparently the cylinders served as habitats for the Chellaquol. The Chellaquol ship grew and grew and grew. Finally it came abreast of a two-hundred-million-year-old Derasay hulk from the Forty-Fifth Florescence. *It's a monster!* The oncoming giant dwarfed the kilometer-long Derasay hulk.

By rough comparison to the Derasay hulk, Billy estimated the Chellaquol ship was about twelve kilometers long by at least three wide from cylinder to cylinder. But it would fit into the twenty-kilometer-long Central Dock—just barely. Could it be a generation ship? Could they lack suspended animation capabilities? Or perhaps they slept the light-years away and intended to plant a colony? Questions whirled about in his mind, each with implications for profit and loss to an astute Factor. He got an idea.

"Factor Solaquil, that's a generation ship out there. What does the House of Tet think of such visitors?" He still detested the orange salamander after its behavior on Silsilaa, but business was still business. If anything, Zilkie had taught him the value of pragmatism. An orange pressure suit stirred among the line of waiting aliens—four arms and two legs moving slightly as Solaquil turned to eye him.

"Human, you state the obvious. We have known that for several months. What are you doing here?"

"Seeking Trade rather than offering insults. One would think the House of Tet could honor the Protocols of Trade and the Arbitration Guild." This wasn't working, but he wouldn't let the Tet intimidate him. Its studied refusal to use his title and name was actually very juvenile. It must really hate him. Or resent him. Or maybe both. Why?

"We do honor the Protocols," Solaquil replied with a hiss. "It is you Humans who can never know the value of traditions, of customs honored for millions of cycles. Be silent."

Billy, contrary to his training by Zilkie, Ding, and Tsorel, tensed to verbally lash out. But a flashing circle of white lights around a portal in the middle of one of the Chellaquol cylinders caught his attention. It was the signal he had been waiting for.

A touch, and his suit jets activated, thrusting him harshly toward the projected intersection point of his suit and the oncoming ship. Billy looked behind and saw that only Factors Namidun, Solaquil, and Zekzek had been as quick as he in computing the necessary trajectory. The others belatedly followed. If Billy could be third or fourth into the entry portal, perhaps he could carve out a service need in support supplies. The old-line Houses represented by his three competitors would probably dominate Trade in major items like fuel, artificial gravity systems, and suspended animation techniques. But aliens in transit for nearly four hundred years were bound to need many, many things. Services which could be picked up by the quick Factor with a low personal overhead!

A black taxi ovoid passed by him silently, curving toward the Chellaquol. Port Authority, BioSystems, and Defense representatives, no doubt. They would make first contact, explain the Rules again and lock the control boards of the weapons systems. Based on their earlier tachyonic communications with the Chellaquol ship, there was no need to expose test species, microbes, and bacteria to the Chellaquol atmosphere. The Factors would be taking a slight chance, but the algors had determined there was no need for a Defense screen. It was an acceptable risk.

Then a forty-meter-round portal loomed before him, requiring actions rather than thoughts. Billy's fingers carefully touched chest pack pressure keys, briefly subjecting himself to three Gs of deceleration. Trading discomfort for time, he'd learned from Tsorel, was common among Factors.

The portal door split in two at a horizontal seam, its massive metal halves retracting upward and downward. Billy looked inside and saw a fairly normal docking bay lit by actinic white and blue lights. Small transparent windows like eyes glared out at him from along the inner wall. Behind the windows he could see large lumpy shapes covered in pressure suits. Metal landing platforms extruded from the walls near the entrance, and the black ovoid already rested on an upper platform, its occupants inside and going about their business with Chellaquol Command personnel. Zekzek, Namidun, and Solaquil coasted to a landing on another platform. Billy followed them. Billy and the other three Factors entered an airlock at the far end of the platform, and cycled through. They cracked their suits and stepped out to meet their first Chellaquol.

Six aliens faced Billy.

The Chellaquol stood on six stumpy, elephantlike legs which supported a short, sausagelike body covered by a hairless blue-gray hide. Their heads were broad, slightly curving surfaces of bone, with six little eyes on tentacles peeking around the protective face-horn. The shapes of their mouths and teeth below the face-horn were hidden since all six Chellaquol stood silent, motionless, looking dispassionately at Billy and the three senior Factors.

The silence stretched. Billy acted.

"Honored Visitors, I am Billy, omnivore, predator, human species, and D-L food chain-based." He hoped his language synthesizer, a Twenty-Third Florescence device of the Garamin aliens, would work as advertised. "Let me offer you the discreet but comprehensive services of the House of Skyee. No service or need is too small or too large for us! We exist solely for the satisfaction of our clients."

Still no response, no indication whether they understood. He plowed on.

"Today we can deliver to you specially tailored biochemicals guaranteed to invigorate any life support system! We also offer relaxing trips through the sensorium environments of most Florescence species now aboard the Shop. Or perhaps you are interested in the latest antisenescence drugs for carbon-based lifeforms—we guarantee a doubling of any species's normal lifespan!" he suggested, hitting them last with the standard Life-Extend offer. This would be from his own personal Trade goods remaining from the Silsilaa Hunt.

His voice came out as hooting, bellowing sounds from the synthesizer disk stuck to the outside of his red pressure suit. Billy's globular helmet was laid back, exposing his nose to an odor reminiscent of some farms aboard the Shop. He tried not to breathe too deeply.

The Chellaquol started backward at the sound of their language spoken by Billy's comdisk. He waited patiently.

Factor Namidun didn't even glance sideways toward him. The insectoid seemed unaffected by Billy's lack of etiquette, by his refusal to quietly wait for whatever crumbs the main Houses would leave him. Namidun's confidence would be arrogance in any species other than the Ketchetkeel. But Solaquil was not nearly so impassive.

The Tet's forked tongue flickered out past sharp-edged teeth, followed by a guttural hiss. His alien's long, flat snout slowly turned toward Billy, bringing him under the basilisk gaze of two utterly black eyes with orange iris slits. Billy, recalling a similar look on the carnage-strewn landing field of Silsilaa, again felt a cold wind rise up his spine.

He jerked his eyes away from the glacial look of Solaquil to see how Zekzek was reacting to his impudence.

The Melanon's leaves chimed metallically, creating a soothing sound that went untranslated by his personal comdisk. Perhaps it wasn't translatable in human referents. But it did seem to make Solaquil break its gaze.

The Chellaquol closest to the Florescence group finally spoke, pulling him back to the Trade at hand.

"Billy Human, we Chellaquol be herbivores, D-L food chain-based, herd beings. We refuse your antiaging drugs —such transgression of divine law is not permitted to us." Six eyes on little tentacles stared at him from around a face-horn. "Our True One demands piety, reverence, and the spreading of His Word by his Herd. To this end we journey to you, to show by our example the True Way. Will you be an Acolyte to our True One?"

Oh damn, oh damn, religious fanatics! That explained why they had no artificial gravity and probably no Suspense techniques. Only the technology needed to bring their divine word to alien infidels. He briefly wondered if they converted by the word or by the sword?

Billy stepped a few paces ahead of the piercing gaze of Solaquil. "Honored Visitor, I know nothing of your Way, so I cannot be an Acolyte." How would they take rejection? "But my House can arrange proselytizing tours of the

Grand Arterial for your representatives. Visits to open habitats to preach your True Word are possible. For only a modest extra fee I myself will escort you and your entourage to all open areas of the Shop. I am certain your Word will be of much interest," he diplomatically suggested. "Are we agreed upon this Service?"

Now even Namidun looked his way, interested no doubt in selling these country cousins enough fuel so they could cruise Orion Arm forever. Far away from the Shop. Far away from aliens long used to periodic missions of salvation by races who felt they had a direct line to truth, to the One True Way. Such races were carefully dealt with, evaluated for possible messianic impulses, and then hurried on their way if found relatively harmless.

Too bad. Religious monomania rarely offered much market for the many services of the Retread Shop. But while they were here, at least they could leave behind some barter credit.

"Billy Human, we accept your Service," said the one who'd spoken first. At least they knew basic Shop protocol. "I am Torolen, Chief Speaker of the True One's Word." The Chellaquol shuffled on its six legs, perhaps nervously—or was it just a custom in its society? "We offer six tons of fresh dextromolecular-levomolecular foods, ten kilos of germanium, and twenty varieties of food seeds native to our homeworld for your assistance. Do you accept our terms?"

The Chellaquol's offer of a Trade deal elated him. Billy walked forward toward the alien, put his ungloved left hand on its face-horn and carefully urged it off to the side to negotiate a refinement of terms. Behind him he could hear the hooting sounds of the senior Factors jumping in to offer their own deals to the remaining Chellaquol Trade representatives. From the confusion it sounded as if their black market language tapes fell far short of his language synthesizer. Namidun should have accepted his offer.

Billy knew that Namidun, Solaquil, and Zekzek would

monopolize most major services likely to be needed by a generation ship of traveling preachers. He felt satisfied with his share. Showing an alien about the Shop was certainly one thing a former thief could do very well.

Chapter Eighteen

"Factor Billy, where do these aliens gather? We would share our word with them," asked Torolen as the Chief Speaker and twelve other Chellaquol thudded down the Grand Arterial near Dock Three. Billy was tired. He'd spent the last six hours showing them the docks, the commercial urbi, the industrial zones, the Farms, the Grand Arterial, the administrative compounds in the interior of the Shop, the Suspense caves—almost everything there was to be shown about the seventeen thousand aliens of sixty-four species currently crawling over the Shop.

"They don't," Billy said. "Rather you have to understand that most aliens stick together with other members of their species." Surely these herd-types would understand that. "They live in Houses, habitats, compounds, clantowers, any place where they can re-create a simulacrum of their culture. Otherwise they would become insane."

"Why? We find you aliens to be peculiar, but you don't provoke insanity in us."

How could he explain to a herd-being who had obviously never spent time among aliens? Torolen thought itself a sophisticate, traveling the deeps between the stars. In reality it was a novice. A memory stirred.

"Torolen, how would you feel if suddenly the herd were gone? If there were no other Chellaquol around? If nothing *looked* like you?"

"IMPOSSIBLE!" bellowed the Chief Speaker. "We are the Herd—it will always exist! Why do you tell stories to me?"

"Because if you want to secure acolytes, you must understand this place. You must understand we are all slightly insane." Billy realized, with a start, that one of his problems over the years had also been maintaining his own sanity. How did the other aliens do it, even with the benefit of memory crystals and single-species habitats? Was this the price of maturity—the ability to see oneself as others saw you?

"Insane?" asked Torolen. "Oh now I understand. You have not the Herd, nor knowledge of the True One's Word. That's why we are here. We will save you from yourselves."

Billy kept silent, knowing better than to argue theology with aliens, or to confuse religious missionaries with the facts. Such as the fact that there were many herd-types on the Station. It didn't matter—either the Chellaquol would adjust to the different reality of the Shop, or they would leave sooner than they planned. As the slow commuter glideway carried the group outward from the Central Dock area, he looked around at the passing ships, awnings, and Trade platforms. The other Chellaquol in the group kept silent, whether in cultural shock or in deference to Torolen, he didn't know.

"Are you sure there is no place where many aliens gather?" pursued the Chief Speaker.

Torolen irritated him, since of course he wasn't absolutely certain. There were parts of the one hundred twenty-kilometer-long by thirty-kilometer-wide Shop that he hadn't been to. As he'd learned from his testing at the House of Skyee, the Shop was an ancient construct which few knew comprehensively. That realization finally gave him an idea. There *was* one place, one to which he'd been long invited but had been too busy to visit.

"There may be such a place," he said. Billy brushed his fingers through loose black hair, enjoying the feel of freedom. At last he was on his own, supporting himself among aliens. His formal red jumpsuit with its sash belt and Hunt earring proved his accomplishments. Today would be a good day.

"The Melanons occupy a habitat in the deep interior of the Shop," he continued, "where it's said they tend over the remains of the first Kokseen Shop. A friend of mine once invited me to visit. Want to go?"

The Chellaquol swung its face-horn around to look at its herd-cousins. The tentacle-eyes moved in complicated body language, answered briefly by assorted wavings from the others. Torolen's pebbly gray neck swung its face-horn back to Billy.

"We will go with you. It's our tradition to speak before a gathering before each of us goes on individual missions. Lead us."

Billy, hands on his hips, faced the six-legged herbivores and smiled. If these aliens ever were stupid enough to wander the Shop by themselves, there would be a need for funeral services Chellaquol-style. He turned around and headed off the glideway for a side tunnel he'd seen before, the Chellaquol lumbering delicately after him. The tunnel led to one of the main dropshafts into the interior of the Shop. It was a long journey, but he missed Zekzek. Maybe he would bargain with the blue-leaved Melanon for a finder's fee if the Chellaquol bought Answers from the Tree.

The trip into the depths of the Shop was a special experience for Billy. He'd been as far as ten kilometers down, well into the life-support sectors of sludge rivers, osmosis-bypass tanks and non-sapient fungoids liquefying organic waste. But there were other levels, other areas. As they walked deeper into the Shop, they saw a broad hall of self-aware algors silently floating on maglevs. The algors were one of the decisive Powers aboard the Shop—and quite oblivious to the passage of mere mayflies like Billy and the Chellaquol.

Then a flight of Dorselliens flapped overhead in a low-G

passageway. Leathery-winged, whip-tailed, dull gray in color, they headed toward their habitat. Tracglobes for the methane, ammonia, and chlorine breathers grew more numerous as they approached a part of the station reserved for exotics. Then silent echoing tubeway halls led them into a giant chamber easily three kilometers high.

The chamber held hundreds of aliens.

"Factor Billy!" Torolen cried. "This is what we seek. How do we address these unfortunates?" The Herd gathered excitedly around Billy, ready for its missionary purpose.

Billy ignored them, looking instead upon a rare sight. Ahead of them in a broad, shallow basin stood, rolled, clumped, hopped, and flew hundreds of aliens from dozens of different species. It was a vision he'd never seen before. And all of them were moving toward something in the center of the chamber two kilometers away, an object blurred and made indistinguishable by distance.

"You don't, Torolen. At least not yet," he hastily explained as eye-tentacles shot up sharply. "Be patient. Let's join the crowd and try to understand what brought them here. This is a very rare event. I only suspected the Kokseen remains might draw a crowd. But this is incredible."

Billy swiftly walked forward, assuming the Chellaquol would follow. Like a child in a candy store he looked right, left, up, and down. He recognized Sorep, Gordin, Hecamin, Dok-aah, Mycrons, Ta-aakens, Bareens, Slizit, Hokkens, Nakals, Ketchetkeels, Kerisen—and scores of other species he'd only heard about.

And of course there were the Tet, at least forty of them in an orange phalanx that moved forward in a complicated dance-walk that involved three steps forward, two sideways, one back, a deep bow, and a hop. Then it was repeated. A few other species engaged in their own ceremonies of approach. What had he wandered into?

"Factor Billy, are these aliens worshiping?" Torolen asked, much too loudly. Billy glanced at a nearby pack of Gordin tracglobes and sighed.

He repressed the temptation to yell at the Chellaquol.

Factors had to be more in control than their customers. And he wasn't too sure what action would set off the assembled aliens.

"Yes, in a way, Torolen. Do you remember the story of the Kokseen from the orientation crystal Port Authority sold you?"

"We do. Although without the faith, we understand these Kokseen did much for all sapients."

"Quite." Billy wondered how they would react if they knew of Ayeesha's *Tale*. For that matter how would the rest of the Shop react? How would this group of believers in the near-mythical Kokseen react? "Torolen, we're approaching the physical remains of the first Shop, which was built by the Kokseen. It's not very large, but it is the kernel around which this whole station has grown over the last five million years. Now do you understand the need to be careful?"

He looked over his shoulder and saw the Chellaquol eye-talking to its cousins. A forest of eye-tentacles shot up. The Chief Speaker looked back toward the predator leading its Herd.

"We understand, Factor Billy. This is just a Reliquary of heathens. We can be patient."

Billy shook his head in amazement. It always surprised him how some species could be so blind to the implications of the habits of other aliens. Some aliens, he knew, acted as if other species were only cute little animals or pets that didn't know how to be civilized, or who were in need of conversion to their way of living. The aliens stupid enough to actually try to impose such customs were either dead, out of business, or in Suspense, unable to cope with the reality of the Retread Shop.

They passed the Tet phalanx, several other groups of strange species, and approached the center of the chamber. Over the heads of the multitude, Billy saw a low black mound. He strained to see, wondering if it was what they sought.

"Billy! Friend! Have you come for Answers?" called out

a blue-leaved bush to his right. It was the distinctive com-disk voice of Zekzek, and Billy stopped.

"Zekzek! It's great to see you." He noticed the Melanon wasn't moving, just hovering on its lodestone as the crowd continued to pass by. "What brings you here?"

The bush shivered its leaves in a chiming laughter.

"I live here, remember? The Tree resides in a habitat on the other side of the Reliquary. What brings you here, if not Answers?"

A hooting cough from behind him reminded Billy he had customers to tend to. He stood up straight in his formal red jumpsuit, feeling a bit on stage, even with his friend. He glanced back at the herbivores.

"Zekzek, these are the Chellaquol from Megan system, recently arrived at the Shop, and *my* Trade customers." Billy emphasized the possessive—the Melanon might be a friend and a former trade partner, but it also had goods for sale. "Their Chief Speaker is Torolen, who seeks to an-nounce their One True Way to this crowd. They seek aco-lyte converts to their faith. Care to help?" He stepped to one side to allow room for Torolen to join them in a small island of stillness among the moving crowds.

"*They* want to speak to these?" chimed the Melanon's blue leaves in astonishment. "Do they not understand the rarity of this event? Every one hundred cycles much of the Station gathers to feed the fusion plants of the *first* Station with offerings of deuterium. There can be no interruption of this ceremony!"

Billy put his bare hand on Torolen's face-horn, stifling an outraged comment before it could be made. Some aliens were taking notice and apparently understanding the con-versation on their own comdisks. Messing in someone else's religion was not what a Factor did—not if he wished to live.

"Thank you, Zekzek. I think they understand now. Per-haps we can follow the crowd and observe the ceremony. Afterwards perhaps the Chellaquol can speak to those leav-ing in the tubeways?" Billy almost pleaded. He wasn't sure of Zekzek's status here, but he was certain the Melanon could either help a lot, or hinder completely. Would its greed win out over its piety?

"Welllll—it can be permitted." The bush rocked on its lodestone preparatory to moving inward. "There is of course a fee for use of our tubeways for proselytizing. And we offer many Shallow Knowledge Answers about what is religiously attractive to most Shop sapients. Torolen, do you wish to buy Service?"

Billy put his hand back on Torolen's face-horn. The Chief Speaker glared at him from four of its eye-tentacles. It was getting irritated with his protective coddling.

"Zekzek, as Factor for the Chellaquol and for the House of Skyee, I accept your Service offer." He felt Torolen stop struggling to speak; maybe it would be satisfied. "We can discuss payment terms later. Shall we see the ceremony?"

Zekzek, without further comment, leaned on its lode-stone and floated toward the low black mound Billy had seen earlier in the center of the chamber. Torolen and the other Chellaquol ambled along behind, their six legs churning in syncopated movement. Billy felt glad he had only two legs to move; no doubt Zekzek appreciated hav-ing none at all.

He looked about alertly, noticing that the crowd of aliens was growing. They came from the tubeways on two sides of the chamber and moved forward, without returning. There must have been at least a thousand pass him already. Did every alien on the Shop believe? Or was it simply good Trade politics to be seen at the Kokseen Reliquary?

"Billy McGuire Factor, let me precede you," ordered Zekzek. "For a fee I will take your group to an overlook veranda inside the Reliquary so you may study the first Shop at your leisure. Agreed?"

He nodded absently, knowing the yellow-branched bush could percept him through its own electromagnetic fields. Anyway the low dome had grown to a giant curving roof reaching far up into the chamber airspace. Broad arches stood open, allowing single-file streams of alien bodies and tracglobes to enter. To his surprise Billy saw a few algors in line. Moving forward, Billy followed the Melanon toward a side access-door that irised open at the bush's approach. He heard the subdued thumping of the Chellaquol behind him. Billy would bet the herbivores were in sore need of the reassurance of the home Herd. He looked at the dome just before they entered.

The dome curved upward in a flawless mathematics, like the upward curve of a falling drop of water. Its black sides seemed strangely depthless and drew the eye upward to an infinity touched randomly with infinitesimal stars, vague clouds of space-drifting molecules, the tiny sparks of life. The opaque dome seemed suspended in space, although it touched the floor of the chamber on all sides, a two-kilometer-high curve that rose steadily up before them to become an unending black wall. Then they passed through the iris door.

Inside the dome they walked into a total blackness relieved only by dark red lights at their feet. He hoped the Chellaquol could see into the infrared spectrum. If not, he'd soon hear them stumbling around. And there was a sense of depths that opened beyond in the touch of rising cool air. Zekzek's faint blue leaves chimed at him, throwing back some of the light that the photovore had eaten earlier. Zekzek glowed slightly, leading the way for Billy and his customers.

Billy saw shadows loom and dwindle beside them as they passed interior walls. A foreground light grew stronger. He looked up at the dome roof. It looked like his dad's memory of a night sky on Earth. Stars sparkled. Eternity beckoned. He broke his gaze to wonder what held up the high roof. The natural shape of a geodesic dome could never carry that kind of weight. Before he could speculate on the tensile strengths of exotic alien metals, the floor fell out from under them.

The Chellaquol softly hooted in alarm, shuffling uneasily on the new surface. Billy sympathized—he didn't like walking on glass, or thin air, or a repulsor field. Or whatever it was that made up the veranda. His boots yielded slightly at each step, an unnerving unsolidity to whatever surface supported them above the black depths beyond the veranda.

"Torolen," he whispered, "quiet your people. They're safe only so long as we don't draw attention to ourselves. Let's look and then be gone." The Chellaquol calmed down although they obviously didn't like it. Zekzek led them through various groups of aliens clumped on the veranda, then worked its way forward to the edge.

"Billy, Friend, see our Reliquary. Is it not beautiful?" the bush crooned to him with chiming leaves. The orphan looked out at a sight from a dream-memory. He shivered.

In front of and below him floated a tubelike space station, hanging weightless in the natural zero-G of the Shop outside its habitat gravity fields. Billy stretched out his hands and felt the glassy smoothness of a pressor field. He felt certain the one-kilometer-long Kokseen artifact floated in airless vacuum, its interior open to space, waiting for absentee landlords to come back, to come home. Only they never would. He and Ayeesha knew they wouldn't. But the rest of the Shop wasn't so sure. Aliens all, they revered the Kokseen and anything they had made. The ground-effect transport from Silsilaa had made him rich: what would the direct memories of Ayeesha gain him?

The bronze color of the Kokseen station glared back at him, in a pale yellow brilliance, as if it had a life of its own. The burr-lines about the station's modules raised the hair on Billy's neck, reminding him of the lifelike automatons who jealously guarded their creators' possessions on Silsilaa. He wondered if others waited deep within, inactive so long as the depths of the station were unplundered. The sight made him wonder what secrets the cyan-colored and sapphire blue crystals of *Star Riches* held. It was time, soon, for him to find out the true value of his Hunt goods.

He watched the lines of aliens approach the pressor field, lay down globes, tubes, and boxes of deuterium, then swiftly retreat. Dozens of suitless Melanon bushes floated in the airless space between Billy and the old Shop and swiftly carried the offerings inside, before returning on their maglev disks for more. Billy had glimpsed far, far more of the inner wellspring of the Retread Shop than he cared to know. This had the scent of the ages about it, a sense of eternity. He pulled back his emotions and rejected it.

"Factor Billy, do your customers wish to purchase commemorative holo-cubes of this wondrous sight?" Zekzek asked.

"Uh—yes, Zekzek, they probably do. Torolen?" There was no answer. He looked back at the Chellaquol in the shadows of the veranda, squinting his eyes against the pale yellow brilliance of the Kokseen Reliquary. He found the Chellaquol in the dark background of the Reliquary. They were not standing, instead lying collapsed on their legs, simply staring at the Kokseen Shop. "Torolen?"

The Chief Speaker turned its face-horn toward him.

"Billy Factor, we will buy these images the bush offers." The Chief Speaker, raised in a religious society that moved to very definite, very restricted patterns of social behavior, and nurtured on the word the Herd would bring salvation to the universe, looked old and shrunken. "We will not proselytize today. Return us to our ship. This must be shared with the Herd."

"Zekzek," he softly called, avoiding any look at the Reliquary, "send the cubes to the House of Skyee with a statement of your fees for today. We'll credit your account. Now, can we leave?"

The blue-leaved, yellow-branched bush floated silent before him. Staring with its leaves perhaps. Then it replied.

"Yes. Follow me."

Billy, Torolen, and the twelve other Chellaquol followed Zekzek through another accessway, emerging into the open on the other side of the dome. Several hundred meters beyond them thousands of Melanons writhed together in the body that was the Tree. But his friend led them away from the Tree, over a stretch peopled with aliens returning to the new, younger parts of the Shop. Zekzek stopped before a tubeway entrance. It said no parting words.

Billy and the aliens quietly walked down the tubeway,

alone with their thoughts. The Chellaquol, he suspected, had an uphill battle to gain any acolytes against the incredible pull of alien gods and goddesses called Kokseen. Perhaps they understood that now. And Billy—he had more than money to worry about. Ancient memories still stirred him. Shrugging, he picked up his walking pace. As they entered a cross-tubeway, Billy caught a flash of orange skin and glittering black eyes. He turned his head to see Solaquil and some of its clutch-mates lounging against the tubeway wall, watching him pass by. Solaquil's eyes stared at Billy—eyes filled with an unnameable alien emotion that he only partially understood. But the gaze again roused his hackles as his predator nature responded instinctively to the powerful alien.

He shivered, feeling very, very alone.

Chapter Nineteen

"The Arbitration Guild announces an incoming projection auction from the Bareen habitat," Billy heard as he sat next to Zilkie, Melisay, and Ding do-wort with Keen so-thorn in attendance, on the curving stone bench that overlooked a low central pit. A Factor surrounded by three Merchants, he felt very junior again. But he was happy to grab at any chance to be inside the Guild's auction chamber, rather than watching like most Factors from the observation gallery above and behind him. The fact that Zilkie never did anything without a reason, including inviting a Factor for a competing House to join it, did not escape him.

Billy looked around the Guild hall, seeing the forms of a Hecamin felinoid, two green-furred Soreps, Namidum katun the Ketchetkeel, Solaquil the Tet, the tracglobes of a

Gordin starfish and two Ta-aaken monitor dragons, and Memra the Dorsellien. Damn. He hadn't realized either everyone was getting a promotion, or the aliens he'd thought Factors on the trip to Silsilaa had actually been Merchants. But then he'd never really socialized with many of them. It was an oversight the House of Skyee and Tsorel had lately berated him about. Sharing food, drink, and lies with aliens, the Mycron quietly instructed him, lubricated Trade deals as much as it did among humans. That was why he'd immediately accepted Zilkie's out-of-the-blue invitation to sit in his reserved alcove at the auction hall.

"What are the Bareen offering that is of interest to you, Merchant Zilkie?" he asked the alien standing to his right. The swirling topknot tentacles went still. A few fish eyes glared down at him.

"Doesn't the House of Skyee teach manners?!" the Cosex quietly hooted. "Sit and watch—you will learn soon enough."

Billy sat. He avoided looking left at the black-and-white-striped fur of Melisay, or further left at Ding and Keen so-thorn. While any auction sale in the Guild hall was important, it couldn't be extraordinary. She would have left her husband at home. He glanced down to the central stage pit. So often when he saw Ding and her mates he was reminded of his lonely state. Fantasies weren't satisfying him anymore. When the *hell* would the other humans get here? He tried to distract himself by speculating on when the Chellaquol would come out of their ship, where they had been huddled for the last month since their visit to the reliquary. The black ovoid auctioneer floated onto the stage.

"Merchants, today comes the Bareen with Life-Extend, universal biomed drugs, and MHD power units from the Forty-Second Florescence," announced the ovoid. "The signal arrives."

The black ovoid, silent again, floated off statge into the shadows of the pit. Someday he would have to learn more about the Arbitration Guild and its members. A humming whine rose quickly up into the human inaudible range and the hall darkened. Billy looked out expectantly. An image took shape.

"Fellow Merchants—we greet you!" squealed a brown ball cluster that Billy recognized from the fur pattern as that of Ika/Ikam, former Factor and gentleman-partner aboard the *Star Riches*. The alien must have done something unusual to earn a promotion to the status of Merchant. Billy had been fortunate in having a powerful sponsor, one who could shorten the usual ten years it took to go from Novice to Merchant.

"As announced," said Ika/Ikam, "we offer a universal biomed healer usable by all carbon-based lifeforms, some delectable MHD garbage units of the Zorsen from the Forty-Second Florescence that still work, and"—the ball clump paused dramatically—"Life-Extend! Who will start the bidding?"

"One *toron* of deuterium for a case of the healer!" yelled Namidun.

"We offer a half *toron* of D-L food for the MHDs," sang the voice of Memra.

"The House will give a full ATMM overhaul and AM refueling for all of your Life-Extend!" yelled Solaquil from a bench-seat across the pit. The alien's overgenerous offer briefly drew Billy's attention away from Zilkie. He saw obsidian black eyes glare out at the whole chamber. But Zilkie the Cosex stayed silent, as did Melisay and Ding. He wondered what was going on.

"Solaquil," squealed Ika/Ikam, "will you add to your offer two globeships with all weaponry to protect our habitat?" That, he saw, got Zilkie's attention. The tentacles suddenly went into overdrive, green whipcords fluttering like grass before a wind. Billy wondered why the Bareen wanted to supplement the deadly protection already offered by the algors.

"YES," the orange salamander immediately replied. "Is Service accepted?"

"YES," yelled the Bareen.

The rest of the goods went quickly and at more normal

prices. Soon the Bareen had sold all its Trade goods and the hologram winked out. The orange full lights of the hall came on. Billy looked around at Zilkie and his two still silent trading friends.

"It is as you suspected, friend Zilkie," barked Ding do-wort from his left. Her four brown eyes still stared at the empty pit stage, but the fan ears were angling toward the Cosex. "The Tet are moving again."

"Moving?" asked Billy, dying to know even if the Cosex got angry. "What's this all about?"

"Billy," purred Melisay softly next to him, "come back with us to the Food shop. We will discuss it there."

Left with the choice of staying, leaving a mystery unsolved, or following the already moving aliens, Billy followed. He might not have nine lives like an Earth creature called a cat, but he was curious. Perhaps too curious for his own good.

The forest room and eating pool brought back memories to him. Memories of hunger, need, and loneliness. But also good memories of a special friend called Melisay. Billy looked at the group as they all sat around the pool. Zilkie, as usual, ate, its worm-toes wiggling in the nutrient-rich sand.

"Billy," hooted Zilkie, "how many sapients are currently at this Station?"

"Seventeen thousand one hundred and thirteen, from sixty-four different species and forty-three civilizations." The question puzzled him. Why did the Cosex want data freely available to all by simply asking the Port Authority algor?

"And how many of them are Tet?"

"Four hundred and seventy-three."

"Are you sure?" asked the Cosex. Billy stared at suddenly still tentacles. What was going on here?

"No, but that's the figure reported by Amadensis a month ago when I last asked. Why?"

"Do you remember the conversation we had when the

Hisein came? About how many other cases there had been when aliens wouldn't reveal their culture to us?"

"Yes." Why couldn't the damn tree-anemone give him a straight answer for once! Billy looked anxiously over at Melisay, Ding do-wort, and an inactive Keen so-thorn. The lack of sex should have told him earlier.

"Three hundred thousand cycles ago there was another conflict with visitors." The tree-anemone bent its green topknot down to stare at him from scores of silvery fish eyes. It was damn unnerving, even after the Walk of Recognition. "They were reptilians from farther out toward Orion. It was their first contact with the Florescence, and they were paranoid. Their ship, contrary to the Rules, began to swing about, bringing its main drive closer to the Station." The Cosex swung its topknot up, pausing, as if the memory of another conflict was hurting it. But why— since it must be only a purchased memory from another sapient or a record in a vidcrystal? "The Tet attacked the Daks with their globeships, utterly destroying them. Then they marched down the Grand Arterial to the meeting hall of the Council. And they demanded full control over Station defense."

"What happened?" Billy was absorbed. Old history this might be to Melisay and the Kerisens, but it was new to him. It definitely wasn't in the orientation crystals or the open libraries.

"It was denied them of course. Only the algors can be trusted not to favor another organic, not to use powerful weapons as a tool to increase one's Trade." Zilkie silently laid a green cord tentacle on Melisay's shoulder. "Since that time they have seethed with resentment. They are a very old race, and they have been aboard this Station for at least two million cycles. They resent us recent arrivals."

"So how does ancient history relate to the auction today?"

"The Tet," answered Melisay for Zilkie, mind-in-mind, "are buying up all the Life-Extend they can find. They seek a monopoly on the ability to life-extend. With it they can gain allies like the Bareen, who are vulnerable in their orbiting habitat. And with allies they will try again to take control."

"Only *this* time," barked Ding do-wort, flapping her glide-skin in emphasis, "we are preparing for them. We newcomers are sick of arrogant old fossils trying to dominate the Station!"

Billy carefully looked at his friends, now very alien except for their determination and anger. Zilkie's tentacles writhed strongly, Melisay's teeth were bared, and the two Kerisens were absorbed in each other as if it were the only way they could relieve the depth of their feelings. He wondered—if their species, on board the Shop for hundreds or thousands of years, were newcomers, what did that make humans?

"Why are you telling me this?" he asked. The Cosex's tentacles slowed their rhythm.

"Because the Tets hate you and all Humans—you don't fit into their Traditional, status-oriented view of reality where newcomer races show submissive respect to ancient races like the Tet," hooted the tree-anemone. "Because Humans are coming on an asteroid habitat with other aliens to visit the Shop. And because such an event—the arrival of nine new alien races at once—can be dangerous. The Tet will be waiting. We think they will again seek control of the Station."

"Other than my survival, why is this important to the House of Skyee?" he asked, buying time as he tried to think of all the implications of what the Cosex was saying. "Why can't the Council handle the threat? They control— or at least deal with—the algors. What's the problem?"

"Young Factor," softly barked Ding from her embrace with Keen so-thorn, "we all like you. But more important, we all want Trade with *Hekar*. So take this as a friendly warning—watch out for the Tets!"

The warning seemed to be the whole purpose of the invitation to the Guild Hall and the visit to the Food shop. Billy stood up, uncertain what to do, but knowing his survival was once again threatened.

Glancing to his friends Billy nodded his head, then

turned and headed out through the purple, yellow, and green foliage of the forest-apartment. His mind felt full of mixed emotions about aliens who cared, but also who saw him as a means to an end. Had his rise in the Shop simply been a carefully orchestrated attempt to use him, to gain an opening when the other humans came?

Billy clumped down the metal rampway into the bustling crowds of Zilkie's Food shop. It was time to go home and think.

"Billy, may I enter," called the deep bass voice of Tsorel from outside his tower room. He looked up from inside his rest unit. The time monitor on the room's black granite wall showed it had been four hours since he'd arrived, lain down, and begun staring at the holo-cube pictures of Jason and Sarah McGuire. He drew the damaged cubes closer.

"Enter." Taciturnity wasn't only for aliens. Billy looked up warily at the blue giraffe as it flowed in on twelve legs. Red eyes looked down at him.

"Billy, do you remember those Chellaquol light-sculptures you recently sold on the Arterial?"

"Yes. What's the matter? Didn't the Hecamin female dominant like them?"

"She did. But Solaquil has filed a protest with the Arbitration Guild. He alleges you lacked proper authority from the Chellaquol to dispose of their Trade goods."

Billy stored the cubes, climbed out of the rest unit, and started pulling on his jumpsuit.

"No way! He was there when Torolen engaged me for personal services." Billy pushed his parents' memory crystal necklace under the suit's high collar. "Since they've been holed up on ship, I sold some goods he left in our storehouse to pay for his dock fees. That's all." He added his dad's bowie knife to the blue sash belt, then the sono-gun from Silsilaa as an afterthought. His left hand caressed the gold earring in his left ear. It reminded him of his accomplishments. Things *he* had done himself, on his own.

"Of course, my friend," said the Mycron, its long eye-

lashes fluttering across the red-glittering eyeband encircling its elongated head. "But we must go to the Guild to
contest the claim. The Elder Merchant told me to bring the
full influence of the House to bear. Don't worry—your
name will be cleared quite soon!"

Billy, now fully dressed, followed Tsorel out to a taxi
ovoid. He felt within him a hard, harsh feeling welling up.
A feeling he'd felt only once before.

Years ago, when he'd left the compressor station and his
vandalized hiding place.

Chapter Twenty

Billy sat next to Tsorel on the transport deck of the automated taxi, acidly amused as the Mycron folded twelve
legs under itself. He heard a burst of static as a call came in
through his wrist comdisk.

"Billy, anyone else within local percept range, we Melanons call the faithful to defend the Reliquary! The Tets
attack! Help us!"

And try as he might, he couldn't again raise the voice of
Zekzek, or any other Melanon. Billy looked at the Mycron.
"Should we go?"

"Of course—the complaint against you is minor. This is
the Reliquary! I'm reprogramming the course now—hold
on."

He held on to floor straps as the ovoid canted at a thirty-
degree angle, side-slipped out of the Grand Arterial into a
side tunnel, and then dropped down a gravshaft like a rock
next to a black hole. Billy wondered when the local iner-
tia-fields would catch up to the taxi's overdrive mode. He

looked out the transparent dome to see what they were passing.

It was a mistake.

"Tsorel—polarize the dome! Or I'll be sick all over you!"

With a flick of its tongue the herbivore touched a pressure switch on the C-cubed unit controlling the ovoid. The interior darkened. He opened his eyes, after-images of rushing walls still causing nausea. Billy, looking across again, saw curiosity written in the cant of the Mycron's ears. But it was too polite and too alien to press for an explanation. And he wasn't about to describe his last ride on a Melanon taxi. This wasn't the time for humor.

"Tsorel, will you fight?"

"Not offensively, young predator. That is for you omnivores. But the Herd body will surround the Tree and offer up our flesh. And our tails will take their toll as we die!" A cracking thump drew Billy's glance back to the taloned tail and razor-sharp hooves. The Mycron would fight in their own way. And Tets would die. He felt the intertia field jerk as the taxi harshly slowed. Then they again felt the usual Shop compromise gravity field—one his parents said was about seven-tenths that of Earth. Billy looked out the newly transparent dome as they rocketed out of the tube-way into the Reliquary chamber.

Carnage greeted them.

He saw blue Ketchetkeel bodies lying broken and burned. Several Bareen ball clumps oozed red blood. Three Hecamin dominants rolled and twisted among a group of six Tet, their neck tentacles ripping flesh from the enemy. Tet blood, he saw, was coppery green. Alien screams, yells, and moans crackled over the taxi's open comlink. Billy's stomach tightened.

The taxi swiftly covered the four kilometers to the high black dome where the final defense was being mounted. He saw scores of Tets attack other aliens with hand beamers, while from a nearby tubeway rattled a ground-effect laser mount outfitted with a forty-centimeter XF laser. He wondered how long the mysterious metal of the dome could stand up to a twenty-thousand-watt laser. Then the taxi dropped down onto the other side of the dome, the side where he'd earlier seen the Tree. Billy saw only a few bushes left. Where were the rest?

"Have you come to defend the Reliquary, sapients?" chimed a Melanon as Billy and Tsorel tumbled out of the taxi's slowly rising hatchway. The bush floated on a lodestone like Zekzek's. Its blue leaves all canted toward him in an unusual pattern that tickled his memory.

"Yes," yelled Tsorel. "I am of the Herd—let me inside to join them. We will stand before you!"

"Yes, I am," Billy reluctantly said.

The bush relaxed its leaves. It swiftly began sliding toward the nearby dome wall. An entry irised open.

"Then come with me. Those outside were not enough to fend off the Tets. Soon it will be our turn."

Billy and Tsorel followed, the silence of the interior dome unusual as the entry closed on the outside screams, roars, and yells of sapients killing each other. The sound of death had been—strangely attractive.

"Billy, there's the Herd," called Tsorel, already moving away with tail held high. "Good Hunting!" it called back to him.

The Melanon also moved away, heading toward the free-floating Kokseen station and the surrounding pressor field. Billy looked around the orange-lighted chamber, wondering whether anyone was in control of this battle. War memories of his dad and his own experiences from Silsilaa rose up about him like guardian sentinels. There really was only one place to be when the Tet broke in. He ran toward the opposite side of the dome where the archways stood bared by alien steel and joined a crowd of aliens sheltering behind an overturned pallet-floater. Their weapons faced the main archway entry. Already it glowed lava-red.

Billy dimly sensed a seething mass of hundreds of Melanons behind him as he knelt among jostling alien bodies.

The bushes were doing something, but what he didn't know. All *he* cared about was that Solaquil might be one of the Tets he could kill today. He carefully raised the sono-gun, gripped it with both hands, sighted on the central archway, and waited.

In seconds the metal vaporized with a burst of released energies. Billy felt a thunderclap rush past him as heated metal gases fled from the laser mount. He ducked, closed his eyes, and held his breath, careful to not breathe in the gray gases. Billy's right thumb lightly touched the pressure stud. His eyes opened.

The gas-veiled laser-mount, its firing stopped in order not to damage the object sacred to all the aliens, blew apart in shards of skirting, metal, xenon-fluoride gases, and ca-pacitors. Orange flesh preceded the flying shrapnel. Billy felt a dull pain in his lower left leg and a sharp ache in his right side. He kept firing at the crowd of Tets gathered behind the ruined weapon. Then the sonogun's partly drained energy pack died.

Aliens around him surged forward to meet the incoming orange tide. Billy saw only a few hundred left on each side, but all gathered together at the main entrance. He and the others waded into the Tet, ready for hand-to-hand com-bat.

He flicked the bowie knife forward and upward, disem-boweling a Tet, then he ducked to avoid a thrown weapon and swept around in a full circle as Tenshung had taught him. Only this time the sweep of meditation had a more deadly purpose than the indrawing of one's self. Green blood showered him. Billy danced nimbly to the left, slashed, then moved to the right, slashed, jumped forward a few paces and repeated the pattern.

Slash, slash, slash—his eyes saw only orange and his nose smelled the warm odor of green blood. Then a blast of light from behind him struck out to impale the unen-gaged bulk of the Tet, barely missing him. He saw the Tet catch fire, flesh cooking. They ran screaming out the arch-way.

"Billy . . . Billy . . . *Billy!*" he heard from far away.

But no one was near. Dazed, he squinted his eyes against the sullen bronze glare of the Kokseen station. He saw Zekzek and Tsorel and a few other aliens gathered nearby. They looked at him strangely.

"What?" he croaked, mouth quite dry. He lowered his aching right arm. The knife's blood runnel stopped dripping.

"You were yelling," chimed Zekzek.

Billy looked closer at his friend and stepped forward. They all moved back a bit.

"What?—Did we win?"

"Yes," said Zekzek, "we won. At a cost. Look."

Billy looked. Behind Zekzek he saw a pile of Melanon bushes, their lodestones gathered about them. They looked dead. Then he remembered—they were photovores! The light blast from behind must have been their full body-charge, delivered as laser light from parabolic-shaping leaves. As many others moved about as were still. It seemed far too many Melanons had died to protect the Reliquary.

"What was I yelling?" Billy asked, his memory clearing. He wiped the knife off and stuffed it back into the sash belt. He glanced around, wondering where the sonogun had gone to. But the crowd of battle-scarred aliens still encircled him.

"You were yelling, 'Solaquil, where are you?!' over and over and over again," said Zekzek. "Billy, the battle is over here. Solaquil leads it elsewhere. The Tets have retreated to their outside habitat."

"Then let's go get them."

"No. Not yet."

The bush seemed strangely reticent—what was the matter?

"Billy, are all Humans like you?" asked the blue-leaved Melanon.

"Like me? How? What do you mean?" *What the hell kind of gratitude was this?* Billy looked around, noticing more aliens had come up to join the crowd. What was so unusual about a biped omnivore predator?

"The killing—it was necessary," said Zekzek. Billy nodded his head in agreement with the bush, impatient to tend to his wounds. "But you didn't stop when the Tets fled. You followed them, slashing at them. You *liked* it."

Billy grew cold. Who the *hell* were these aliens to sit in judgment on him? They'd asked for help. He had given it, here and on Silsilaa. It puzzled and angered him.

"Maybe I did. But I defended the Reliquary. What's so special about this old Shop other than its rarity value?" he asked, trying to move the discussion to safer ground. Aliens rustled, thumped feet or otherwise showed startlement at his words. Damn! Why did human curiosity bug the aliens?

Billy saw Tsorel, covered with someone's green blood, and with two of its legs cut and bleeding yellow blood, push its way through the crowd. The Mycron glanced his way, then over to Zekzek. His House friend seconded Billy's question.

"Zekzek, perhaps it's time for the Human to know. Perhaps we should all know. Will the guardians let us in?"

"The Tree . . . tells me it is permitted." The Melanon canted on its maglev lodestone. "But one of us must accompany you, otherwise the Reliquary will strike at you."

"What?" Billy yelled, falling in with the group of about thirty surviving aliens as they headed across the inner dome's perimeter toward the station. "The station can defend itself? Why all the bloodshed then?"

The Melanon chimed back a terse answer. "Yes. The station is tuned to allow entry only to our cellular form —any other lifeform that enters without us dies immediately."

The floating bush halted in front of a C-cubed console, touched its surface with a few gray sucker roots, and then floated down a pressor field tubeway that extended across the abyss to the Kokseen station. The tubeway filled with air and slight warmth. Quickly water moisture began steaming and liquefying on the station's yellow metal from the sudden influx of an atmosphere. Billy wondered how efficient a five-million-year-old Kokseen eco-mentat could be. Still irritated, he pressed the Melanon for an answer. "Then the Tets couldn't have controlled the Reliquary by themselves?"

"No," said Zekzek. "But controlling *access* to the Reliquary was their true objective. After all, they are of the faith too. They are just too zealous."

Zealous? Billy would have called them insane. And maybe they were.

"Then aren't you as much to blame for the deaths as I?"

"No. The faithful had to fight. You liked it." The Melanon led the way into the old Shop. Billy followed, part of the group, but separate still.

He kept his mouth shut. Even after years among them, Billy still found the aliens of the Retread Shop puzzling in their thinking. They were not always linear in their thought patterns. Nor were they always logical. He conveniently forgot his dad's warning that humans also were neither logical nor predictable.

The crowd walked, rolled, and flowed down an interior tubeway in the station. Zekzek came to a gravshaft, dropped two levels, and led them onward. They rounded a curve, then stopped. Billy craned his neck, trying to see ahead.

"What is this?" called out a raspy voice.

Looking back, Billy saw a surviving Hecamin female dominant bringing up the rear. From the twining pattern of her neck fur, he could tell she belonged to the Clan of Dorimanen the Cloud-Walker. Years ago, he'd played with a cub from that Clan. Before his parents died. Before the Shop turned cold and indifferent. Shaking more memories off like raindrops at one of the Farms, Billy pushed forward to the front of the crowd. A massive bronze hatch barred their entry into the central part of the station. Twenty-eight other aliens crowded around and behind him.

"The entry to the Reliquary, of course," chimed Zekzek. Its sucker roots stretched out to key-in a code pattern on the security console in the middle of the hatch. The oval hatch swung open slowly, with a grinding squeal of metal on metal. Billy wondered if it had been opened before in five million years.

He stopped wondering when he stepped inside.

Ayeesha stood before him.

"Ayeeeeshaaa!!!" Billy called out instinctively, before he could think.

"Billy! shut up!" called Tsorel from behind.

Zekzek floated before them, then halted before an upright, transparent Suspense canister. It held the body of a very beautiful Kokseen. He recognized her from the tattoo of *stretzels* on her thorax. Could she still live, or was this just her mummified body?

"Billy," chimed Zekzek from a stasis-monitoring console in front of Ayeesha, "what was the meaning of the sound you just uttered?" The Melanon's comdisk voice seemed, somehow, to hold both curiosity and menace.

"Oh—um, uh, just the name of a Kokseen I saw engraved on a statue on Silsilaa. Before we found the automaton. Remember?"

The bush ignored his question to address the group.

"Faithful Sapients, look upon the true Reliquary! Now you share with we Melanons the wonder of seeing our Progenitors. You shared blood, now share our Knowledge!" chimed Zekzek, blue leaves flickering in the pale purple light of the room. No one answered the bush. They all looked at the Kokseen. Whether with eyes, radar, empathy, or other senses, they percepted the last Kokseen in home galaxy, drinking in that which had only been known before from carvings, pictures, vidimages, or a few rare vidcrystals. The crowd scurried forward, surrounding the dais-mounted canister.

Billy stood in the back of the room. He'd moved there after the first flash of recognition. He leaned against a cold metal wall, wondering how the Tets would like to fight a living god. And one who had very sharp mouth-palps. He glanced down as Zekzek glided up to him, leaving the faithful to their transcendent experience. Billy didn't need the sight—he had his memories.

"Billy, I offer you a Trade. Knowledge of who killed your parents in return for what you know of the Great One. Agreed?"

The offer brought all his attention down to the floating bush. The alien he'd thought was his friend. Why hadn't the Melanon told him before?

"Agreed." He stepped forward, drawing very close to the Melanon. "That is Ayeesha, first of her race to mind-meld with the Glakh Repository ship. I know her memories."

The bush's blue leaves had gone absolutely still. The lodestone dropped to the deckplates with a thud.

"Now, *you* tell *me!* Who killed my mom and dad!" he screamed, tears running from gray eyes.

"Sooooo . . . that is the way," finally chimed the yellow-branched bush as it struggled back onto its rock. The lodestone shook with re-energization as it lifted up. "I knew you never studied the Kokseen script from the *Star Riches'* library. But I never suspected you already knew it. What is she like?"

Billy looked up at Ayeesha the orphan. He remembered.

"Like the wind Mariah, like the crackle of lightning, and like the heart of a nova! Now, *tell* me—who killed my parents?"

"Solaquil the Tet."

Billy shook with rage at the name.

"The Tree only recently learned this as it was reviewing all monitor vidcrystals dealing with Humans," said Zekzek as it retreated before his predatory step. "The Tet was clearly tracked going into your parents' ship, setting a ta- chyonic pulse signal link to cut off the thruster reactant flow, and then leaving."

Billy stopped cold. A tachpulse signal link! No wonder the surprised pressor operators couldn't help. Metal walls could not stop a tachpulse. His parents, Billy realized, had been killed with a tachyonic binary signal whose residual echo was already spreading across the local group of galax- ies. Unintelligible after the passage of millions of light- years. It would still resonate within him.

Hatred filled him. He turned to leave, wanting revenge. The bush followed him into the tubeway. "What will you do, Billy?"

"Hunt well."

Chapter Twenty-one

Space battles rarely last long. This one had already lasted six hours. Billy was starting to come down from his blood lust high.

He looked out of Zilkie's antiquated service lighter through the direct vision port at flashing free-electron laser beams, yellow proton beams, smart torpedo remotes trying to evade electronic senses, and great, red-glowing balls of plasma that inexorably splashed against the immaterial pressor field surrounding the globular Tet habitat. So far, the algors' Defense Screen had protected the Shop and the other exterior habitats from the Tets' neutronic antimatter beams. But the offensive ships of much of the rest of the Shop, including several multikilometer-long Ketchetkeel dreadnoughts, had failed to seriously damage the shield-protected habitat. No one, until now, had known the Tet possessed such a powerful defensive screen. And since no one from the Ship dared use antimatter—for fear the algors would lose all patience with the mayflies—the battle had developed into a standoff. He looked back to the Attack console in front of his accel seat.

Despite this frustration Billy had loved impaling two orange globeships on Zilkie's old hydrogen-fluoride gas laser, watching the console vidscreen as they exploded in gouts of gas and vaporized metal. His neuro-link connection to the ventral laser blister gave him a feeling of power, as if he had only to reach out and his enemies would die.

The three of them worked well together. The tree-anemone and Ding do-wort either set up fire-control computations or deflected solid kinetic energy weapon counterstrikes with their own pressors and tractors. And Billy—he attacked like the predator he was.

And he enjoyed it.

"Zilkie," called Tsorel over the lighter's comlink from a nearby House of Skyee armed merchantman. "There are no more globeships left. And the Tet screen absorbs our blows. Why do you predators still attack?"

Billy, in a lull while the laser's blister mount smoothly rotated with the lighter's downward dive toward galactic south, thought of revenge. Of hatred. And of what life had been like for him as an orphan. It gave him all the reason he needed.

"To tempt Solaquil into something rash," hooted the Cosex back to the Mycron. "The next time the screen sublimes to let the AM beam out, we'll attack. Maybe the backup pressors will be less quick than our beam."

The blue herbivore didn't bother them anymore, the motivations of predatory omnivore plants and animals perhaps too alien for it. Billy didn't care. He wanted more revenge.

Billy's Attack console vidscreen flashed orange, signaling detection of the precursor subatomic particles endemic to a pressor screen sublimation. He would have only a few seconds, but maybe he could reach in and toast Solaquil. Wherever he was in the habitat.

Then the console showed a purple neutronic antimatter beam of four centimeters diameter shoot from the Tet habitat. The beam, powerful enough to destroy a small moon, passed through a too-slow remote torpedo and disappeared into the algor Defense Screen behind their craft.

Abruptly a black tentacle reached down from galactic north, intersected the steady purple beam, and slowly followed it back to the habitat. The beam quickly shut off. The pressor screen reappeared. Startled, Billy looked up and out of the roof's direct vision port.

He saw an asteroid falling on him.

"ZILKIE! Maneuver core-ward! Now!"

The lighter quickly shifted trajectory.

Billy kept his eyes fixed upon a brown crystalline asteroid. Then the Shop came into view between them and the asteroid. The boulder that his senses insisted was falling on him was at least eighty kilometers across. The asteroid slowly took up position between the Ship and the Tet habitat. Billy, astonished, watched as small black tunnels reached out from the asteroid to almost negligently snap up the offensive remotes, englobe a few fusion-tipped torpedoes, and intercept several ion and proton beams spearing out from the Tet habitat. The black tunnels absorbed everything. He saw the Florescence ships scatter back behind a retreating Defense Screen of algors like minnows in Zilkie's food pond.

"Cosex, what in the name of the three suns of Miyar is that?" barked Ding do-wort.

The Kerisen still sat in her accel seat. So did the treeanemone. The two aliens watched the bow viewscreen and the upper direct vision port. Billy had just two eyes, both of which had to focus in the same direction. He watched his friends.

"A Zotl," replied the master Merchant in the softest, quietest voice Billy had ever heard.

He looked out the overhead port with great interest, the battle nearly forgotten. Memories from Ayeesha's *Tale* stirred. What would it be like to share memories with an intelligent silicon asteroid born during the First Florescence? How many other beings did it carry as memory engrams impressed into ageless crystals? What was it like to live for four and a half billion years? Billy thought the Zotl would make even the arrogant algors take notice. Especially since the Zotls had been the first to create the entropy tunnel, later an entropy globe, for the near-lightspeed ATMM stardrive. The black tunnels, he realized, were incredibly long entropy tunnels.

"What do we do, Zilkie?" crooned Ding, her yellow fur rippling about her as she stretched her four arms in anxiety, her accel crash locks manually released. Billy agreed. What did they *all* do now that one of the greatest beings ever known to the galaxy had come visiting? Zilkie's tentacles, quiet from the first sight of the Zotl, now began to move, lazily writhing in the air as if they considered something very profitable.

"We wait until it's fed."

"Fed?" asked Billy. "How do you feed a triple-damned *asteroid* that is solid silicon crystal?" His voice rose with a touch of hysteria. He had to watch himself—control, control until the other humans came.

"Billy, you try my patience," hooted the Cosex from within its crash-cushioning. "But since we have nothing better to do, I will explain." The tree-anemone's tentacles split open to reveal a bank of eyes looking at him. "Simply put, the Zotl feeds on raw energy. Lots of it."

"How does it get this energy?"

"By sucking on suns," said Zilkie.

"Impossible! Nothing can fool with a star!"

"Billy," the Cosex patiently explained, "with a Zotl, nothing is impossible. They generate an entropy tunnel much larger than the minor ones you've seen snacking on our weaponry. With them they can suck on the coronosphere of a star and eventually the body itself. Don't worry—it takes only a tiny bit. Just enough to replenish its transuranics and mascon reserves."

Billy wasn't reassured. He looked down at the Attack console readout display. Then he looked back out the overhead vision port. "Zilkie."

"What?"

"There is no sun nearby except for Cebalrai. There's only us. And the Shop."

"Little thief! Don't worry—you'll live to conquer Solaquil. Look, here comes its food."

Billy looked at the lighter's bow viewscreen, then out the view portal. He saw a Ketchetkeel dreadnought moving across the north galactic pole of the Zotl like a tadpole across an ocean. It pushed before it a six-kilometer-wide hulk of the Forty-Fifth Florescence, only recently stripped down to base metal. Then a small, silvery globe puffed out of the belly of the largest starship he'd ever seen except for the crude Chellaquol ship. The silvery globe drifted lazily toward the hulk.

"Ding! Polarize the portal. Everyone—close your eyes just in case!" hooted the Cosex.

Billy resisted the urge to look again out the portal. He squeezed his eyes shut. There was a brief flash of the whitest white he had ever experienced. The orphan opened dazzled eyes, wondering.

"Zilkie, what happened? What went wrong?"

"Nothing. Look."

He looked out the viewport just in time to see a ten-kilometer-wide black globe swiftly shrink in size, the connecting entropy tunnel already pulling it back to the Zotl. Billy looked his question at the tree-anemone. The Cosex's whipcord tentacles danced over its NavMentat console, setting up the return course, while Ding crooned an unintelligible lullaby of sounds. But Zilkie finally answered his look.

"Its meal was the meeting of four liters of antimatter and that Da-ubadah hulk out there. Understand now?" The Merchant returned to piloting the lighter back to Dock Ten.

Billy understood.

His heart hammered at the realization of so much power contained in such an alien form. He still dared wonder if it would share memories with him. Just as he turned to shut down the emergency MHD generators, Billy heard words in his mind.

Thank you for the meal, Life.

The voice wasn't that of the Elder Merchant. He knew it couldn't read minds against the will of the host sapient. But if not the Noktoren, then who? The Zotl?

A very subdued assembly of Factors, Merchants, senior species representatives, algors, tracglobed aliens, and Melanons encircled the Council meetplace in the center of the House of Skyee's main plaza. Billy stood to one side of the plaza, the black granite stones of the clan-towers behind him, the central urbus before him, and the crowd in between. He watched as the gathered powerful flew, hopped, rolled, thumped, or walked about, waiting for daa-lumka-liche ka-ka-Hak! to show up.

A thunder of displaced air and a splashing of waters from a nearby tank alerted him. The Noktoren, impressive as always, had simply teleported into the round transparent tank, dropping the last meter into the water. So far as he knew no other race could even come close to the psy abilities of the Noktoren. Maybe it was good their home planet was so far away.

A laughing echo in his mind teased him. Damn! The Elder Merchant didn't know the meaning of privacy!

Neither do you, little thief. Did you enjoy the blood-letting?

He stubbornly ignored the two-thousand-year-old ruler of the House of Skyee. It might cost him a commission, but he would control himself. He would simply observe what the alien powerful decided to do about homicidal Tets and a nearly all-powerful Zotl.

"Honorable Sapients," boomed the comdisk voice of the Noktoren, "welcome to the six thousandth, four hundred and twenty-third meeting of the Council of Control." Waves sloshed over the tank. Billy saw a great gray fluke briefly appear over the tank's rim. "Trade has been good, but now it is disturbed. The Zotl's Components say the Self is still sleeping, waiting. They say be patient, ignore the Tet, and wait until fullness comes. What say you?"

Billy noticed Zilkie, Melisay, Zekzek, Ding, and three husbands gathered together a few score meters away in the thick of it. Zilkie stood next to a Bichuen drone and its Zorell dominant, but the Cosex's tentacles lay nearly still.

"What are we waiting for?" he heard the muted, rachety voice of Namidun ka-tun call out. The blue praying mantis briefly opened and closed its saw-toothed grip-arms. Thinking of the dreadnoughts and the sector-wide influence of the insectoids, Billy gave thanks the Ketchetkeel had been on their side. Other aliens in a medley of voices, light band flashes, and smells asked the same question.

"We wait for new visitors still a few months away," said the Noktoren. "They belong to nine species new to the Florescence. They come on an asteroid starship called *Hekar*."

Billy quickly looked away from his trading partners to stare at the tank. Why did the Noktoren think the Zotl would be interested in a few new aliens? It probably counted scores of races in its engrams. The Components themselves, he'd been told by Amadensis, were simply aliens of earlier Florescences who'd freely chosen immortality with the Zotl and a slow cruising of the galactic arms on whorls of magnetic impulse rising from the core.

The Council of Control didn't look all that impressive to Billy. Simply a score of aliens of varied shapes, species, and habitats who gathered in a loose cluster about a few algors; the purple algor globes both translated and represented the inorganic community. And he remembered the Council hadn't been able to persuade the Chellaquol the Shop was safe. The bewildered missionaries had left months ago, seeking safer converts.

Movement drew his eyes. A Gordin Counselor in a tracglobe asked the obvious question.

"The hungry ones—they hunted us—what with them do while waiting?" asked the anonymous methane-breather.

"There is blood debt owed," rumbled a rusty red Hecamin male dominant member of the Council, neck-tentacles twisting in agitation. The quadruped's prehensile tail and neck tentacles insistently tapped the black flagstone of the plaza. Billy sympathized—he too owed a blood debt. A purple-steel algor globe floated up to the Council from the outer fringes of the crowd.

"Sapients," he heard Amadensis's distinctive voice interrupt, "there have been conflicts among the organics before, and they were resolved. There will be other conflicts. But Trade is best." The maglevs elevated the algor even higher than its usual half meter off the ground. "I suggest a rest, a pause—you organics can always kill each other in the future. Why are you always in a hurry to shorten what entropy has apportioned you? Be patient."

Billy wondered if Amadensis only spoke for itself or for most of the several hundred algors residing in and near the Shop. He knew little about the algor society, except that it truly held the balance of power between the competing alien species. Control of the antimatter weapons and most service mentats gave the inorganics a stranglehold—when they wished to exert it. But they rarely interfered—apparently the doings of organics both entertained them and reinforced their own perceptions of superiority. He suspected the Council acted mainly as a negotiating team for the organics.

"That's good advice," the Noktoren again boomed out over the comdisk. "We're at stalemate now, and the Zotl absorbs any weaponry from the Tets. Why not await the arrival of this *Hekar* and see what new factors enter our game?"

Billy closely watched Zilkie, Melisay, Ding, and Zekzek. He wondered why none of them had brought up the tachpulse facts that *Hekar* was as big as the Shop, that it was partly controlled by an algor of its own, and there were over thirty-four thousand sapients aboard the starship. Twice as large a population as the Shop. He felt such a visit was rare in the history of the Shop. In fact, now that he thought of it, the coincident visit of a Zotl and such a multispecies starship seemed unique—at least for this Florescence.

"Agreed—"

"Satisfactory—"

"The debt still holds, but we accept—"

"Maybe the Melanons can replace the stardrive overhaul Trade niche—" came a clustered group of voices from the Counselors.

Billy sighed. He felt tired. Too tired even to think of going after Solaquil on his own. The revenge desire still burned in him, but it was like embers, waiting to flame again. And whatever his feelings, he could do nothing against the Tets on his own. He too would have to wait. He looked across at the gathered Traders of the Retread Shop. They all, he thought, had power and now they wanted to keep it. Only when the humans came would the power equations change. He would be patient—a while.

Three light cycles later Billy stood on the control deck of a House of Skyee merchantman as it hovered near the Zotl. The trading ship was trying to pretend to be part of the Shop's encircling Garbage cloud of hulks, habitats, C-cubed units, slag fragments, discarded fuel tanks, and anything else someone had left behind over the last five million years. Billy was functioning as an observer for a spy flight controlled by a tracglobed Gordin named Nak-alumin. Memra the Dorsellien, Tsorel, and several other alien Associate Factors of the House served at crew posts on the domed control deck. The deck layout was very similar to *Star Riches*—which was to be expected given the inherent conservatism of ancient cultures and the reliability of Kokseen technological patterns.

"Detection—boson deep-scan results—elucidate now," Billy heard Nak-alumin curtly demand from its Control Nexus platform.

Billy looked right at the recovered Memra serving at Detection post. How did the Dorsellien use its shortrange telekinesis to percept the electronic and photonic potential changes in the pedestal? He wanted to ask, but the gray deltoid hovering on a maglev disk in a low-gravity local field had other things to do besides satisfy his curiosity. Its mouth sensor tendrils twitched.

"Pilot-Captain," called Memra to Nak-alumin, "the scan shows numerous concentric layers below the surface, apparently composed of pure hexagonal silicon crystals." The Dorsellien lazily flapped its delta-winged body, straining for the simulacrum of the clouds. "The crystals lie in concentric layers below the outer surface. There are no large air pockets. However"—Memra's translated voice sounded excited—"there *are* mass concentrations detected. At four various levels. Transuranics are present!" Billy stood entranced, caught up in the knowing—never before had he encountered a noncarbon-based lifeform, least of all one so strange as the Zotl. "The transuranics are all long half-lives. There are high gauss magnetic fields rippling in all directions, and radiation flux levels are two to eight MeVs."

"Detection—Zotl is massive—why no detection—elucidate," demanded Nak-alumin.

Billy wanted to hear more. Like how could such a lifeform generate a magnetic repulsion drive field that could grab hold of the nearly nonexistent fields of interstellar space and use them to achieve lightspeed velocities? He listened intently from the Comlink console where he stood.

"Port Authority says Zotl entered masked." The cloud-dweller increased the rate of its wing-flapping. "Neutrino, quark, and lepton release was minimal, there were no EMF signals, and the Tets had all their attention."

"Excrement!" yelled the Gordin.

Billy looked back toward Nak-alumin, seeing its red starfish form writhing, partly obscured by white methane gases. A central yellow compound eye stared back at him and Memra. "The Zotl appears suddenly—how? Research answer—now!"

Billy quickly turned his attention back to the bow viewscreen, studiously watching a hologramic depiction of the Zotl as it appeared to electromagnetic and lightspeed-accelerated subatomic senses. A sectioned ball representing an eighty-kilometer-sized lifeform slowly rotated before his eyes. Readouts flashed listings of lanthanum series isotopes and exotic trace elements. Billy thanked his luck he didn't work for the Gordin. It was too much of a taskmaster for his taste. The main tubeway access door to the rear hissed open.

Looking, he saw a blue-leaved Melanon on a distinctive lodestone enter.

Zekzek quietly floated up to Billy. He silently looked down at the bush. It was hard to realize just how powerful his former friend was. Particularly when it coalesced into the Tree. Its presence aboard the merchantman didn't surprise him—the Melanons were calling in many owed favors after their deadly victory at the Reliquary. He just wondered what it wanted from him.

"Billy," Zekzek chimed, "we have unfinished business with you. Where are the Great One's memories?"

"In a safe place. Where you can't get them, I hope." He nervously combed his loose black hair with one hand, the other tugging at his red jumpsuit to make it fit just that much better. "Do you offer a Trade?"

"We do not Trade for the memories of the Revered One!" The bush's gray sucker roots curled and twined about the lodestone, seeking an answer. "Billy, we *must* know her before we awaken her!" the Melanon pleaded. The statement drew his full attention to the alien. "Please, will you freely help?"

"Why wake her?" he asked, playing for time. What would happen on the Shop with a live Kokseen running loose? A Zotl, the Tets, Ayeesha, an asteroid starship, humans, and his revenge Hunt were becoming too intermixed.

"We—the Tree—seek the Deep Knowledge of where the Progenitors went. We must know!" the Melanon's leaves chimed loudly on the suddenly quiet control deck. Billy dared not look up to where the Gordin ruled. What could he say?

"All right, freely given, like my blood at the Reliquary." Billy looked appraisingly at the bush, hoping to rekindle in his offer a bit of their earlier friendship, damaged now by his discovery the Tree had known his parents' killers—and not told him. "But not now. Wait until we return and things settle down. Now please—be quiet!" he whispered. The bush complied, floating silently.

Billy McGuire Human, Factor of the Retread Shop,

predator omnivore, thief, and orphan looked at a control deck side screen. It showed a natural light view of local space. He saw the glittering starry band of the Milky Way shining brightly, peeking through intervening dust clouds. Billy looked longingly outward toward the core, toward new worlds and suns. But most of all he wondered what he would do when the humans came.

MERCHANT

_____

_____

_____

_____

Chapter Twenty-two

"Ding, may I enter?" Billy called, standing in front of the Kerisen's office door in the Dock Twelve Merchant's Refugo. It was two months since the battle with the Tets, and he needed a friend. He needed advice. And while Zekzek had become much more sympathetic after experiencing Ayeesha's memories, Billy needed to talk to an animal, a mammal—not a bush. The silvery metal doorway irised open.

"Enter," called out Ding do-wort.

Billy walked into the reduced gravity of a carpet-strewn, lightpicture-decorated front office. Ding, as usual, sat on a giant blue and red cushion, surrounded by blinking terminals. There was no sign of Keen so-thorn or any of her other seven husbands. She spared two of her purple eyes to look at him, fan-ears canted his way.

"Do you offer Trade, Factor Billy?"

"No—uh, I mean, maybe I do." He stopped, realizing how stupid he sounded. It was time to be more than just a silly orphan who felt sorry for himself. "I mean—I need advice. I need a friend. And I was hoping you could help. What's your price?"

The yellow-furred Kerisen briefly switched two more eyes his way. The bullet head canted fully toward him. She kept only two of her arms busy entering data.

"Modest—knowledge for advice. You tell me what you saw in the Reliquary and I will offer advice. Agreed?"

"NO!—I mean, I can't. I promised Zekzek." Ding's purple eyes seemed to flare with interest. Billy desperately considered his options. "What if I share the images from a

Kokseen starchart crystal I got from the *Star Riches'* Trade?"

"Satisfactory. Anyway"—Ding turned her upper body around to face him, yellow glide skin rippling with the movement—"I like you. You intrigue me, and I think Trading with Humans could be both fun and profitable. Remember the secret I told you over three cycles ago?"

Billy blinked gray eyes. Had it really been almost four years since he'd first met Zilkie, Melisay, Zekzek, and Ding do-wort? He would soon be twenty. Time for a birthday. If only he could find someone to share it with. He nodded back at Ding.

"I do—you said 'the meaning of existence is to have fun'—right?"

"I did. And you amuse me. Our escape from Silsilaa was the most fun I've had in sixty cycles!"

"*That* was fun?" Billy barked, sitting down on a lavender pillow a few yards away from the Kerisen. It looked like he was in for a long visit. "It scared the hell out of me! What's so funny about being shot at?"

"Why, little sapient, the thrill of coming so close to knowing the universe's ultimate joke!" All six of Ding's purple eyes now focused upon him, the terminals left unattended. "Death comes to all, but once our memories are recorded, why not tempt it?" He wondered if the Kerisen was insane. "What other purpose do you think entropy intended for us to have, than to be the self-aware fingers of one hand tempting the death-dealing fingers of the other hand?" The Kerisen stretched wide her four arms, exposing the velvety smooth inner fur of her glide skin to his gaze. Four hands, each with four fingers, counterpointed her speech with frantic finger movements, each handfoot its own puppet show to the others. Billy felt the wind of an alien culture touch him.

"I see." He slowly stroked the small beard he'd been growing the last year. "That's an interesting concept. But I still need advice. Will you help me?"

"Tired of my stories? All right—tell me what concerns you," she urged. The Kerisen turned two arms and four eyes back to the Trade terminals, back in her business persona, back to earning more barter money.

"The other humans are only a month out from the Shop. The House of Skyee wants me to tachpulse talk with them, to set up Protocols." He blinked again, remembering a long-ago encounter with a silent octopoid. "But I'm... afraid. It's been so long since I talked to real humans, I'm not sure what it will be like. How do you think I should open discussions?" he lamely asked.

Ding threw her yellow head back and opened wide a V-shaped mouth in a barking laugh. "Oh my young, young Factor! Such problems at a young age! Tell me," she asked, moving a third purple eye to join the first two in spearing his wilted spirits, "aren't there eight other alien races on this *Hekar* starship?"

"Yes."

"And what are their basic classifications?"

"A second humanoid race with fur, an eight-legged crustacean race, an eight-tentacled octopoid species, a three-eyed flying reptiloid raptor, and a multilegged empath, all omnivore predators." Billy paused, remembering the sparse data sheet he'd received from Zilkie and Melisay after his return from Silsilaa. "Also there's a six-legged carnivore type, a silicon-based amoeboid species that breathes methane, and a barium titanate crystalloid race with a gestalt mentality."

"And why do you think you will have any trouble dealing with the *Humans* when you can Trade with the likes of such aliens!?" Ding turned all but one eye back to her terminals. "The answer is simple. Approach your Humans as if they were simply another alien race, which they are. To me, at least. Understood?"

"Understood," Billy thoughtfully echoed back. He got up from the cushion and headed toward the front door. Caught up in thought, he ignored etiquette and started to step out into the Refuge corridor. Then he heard the sound of bodies thumping together. Billy looked back to see Keen so-thorn busy with Ding. Both aliens each spared only a single purple eye for him.

"Ding, why do you live here, at this Dock, rather than with the rest of the Kerisen in the habitat below Dock Seven?" he asked.

"Why . . . because I'm insane, young sapient." The Kerisen gave him a tooth-filled grin, while Keen so-thorn's mobile eye glittered at him. "At least my people think I am to choose to spend so much time among aliens, among beings who can't see the great joke." Ding's hands and fingers left the terminals to spread wide, matching the outstretched arms and glide skin of her senior husband. Together they rocked on the pillow, all thoughts of business banished in mutual pleasure. "But then I like to consider myself a missionary for our point of view." All six eyes slowly winked back at him. "Who knows—I may even make a convert."

Billy carefully backed out of Ding's office.

This was too weird. An alien jokester he could take. But an alien who truly, absolutely believed in her ideology— that was not the kind of friendliness he sought. He touched the pressure switch in the hall outside, closing the door on a scene that made him ache for a *woman* of his own species, but a scene whose cultural underpinnings were far different from those accepted by humans. Billy the Factor turned and walked down the hallway, heading for the bar and the simple distraction of drink. He had his advice and had renewed a friendship. But like all things it had a price. Billy wondered what it would be like to share memories with Ding, when she remembered to ask him to share the Kokseen starchart with her.

The House of Skyee's Comlink center occupied a pyramid of stone, metal, and crystal that shared the place of honor about the Noktoren's geodesic dome. The trip to the central urbus in a House taxi was simply one of the fringe benefits of his Factor status. But the silent walk into a semidarkened Comlink room, consoles and pedestals flickering with electronic and photonic linkages, all crewed by aliens of at least seven different species, was different. The familiar form of Tsorel cantered up to him from near the central tachpulse dais.

"Billy McGuire! It's good to see you, Factor," said the blue-skinned herbivore. The giraffe angled its eyeband down to look at him with all twelve red eyes. "Are you ready to make Trade contact with *Hekar* and the Humans?"

"I guess so." He walked up to the dais, stepped onto it, and faced the end where the return hologram signal would heterodyne in. "Why the humans? Why not Trade contact with any of the other aliens?"

"Billy, don't be stupid, because you aren't," said Tsorel. "We contact the Humans because they're the only race with a representative aboard the Shop. You know this," the Mycron quietly admonished him. He did know it, but he still felt uneasy. Enough—it was time for a true Factor to work.

"I'm ready. Send the tachpulse precursor."

"Done—signal is acquired—holo is incoming," chittered the voice of a Gordin tracglobe as remote manipulators lightly touched the tachyonic console. Billy looked away from the red starfish to the incoming signal. He nearly collapsed on the dais.

A woman stood before him.

Long black hair framed an oval-eyed face with delicate features. Jet black eyes stared out at him. She was dressed in a *yellow cheong-sam*—a form-fitting dress of silk, his parents' memories whispered to him. Her body aroused him. Fingers clasped together before her slim waist, she spoke to him.

"Forty-Seventh Florescence Trading Station, this is Falling Waters Nakashimi, current bridge Liaison for the Compact starship *Hekar*." Pale pink lips moved, forming words that engraved themselves into his heart. "We have your signal. What is your wish?"

"Uh—we—I mean, we wish to establish Trade Protocols for your arrival here at the Retread Shop." Billy spoke in a rush, jerking his mind back to his work, trying to focus on the shapes of the weird Compact aliens that he could see moving about in the background behind the human woman. One of the reptiloid raptors, great leathery wings slowly flapping, occupied a Control Nexus-analogue station to the left rear of Falling Waters. "I'm Billy McGuire Human, predator, omnivore, and Associate Factor of the multispecies House of Skyee Trading enterprise. We welcome you to this part of Orion Arm. On behalf of the Elder Merchant, we ask permission to speak to your humans—we would first work through them, if it is acceptable?"

Falling Waters frowned slightly. A small tongue licked her lips. Then the black eyes glanced back over a beautiful shoulder to the winged alien at the Control Nexus dais. Billy saw a compound eye on the left side of the alien's head look directly at the human Liaison. Scale-covered oval ears flared out, perhaps in a sign language signal. The woman seemed to get her answer. Falling Waters turned back to face him, a neutral look on her face.

"Billy McGuire Human, your request is granted. We will switch this signal to the human habitat and the attention of our first Liaison. However"—her pause disrupted his rapt attention; Billy put business foremost in his mind—"be aware the *Hekar* is a cooperative entity that permits separate contacts by each race. All may Trade independently, so you or other Florescence aliens may be contacted by our member races. Good Trading!"

The tachpulse holo briefly dissolved, taking away the image of Falling Waters and wrenching his heart. Billy steadied his stance, hoping his formal red jumpsuit, blue sash belt, and Hunt earring would complement his image. He tried to be wise beyond his years.

The new signal completed his emotional devastation.

Billy saw a man and a woman sitting in redwood chairs inside what seemed to be a Comlink center. They both looked very, very old. The man, dressed in bluejeans, a red plaid cotton shirt, and leather boots inscribed with distinctive designs, looked animatedly at him with twinkling gray eyes. The woman, sensuous despite an apparent age of at least a century, was dressed in a pale yellow toga with a clasp at her left shoulder. The right shoulder next to the man was bare, and part of a breast swelled out to entice him. She had green eyes, pale red hair, and a wide grin on her face.

"Jack, look! It's a human boy! How could he have gotten there ahead of us?" the woman said in a deep, musical voice which, despite age, still held a strong hint of laughter.

"I am a man, not a boy, and I'm Factor Billy McGuire Human," he asserted. "Who are you, and do you represent the humans in Trade?" It was time to make progress. No one from the onlooking House of Skyee aliens had pressed him, but Billy knew they were anxious. They all wanted to tie up an exclusive representation and factoring agreement, if possible. If not, they could at least acquire information that could later be sold to other competitors.

"Yes, Billy McGuire Human," rumbled the deep bass voice of the swarthy-skinned man as he leaned forward in his seat, his left hand lovingly entwined in the woman's right, "we do, at least to a degree. I'm Jack Harrigan, former newsman, then Liaison to the aliens, now myth-figure to the ship-born ones. And"—he turned to look at the woman—"this is my wife, Colleen McIntyre, former journalist, lover of aliens, and lifemate." The man's finely wrinkled smile turned serious. "We come from the time of the First Contact, from the late A.D. 1990s. What's *your* birth-time?"

"I—my parents, I mean, came from the third Garbage Hunter launch of 2077, but I was born in flight while under stardrive." He shrugged, trying to remember the Empire of Ch'in time referent that would translate into the archaic Gregorian calendar. Then his mind tossed up the figure. "I was born in Year 2889 of Kung Fu-tzu, Day 12 of Cicada Month, which is—March 4, 2338. Why do you ask?"

"So we can better understand your culture, Billy," said Colleen, now also serious. "With humans of all different birth-times sailing the deep in sub-light vessels, you can meet people from your future or your past. You, young man"—he liked how she emphasized the word *man*—"are from our future."

"But don't you know our history? The tachpulse signals

still come from Earth, from the other Garbage Hunter ships, from colonies up to ninety light-years out." Billy shook his head in puzzlement. "Humans are spread widely compared to a few hundred cycles ago. What began with *Hekar* is now a great series of ripples, spreading ever outward."

The steel gray-haired man looked puzzled, then slowly smiled. "Thank you, Billy," said Harrigan. "We do know our history. It's just that we humans on *Hekar* feel ... special in a way. Our culture is unique. We live among thirty thousand aliens of eight different races." The man's gray eyes looked distant. "They are our brothers and sisters in a way."

"I understand. But there are seventeen thousand aliens of sixty-four different species aboard the Shop, and I feel special too as the only human here." Had he engaged in enough non sequitur small talk? Had he put them at ease? Was now the time to pull the fishing line in? "I represent the House of Skyee, some of whose members you can see behind me in the Comlink center. Skyee is the *only* multi-species Trading House here. It's the one that accepted me as a Factor; it controls many ships and resources; and it would like to Trade with you. Profitably. And to the mutual benefit of you humans, your ship, and the House. Are you willing to discuss Protocols of engagement, service, and fees?" Was their concept of Trade close enough to that of the Florescence that they understood? Brown thumbs stuck in his sash belt, Billy felt nervous.

"Billy McGuire Human, I remember the green hills of Tennessee and the Smoky Mountains," pronounced Harrigan; the gray eyes smiled. "There's an old saying not unique to country folk. It is—don't try to teach your grandmother to suck eggs. Understood?"

Billy didn't understand. An idiomatic saying obviously, but what was its meaning? Since they were all speaking English, with some help from the comdisk to clarify the differences the language had evolved over three hundred years, he couldn't expect the algorithm to do more. And his parents' memories didn't explain the reference.

"What do you mean, Jack Harrigan?" he finally asked.

"It means—we're Traders too, young man." The lean, well-muscled male crossed his legs and reached down with the free right hand to pick up a drink glass from the stone floor of the other Comlink room. "Don't try to pull the wool over my eyes"—what the hell did that mean?—"with fancy phrases that mean something in your alien culture but not a lot to me. Instead let's speak straight." Harrigan grinned over at the woman Colleen McIntyre. "We have the knowledge base of our race, biologicals from the Amazonian jungles your friends there never saw, booze that'll make a snake drunk, and whale-songs that will break your heart. What do you have to Trade in return?"

Billy grinned. He liked Harrigan's direct Trade style. It was an effective variant on the Forthright Assertion 2M Style. They could do business.

"How about two planets full of deuterium, *torons* of lithium six, sapients who can overhaul your ATMM drive, black hole reservoirs, thousands of kinds of D-L seeds and foods"—he couldn't forget Zilkie's specialty; the master Merchant would surely give him a nice commission on any human business he sent the Cosex's way—"rebuilt and overhauled Garbage technology from the last twenty Florescences, and bonded warehouses where goods can safely be stored during negotiations. Interested?"

The holo images of Jack Harrigan and Colleen McIntyre smiled at him. Their clasped hands, he saw, gripped tightly. They reminded Billy of his parents.

"Damn right I'm interested! And the rest of these wacko Compact aliens will be also. But we got to you first. What's your cut, Billy the Factor?"

He smiled back. This human knew the basic Rule, knew you don't get something for nothing. The House of Skyee would be proud of its newest Factor.

"Only twenty percent of anything of yours I can sell here. Are we agreed upon representation and service?" Billy alertly watched, wondering how much the Noktoren would mark up their goods.

"Agreed, Billy McGuire Factor," said Harrigan with a

glance off-screen at his habitat. "Our human Council has given me plenipotentiary powers to deal for us. And the first thing you can Trade me is your basic orientation program for sapients new to your station. You have one, don't you?"

Billy smiled again. This Harrigan was shaping up to be a challenge. It was time to invest some of his own funds in this venture.

"Of *course* we do after five million years of Trading! I'll tachpulse the vidcrystal to you free as a sign of my goodwill, at my own cost." Harrigan and McIntyre both looked silently at each other, eyebrows raised, then out at him. "It usually runs with an algor in interactive linkage, but the nonaware part of the program will make adjustments."

"Fine. And don't worry about the algor—we have one of our own, if we can tear it away from its research program into how organics could ever have created it," said Harrigan, looking a bit tired. Billy could see the wrinkles in the man's suntanned face, and recalled both Jack and Colleen had remained seated. Were they invalids? Somehow he didn't think so. "My associates here have prepared a long list of items we wish to Trade for, and various goods and services we can offer in payment. We'll tachpulse it to you in binary encryption on the end of this signal. Satisfactory?"

"Quite satisfactory," he replied, briefly looking off the dais at Tsorel, the Gordin, and a tight ring of senior House representatives. "Is there anything else we may Trade you or that you wish to know?" Courtesy was everything when dealing with aliens, especially with human ones.

"Yes, Billy," called out a serious Colleen from her seat. "How long have you been without other humans?" The question tore his heart out. Billy's face turned savage, then studiously neutral.

"Eight years since my mom and dad died. Why do you ask?"

"Well"—the woman tentatively smiled a freckled grin at him, full of good cheer—"we're just a little startled to be talked to as if we were aliens by another human. That's all."

"I see . . . Is there anything else you wish to know?" he asked very quietly. Billy's innerself reburied his memories of family, of hopes, of the times before he was orphaned. Harrigan's gray eyes looked back sharply at him, seeming to sense the Trade contact was at an end.

"No—not for now. We'll call you over the next month with suggestions on barter equivalencies. And feel free to call me," the man offered. "I'm attaching my personal residence number to the binary datastream. Use it—anytime you want to talk. Or just see another human."

"Thank you." Billy wasn't quite sure this kind of intimacy was right for a Factor with his customer. But then their ways were new to him. He made allowances. "Good Trading to you, and the House of Skyee will lavishly welcome you to the Grand Arterial. Good-bye."

Billy stood silent for long seconds after the holoimage winked out. The Trade contact had gone exceedingly well; there was a high probability of sole Factor representation for him with the humans. But what about the rest of the House?

"For a predator, you can be almost graceful in the Hunt," softly commented Tsorel from behind. He turned around. Ten alien House Partners hovered around the Mycron as it took the lead in handling him. "That was well done, Billy Human. With this opening we may acquire the business of some of the other aliens—perhaps the reptiloid raptors would like to live-hunt some game along the Arterial," Tsorel mused, gripped by unpacifistic thoughts. "You will keep all this confidential, we assume?"

"Of course," he assured them. "Except for the Cosex and Melisay, to whom I still owe much. Is it permitted to give them the outline of the humans' food preferences?" The blue giraffe swung its scaly neck down to closely appraise Billy. The eyelids slowly blinked several times in complicated syncopation.

"It is permitted, Billy. But remember—we are your House."

"I'll remember." He stepped down from the dais and headed toward the Comlink's main entrance. "You'll send me a hard copy of their Trade list?"

"Of course, Factor Billy. Good luck with the Cosex. And good Hunting," whistled the Mycron.

He didn't look back, knowing the aliens of the House of Skyee wouldn't mind, knowing they could follow him anywhere he went in the compound with monitor systems emplaced millions of years ago. The sense of age, of antiquity, of hoary beings toying with the emotions of novices rose up from the dead flagstone floor to invade him. Billy quickly walked to the waiting ovoid, anxious for once to be back on the Grand Arterial.

He found Melisay sitting alone by the Food shop's eating pool. Cross-legged, with muscular arms wrapped around blocky knees, she rocked silently. The black-and-white-furred carnivore looked up at him with four brown eyes.

"Hello, Billy. Have you come to listen to the forest with me?"

"Melisay, no, I hadn't planned to. There's business news for Zilkie. Is he here?"

"No—he speaks now with the Melanons at the Reliquary. Come sit by me until he returns. Please?"

Billy, looking upon the Tellen bear with the eyes of memory, understood. She needed a friend. She needed the company of another mammal. She too sometimes felt lonely, the only one of the *brach-ahn* to walk through the stars. He tugged open the neck of his jumpsuit, loosened the sash belt, and sat beside her, looking outward.

The forest he saw looked endless. Giant green ferns, purple trees, yellow toadstools, and orange moss-covered rocks carefully, delicately fooled the eye into thinking this was a true forest, a continent-wide stretch of plantlife that breathed and lived for the planet. The images brought to life Melisay's memories of Homeworld, of a people called *brach-ahn*. He solemnly and joyfully remembered.

"Billy . . . will you show me your people when they come?"

"Of course, Melisay. Of course. But why humans—why not the other Compact aliens?"

"Billy, how many times have you shared memories with another being?" The Tellen bear turned her stocky head to look directly at him. The furry fan ears betrayed her mood with nervous twitchings.

"Once, no, twice, in a way," he said, remembering Ayeesha of the *stretzels*. "Why?"

"I have shared memories with over two hundred sapients of one hundred eighty species." Billy looked wonderingly at her—he'd never suspected. "And in all that time only three aliens have ever cried with me." Brown eyes sucked his soul downward into great pools of caring. "First was with Zilkie when I touched him. Second was with Ding do-wort over three hundred cycles ago. The third time was with you."

"That's . . . wonderful, Melisay. But why the rarity? Why didn't the others empath with you?" he asked, trying to gain time, trying to understand what Melisay of the dead sisters was trying to say to him.

"I don't know. I'm not Technological like you others. I just feel and sense and know the life about me." She paused, looking back at the world-forest. "I have skills—like navigation and piloting, the healing touch, and a little foresight. But no other aliens except you three have ever resonated with me, shared fully my feelings, understood my sorrow, *known* my loss!"

Billy once again understood. She was an orphan too. He looked back out at the great world embodied in a small one. Melisay stayed sharp in his mind's eye. He had no need to physically see her.

"I get so lonely," he confessed. "But now with the other humans coming, I feel like running. Even talking to them feels . . . strange," he recalled. "The House of Skyee asked me to handle a Trade contact with *Hekar* and the humans, and I did. Quite well, actually," he mused. Melisay's warm paw-hand lightly touched his right thigh, reassuring with contact. "But it felt alien to me! My own people and I didn't feel them! Why?" he cried out.

Melisay turned fully to face him, reaching out with both furred hands to gently take hold of his face. She looked at him, brown eyes reaching out. He reached back.

"Billy, it's all right to be lonely. To be alone. To be the only one of your kind here." She blinked, shedding a tear down a blunt muzzle. "But what is *not* all right is to give up, to forgo hope. Billy," she said insistently in Trade *lyol* speech so her words came directly to him without the interference of the comdisk, "I care for you. I need you and your feelings. Whatever happens when the Humans come, we are soul-linked forever. Where you will go, I go, and so will Zilkie. Do you understand?"

He looked deep into her eyes, tears streaming down bearded cheeks. Billy the orphan understood. At last, he was loved again.

Chapter Twenty-three

Three days later Billy was back at the Food shop. This time Zilkie was there. And the Cosex's topknot of tentacles were barely moving. He wondered who had upset the touchy plant.

"Billy Factor," hooted the green predator from its four sound sphincters, "do you think these Humans of yours will take sides in our local dispute with the Tet?"

"Not unless they're fired on." What the hell was the Cosex really trying to find out? No visitor to the Shop engaged in unprovoked violence—the Shop's weaponry was simply too powerful.

"Ummmm...no, that would be too dangerous to arrange...we know they have AM projectors. No!"— what idea was the meat-eating plant toying with?—"We will simply park them on the side opposite the Zotl and the Tet, and then—"

"Zilkieee," he exasperatedly interrupted, "just what are you talking about? I just told you I'll Factor all their Food needs to you for only a modest commission. What's this talk of antimatter weapons and side-taking?" He looked around the back office, remembering the uncertainty that faced a certain young boy who once slept there. Things had most definitely changed since then.

The Cosex stopped its shuffling about on worm-toes. The green whipcord tentacles lifted a bit. The plant stiffly leaned his way. A bank of fish eyes glared at him.

"Little Factor, don't you Humans know courtesy? Don't interrupt!"

"Go to hell, you arrogant plant!" he shouted back, angered by the suggestion he was still an apprentice to the plant. He had suffered too much to be treated like an orphan child again.

"What . . . what . . . you defy me? Why it's about time, little sapient." The Cosex's eyes twinkled in the orange light. "Good, now we can discuss what really matters."

Billy was confused. The plant had always been touchy with him. Why the change?

"Discuss what?"

"Why, how to deal with the efforts by the Tet to develop a coalition of ancients against us newcomers, and how you will handle your upcoming appearance before the Council of Control."

"What!"

"Haven't you been comlinking with your House C-cubed/I network? All the best Trade intelligence and rumors are on it," the Cosex calmly informed him.

"No . . . not recently. I've been too busy." He recalled how he and Melisay had simply lain next to each other after their sharing, holding on, warmth to warmth. He'd fallen asleep next to her. "Anyway the Zotl protects us from the Tet. Why worry about them? And *what* is this about an appearance for me before the Council?"

"Billy McGuire Human Factor"—the formality of the

Cosex's speech startled him—"we are *not* safe from the Tet. Only their weapons. But not their politics. Not their maneuvers. And the Council is anxious over the upcoming visit by *Hekar* and the Humans. *You* have upset them. And they seek advice and answers."

"Me—I upset them?" The Cosex's statement on the Tets worried Billy. Could Solaquil really reach out to him from the orbiting habitat? "How? And when do I see them?"

"In thirty *micoms*"—and he wasn't even in formal dress; Billy started pulling his hair into a tail and combing his beard with his fingers—"and you upset them simply by being Human. They're not used to a newcomer sapient rising so quickly in the meritocracy of Trade." Billy could have sworn the Cosex's voice held a hint of smugness.

"So when do we leave? And how do you want me to act?" he asked. He should have known better. The Cosex would have smiled if its body had a face.

"So glad you asked, little thief." The silvery fish eyes looked down at him as the Cosex glided up close, wrapping a few tentacles around his shoulder. They were uncomfortably tight. "Let Uncle Zilkie advise you."

Billy was "advised" all the way to the Council of Control meeting.

The Council meeting hall was an old, rehabilitated Dok'aah habitat block that still had the smell of the snakes about it. There was no furniture, except for C-cubed units before each member, and the compromise gravity-light fields were a pallid half-G and dim red. The aliens he saw were as weird as those at the Walk of Recognition.

"Colleagues," began the Cosex as it stood in front of him and to one side, "I have brought the Human Factor Billy McGuire as you requested. You can see he wears the colors of the House of Skyee"—Billy looked down, remembering how he'd let Tsorel paint them on his light beige jumpsuit—"and he has already made tachpulse contact with *Hekar* and the Humans. What is your pleasure?"

Billy quickly inventoried the Council. The Noktoren was absent. But there were a Sorep, two Dok'aah, a Melanon,

Namidun the Ketchetkeel, a Gordin, a Dorsellien, a Heca-min female dominant, a Bichuen drone and Zorell domi-nant, a Mekanen, a Ti-keel floater, a chlorine-sucking Nakal crustacean barely visible in its tracglobe, a dielectric Galian crystalloid whose yellow facets glittered in the light, and the miniature purple tornado of a Minoren gas-oid. He hoped neither the Mekanen death-eater nor the Minoren were hungry.

Then he looked again. The Council membership lacked a Bareen, a Tet—of course—and a few other of the an-cients. The aliens before him were, by a slight majority, newcomers. Only at the Station for the last half-million cycles. What could it mean?

"Our pleasure varies," came the reedy voice of the green-furred Sorep as its prehensile tongue whisked out to smell-sense the air, "according to our biologies, master Merchant." Billy noticed that all the aliens with eyes or their equivalents were staring at him; even those for whom staring was a social taboo. "Tell me, Human, what do your people want?"

"Trade, of course. That's what all intelligent lifeforms want, right?" He hoped the answer would suffice. The one-meter-high pile of fur stirred, revealing four small legs. The front two had three-fingered hands held close to the chest while the rear two sported sharp-looking claws. The two blue eyes of the Sorep looked back him.

"Most do. Some don't. Like the Hisein. Others want more—they want to control the faith. Like the Tet. You understand?" the reedy voice asked again.

Billy slowly scanned the semicircle of seated, standing, or tracglobed aliens. He sniffed the air. There was a smell of threat here that even the House of Skyee aliens didn't arouse in him.

"I understand." He did really. These were the people who controlled the Shop, who had the power, and who grew rich or whatever was important in their cultures. They weren't about to lose it, either to outside upstarts or to fanatical ancients. "How may I assist the Council?"

"Your Humans," called Namidun from the side opposite the Sorep, "what do they need in Trade?"

"Honorable master Merchant, you know I cannot break the seal of bond service with my House"—Billy saw the Ketchetkeel mantis stiffen slightly—"but my advice is available for only a modest fee. And spectroscopic observation of *Hekar's* drive flare should easily tell you their fusion pulse/ATMM drive uses deuterium and lithium six like nearly—"

The sound of alien laughter over the comdisk interrupted him. Billy carefully looked around, trying to match the sounds with the few body movements showing on the aliens. It was hopeless; he did not know enough of their body languages.

"Merchant Zilkie!" he heard the Sorep call out. "You and Ding have taught the Human well! Its arrogance is pleasant to hear. But now to real business." The Sorep turned its snouted face to look at its fellows surrounding Billy. "My associates can buy or not buy the Trade list your Humans encrypted to the old Noktoren. But I care most about how to handle nine different alien species, only one of whom we have any knowledge—you Humans. Billy Human"—the blue eyes turned back to catch him—"what are you Humans like?"

"We are . . . curious, master Merchant." What could *he* tell them about a species he barely knew except from his parents' memories? "We are also argumentative, arrogant, predatory"—the Ketchetkeel and the Melanon rustled in knowing agreement at that statement—"sex-driven and possessed of a special sense of our place in the universe. Usually we are fair, but do not harm us—our history is one of making war for fun, profit and pleasure." The Gordin starfish, he saw, had moved its methane tracglobe closer to him; its yellow cyclopean eye stared. "And we love to Trade—my dad once said that for us humans Trade is the pursuit of war by other means."

The aliens were silent. Even Zilkie's tentacles lazily moved about, considering. Had he said too much?

"And what about this Compact of aliens on *Hekar*—what is it like?" asked the Sorep.

"The usual group of weird sapients wanting to Trade." He shrugged. Then he tried to recall early human history lessons heard first from Tenshung and later his mom. "They came to our home system in A.D. 1995—about three hundred Shop biocycles ago—in an asteroid starship that had only one-half lightspeed capability." Vague memories slowly surfaced in his mind. "They Traded with us. Humans acquired the designs for fusion pulse starships, fusion power plants, and Suspense. The Compact stayed in-system for ten years of Trading. They planted a colony of barium titanate crystalloids called Thoranians on our innermost planet"—Billy noticed the Galian had moved its linear induction repulsion disk closer to him—"sent off a small asteroid colony ship filled with amphibian crustaceans—the Zik, I think—to a nearby system called Barnard's Star, and left with a human colony habitat of four thousand."

"They now have an ATMM modulus," called out the Hecamin. "How did they acquire it?"

"They didn't. They developed it on their own." The Hecamin's silent golden eyes stared at him. "I remember that after the aliens left, we humans began to exploit our local system resources. Then we got tachpulse word in . . . 2074, I think, that *Hekar* had been attacked by methane-breathing religious zealots called Xi Booteans about twenty-six light-years out from Earth. The histories say the ATMM drive was developed just before the attack and helped in the escape of *Hekar* from the Xi Bootes system. That's most of what I know."

The Council held silent for a while. Billy wondered if there would be more questions. He was tired of being front and center so much. The tension of trying to say and do the right things was tiresome.

"And these Compact aliens never knew of the Florescence?" the Sorep asked. Its claws, he saw, were leaving scars on the titanium-steel floor of the habitat. Was it nervous or simply sharpening them?

"No . . . at least not until after they left Earth and before they got to Xi Bootes. Sometime around then they got a tachpulse signal from the home system of their Arrik aliens that a Zotl had come visiting." That definitely caught Zilkie's attention; the tentacle topknot writhed furiously, and several other aliens showed body movements suggestive of deep interest. "The Zotl made some kind of contact with these Arrik—they're reptiloid raptors, I remember—and out of it came knowledge of the Florescence. That was passed on to *Hekar,* and ever since then the Compact starship has planned to visit the Shop. My progenitors told me they were taking a roundabout trip." He smiled slightly; it was a good feeling to know something the powerful Merchants of the Shop didn't know. "Not an unusual story, really."

"Hmmph," grumped the Gordin starfish from its tracglobe next to him. "Your Compact aliens—unknown to us were—why?"

"Space is big and we are small, master Merchant," he smugly replied. How should he know why the Ketchetkeel or any of the other Wanderers had missed a cluster of sapient civilizations? From what he knew of the Forty-Seventh Florescence, it happened all the time.

"Zotls are *not* small," quietly commented the Sorep, "and an asteroid starship bigger than this station with four thousand of *you* aboard is also not small." Billy kept his mouth shut. There wasn't anything intelligent he could say about such self-evident facts. "You may go."

"Certainly honorable master Merchant, but"—the Sorep turned back to face him, blue eyes staring again—"I trust my consulting fee of two *torons* of deuterium will be deposited in my warehouse at the House of Skyee?"

"It will be. Now leave us to *consult* with Merchant Zilkie."

Billy did as he was told. He turned around and walked silently on bare feet out of the Dok'aah habitat into a nearby tubeway. A House of Skyee taxi ovoid awaited him. He smiled—it was nice to know the Noktoren could spy as well as the rest of the Council.

* * *

The next day Billy arose early in his tower room, flipped on the C-cubed unit in its center and listened to the status reports on the approach of the humans and Compact aliens. There was a photomultiplier-enlarged normal light image of the asteroid starship in the screen's center, while on all four sides of the screen were running commentary ideograms in *lyol*. They gave readouts on mass, speed, deceleration rate, neutrino leakage levels, gravity wave and graviton emissions, infrared signatures of the nine different life habitats stuck to the outside of the elliptical asteroid, quark, lepton and boson scan characteristics as the Compact aliens looked back at the Shop from several million kilometers away, informed speculation as to the energy and data compression levels characteristic of each alien species, and the combined civilization level exhibited by *Hekar*. He watched carefully as he ate a meal of D-L synthflesh and *esay* grains. Most of it was data he'd learned while still with his parents, but important nevertheless. Billy touched a pressure switch on the unit's upper surface.

"Comlink control, what's the estimated time to arrival of *Hekar*, assuming constant deceleration?"

"Twenty light period cycles, Factor Billy McGuire. Further service?" asked the nonaware C-cubed program.

"What is the estimated volume of *Hekar*?"

"Two hundred and ninety-three thousand, three hundred fifteen cubic kilometers, Human McGuire. Further service?"

Shit! The damn thing was the size of a small planetesimal. The Ketchetkeel would get rich just topping off its tanks.

"Yes, what are the overall dimensions?"

"One hundred sixty by seventy kilometers, Human McGuire. Further service?"

He couldn't resist asking. He had to know. The little boy in him still joyed in the big and stupendous, even when he knew small and quick could be just as deadly.

"The starship's primary exhaust funnel—what is its exit opening size?"

"Four kilometers, Factor. Further service?"

"Uh, um—no. Off circuit."

Billy just sat on his stool, one foot into his jumpsuit, overwhelmed. Most starships he'd seen could disappear up that funnel. And the ATMM modulus had to be large enough to take the plasma flare as it exited at one-half lightspeed. The damn modulus must therefore be as big as most short-range starships. Just what kind of antimatter-matter drive had these aliens independently developed?

He began, slowly, to realize that what was approaching wasn't a starship. It was a world. Actually it was nine different worlds. Along with the desire to know, he felt a little fearful. Billy had the feeling twenty light periods would pass very quickly.

Chapter Twenty-four

"Billy, the Bareens really *do* want to buy your MHD generators," Zekzek reassured him in the cavernous space of Dock Six. "They're just very paranoid and fearful of coming to the Shop. So we go to them. It's simple."

Suited up in his dad's spare suit, neck ring checked out, and helmet laid back, Billy frowned his doubt. The Forty-Sixth Florescence combat exoskeleton he'd bought a year ago on the Grand Arterial fit snugly about him, hardly a bother. He lifted his right arm to flip the helmet down, and the soft vibration—no sound—of chip motors operating within miniature pressor fields briefly touched his skin. They were taking a Melanon taxi with tractor unit attached so he could haul six MHDs out to the Bareens. But Billy felt uneasy—the Bareens were ancients, and they were at best neutral in the Tet–Shop feud. Still, credits were credits, and the humans had come much closer since his Council interview—they were now only a few thousand klicks out.

"Where's the Bareen habitat now?" he asked the blue-leaved bush.

"In the outer nimbus of the Garbage belt, north relative to the galactic equator and up arm," replied the friendly Melanon. "Don't worry—the Tets are on the opposite side of the station, with the Zotl between them and us."

It was precisely because the Tets were nowhere near the Bareens that Billy had even considered the Trade. He looked around for the levitating bush. It waved yellow branches from within a nearby transparent crystalline taxi globe. He walked out on a loading parapet, bent down, gripped the airlock rim, and lowered himself into the globe. The exoskeleton barely even vibrated. He sat down before a C-cubed tractor console.

"You have trajectory clearance from Port Authority and the Defense Screen?" he asked Zekzek.

"Of course. We are the Tree, little one. Such things are never forgotten."

"Then let's go—slowly, please."

For once in four years, the Melanon did exactly as he asked the first time. The globe lifted up, moved out to a secondary exit portal used when it wasn't necessary to open the primary clamshells, passed through the inner seal, the middle seal, and then the outer lock opened. They popped out into the dark. Billy, helmet unpolarized, looked out at the beauty of starlight glinting off abandoned hulks, Garbage parts, a few habitats, and some parked starships. Thousands of pieces of small debris, like silvery grains of sand, reflected back the immensity of space to him.

"Do you have the MHDs under tow, Billy?"

"Of course—such things are never forgotten."

The Melanon didn't rise to his teasing. It was too bad. No matter how friendly the Melanon now was, it still remained a plant. It wasn't quite like Melisay and Ding, or even the gruff Gordin merchantman commander. Now Zilkie though—that was a plant with a difference. Including a sense of humor.

The trip was to last only a few minutes, even at a low speed of five kips. The rhombohedral Bareen habitat quickly loomed up in front of them as they swerved to pass a tumbling Melisuk hulk from the Twenty-Third Florescence. They nearly died then.

"Billyyy—" "Zapp, Crackle"—his eyes saw purple afterimages. Instinct moved his tongue to click on the helmet polarization. Blinded, Billy bounced from one side of the globe to another.

"Zekzek—what *happened*?"

There was no answer.

He blinked weeping eyes. Then he tongued the polarization to half-strength. Billy looked out the crystalline shell at an orange death.

A Tet globeship was rushing out from behind the Bareen habitat toward them. He looked down at the bush. It was lying up against the wall by the C-cubed NavMentat package, lodestone fallen from its taproot grip. The leaves looked wilted.

Billy thrust down toward the C-cubed unit, plugged a cable override into it, and keyed a course into his chest pack. The taxi jerked as the magnetic repulsion field flickered on, off, and then on. It began to move slowly, then quickly. He dove the craft down and behind a nearby Lesser Um'tak hulk. The attacking proton beam that had almost gotten them before flared off the raw metal of the hulk. He tapped a quick course change in, then downloaded from his suit's chipmemory a prepackaged escape and evasion algorithm. Sarah McGuire's memories told him to cross his fingers. He did.

"Billy McGuire Human . . ." groaned Zekzek—how could a bush groan?—"the *Tet!* It's hiding, it's—what happened?" asked the Melanon as it struggled to climb back onto its lodestone. Before he could answer, they were out from behind the safety of the hulk.

"Hold on if you can!"

Billy, sighting the orange globeship closing from south galactic, dove outward from the Shop, acting on a hunch. They wouldn't survive trying to get back to the Shop, unarmed as the taxi was, but there was one possibility. If only the taxi had enough speed.

"Zekzek, we've got a few seconds. That last vector change threw their tracking-lock off. The Tet is behind us. I'm heading toward the humans."

"Billy, the Tree says Port Authority has launched the algors. They will battle the Tet for us."

"Too late." He looked at the orange gas-dynamic screen on the C-cubed unit, then at the repeater signal on his neckring. They both showed the Tet rapidly closing. The taxi was fast, but not quite fast enough.

"Zekzek! The Tets want me. Prepare for Garbage Runner ejection maneuver. *Now!*"

Again, the bush didn't argue with him. He almost wished it had. Then he was out in space, the exoskeleton powered up, small thrusters flaring as he diverted from the taxi's course. Zekzek dived coreward. In seconds he would know the decision of the Tets.

The proton beam flared once more. It grazed the Melanon taxi. There was a barely visible puff of atmospheric gases. His friend's craft ricocheted in a shearing trajectory that seemed unpowered. Then the globeship's nose brightened as it spat a kinetic kill vehicle at him. He had only seconds to live. Then for the second time in his life, he looked up and saw an asteroid falling on him.

Hekar hung above him, its rocky nose streaked with impact scars from sandgrains impacting at near lightspeed. He saw scores of small blisters scattered in equatorial and polar lines about the ellipsoid. Then the twenty-kilometer-wide prime habitats. His telescopically augmented eyes saw one of the small blisters iris open and spit out a small black sphere the size of a peapod. He looked away and back toward the onrushing death of the KKV.

Instantaneous with the perception by his eyes of the light from the small KKV drive as it speared up to him was the overlapping image of the sphere as it passed between him and the KKV. Then it moved toward the projectile and away from him. The KKV curved and dove into the tiny sphere. And disappeared.

Billy's heart was pounding.

He was alive. And he should be dead. People in spacesuits don't survive when pursued by hunterships. He glanced back at *Hekar* in enough time to see the black sphere curve back toward the ATMM modulus at the asteroid's stern. Then he understood.

The Compact aliens, weapons boards shut down as demanded by the Shop, had simply shot a miniature black hole at the KKV. Now the excess gravity well was going to rest in the modulus' reservoir. The sweat on his forehead reminded him that miracles are only miracles for a few moments, then the living have to get on with living. His relief almost cost him his life again. He had forgotten about the globeship.

"Help . . . please . . . help me," he called out stupidly.

Billy saw the miniature orange marble of the Tet ship in the distance as it swung toward him, determined perhaps to ram him or capture him with a tractor. Before it could do either, six red shapes rocketed out from behind him to dart forward in frantic jerks, twists, and right-angle turns that threw the Tet firecontrol off long enough. The orange globeship simply exploded in incandescent shells of metal, gas, and debris as energy and matter weapons from the red shapes speared it. Stepping down the polarization for the second time, Billy looked out at a lone red shape just as it jerked to a halt in front of him.

It reminded him of a globe within two spinning armatures. The metal glinted silvery red. There were no normal-light portals on its surface. And the armatures rotated freely around the globe, without touching it, at constantly varying angles and intersections. Jason McGuire's memories suggested a device called a gyroscope, but it was unknown to him.

"Greetings, sapient," the comdisk within his suit said. "You scan as Human. Are you Billy McGuire, the Factor?"

"Yes." What do you say when your life has been saved

twice? "That was well done. I will do my best to secure a discount for you from the House of Skyee."

"Hey kid," came a distinctly different voice that sounded male human, "we don't need any favors. Just doing our job. Want a lift over to *Hekar*?"

"Please. Can I go to the human habitat?" What should he do now? There was no point in returning to the Shop when he was this close to the biggest customer the Shop had ever had. A memory stirred. "I was once invited to visit a Jack Harrigan—do you know him?"

"Know him? Hey, kid, he's my stepdad. Hang on."

Billy held on to nothing.

It didn't matter. The strange ship's control of tractors was exact, delicate, and perfect. Billy briefly looked down at the new world of *Hekar*. He saw a gigantic rectangular slit appear in the forward side of the starship, then gradually enlarge to reveal a spacedock four kilometers by two in size. He felt like an insect as he was towed into the asteroid.

"Sapient, please do not move after we land," came the strange hissing voice. "There are variable gravity fields present in the hangar deck. My shipmate will escort you."

The landing, a kilometer below the asteroid's outer skin, was silky smooth. Billy landed on his feet, and the exoskeleton didn't even purr. He looked over at the globe as it hung above the metal deck, then turned and looked around at the spacedock—no, hangar deck the hissing voice had called it. It looked similar to the Shop's Docks except for blister emplacements on the upper ceiling.

"So you're the Human alien we've been hearing about," said a male human voice behind him. Billy turned around to see his rescuer. A young man perhaps a few years older than he stood before him in a semiliving flightsuit, collapsible glassine helmet laid back on his shoulders. The man was red-haired and green-eyed, but an Asian epicanthic fold was very visible around the eyes. A Eurasian, the man didn't look too much like the Jack Harrigan Billy had seen during the tachpulse contact.

"Yes, I am the man Billy McGuire," he said, emphasiz-

242 . T. Jackson King

ing his maturity as he recalled the references to kid.
"Thank you again for saving my life. My parents taught me
we . . . shake hands to show gratitude. Will you?"

"Sure."

Billy gripped the man's right hand. Then a slithering
sound caught his attention. He looked up and beyond to the
hovering globe. An incredibly ugly alien was flowing out
of an upper hatch. It looked like his mom's memory of a
centipede. Except it had eleven pairs of legs, there were
two pairs of flexarms near an uprearing torso, the body was
segmented to match the leg pairs, the silvery skin was
scaled, and the alien had no eyes.

"Hello. Are you the one who spoke to me?" Billy con-
versationally asked the new alien. It was a Strelka. The
male dropped Billy's hand and also turned to glance at the
new arrival.

The segmented alien was suddenly, swiftly before him,
the torso elevated above the hangar floor, while the legs
flowed it along. Its torso, topped by a cranium with a
teeth-fringed sucker mouth, swayed slowly from side to
side. Billy, acting on intuition, stepped out from the embrace of the exoskeleton and began swaying from side to
side also, all the while feeling emotions of curiosity and
gratitude.

"Greetings, Sapient," said the sucker mouth. "You honor
me with the dance of feelings. Will you Hunt with me
again?"

"It will be my pleasure and my desire. What are you
known by?" Billy, caught up in the contact, in the rush of
Trade Protocol, didn't notice the human looking at him
strangely.

"Flickering-Blue-Embers, brother-in-thought." The
Strelka slowed its oscillation, lowered its rearing until all
its feet were on the ground, and angled its cranium at him.
It was then he noticed a band of different colored scales
encircling the head. "Come see us at the Hive—the Food
Game is flavorful to sense. Good Trading, Billy McGuire.
Good Trading, Sam Nakashimi."

"You're Sam Nakashimi?" he asked his rescuer, watching distractedly as other aliens briefly appeared and disappeared in the far open spaces of the hangar deck.

"That I am." The mustached lips frowned slightly. "How did you know to dance for old Blue-Embers?"

"I didn't. It was simply the right thing to do. Wasn't it?"

"Young Human, response correct, was," came another comdisk voice from behind him. How many crew did this globe have in it? He turned to look. A transparent quartz ovoid filled with green crystals silently moved toward him, presumably on linear induction repulsion. The Thoranian was about a meter high.

"Nakashimi Human, neurons slow this time, why?" Billy heard the Thoranian ask his neighbor. Wondering how long it would be before other humans came to greet him, he bemusedly watched Sam Nakashimi turn red in the face.

"Suck vac' Syees! Just because you crystalloids think at transluminal speeds doesn't mean we organics can't do a good job." Sam blinked green eyes in anger. "He's alive, isn't he?"

"Sam—Elder Syees," Billy interrupted, "I appreciate the rescue no matter if it was a few nanoseconds slow. But can you direct me to the human habitat and Jack Harrigan?"

The human turned back to glare at him. Then he looked resigned. He made an obscure hand gesture to the dielectric crystalloid. "Come on, Billy, there's a grav dropshaft to an interior arterial near here where we can catch a transit disk. Up yours," he heard the human call back to the Thoranian. The crystal matrix didn't offer a reply.

Billy followed his guide. Sam Nakashimi stayed silent as they walked down a tubeway, stepped into a vertical shaft where he fell downward, slowed, and landed at least three kilometers below the asteroid's outer crust. They came out into a small rock chamber where a series of aliens and a few humans passed rapidly down a tunnel that began on Billy's left and went to his right. Everyone, he saw, stood, sat, or tracglobed on a maglev disk. Billy, eyes watchful, nimbly jumped onto an idling disk at the edge of the arterial right after Sam did. Leaning forward, he noticed, caused the speed to increase.

"Sam, what kind of ship was that you were crewing?"

"A Stinger."

"How does it work? And how do the three of you crew it?" Billy hoped the human would be more communicative. He needed words to supplement the discerning observations his gray eyes were rapidly recording as they passed alcoves, chambers, tunnels, dropshafts, and other installations unfamiliar to him.

"It's simple. We're all neurolinked to each other and the ship. I run the Detection and Drive pedestals, the Thoranian does Navigation and Fire Control, and old Blue-Embers handles the Attack mode." Sam paused, the brown flightsuit tight over broad shoulders in front of Billy. "You know the Strelka—they like to taste the death screams of their prey."

"It's . . . an effective huntership. When did you develop it?"

"Just before the Xi Bootean Conflict." Sam was silent for a few seconds. "It was an idea of Billy !gose-/!lay before he died."

"Who was that?" Billy the Factor didn't even try to wrap his tongue around the sharp, acute syllables that seemed to be the last name of this other Billy.

"A !Kung Bushman who was the greatest survivalist known to old Earth."

"If he was a great survivalist, why is he dead?" Billy hoped he wasn't being rude. But the language of this Sam Nakashimi was a weird mixture of normal English and archaic syntax.

"Because he gave his life for us, for *Hekar*. He led the attack on the Xi Bootean dreadnought. Enough. We're there."

"There" appeared to be the entrance to another dropshaft. Only this one led upward. Sam didn't follow but motioned him to enter. Billy stepped inside and looked up as his body rose. There was a round yellow light far ahead. Then he was in the light, in a half-dome that covered the dropshaft. Billy landed on his feet as the transit device spit him out. Not seeing anyone there to greet him, he walked toward an archway, expecting a monitor eye to interrogate him. Instead the archway irised open.

Billy stepped out.

Yellow light blinded him. Strange aromas and smells assaulted him. Just before his heart froze in his chest, he saw a vision of paradise. He collapsed wondering if this was the heaven of his mom's memories.

"Billy! *Billy!* Wake up!" called an insistent voice.

He felt so relaxed. There was endless time in which to wake up. Why was the voice bothering him?

"Jack, why won't he wake up?"

"I don't *know,* Colleen," Billy sleepily heard a gruff male voice exclaim. "It's not the full-G gravity shock that threw his ticker out of sync. Try again—give him a whiff of that perfume you're wearing."

"Jack! But OK." A strange, nice odor tickled his nose. "Billy, this is Colleen, please wake up."

He opened his eyes. Looming over him was a woman. Then he remembered. It was Colleen McIntyre, the mate of Jack Harrigan. Billy just looked, drinking in the vision of sea-green eyes, long eyelashes, freckled white face, and pale red hair, all framed by delicate wrinkles. The look of concern, of caring, comforted him. But there was an insistent melodic background sound, a deep thumping that soothed his innerself as much as the sight of the woman.

"Hello. What's that sound?" The woman looked briefly confused. She looked up at the male voice somewhere behind him, then back to Billy.

"Earth, young man. To be specific, it's Beethoven's Fifth Symphony. Do you like it?" she asked.

Billy, turning his head, saw he was in a redwood-panelled room. Some kind of cabin, Jason McGuire's memories whispered. There was simple furniture scattered around. And Jack Harrigan's black-haired form stood nearby, dressed as at the comlink center.

"I like it a lot." Colleen, he saw, was wearing a pastel

green toga, clasped at the left shoulder with an intricate device. The toga revealed most of the woman's right breast as she leaned over him. "You could make a lot of barter credit selling recordings to the Dorselliens, the Galians, and probably half the remaining sound-perceptors on the Shop. Do you have others to Trade?"

"Sure we do, Billy Factor," said Harrigan, moving around to sit by Colleen in a split-pine chair. The man crossed his arms and leaned forward over the back rim of the chair, blue-jeaned legs straddling the simple construction. Slate-gray eyes amiably looked him over. "We've got wondrous sounds by Debussy—ever heard *Clair de Lune*? Then there's Tchaikovsky's *1812 Overture*. And the usual run of Mozart, Bach, Beethoven, Rimsky-Korsakov, many others." They were strange words; were they styles of music or song names or composers? "Then the Hindus over in the New Varanansi sector have *sitar* ragas that'll tear your heart apart with longing for love. Haven't you ever heard this stuff before?"

Billy, leaning over on his right elbow, realized he was naked beneath the rough organic fiber of the bed coverlet. He looked over at slightly smiling Colleen. Then he silently shook his head at Harrigan.

"No, Mr. Harrigan. Many of our memcrystals and datadisks were lost in the destruction of *The Pride of Edinburgh*. Jason McGuire—my dad—only had enough time to push Mom and me into Suspense canisters, set the tachpulse beacon, and slow our spinning." Jason McGuire's very vivid, very real memory of the accident loomed before his glazed eyes; Billy was simultaneously in his dad's memories, then his mom's. Then the touch of the woman jerked him out of reminiscing.

"Jack . . . I think Billy needs time to rest, time to have only one other human around while he adjusts." He saw Colleen look over at Harrigan from her footstool next to his bed. There was a special look in her eyes as she somehow gave a silent message. "Why don't you go visit Sargon at the Horem habitat—he'll want news about that orange globeship and whether *Hekar* faces any threat from this Shop. I'll call you when Billy's ready."

"Sure."

Harrigan stood up, still sprightly despite the delicate wrinkles evident on the skin of his bare arms and face. Billy wondered just how old these humans were. Just as the male was about to go out of the living room, he turned and looked back at Colleen with a wry grin on his face.

"Lover, remember he's human *and* alien. Don't let your enthusiasm for new experiences blind you to the need for a unique approach."

"I won't. Give my love to Sargon and Bethrin."

Billy, still leaning on his elbow, closely watched the curves and shape of the woman's neck as she gracefully turned to talk to her lifemate, then back to face him. The red hair was long, curly, and thick. The small upturned nose wiggled at him.

"Billy," she said, standing up. "I think it's time for a bath for you. We have a redwood hot tub out on the deck —come on."

Colleen McIntyre calmly unsnapped the clasp, dropped the toga to her feet, stepped out, and stood before him. He stared at her, eyes darting all over. Billy felt his desire rising beneath the blanket.

"I—um, ah, fine!" He sat up, throwing back the blanket. His dad's memories told him not to look down at himself, to just be naturally naked when around a woman. "Where's the deck?"

"This way," she said, turning and walking to the far end of the rectangular room where a sliding glass door led to the outside. Billy stood up, feeling a little shaky, then felt better as he realized the Harrigans must have set the local grav-field at a comfortable seven-tenths G. He followed the luscious swaying hips of Colleen McIntyre. If his attention hadn't been entirely on her body, he might have fainted again at the yellow-lit sight that greeted them.

He stopped, eyes overloaded.

Out beyond the deck he saw the paradise he vaguely

remembered from the half-dome entrance. Around him stood a grove of giant redwoods, lacy green ferns clustered around their base. A small green meadow with wildflowers waved in a cool breeze. Looking past Colleen—who was stepping into a round tub filled with swirling blue water— Billy saw rice paddies, a curving river, rolling and lightly jungled hills, wooden buildings of unique design in one sector, wheatfields, a lake, stair-stepped condos on the far side of the twenty-kilometer-wide habitat basin, and many, many other sights his parents' memories couldn't name. Breathing deep, smelling the lilac scent of the wildflowers, hearing the rustle of the redwood branches high overhead, feeling the roughness of the redwood deck flooring—he felt at ease. He felt rewarded. Billy looked down at Colleen. Her green eyes looked back with interest and desire. He carefully walked the few paces to the tub, stepped into the blood-warm water, and sat down next to her on a below-water bench.

He was drawn into the embrace of a very special, very gentle, very loving woman.

He awoke to the call of songbirds. Colleen lay next to him under a thin sheet, snuggled up onto his chest. He softly caressed her wrinkled cheek. Green eyes opened to stare deep into his soul.

"Morning. Did you sleep well?"

"Yes," he tenderly replied. "Colleen, you were wonderful. And now I understand what my parents had. But why? Why did you take me to you—a stranger?"

"Billy, we're all strangers beneath the arch of entropy." She rubbed red hair against his left shoulder. "Each of us is an island unto himself, seeking a bridge to the other islands. Alien to alien, human to alien, we all need to reach out." Her left hand moved beneath the covers to caress and arouse him. "But for humans—for people, making love is a very special kind of closeness. It's how we reaffirm ourselves. How we throw back the night. How we cry out against the onrushing tide of dying. We all must have it. Is it so different with your alien friends?"

"No," he said remembering Ding and Keen so-thorn, remembering Melisay and Zilkie.

And together, they comforted each other.

Chapter Twenty-five

Billy and Colleen were sitting in lounge chairs on the deck, looking raptly at Earth, when Jack Harrigan returned. He heard the first Liaison call from inside the A-frame cabin. Human voices again, after so many years.

"Colleen, we've got visitors. Roust yourself, lover. It's Sargon and Bethrin." Billy reluctantly looked away from the sight of humans—Asiatics he thought—carefully tending rice seedlings. He was curious to see what the Horem looked like.

"Jack," called Colleen, "we're on the deck. Come on out." She got up, moved her chair to the corner opposite the tub, arranged some cushions and winked at Billy. He winked back. She smiled. Jack Harrigan walked out onto the deck.

"Billy, meet Watch Commander Arix Sargon Arax"—a tall, short-furred humanoid stepped around Harrigan to grasp his hand—"and Clan Mother Lux Bethrin Arax." A feminine version of Sargon, with six breasts in two vertical rows amply filling a blue toga, also came foward from the cabin interior to shake his hand. Standing, Billy looked expectantly over at Harrigan.

"They couldn't wait—they had to see the first non-Compact human we've had aboard *Hekar* in several hundred years." Harrigan, arms crossed over a plaid cotton shirt, looked on as he stood next to Colleen. Everyone, he noticed, was looking at him.

He looked back. The Horems' short fur covered the aliens everywhere except for palms, foot soles, and lips. The bullet head was earless, but he saw indentations on either side that might be auditory receptors. Atop the head was a yellow-flecked, feathery crest ruff. The nose between two golden eyes was broader than a human's but strongly arched. Sargon smiled a ghastly imitation human grin full of extra incisors at him.

"Hello," he stoutly greeted his new alien customers. "I'm Billy McGuire Human, omnivore predator and Factor for the House of Skyee. Do you command this starship?"

"Only one-third of the time"—Sargon grinned back at him—"and then it's at the pleasure of our Compact Council. Two other sapients share Command duty with me on different watches. Shall we sit and discuss our futures?"

At his nod the Horems pulled cushions under their knees and sat down, feet and legs tucked under. Billy sat on one lounge chair. Jack sat in the other, Colleen curled up into Harrigan's lap.

"Sargon, you mentioned futures. What do you want to discuss?" Billy decided to adopt a direct style.

"How about the hostile orange globeship that attacked you? How about the algors clustered between us and the Shop with a forty-kilometer-wide entropy screen extended? Or"—the alien paused, feather-crest rippling in complex patterns—"how about the evidence of recent war making that our sensors picked up several million kilometers out? We live to Trade, but this is our world, our home—we will not endanger it."

Billy gulped. A look at Harrigan and McIntyre told him he was on his own. Sighing, he did his best to explain five million years of Trade politics.

"Watch Commander, those are good questions, and I understand your concern for safety. Do you recall the orientation program we sent the humans?" He ignored Jack's sharp look.

"Yes."

"Then you must know the Retread Shop is a complex ecology of wildly differing lifeforms, of carnivores, herbivores, and ominvores, of diurnal and nocturnal species, of social and asocial cultures." The Horem's golden eyes looked intently at him. "What makes it worse is that many have been here for hundreds of thousands or even millions of years, periodically going into Suspense when Trading slackened or when they got bored. Then there are the algors." Colleen and Bethrin were both now sitting stiffly forward, intent on his words. "They live as long as they wish, they see us as transients, mayflies my mom said, but still they protect us, help us and sometimes Trade their knowledge with us. A few even make organic friends."

"Remarkable," said Harrigan, "but what does this have to do with the violence?"

"Everything. The Shop is not only a hotbed of competitive organics and inorganics out to get the best Trade deal they can, but there's now a conflict between the ancient and newcomer races. And mixed into it is the question of who will control access to the Reliquary, the touchstone of the faith here."

"So who are the players?" asked Colleen.

"The Tets are the orange globeships, and they are both ancient and anxious to control access to the Reliquary deep within the Shop." Harrigan, he noticed, was pointing a bracelet with a turquoiselike stone at him; probably a sound recorder. "They resent anyone who hasn't been here more than a half million cycles, and they claim the right to take over from the Melanons the control of access to the Reliquary." Now Bethrin's yellow feather-crest was flaring. "Our Council of Control is dominated, at the moment, by both ancients and newcomers who are . . . pragmatic; they don't want business disturbed." Harrigan sagely nodded his head while Colleen shook red-glinting hair in the yellow sunlight. "My friends, a predator plant named Zilkie, his carnivore mate Melisay, Zekzek the Melanon, Ding do-wort, a few others—and I are simply trying to make a living, to gain riches, and to prevent the Tets from taking over the Shop."

"What about the Zotl? Why is it here and what does it want?" asked Sargon. The alien, he saw, was stroking its chin in a very human mannerism. Just what kind of multi-species culture had he run into here?

"It's here because it wants to be—you know them from the Arrik encounter. As to what it wants?" Billy shrugged his shoulders, feeling the stiffness of a newly cleaned jumpsuit. "Its Components say it is waiting. For your arrival."

"What!" yelled Harrigan.

"True," he said. "Somehow it knew *Hekar* was coming here. And once here, it plans to talk to you." Billy, thinking of Ayeesha, of the Noktoren and of a soft quiet voice he'd heard during the battle, asked a question. "Jack, how does a Zotl talk?"

"Uh—that's a secret of ours, for the moment." Harrigan looked down at Colleen, then hugged her. "So what do we do? Can your Shop Trade with us, or not? You have our list—we have needs."

"I know. And I'll Factor them for you. Don't worry, we'll Trade with you, and this little affair—"

"Master Harrigan," interrupted a crisp human voice with very sharp enunciation, "you have a visitor at the front door. Shall I let her in?"

"Yes, Jeeves. Release the door locks." Harrigan looked over at Billy and grinned a rueful look. "That's Jeeves, my house computer. It's patterned after a classic celluloid film English butler."

"Uncle Jack, where are you?" called a delicate musical voice he'd heard once before. Billy's heart beat fast. He looked to the sliding door.

"Out here, Falling Waters."

"Hello, Uncle." The woman of his dreams, of his hopes walked out onto the crowded deck as the two Horem moved to the side. Her long black hair was tied up this time in a very intricate pattern of ringlets, curls, and buns, fastened with combs and ivory pins. But she still wore the yellow silk *cheong-sam*. "The Bridge sends me. There is a tachpulse message for Billy McGuire."

Billy watched with fascination as she walked toward him. Her high cheekbones pleasantly balancing the black eyes and red lips. She handed him a metallic message form.

"Thanks, Falling Waters Nakashimi." Before he looked at the message, he asked a question, trying to stretch out the period when her sole attention would be on him. "Do you have a brother or relative named Sam Nakashimi?"

"Yes." Her neutral look suddenly transformed into a radiant smile. "He's my brother. We have the same father." The Asiatic slightly angled her head, glancing around the group. "Colleen is his mother, while Petal Blossoms Yamamoto was mine, and our father is Yasuhiro Nakashimi — chief scientist of the Research department."

He was confused. How could so many relationships exist among these humans? "But—"

"Billy, don't try," interrupted Colleen. "I'll fill you in another time on our family-birthing practices. What's in your message?"

"It's from the House of Skyee," he replied, looking down the close-packed *lyol* ideograms. "The Tet have gotten into the Shop. They're heading for the Reliquary. Zekzek asks for my return." Billy looked up, realizing that for a few moments, he had been surrounded by three humans and two humanoids, and it had felt comfortable — natural.

"Can you get me there quickly?"

"Yes," said Falling Waters. "One of our Stingers is waiting at the top of the habitat's support pylon." She pointed behind him to a four-kilometer-high spear of metal that reached up to the blue-painted, domed roof of the habitat. "I came in a ball-taxi — we can be there in only a few minutes."

"Then I'm going." Billy looked around at the gathered people, catching in his mind's eye their distinctive look, their attitude, the feelings clinging to them like vines about a waterhole. Sargon, Bethrin, Harrigan, and Colleen — they had saved his life and befriended him. Colleen, especially, had shared a great gift. But it was time to go back to work. "Good-bye, all. When things are settled, the House *will* make you welcome!"

He walked after the woman into the cabin, through the living room, past the alluring smell of coffee perking on the electric range, and out the front door to the waiting ball-taxi. Thinking ahead to the upcoming confrontation, he let his legs carry him into the two-seater craft. The entry-door closed shut, cutting out the sounds and smells of Earth. Billy looked over to seated Falling Waters as her slim fingers swiftly coded their destination into the chip-pilot console.

"Falling Waters?"

"Oh, yes." She looked over at him, no longer guarded, no longer formal. "What?"

"Will you hold my hand while we travel?"

She looked back at him warily, then understanding suffused her face. A slight hint of caring leaked out from black eyes. She sat back in the accel seat, letting the crash-straps automatically enwrap her form. Her left hand reached out to him.

"Yes. It's hard to be alone, isn't it?"

Billy looked out the transparent dome at the blur of green vegetation. Yellow, natural light from the ceiling radiator washed over him. He felt the warmth of her hand in his. "But I'm no longer alone."

The Stinger, passed by Amadensis in the Defense Screen, darted through the Garbage cloud, heading for Central Dock. The House had a separate, private portal near it that led directly into the Compound's airspace. From there he knew they could catch a gravshaft that would access to near the Reliquary. At least the human craft, stuffed with Billy in his combat exoskeleton, Sam, Flickering-Blue-Embers, and Syess, was small enough at twenty meters across to fit through the primary tubeways. He still hadn't made up his mind whether to ask for fire-support from the Stinger.

"Through here, Billy sapient, is?" asked the Thoranian.

"Yes," he replied, crash-webbed into an auxiliary accel

seat behind the centrally mounted crystalloid. The interior of the Stinger was a series of two partial shells to which were stuck equipment consoles, power cable runs, Sam's combat chair with Remotes neurolinking, and the Strelka's fluid-filled combat harness sack. Vidscreens flared everywhere in normal-light, infrared, UV, lightspeed-accelerated subatomic levels, and versions that looked like the picture of his guts turned inside out. Nauseated, Billy wondered if there were certain alien image concepts humans should never experience.

"Sensors report a large gathering of lifeforms just ahead in a deep chamber," reported Sam. Billy looked toward Sam, seeing their approach in one of the few normal gas-dynamic screens of the craft. The darkness of the tubeway was bright with far infrared sparkles. "Breakout in four seconds!"

"Breakout!"

"Up axis—now!" called Flickering-Blue-Embers. The Stinger jerked upward at a right angle, the inertia compensators balancing perfectly the stresses upon their bodies. A yellow beam flared past, missing them. "*Attack!*" screamed the Strelka.

Billy looked back at the screen, realizing the Tets had managed to infiltrate at least one laser-mount. The politics of involving the humans in a Shop fight were now irrelevant. They were fighting for their lives.

Masses of alien bodies churned over the killing field again. Tets, Mycrons, Kerisens, Dorselliens, Ketchetkeels, Bareens, Soreps, tracglobes from at least four different atmospheres—Billy sickened at the sight of at least forty different alien species engaged in killing each other. He had had enough of killing, of blood, of revenge. It was time to end it.

"Embers, kill only the orange salamanders, the brown fur-balls, and anyone else trying to move toward the black dome over there." He thought a moment. "Can you use pressor fields to push the defenders back so they won't be hurt too much?"

"Can be done, Human. Oh, the taste of the mindscreams is delicious here!" he heard the centipede exclaim.

Billy gripped the armrests of his accel seat, hoping the Strelka could control its empathic lust for death. He wondered whether the Strelka would win, if faced with a Mekanen.

Flashing explosions lit up several interior screens in multiple light spectrums. The Stinger shook as several KKVs rocketed out, selectively aiming for aggressor targets buried among defenders. In seconds it was over. A Huntership controlled by three neuro-linked sapients with combat experience is an overwhelming match for two laser-mounts and hand weapons.

"Descent location, where, is?" asked Syess.

"Over there by the black dome—in front, this time, I think," replied Billy. Already he could see the blue leaves and yellow branches of Melanons gathered about the main archway, prepared for a last light-charge blast that was no longer needed. Other newcomer races held positions nearby, lay wounded, waved tentacles their way, or watched alertly for Tet remnants. He saw Zilkie, Ding dowort, Keen so-thorn, and seven other husbands, Melisay and a Melanon bush that must be Zekzek, all gathered to one side of the Tree mass. Tsorel, a few other Mycrons, several Gordin tracglobes, six Ketchetkeels including Namidun ka-tun, and many other aliens held the other flank of the Tree. They all looked—as far as he could read the body language—to be exhausted. He suddenly realized Sam was hanging near him from a strap—they had landed.

"Billy?"

"Yeah, let's go outside."

His first friends looked over at him as he slid down from the lower airlock portal. Zilkie's tentacles were weakly waving, several had been scorched and two were severed half-way down, leaking viscous green blood. Melisay's fur was singed on one side; she held her left arm with her right. Four sad brown eyes caught him from across the dirt and grass.

"Billy? Oh, Billy—you live!" A tear ran from one eye.

"Zekzek said you had survived, but we thought the globe-ship got you."

"It's all right Melisay. It's over. The fighting is all over," he reassured her. For a second he even believed it. But everything has a price.

"*Not* while I live, little grub!" screamed a shrill, wavering voice behind him.

Billy whirled about, dropping into a combat crouch, feeling for his knife. It wasn't there. But the exoskeleton whirred like a second skin. He saw Solaquil and a phalanx of twenty bloodied Tet coming over a small hill.

"*Destruction, orange ones, desired?*" came the booming electromagnetic voice of Syess the Thoranian from inside the Stinger. Sam and Flickering-Blue-Embers, halfway between him and the craft, ran back to the Hunter-ship. The bronze armatures whirled about the globeship, weaving an ominous spell.

"*No!*" Billy called out.

There was a revenge Hunt to be concluded here. But his stomach ached at the thought of more blood, even the coppery green blood of Tets. The phalanx and Solaquil, clad in weapons harnesses, had abruptly stopped at the rise of the Stinger into attack mode. Billy remembered one of the lessons of Tenshung, when the old Asian was teaching a wise ten-year-old the ways of the world. His first mentor had said killing was part of life, not to be sought, but also not to be run away from when necessary. And he had said the best time to kill, the only right time to kill, was when it turned your stomach. When you hated what you had to do.

"Solaquil, settle this with me *now*! Or you will all be destroyed," he yelled out to the Tet. "Do you accept my challenge?"

Two-thousand-year-old black eyes with orange iris slits gazed back at him across the field. But they no longer made him fearful. They were simply the last distasteful job he faced before he could go on with his life.

"*Yes!*" The Tet bounded down the slope, four arms outstretched, reaching for him. Billy glided forward, blood pulsing with adrenaline. Time stretched.

"You should have brought a weapon, grub!" screamed the Tet as it came near. The great hind legs tensed for the death leap. He saw the Tet were true carnivores—with very sharp teeth and claws.

"I did—myself," he softly called back. Billy moved sideways, dismissing the chastising memory voice of Tenshung, who would never have approved of such boastfulness. The Tet leaped.

Billy jumped into the air to meet the murderer of his parents. Curling up in a partial ball, he struck out in a flying kick at the bulging orange abdomen of the Tet. They came together in a whirling of limbs.

When they hit the ground, Billy had two broken ribs. Two of the Tet's arms were broken and coppery green blood welled from the salamander's muzzle where his head had butted it. They rushed together again.

Billy had the Tet's throat in his mouth, chewing and biting into its airway. An alien larnyx crunched. Blood tasted sweet and sour. He pulled with his jaws, hard.

He looked down at the alien under him, quivering in the muscle spasms of death as it drowned in its own blood. Black basilisk eyes gleamed one last time at him. Then they dimmed. Billy spat out the flesh.

The orphan stood up and looked at the other Tets. They milled away from him. He looked around for his friends.

Sam looked at him strangely, a concerned look in his green eyes. The oscillating form of Flickering-Blue-Embers swayed next to Sam, lost in the emotional thrall of death. Billy looked back at the dome to his alien friends.

Zilkie had come closer, perhaps readying to help with its tentacles. The topknot writhed lazily in a pattern he'd never seen. Melisay, limping, looked sorrowfully at him. She cared for his hurt. Ding and the other Kerisens, he saw, were madly embracing—trying perhaps to deny the inevitability of death or just enjoying the greatest joke. The Melanons, including Zekzek, were floating away from the archway door. Something was happening inside the dome.

"Who fouls my nest with killing?" squealed a high-pitched voice that wavered into the ultrasonic.

Ayeesha came out of the dome.

The Kokseen's yellow cranium, five blue compound eyes flashing, swayed from side to side. The primary and secondary mouth-palps flashed about an oval mouth. Behind the head stretched a lavender thorax and gray abdomen swelling with girth. The six massive legs held her three-meter-long body a yard above the ground. She seemed very angry. Billy dropped into a crouch on all fours, shuffled forward to catch her attention, and lifted his head. He crooned to her.

"Eeee ayoooo cccc—ayeeee, help me Great Mother," he called out to Ayeesha, squealing the *stretzel* distress call as best he could. Would it work?

"*Stretzel!?* Little one, who hurts you?" hummed out the question. She came closer. Everyone stayed frozen, entraced by the living reality of the true progenitors.

"The orange ones, Great Mother. They attack your home. We tried to protect you."

"Murdering lice!" Billy heard Ayeesha scream out, rapidly passing into the ultrasonic. He saw Melisay press hands over her fan-ears in pain. The Kokseen pranced closer to the orange phalanx.

"Where are the Caretakers? Where is the Tree? Have you hurt them?" screamed Ayeesha. "If so—they will pay—now answer—me!" Billy heard Ayeesha demand, part of her words lost as the comdisk failed to keep up with the high cps fluctuations of true Kokseen speech. Melisay, he saw, was being held by Zilkie. He had to help.

"Great Mother, judge them quickly, for one of your defenders hurts from the high speech. The Tree, the Melanons have kept safe the Reliquary—look behind you, then look at those who sought to harm your nest." Billy slowly stood up, hoping that the Kokseen was now fully awake from her Suspense decanting. Maybe it would rationally see them as fellow sapients, not just as threatening predators.

Ayeesha's great body swayed, reared up on its two hind legs, twisted to look back at the silently floating Melanons, and then turned to face the Tets. One salamander had come forward, reverting to the ceremonial walk he'd first seen when visiting with the Chellaquol. The erratic movements ended just meters away from Ayeesha.

"Great Mother, please understand—we sought only to preserve the faith. To keep the traditions. To prevent newcomers from defiling—"

"Silence!" screamed Ayeesha. The Tet fell to the ground. Coppery green blood flowed from its two small ears. It writhed in pain on the ground. Billy saw truly just how deadly ultrasound could be.

Ayeesha dropped down onto four of her feet, elevating her flexible upper thorax and cranium to look around at the crowd of sapients. Forty or more species had silently gathered from across the fields, drawn by the sound of his battle with Solaquil. At least two thousand aliens slowly milled around Billy, the humans, the Stinger, Zilkie's group, the Melanons, and Tsorel's House of Skyee group. Ayeesha's blue compound eyes flashed at them, then she turned toward him.

"Almost-*stretzel*, how do you know the danger call?"

"I . . . remember Gamafore. I too am an orphan. Will you succor me?"

The Kokseen finished dropping down onto her forelegs. She pranced up close to him. The secondary mouth-palps, those insectoid inventions that served as very deft fingers, briefly reached out to touch him. His bare hand felt a dry, cool touch.

"You too are alone?" whistled Ayeesha in a low timbre.

"I . . . was, for many years, until more of my race came." Billy pointed to the Stinger. "They helped put an end to the violence. We are all tired of the killing. Will you help?"

"Yessss . . . I will help." Ayeesha looked out at the gathered Tets, the phalanx now broken. The orange tide had spent itself.

"You, aliens. This is my nest, my *home*. Leave it *now*," she squealed at the Tets. "Or your bodies will soften my trail!"

The Tets scattered, totally dispirited. Soon they would

leave the Shop. At last the Shop could return to its usual, simple, cutthroat competition. Where only money was lost, and poverty was the most serious penalty.

"Alien, almost-*stretzel*," Ayeesha called to him. "You know *The Tale of Ayeesha*. Will you share memories with me?"

Billy, startled, looked across at the insectoid. He wiped Tet blood off his lips with his sleeve. "Do you mind predator memories, Great One?"

"No. They are the most flavorful of all. Come into my Home."

He walked after her, wondering if she realized she was a living goddess to the surrounding aliens. Hundreds of other aliens followed them inside until they came to the pressor fields. Then only he and Ayeesha went up an immaterial tubeway into the first Shop. Happy, at peace, Billy never looked back. He looked forward to the exchange, wondering what it was like to be part of the first flowering of a great civilization.

Chapter Twenty-six

The park of the Hecamin was peaceful for Billy and Falling Waters. They sat under a tree with long weeping branches, yellow leaves, and a russet red trunk amid golden alien daisies. Billy looked over at the woman who had been his lover the last three months, the time since he and Ayeesha had come out into a changed world.

Colleen's stepdaughter wore one of her mother's Clan MacLaren tartan skirts, with white blouse and black boots. Her long black hair hung loose, waving slightly in the breeze. The whitish yellow Hecamin home starlight made her skin glow like deep burnished ivory. Her black eyes gazed across the habitat, watching the family packs of four-legged, golden-furred carnivores frolic among similar trees and low hills. The laughter of blue water glistening in curving streams called to them. Her left hand held his tightly.

"Billy, why won't you come to live with us on *Hekar*?" She turned to face him directly, a few tear-tracks still marking her cheeks. She had stopped crying several hours ago.

"Because . . . I am more than just human." He leaned his head on her left shoulder, seeking solace. The touch of her hair curled around him. "My friends, the ones who helped me survive, are here. Zilkie, Ding do-wort, Zekzek, Tsorel, and Melisay—they are so special to me." Falling Waters put a hand under his bearded chin, lifted, and struck deep into his soul with her look.

"You are special to me. I am a woman. I can give you what no alien can!" The tears were falling again, like pearls on black satin. "Oh Billy." She leaned her head against his, each nestled in the crook of the other's shoulder.

Moving by instinct, by desire, and by caring, Billy caressed her. "Falling Waters . . . there's still time for us. Let me give back to you what I can, while I can."

Jack Harrigan and Colleen McIntyre walked along the Grand Arterial, passing up the option of low-speed glideways. They were exploring. And they were having a grand time. Red hair was not common among those aliens with hair.

"Jack, look there! That sign says . . . 'Life-Extend', according to this *lyol*-English dictionary." The one-hundred-and-twenty-year-old woman looked up at the older man. "Do you think it's better than the *kliss* antiagathics of the Sliss?"

"It's worth a try, lover," said the swarthy-skinned ex-newsman. He grinned at her. "Why live longer—looking for new lovers?"

The woman jabbed the man in the ribs, then wrapped her left arm about his waist. She stuck her tongue out at him, then grinned a freckled smile across wrinkled skin. "Do you have that barter credit chit Billy gave us? The one with the House of Skyee ideogram on it? Let's stock up—I want to see what the future is like."

The human male and female walked up to an open basin over which a nameless Dorsellien flapped its wings. The cloud-dweller increased the tempo of its flapping as its TK moved vials of the life elixir front and center before the customers. Its great gaping mouth and tendril eyes tasted the flavor of new aliens.

When the Trade was done, the Dorsellien barely managed to show enough profit to pay for storage, lab fees, and the commission to its boss. Its wings weren't flapping quite so vigorously. And the man and woman were skipping down the Grand Arterial, laughing.

Ayeesha of the Kokseen paced up and down the hollow, echoing corridors of her Home. She was bored. The Caretakers were as conservative as ever, rarely venturing into her abode, and keeping out most of the weird aliens who lived in the burrows of her overgrown station. They meant well, they were as curious as ever, their Answers Shallow and Deep were still the marvel of her tertiary memory ganglion, but they were not . . . adventurous. She looked down the primary tubeway at the old Control Bridge, its entry portal irised open. A blue-glistening hologram of near space slowly rotated before her old Control Nexus, showing the massive new station, the Zotl, the asteroid starship *Hekar*, the Garbage cloud and tiny specks of life moving about. Trading. Learning. Hungering after something. Now inside the bridge, she looked up at the domed ceiling, seeing the painted mnemonic story of the Kokseen.

Honored throughout the one million, eight hundred thousand and ninety-five cycles of her race's history, Ayeesha of the *stretzels* had been left behind by the great trek. The planet Hamiden had moved to the portal and disappeared. She had no desire to return to the orange light of

Lamiseen, now left orphaned by its lifeplanet. Her duty—
to see that the new ones carried on the Florescence that had
cost her race so dearly—was now done. Their childhood
was over. Adolescence was soon to begin.

In the holopicture, one slightly larger speck drew her
three primary eyes. It was a Kokseen forerunner ship, built
to trek the spiral arms and never return. The bronze-col-
ored starlight, along with the Human Billy McGuire's
memories, awoke an idea. She thought long and hard.

Melisay **brach-ahn** Corhn sat in the Food shop's upper
floor, rocking by the food pool, staring out at the forest. It
seemed to be getting smaller. The colors were growing less
vivid.

My love, why the sorrowful heart? called Zilkie in her
mind.

*I need a world, Zilkie. A true world. I need many
worlds, many forests. And I miss Billy.*

The Cosex sent feelings of consternation, sympathy,
wonderment, and encouragement. He had always been
sensitive to her needs. She had also tried to tend to his
needs, his desires. But the plant phylum was so strange.

Zilkie, show me where you are now.

Images of the Council of Control in a meeting came to
her. Alien forms. Alien concepts. Alien hungers and desires, filtered through the five nodes of the Cosex's own
brain, came to her. They were arguing again—that she
could tell. The presence of the Zotl, the Humans, the now
avidly trading eight other alien races of the Compact, the
peculiar mind of the Compact algor called *Hekar*, the departure of the Tets—all these things and more had upset
the steady rhythms of millions of cycles. And the presence
of a living god among them, of a faith walking among
them rather than safely tucked away in the Reliquary, *that*
was the most disturbing.

*Why don't they just go into Suspense and wait until it all
settles down again?* she asked the Cosex.

Some have done so already, my love. But power is an

*addiction, a drug more powerful even than Life-Extend.
They wish to control that which is uncontrollable.*

Melisay sent back a mind picture-word that Billy would
have translated as "Pshaw."

She turned back to her own thoughts, those of the Cosex
receding to a dull background roar. She thought of Billy
the Human—at least he was learning to grow face fur.
Melisay wondered if he would leave her.

Billy McGuire Human sat alone in the black stone-
walled tower room of his House of Skyee residence. A
redwood chair, courtesy of Jack Harrigan, enveloped him
in special wood smells. The smells of Earth. He ran a
finger along the rough-cut surface, feeling the grain scratch
back at him. When he looked up he saw his rest unit, a red
granite table, and the C-cubed unit. The unit whispered
market quotes, current bonding rates, upcoming auctions at
the Arbitration Guild, the markup the Ketchetkeel were
charging the Compact to replenish *Hekar*'s 20-percent low
tanks, the antics of the Arrik alien raptors as they flew
down the Grand Arterial hunting live game, all these tidbits
and more called to him.

But he ignored the machine. He even ignored the after-
image of Falling Waters that insistently overlapped nearly
everything he looked at. Even his stacked cases of Life-
Extend looked pale to him. The physical signs of his early
desires, of a name achieved among the aliens of the Retread Shop, were as nothing compared to the cyan-colored
vidcrystal he now held loosely in his right hand. In his left
hand were his dad's bowie knife and the necklace of human
memory crystals. Billy had sat there alone, for hours, after
memoryviewing the last of his Trade goods from *Star
Riches*.

The cyan crystal had been of a type he'd never seen
before. For lack of a better label he had called it a theology
history lesson. It spoke of beings of pure energy—not
plasma like the Minoren gasoids—who were known to
every Florescence, who had outlasted every Florescence,
and who supposedly knew the secret of faster than light

stardrive. The duty of these energy beings—called simply the Guardians in the crystal—was to watch over the Winnowers at the end of each Florescence. The Guardians' job was to make sure the Winnowers—who helped complete the natural extinction of sapient life at the end of each Florescence—did not stick around, did not seek exception from the universal rule. And the Guardians supposedly lived nearby in Sagittarius arm, only four thousand light-years away.

Billy knew it was a theology crystal—not factual data—because no other history from any Florescence even spoke of such beings. The only beings who could outlast a Florescence were the Zotls. And it was said they lived even before the First Florescence came into being out of the energy pulse from the infalling of the first three-kiloparsec arm into the galaxy's central black hole. But still, Billy McGuire Human, Factor, omnivore, and predator, doubted his certainty. All he knew for certain was that the universe was *always* stranger than any sapient had ever conceived it. He reached over and touched the C-cubed unit.

"Comlink center, connect me with Jack Harrigan, Human habitat, *Hekar*."

But before he could speak over the open tachpulse line, something came into his mind.

Self1 felt the beating of the life motes below, above, and around it. They were tiny, the gravity wells were almost nonexistent, but the nexus was achieved. It had heard enough from its monitoring. The desire had flared in at least one mind, and others would follow.

Only the outer four Component echelons were activated, and a few dozen Transition foci sufficed to handle tachpulse communications with the lifeforms scattered about it. The inner cortical layer of Self2 and Self3 were still asleep—only the energy of a primary fusion flare would suffice to bring the entirety of itself to full awareness. But the upper reservoirs had fed on antimatter recently, and lesser energies were sometimes fed to it. There was enough to begin the Dance.

Self1, sometimes known as a Zotl, reached out with its mind to each and every one of the fifty-one thousand, two hundred and nine lifemotes of the Retread Shop, Hekar, and attendant habitats.

It was ready to talk.

Billy, Melisay, Zilkie, Ding, Zekzek, Tsorel, Jack, Colleen, Falling Waters, and thousands of others all heard the same message.

"Life, we are Self1. Your gifts of food are appreciated. We hunger more. Please approach us with more food so that we can more easily percept each other.

"But until then, we issue an invitation.

"We go to seek those who oversee the Winnowers. The minds of the Guardians are immanent. Their travels are instantaneous. They are nearby. And we want to play one last time with the progenitors of the First Florescence before the trip into the long Dark.

"We seek mobiles who can act for and with us. Short-lived though you be, the desire lives within you. The Dance of curiosity, of creation, of knowing, and of humbleness swirls among you. Will any among you come dance with us and play with the Progenitors?"

Billy came awake sitting in his redwood chair. The invitation of the Zotl still sang in his mind. Its beauty so far surpassed the luminescence of Beethoven's Fifth Symphony that there was no comparison.

He stood up, still dressed in his formal red jumpsuit. The necklace went around his neck. The knife into his blue sashbelt. A finger touched the Hunt earring.

There was no need for such personal reassurance. He knew where the Zotl was going—the blue starchart crystal he'd shared with Ding a month ago showed the way, he now realized. But a human lives to certain patterns, certain rhythms. And, while his alien half swayed and flowed to its own beat, his human half felt comfortable. Billy stepped out the door, looking for a taxi ovoid.

Already he was planning the greatest Garbage Hunt ever conceived. All he needed were some old friends, some new friends, a goddess, a ship of his own, and a moving world called *Hekar*.

He hoped Jack and Colleen liked adventure.

Chapter Twenty-seven

Zilkie was waiting for him at Central Dock's interior departure platform, the painted *Star Riches* looming above and behind the Cosex. Billy, finally ready to lead the Sagittarius Garbage Hunt after two months of harried preparations, wondered what he would say. The tree-anemone was staying behind, while Melisay was going with him. As were *Hekar*, the Zotl, and Ayeesha. Zilkie's green whipcord tentacles slowly moved in a new, never before seen pattern.

"Little thief, you must yet attend to a few details," hooted the alien, scurrying toward him on pale green worm-toes. The tentacle topknot sped up. A bank of silvery fish eyes looked across at him. With a start he realized he had grown over the years—he was now nearly as tall as the Cosex.

"What details?"

"Why, the designation of Benefactor and the agreement on the Charter, of course." The green tree-anemone bent over slightly, giving him a full view of the topknot, the eyes hidden at the base of each tentacle, and Zilkie's glistening green throat-mouth. Then it straightened, the circular rings of plant-flesh that made up its trunk bulging with strength. He wondered just what the hell his former mentor was talking about.

"I earned my berth aboard *Star Riches*, I'll lead the Hunt and the craft belongs to Ayeesha." Billy was impatient to get going. His first Hunt earring tinkled at his left ear. He looked forward to adding another.

"Not quite, my young Human." The tree-anemone's tentacles slowed nearly to a stop. "Anyway, someone special awaits you. Look behind you."

A dull rumble of thunder greeted his ears as Billy turned to look into the massive cavern of the spacedock. He saw a globe of blue water at least three hundred meters across, hanging, held together by the lack of gravity. Inside the globe was the torpedo shape of daa-lumkaliche ka-ka-Hak! Its leathery black skin sported new white barnacles about its tail-fluke, while the fist-sized black eyes looked at him from either side of a broad, shark-tooth-filled mouth that was wider than he was tall. The wedge-shaped mouth lazily opened, closed, then the Noktoren turned within the globe to broach its left side. Billy heard a crinkly sounding voice in his mind.

"Leaving without saying good-bye to your Benefactor? Leaving without your charter?" bellowed the Noktoren in his mind and probably also in Zilkie's. *"Cosex, perhaps you encouraged the arrogance of this young sapient too much. Perhaps we should have left it to scavenge in the tubeways of the Shop?"*

Billy, black hair rising on the back of his neck, looked over at Zilkie. At his first mentor and friend after his orphaning. The tentacles were moving rapidly in a pattern he recognized as amusement. The Cosex didn't reply to the Noktoren's rhetorical question. But he did.

"What do you mean, Elder Merchant? Have you . . . maneuvered me? Did *you* order my parents killed?" he screamed. His left hand went to the knife at his waist. His gray eyes judged the leap distance to the Noktoren.

"Wait!" bellowed an imperious voice in his mind; the strength of the mind-voice was such he could barely stand up. *"Little thief, neither I nor the Cosex nor anyone here other than Solaquil had anything to do with the death of your progenitors."* He saw massive gray-black flukes

break the surface tension of the water globe, then disappear as the thirty-meter-long Noktoren swam in a tight circle in the blue water. *"Their deaths were regrettable—the Council had hoped they would survive until Hekar came. They didn't. You did. So our plan remained the same—allow a member of a sapient newcomer race whose other members would shortly arrive at this Station to compete and Trade among us."* The black pig-eye was now only twenty meters away, quite near the water-air boundary; he felt empty and confused. *"We honored you, on behalf of your race. Don't you understand?"*

Billy, rocking on the balls of his bare feet, stood with thumbs stuck in his sash belt, mind racing. The implications were depressing. He ran a hand through loose, long black hair.

"How did you honor me? By leaving me to starve? By letting the Tet Hunt me?!"

"We honored you," said the crinkly voice, now overlaid with the distinctive mind-sense of Zilkie, *"by not making things easy, by leaving you to your own devices for four years, by giving you a chance—not a guarantee—to advance in Trade."* He saw the Cosex had come closer to him; a long green tentacle reached out to lightly touch his shoulder. It felt . . . friendly.

"But I could have been killed!"

Great bellows of laughter welled up in his mind. He saw the Noktoren also had a sense of humor—if an alien one at that. He almost smiled himself.

"Billy McGuire Human," said both aliens in one mind voice, *"we could all have been killed! Don't you realize there are no guarantees? No, what you achieved you did on your own. And the conflict with the Tets—well, sociopathic projection is an inexact science, even when one can see a few minutes into the future!"* The black pig eye blinked at him. *"But now that our entertainment is over, it's time to go back to work. Here, Human, you have earned this. Put out your hand."*

Billy put his left hand out, palm up. A miniature rumble-crack of thunder preceded the teleportation of a gold wire necklace and medallion. It dropped heavily into his hand. The metal felt cold to the touch, and wet. Bringing it to his nose, he smelled a sea scent. He remembered a long ago Trade, his first Trade.

"Merchant Billy McGuire, Human, omnivore, and predator, are you ready to act for the House of Skyee?" He looked down at the Merchant-rank medallion; he wondered just what the Elder Merchant had Traded Amadensis for the gold wire of his old necklace. He looked up at both Zilkie and the Noktoren.

"Yes."

"Then take this as your Charter. . . . You are to go with the Zotl and Hekar, locate the ones who oversee the Winnowers, learn the secret of faster-than-light travel if it exists, and return to this Station." A fluke slapped the water surface, creating a crack-snap sound that echoed across the spacedock; he looked around, noticing that no other sapients were within a kilometer of them. *"And as your joint Benefactors, the Cosex and I have loaded onto Star Riches a few things that will aid your Hunt—two new TALs, several cases of Life-Extend, universal biomed healer, spare tachpulse pylons, songs of the Noktoren, a few weapons, and a complete fuel load."* The Cosex's tentacles were writhing in a pattern he knew best as gleeful satisfaction.

"How long do I have to find these . . . beings?" Billy, pleased with his Merchant status, still wondered where the hidden price was. The Cosex and the Noktoren, it was now apparent, never left anything to chance.

"Not long," hooted Zilkie, "there are only ninety-four million cycles left in the Florescence." Silvery fish eyes glinted at him; the tentacle on his shoulder tightened slightly. "Of course we expect you to be fairly quick—the system is only across the Dark in nearby Sagittarius Arm. By the way—just exactly *where* is it located?"

Billy smiled, looked up the tentacle at Zilkie, then across at the water globe and daa-lumkaliche ka-ka-Hak!

"Benefactors, you don't get something for nothing. Do you wish to Trade for the starchart?"

The crinkly voice in his mind laughed. The Cosex hooted as its tentacles wiggled in amusement. Billy smiled a broad grin like the one he often saw on Colleen and Jack. It was fun to be human—some of the time.

"Noooo . . . ," said Zilkie, "we can wait for your return."

"Even if it takes several millennia?" he asked, turning serious. The Shop had been his home for so long. Now he was leaving it. But here, in the competitive embrace of two aliens, he finally understood a simple lesson. Home was where his friends were.

"Little Merchant, millennia are but brief echoes in a Florescence. We will await you." replied the Noktoren. Billy turned to face the Cosex.

"Zilkie, any words for Melisay?" It was, he realized, a stupid offer—the Cosex was always in the Tellen's mind, no matter the distance. But it was the human thing to do to make the offer.

"More for you than her, my young Human." The green whipcord tentacle left his shoulder to join its neighbors as the Cosex slowly retreated on worm-toes. "Tell her—what are a few thousand years? I will but sleep, and when I awaken, my Melisay will be there." The Cosex sped up its departure, heading for a down ramp and the entrance to the observation galleries. Billy heard the sound of thunder.

Instead of looking to where the Noktoren had been, he looked up at the bronze beauty of *Star Riches,* its upper hull decorated in fresh yellow, lavender, and black colors. It was time to report. It was time to leave with his friends, old and new. He hand-signaled one of the spacedock's tractor beam operators and felt himself lifted up to the open cranial segment hatch. The one he'd entered on his first Run.

The sound of Beethoven's Ninth Symphony greeted him as he exited the tubeway entrance onto the control deck. It seemed the songs of Earth were popular among aliens. And it suited a starship run by a goddess.

"Almost-*stretzel* Billy Human, shall we go Hunting?" whistled Ayeesha from her Control Nexus dais. The Kokseen's yellow, lavender, and black colors were radiant under the natural orange light of the bridge. For someone who'd shared memories with him, she was turning out to be a damn hard taskmaster.

Billy McGuire the Merchant walked over and sat in his accel seat at *Star Riches'* Detection console. He fitted a memorynetlike skullcap onto his head. He closed his gray eyes, relaxing, seeking the alpha state. The bridge vibrated underneath him as the Kokseen forerunner ship was pressored out of Central Dock. He opened his eyes.

The right side of his brain was now neurolinked to the Detection sensors. He saw in EMF, UV, IR, and yellow visible light screens the nearby Garbage Cloud, the tubular hulk of the Shop retreating behind them, the massive jacobi ellipsoid of *Hekar* as a thousand-kilometer-long white flare of antimatter driven plasma slowly pushed the planetesimal along their heading, and the brown crystalline mass of the Zotl as it silently matched their every vector and speed. In only a few *dicoms* they were clear of the accumulated debris of five million cycles of childhood. Ahead of them were only the stars, the dark between the spiral arms, and the unknown. He finally answered his memory-friend.

"Yes, Pilot-Captain, let's go Hunting!"

Billy looked around one last time at the bridge crew, feeling deep warmth for every entity there.

Melissay of the **brach-ahn** sat before him at the Navigation console, her healed arms deftly inputting coordinates and thrust parameters. The black-and-white-striped fur seemed to glow with happiness. The fan ears alertly quested for sonic and subsonic signals from the instruments.

To port under the painted high dome was Tsorel trill-aa of Herd Myden at Life Patterns, its long purple tongue deftly stabilizing the Suspense fields. Next to the blue-skinned herbivore was the tracglobe of Anaxarion the Gordin, third clone of the merchantman captain who'd taken him sightseeing in the Garbage Cloud. Farther back on the port side he saw the floating crystal ovoid of Syess the

Thoranian, green crystals glittering within a cloud of radon gas—the Compact alien must be hungry, he thought.

Twisting his head to the right, Billy saw at starboard Dalithun ka-tun, first offspring of Namidun. The blue praying mantis waved a grip-arm at him from the Power pedestal. Then came blue-leaved and yellow-branched Zekzek at Defense and Flickering-Blue-Embers at the Attack pedestal. Billy, who now knew just how much the Strelka could "see" with its sensorium strip of specialized scale-cells, hoped the empath was enjoying the diverse mix of sapient thoughts and emotions.

Looking far back to the right, the Merchant saw the purple-colored globe of Amadensis at Tech Assessment—the algors had, at the last moment, decided to send a representative along with the mayflies. Just in case there really were beings who knew the secret of faster-than-light stardrive. Amadensis, he'd heard from Ding do-wort, seemed to have a case of schizophrenic indigestion from the personality feed of the Compact's *Hekar* algor. It consistently exhibited multiple personalities, none of which he was familiar with. In time it too would adjust to an alien double-identity.

At Comlink was the best friend of all. Falling Waters Nakashimi, her black hair done in a style called *geisha*, stood within the clear panels surrounding the tachpulse and normal space Comlink pedestals. Her slim fingers lightly touching a few pressure-keys, black eyes looked back at him with the look of love. The blue herons sewn into her white silk kimono seemed as alive as she was.

A loud thumping noise drew his attention away from his lover. The Kerisens were at it again. He looked past Ayeesha to the post opposite his.

Ding do-wort, with Keen so-thorn on her back, her six purple eyes all looking in six different directions, fed multiple inputs into the Tactical pedestal. She seemed to thrive on the challenge of coordinating the drive impulses of *Hekar*, the Zotl, and *Star Riches*—with their vastly differing masses and greatly varying rates of mass acceleration. Her seven other husbands were back in the thorax segment in Suspense or preparing the tsa'Lichen TAL for possible use. There was much yet to learn, he realized, from a Master Trader and senior Merchant such as Ding.

"Dalithun, commence full stardrive now!" whistled Ayeesha.

Billy stopped his musings. He turned full attention and his left brain side back to the tasks at hand. Watching the colors of the stars slowly change as they gradually became relativistic was a favorite recreation of his.

Hours passed. He enjoyed watching the rainbow of stars as he dealt with the duties of avoiding miscellaneous debris. Then it was time to close down the ship for four thousand years of voyaging.

The cabin Billy shared with Falling Waters was tidied up. The holo-pictures of Earth, of the human habitat, of Jason and Sarah McGuire and of alien friends were all in their proper place. Falling Waters was all ready in Suspense in the central hold, protected from stray radiation by its interior location and extra collapsar shielding.

The purple sparkle of a tachpulse precursor glittered in the air above his C-cubed unit.

"Billy, Billy, are you there?" called out the gradually solidifying images of Jack Harrigan and Colleen McIntrye. They were holding hands. The solido image was coming from the deck of their A-frame, judging by the scatter of cushions, chairs, and hot tub in the background.

"I'm here, folks. Is *Hekar* ready?"

"Do chickens have teeth?" roared Harrigan with a great bearded smile. He wished his friend, new mentor, and husband of his mother-in-law wouldn't use so many archaisms—the comdisk algorithm just couldn't handle them. Billy grinned back.

"Do aliens have tentacles? I don't understand what you mean Jack, but I gather there are no regrets?"

"No regrets, Billy," called Colleen in a throaty contralto voice. "Exploration and seeking new Trade opportunities are what *Hekar* is all about. Our Council loved the idea— local space has suddenly gotten crowded with the discovery of you Florescence types." She wrinkled her snub nose at him in a simple, caring, loving gesture. "It's time we humans took a long walk and left baby steps behind. It's time for us to find more islands to touch."

"True. See you in fifty years at the first awakening." He waved to them, even after the purple sphere winked out. Then he walked out of the cabin, down the primary tube-way, past the twenty Suspense-held alien gentlemen-partners who'd signed on, and up to a horizontal canister that held the love of his life.

Billy McGuire Human stood looking down through the view-port at the silent, white ivory stillness of Falling Waters's face. Black eyelashes sealed her dreams away. Black hair lay about her neck like ebony sand upon a rocky beach, both hiding and revealing at the same time. He sighed. Then he turned to the waiting canister next to her, climbed in, and lay back on the semiliving biomass that would massage, refresh, and sustain his body. The cover began to close over him, reflecting back his memories.

Memories of Sarah and Jason McGuire. Memories of a frightened little boy. Memories of a young thief. Memories of death, anger, hatred, desire, and hope. Memories of Ayeesha of the *stretzels*. They all enveloped him, riding with him into the night.

His last waking thought was that Ding was not quite right. Life wasn't just a great joke. It was more a call to the puppets to cut the strings, to reach out and push back the night, to find that one special island of love, of caring and of sharing that held all entropy's children.

It was a long, echoing thought.